THE ESOTERIC LEGACY
OF CORVEAUX MILLIONS

NEO METRO
PARAGON CODE

Written and Illustrated by
Corveaux Millions

Edited by
Corveaux and Luna Millions

NEO METRO
PARAGON CODE

TABLE OF CONTENTS

Long after the *Great Shift*, much of humanity's history was lost in what were the final wars. Countries then redrew their borders, and those borders made new territories.

Countries then dissolved when powerhouse corporations purchased the war torn land, and created their own private freelance nations. My father defined it as an evaporating land war that the world governments had lost horribly due to the financial crisis that ensued.

In the end, the world became divided along the new meridian. The United Northern Provinces, and the Southland Territories.

He said it was 'better days' before the Epoch.

He was part of the United Northern Alliance's military sciences division, and one of the few people who lived to survive inside the dome afterwards, and have a family.

It was, in part, due to the Paragon Corporation, and him having worked for them, as well. During the last wars, the Paragon Corporation destroyed the competition by only arming the Northern Provinces with their superior light-based weaponry and armor.

This caused fear in the under-equipped Southland colonies, forcing them to hire soldiers to fight their war; giving rise to the savage Southlander mercenaries.

All killers for hire.

He would tell the stories of how the world had become a dim reflection of its former beauty, and how the Epoch had splintered Earth and humanity.

I would sit and listen with an open jaw, as he told me stories of shocker fire, light cannons, explosions, and the moon.

Every time, he would always stop, when he got to the moon. It seemed to be a bad memory for him. As a child, I thought it was because we could no longer see it, and it made him sad.

My favorite parts of his old stories were of the Countess, and her Meridian guards. The way he told it, they were like something out of a fairytale, but he swore the stories were true.

During the land purchase war, a noble named Victoria Hart, made a major deal along the new meridian line after the Great Shift, rightfully naming it *"New Axis"* and herself, its' sovereign Countess.

It was said that her guard could withstand any environment, endure any challenge, and that just one Meridian guard was better than even a hundred Paragon Standard Issue Battle Soldiers.

The Southlanders even worshiped her.

She didn't engage in conflict between the divided nation states, but would often intervene in the war to try and avoid the spread of battle. She was a beacon of hope in the last days of the outside world.

He never stopped telling the stories as I grew up. His position with the company afforded me a better education in a rapidly changing world. He had tried to acclimate to life inside the dome, but he missed the outside world, and longed for days when he didn't feel so trapped underneath this glass bowl.

With his help, I took his place within Paragon, but I had never known the same Paragon he had. I had only known the ruling corporation that gripped the city and humanity in its hands, trying to keep it precious and safe, and crushing it at the same time.

I was never sure if it was how much he longed for the outside world, or how good he told the stories, but the red Earth outside consumed my life; although, I lived comfortably in Central D, Paragon office estates. He had since moved into retirement, and I visited him regularly.

I would tell him the stories of the United Northern Provinces, the Southland Territories and of New Axis and the Countess, because dementia had eaten away at most of the man he used to be, and it helped me hold on to him a little longer.

Most of what he could remember was the fear of being trapped inside the dome, and how terribly the world had almost ended. Those stories consumed his last days.

It had been the way he described the Countess' guards that had made me most curious, and took over my life's work. The Earth, before the Dome, was fragile and changing, giving way to many different new types of battlegrounds for the divided states.

It had made it hard for both sides to fight at times, but never for the Meridian Guard. He said it was as though they moved fast like blurs and were nimble like spiders. When they attacked, it was exact and quick.

I thought of how useful that would be; to be able to leave the city, take readings and study the atmosphere. To try and solve the chaos of the world outside, so that the crowded city within wouldn't keep decaying with lethargy, crime, and apathy.

I would use the knowledge and education granted to me to re-create that ability; to enhance humanity, and give us the power to fix our environment, or escape it.

It would take something like the world had never seen to be able to achieve it. I thought of the Meridian guard, what they stood for, and what the countess had represented before the Epoch.

Hope.

Hope was the antibody that humanity's immune system had stopped producing. Hope was what I would have to create to make the fighting stop.

It didn't occur to me until the day Marcus was proposed to take over Paragon's Science division, and I went to my father's holo-memorial to consult with him about the change in guard.

I was telling him a story of the Northern Science research findings. It was another one of his favorites, and his self-declared greatest discovery.

He had been scanning part of the sky, mostly as a hobby, when suddenly a cosmic anomaly fell, changing the already broken world yet again. A large alien craft crashed into the planet. The impact covered the world in a cloud of dust, and wind storms that have since ravaged the terrain. It was my father that deciphered the alien technology and found the world inside that ship.

The dome.

My father had foreseen the calamity, and used what he already knew to turn the crash into humanity's advantage.

The Earth was no longer a suitable environment, and he helped lead the reformation with Paragon, and Killian Stoddard, herding people to sanctuary inside this glass-covered city. Once inside, society tried to start fresh. Humanity took a much needed break from killing and war, and Paragon erected itself as the leader above everyone else, tailor-fitting the future as it saw necessary.

That was when the rebellion began.

I could still remember it. I was young, but there was a time just after the migration, that the older population from the Northern Provinces and Southland States held onto their grudges and began to fight once again.

Paragon tried to quell the uprising, but, in doing so, only turned attention to itself, giving the people a new enemy.

Paragon instituted several protocols and formed defense teams to suppress the ensuing violence, but it only led to more.

It wasn't until the population had dwindled to a handful that humanity began to come to its senses. Killian, Paragon, and my father had all but given up on a solution, and instead decided that the corporation would have to build a new system of order.

They began to police the people, creating sections of the company with the sole purpose of controlling the population. Paragon then divided the population into residents; those who lived on the outer rims of the city, called the slums, and Citizens; those who lived in Central D, the inner city; a wealthier caste of civilization.

They also introduced a new form of currency, and offered various ways to obtain it. Enough of it could even grant you citizenship, but I didn't have to worry about any of that nonsense. My heritage kept me safe, and as long as I kept pushing the buttons for Paragon, I was allowed to continue my research, and find the answers I needed to fix the human condition.

"Just a couple of more tests and Version A will be ready for trial awareness, father." I said aloud knowing he'd be just as excited about my new accomplishment as I was. The little holographic projection image of my father smiled back at me. As I looked at his memorial, I tried to imagine what he would think of my achievement; being of a similar scientific mind.

"You really should think of a better name." I laughed a little at the impersonation I had done of him.

It felt like time had flown by, and now I was the old man that I always imagined him to be. Paragon and the world was about to go through another change, and humanity would have to endure, yet again.

Only this time, it would have to endure having a little more hope.

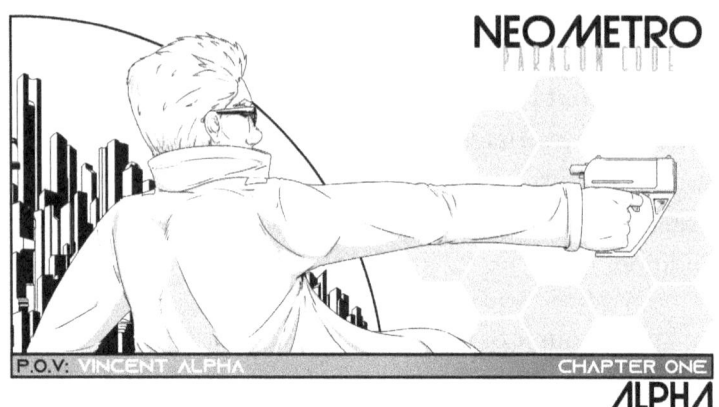

NEO METRO

P.O.V: VINCENT ALPHA   CHAPTER ONE

ALPHA

He was accused of the embezzlement of corporate rations to supply Dox-4 chemists with the needed ingredients to mass distribute *Uphorium* into Central D. Paragon bookkeepers found out while researching an overdue payment on a credit loan he had taken out. This suspect's name was Zane Blanc.

The year is 60AW.

This was the world after the wars.

The air was stiff and the room smelled of vapor and cheap *synthohol* as I entered. I shook the drops off of my umbrella as I folded it, and tossed it into a silver can next to the door. It was a courtesy unused here that made the container look empty and ill-placed.

I knew this dive.

I could bypass the seating area, and walk right to the booths in the back of the room; finding my way around easily.

The neon barely lit the dance floor, while the multi-colored radial lights flickered on and off the patrons; illuminating them for half-seconds at a time. The music wasn't to my taste either. It was some kind of *pre-revelation* electronic noise that was more for volume than enjoyment. This place was lower-class, even for the skirts; a haven for the Dox-4 users. Not the kind of place you want to get deleted in, but that was what was going to happen to Zane Blanc, now.

He had apparently noticed me, not that it would matter. The company coat and tie, tinted glasses combination always gave me away at the door. You could look around at the scantily clad setting and see that I didn't match the status quo for the environment.

Zane shot up and ran, not-so covertly, into the back room. He was putting too much faith into the doorman that guarded it . So, I made my way to the back of the bar and up to the door protected by the wide, rough-looking man. This was all going to be unnecessary.

"Hey guy, this room's for VIPs only. You can't come back here." The overgrown man let me know in a harsh and abrupt tone, while placing his hand on my chest, I supposed for the sake of keeping me away.

"I just need to talk to the man that you let back last." I gestured around him to the door enunciating every syllable in a low tone so that I knew the lout would understand, but in retaliation the doorman grabbed me around the collar with both hands, and pulled my face closer to his. An inept intensity burned in his eyes; something I could only assume was some sort of professional pride.

"You don't look all that important to me." He growled through his teeth at me at the end. His eyes were now small beads as he pierced them through mine. I could only smirk at his intensity.

I grabbed his wrist with my left hand, squeezed it, and sent the man down to his knee. His hands wrenched down my collar on his way to the floor, and he got a good look at the shocker in its holster inside of my jacket. He got an even better look at the emblem on the hilt; Paragon Corporation's logo.

"Do you see that?" I let my smirk fade as I pointed to my VIP card; it would be the only time he saw an official with a lethal weapon. He then nodded. "So, you know what that means, right?" I tightened my grip to assure him of his answer, and he let out a low whimper of acknowledgement.

"I...Apologize...I...Didn't know." He stuttered out, and of course he was lying.

You would have to be daring or slow to not notice the difference between me and these people, but most of these tough guy types were both. Always testing to see if Paragon was watching, and to see what they could get away with.

Either way, he wasn't why I was there, so I let him back up to his feet as he surely wasn't going to be a problem anymore. He stepped aside and let me into the back room, which was more like a glorified set of closets; each covered by a velvet curtain. Of the three little rooms, I was sure he was in the third. The coward he was would set him as far away from me as possible. So I didn't even bother to check the first two as I made my way to the third curtain.

"Zane...I think you know why I'm here." I called out as I drew my shocker, just in case he thought he was going to pull something fast, but I was sure he wasn't that foolish. Still, a pulled weapon is a better form of intimidation than casual conversation, and I was sure he heard the chamber charge in a bolt as I pulled the slide back.

He panicked, "Wait...Wait. I got the credits man. You don't have to bolt me...I got the creds." His voice shook as he thrust out the words, but his fear only reminded me of why I was there in the first place. I had a job to do, and I wasn't a debt collector.

"Zane, we're going to need a little insurance; you're four months past due on a two week loan." I said, just having a little fun.

"What?!" He pulled the curtain back angrily and was greeted by the business end of my partner. His eyes widened, but his thoughts did not curtail. "I ain't giving you Paragon elitists shits a cred I don't owe you. That's crazy."

Crazy is talking with a charged shocker in your mouth.

"Besides you guys will just find another way to get it out of me...right. You're always going to need ole Zane here, right?" He insisted as he bargained with his place in the world. Even for what I was used to, he was getting pathetic. I thought I better cut to the chase before his ego made him think he might get out of this.

"Actually, we're not looking for more credits from you Zane. We need you to be an example." I told him as I peered down the sights of my weapon.

"What do you mean by example? I'll do it, whatever you want." He whispered out desperately looking back down the sights at my shaded eyes. This was the rough part. It's getting to where I can barely look at them. I knew what he was about to do in response, but I would still follow orders.

"At Paragon, we pride ourselves on doing proper business. Making sure appearances are kept." I didn't need to give him the monologue, but it had become a habit. A need I felt to explain myself for the following action. "And we can't have someone come to us for credits, and not pay. Soon, other people will do the same, and it will all be your fault. You understand?"

The tough guy act had become just that at this point, a one man show that I performed to amuse myself with my work; otherwise, there's very little joy to be had. So, I stretched it out at times.

"What are you saying?" he gasped out real slow.

I pressed my shocker into his cheek and used the barrel to throw him back onto the couch in the little velvet draped enclosure. I moved my posture slightly, straightening my back and giving my arm its full extension. Then, he knew what I was saying.

"Wait... don't do it. I have kids. I got a little girl at home..." He wept as he crawled onto his knees on the floor below me, and he pulled credit chips from his pockets. His hands shook nervously, dropping them at my feet. My extended arm followed him downward as he slithered towards me on hands and knees.

"Please...I can't die...they need me." He muttered it as his nearly paralyzed hands were grasping at my pant leg. This man was pleading for the lives of his family. If it were only him, it would make my job so easy, but this is what I've dreaded lately. My job is to take the lives of those I'm told, and I don't have any other choice. I never have. I grew up in Paragon, and it was what I did. Now, all of the sudden I have this man's family clouding my once impenetrable conscience, and he's not the first.

I wanted to give him his life back. I wanted to take the money he owed back to the company and call it a day, but I couldn't. If I left this place and Eddie suspected anything, it would get back to Marcus. Then, Zane would no longer be the one having to worry about Paragon coming after him. If I didn't pull this trigger right then, I would be swapping places with him, right there.

Somehow, that thought coursed through me for an eternity in an instant. *'Maybe that's ok'.*

I raised my shocker, and my head went up with it; disobeying my orders for the first time in my life. Time slowed as my eyes focused on the flickering red bulb above. In that instant, I knew I could be more; more than just the killer they had made me to be. More than Paragon's hungry lapdog settling for whatever scraps they threw at him; more than just a monster without a conscience or sympathy for the so many lives he's taken. All of their faces came back in a quick flurry, each dancing up-tempo through my mind. All at once, I knew I was making the right choice.

"Get up." I muttered it out at Zane, the man that still wept on the floor. His eyes grew big as his face looked skyward toward mine.

"You're not going to kill me?" He questioned hastily. I flinched behind my dark glasses at the question. I realized that I was just as surprised as he was. Never-the-less, I gestured him up with my shocker, waiving him to his feet. He started gathering up his dropped credit chips from the floor around my feet, and stuffed them back into his pockets for safe keeping. "Thanks, that's great! I really owe you, man." His lips curled at the edges as he spoke showing insincerity in his words. He got to his feet, and his eyes met mine. Then, his hand came down on my shoulder. "My little girl owes you, man."

His finger wafted at me from his free hand, while his searching eyes told me a different story. The weeping and the tears probably weren't hard to pull off while he thought I was going to delete him, but his acting had gotten severely worse now that he thought the threat to his life was gone.

Instead, he was being sarcastic; almost mocking me. He turned and started walking for the door back to the main room. I stared at him, watching him, my mind was racing.

Anger started to consume me. This was not 'ok'. I wasn't about to throw everything away over one moment of compassion for a man who didn't at least deserve it. He mocked me with his quick fantasy, but I shouldn't have been taken in so easily. What was I thinking? A family man? In a scab bar? Probably lost on *Uphorium* and running from Paragon? No, he was exactly my type of target. The kind I didn't feel any remorse for. I was just doing my job.

The smug little man continued until he was about to hit the door and make his escape. No doubt he'd run as soon as he made it through the threshold, and that would be a lot of unnecessary work for me. I didn't mind a chase, but at this point I've already run enough circles in my mind.

"Zane, How old is your little girl?" I narrowed my brow as the question left my lips. I wasn't gauging his honesty any more. It was just to make him stop; thinking that I'd bought his ruse, and that all he needed to do now was lay it on a little thicker. I raised my weapon back towards him as he started to turn around.

"Eh?" It was all that he could mumble out, before his glance made my weapon's focus.

Click.

The light from the charge round flickered and danced through the small room.

The credit coins sprayed from his pockets like an open watermane as the bolt pulled his hands to the air. You never get used to seeing how a charge cauterizes the hole it makes so instantly, and with the kind of accuracy I have, he dropped just as fast. My assignment was complete. Zane Blanc was deleted.

I walked over scooping up a handful of the credits from the floor beside his lifeless body. "Hope it was worth it." I muttered out from my indifferent lips. I had never thought credit was worth as much as others' seemed to value it. It was the same as usual. I cared, but not enough. At least I didn't have to worry about Paragon, and my momentary glitch in corporate ethics had vanished.

The doorman didn't raise a brow as I holstered my shocker, and made my way back out into the common area. He knew better and besides, I'd left him with quite a nice little mess to clean up if he wanted his lounge back in operation. Nothing stopped in Club Kelp. This type of place didn't notice what happened in its little dark corners, nor did it care. Everyone there was too busy escaping, and if they forced themselves to notice me, that escape would be futile. I was a walking symbol that showed them who was in charge, and that it wasn't them...not anymore.

So they refused to see me. In the back of my mind, I knew it was for the best. Paragon's control over the entire city was relentless and everyone, even me, knew that.

I grabbed my umbrella from the cylinder at the door, and proceeded outside into the city, and the rain.

Just then, as I stared into the skyline of the dripping city, a quiet sloshing sound came to a stop in front of the door next to me.

Then. there she stood; soaked from the rain. It slid in streams down her hair and coat. She was staring at another awning across the street; for refuge I imagined. She was running from one awning to another trying to keep out of the rain. Her soaked hair being the first thing I noticed, seemed to shimmer despite being smothered down by the drops. Her arms wrapped around the front of her, as if she were trying to keep warm in her coat, and she seemed to be waiting before she crossed. It had just occurred to me that she too, like the others inside, hadn't even noticed me.

A drop from the awning came down on her head, and then she looked up to see me standing next to her, staring at her. I quickly glanced away hoping to make my ogle look more casual than it was. She did the same, only she looked down at the street, hiding her face from me behind her dark silky hair. I didn't know if I had scared her or not with my scrutiny, but I didn't want her to be like the others. I didn't want her to fear me.

I quickly popped open my umbrella and held it above her, and in a way, my own head. I thought it would keep the awning from leaking onto her while she tried to warm herself. She looked back to me and smiled, a gorgeous and delicate smile that held sincerity in it.

"Thank you." She said it to me with a tiny voice as soft as silk. I immediately fell in love with her voice.

I scrambled to say something back. My mouth would only open and close, again and again, as my mind raced for something, anything to say in response. She let out a little giggle as she watched the complexity of my awkward and reaching face, and then looked away covering her smile with her hand.

I didn't understand what was happening to me. I could feel my hard demeanor vanishing, and I had no comprehension as to why or what was the cause. I thought of the moments just before, when my shocker wasn't tucked so discretely inside my jacket, and the dead face of Zane Blanc. I wanted to just ignore her pleasantries, her hair, and the perfect full smile I had just received for my random act of kindness, but I couldn't.

"You're welcome." I rasped out, and even for me, I could tell it was awkward sounding. Most likely due to the fact that I had never said the words before. She just continued smiling when she turned back to look at me. I immediately postured myself straight forward, in what I could imagine, was a rather uncomfortable look. For some reason, it only made the little giggle return. The pink shade on her smooth alabaster cheeks was unlike anything I'd ever seen. I couldn't help but continue to stare out of my peripheral vision at her. I found her to be an incredible sight.

"Ah…" I began mumbling, trying to find some reason to start a conversation with her. Again, my mind detoured back to the seconds before I came outside. The pool of Zane I had left behind. "You're all wet…"

Stating the obvious was the best I could come up with, and she giggled once more. "Yeah, I've been out in it all day."

Her response wasn't as condescending as I would have been, based on the ridiculousness of my statement. So, I took a breath to try and act more natural.

"So it would seem." I used the opportunity to scrutinize her again to notice that her clothes and boots were completely drenched. "Can I give you a ride somewhere? My car will be here in a few moments."

Her cheeks flushed again. It sent an uncontrollable urge through me to wipe them free of the small drops of water that had settled on them. Without thinking, my hand was smoothing them from her face, but it didn't seem to startle her as much as it did me, when the realization of my actions hit. My hand hit a hard pause when I noticed what I was doing.

My eyes suddenly shifted to hers, and for the next few seconds we stood gazing into each other with a strange intent. It was as if those seconds held some unknown truth to both of us. A truth that connected us somehow.

The feeling broke when Eddie pulled up to the curb in front of us in *Penelope*, his black sedan. He used it to escort us around on my assignments. I didn't acknowledge him as the driver's window rolled down a crack, and then quickly rolled back up. His purposeful detraction only made me more aware of his presence. The girl was startled momentarily by the appearance of the massive black car with tinted windows. Then, she began to seem amused as she looked it over.

I reached for the door handle in front of her, and opened the door for her to get in. "After you." I insisted.

Her smile spread wider as she turned to angle herself into the open door, but she still remained looking at me.

"Such a gentleman." She shot back with a snarky tone, and proceeded into the car without a hint of any worry. I closed the door after her, and walked around to the other side. I folded up the umbrella, and entered the car. Eddie was watching us in the rear view mirror, but didn't say a word. I placed my finger on the privacy window controls, and excluded him from the two of us.

This was not like me.

It was more like something Eddie would do. He's the social one, not me. My life was troubled enough with my recent indecisive morals lingering over my work habits. My work. I had almost forgotten for a second about what I did for work. This definitely didn't make any sense for me to be doing.

I stared out the window without looking at her, and time passed without any exchange of words. We both just remained looking out of our respective windows, watching as the rain beat down, and then rolled off the glass. It's funny; the rain. How it is dark and looming like a fate for the whole city. How it can bring people together. How it can tear them apart.

With that thought, I turned to look at the delicate woman sitting next to me, and as I did, she turned to look back at me, as well. We exchanged simultaneous glances. She blushed again, and I snapped my head forward. A moment passed as we sat listening to the pings of the drops dancing on the roof of the car. Until suddenly, she let out a small sigh.

"Coat and tie guy, huh? You must be someone important." She made the observation with some playfulness to her tone.

It didn't help that she used the word 'important' to describe me, as it only put me back at Club Kelp minutes before we met, where I explained to the door guard just how important I actually was.

"Not really." I said solemnly.

The kind of importance I was, people didn't live long enough to know about. Normally I wouldn't care if she knew who I was or what I did, but something made me not want to tell her. Maybe, it was just that fact alone.

"So, do you always pick strange girls up off the streets?" The playful sarcasm she exuded was very odd. Her confidence was reassuring in the fact that she was not afraid of me. Or didn't seem to be.

"Are you a strange girl?" I asked, starting to feel relaxed with her teasing. What I was feeling was unusual and different; A strange sense of ease. Her brows narrowed slightly at the question, and her sarcasm only elevated in her face.

"No!" She said, seemingly playful yet a slightly appalled, and only briefly. "Let me guess, a guy like you doesn't need to, right?"

I didn't understand entirely what she had meant, and I could only imagine the puzzled look I gave her.

"Nice car, expensive suit, mysterious, handsome. I bet you have the ladies just falling into your lap." The smirk she gave was prodding as she dissected me with her eyes.

I only heard the last part, *'handsome'*. It echoed in my mind like a sick joke. No one has ever described me as handsome. *Gruesome* would probably be how most who knew me would describe me.

"Not really." I thought aloud, being dead honest.

Until then, I had never been that close to a civilian woman. I usually left those assignments to Ryne. His ethics on women and children were a bit different than mine.

She was smiling at me. I could only smile awkwardly in return. I didn't smile. I could remember smiling before, but this somehow felt like the first time it had ever happened.

"You're not really the talkative type are you?" She teased the question.

I didn't have to think about an answer to that one. I wasn't a *'talker'*, and never had been. Not even with Eddie, or in briefings or meetings. I had always been all about business until about five minutes before then.

"Not..." I wasn't able to get it out.

"Not Really!" She blurted out in excitement at her clever interjection. She started laughing, amused at herself, or with me, I guessed. She used her hand to cover her mouth while she laughed.

I was *still* smiling; caught up in her at that instant. I was beginning to put everything else that had happened earlier in the back of my mind. Do you ever notice how people scratch the back of their heads when it happens? I had never had an itch in my life.

"I'm just not really that interesting. So I don't really have much to say about myself." I had finally said more than a couple of words to her, but her laugh stopped abruptly as something outside the window had caught her eye.

She then tapped on the glass privacy shield, and Eddie's head angled back as he rolled it down to acknowledge her.

"This is my stop, right up there on the right." She pointed out of the front window giving Eddie some direction, and leaned back quickly into the seat.

Without paying attention to anything other than her coat pocket, she pulled out her datcom, and then rummaged all over her coat looking for something else.

"Ah ha!" She exclaimed, "Here it is!"

She pulled a lightpen from her inside pocket, and then quickly scribbled something on her Com as Eddie pulled Penelope to the curb. The rain was beating down just as hard here, and when I looked around we hadn't gone very far from Club Kelp, where we had started, by only a couple of sectors.

It had seemed longer, but I still didn't want the ride with her to end. She opened the door and stepped out, but turned back midway to look at me.

"Well, you've got my attention, Mr. Mysterious...Com me." She smiled and flicked her lightpen across her device; sending a local transmission from her Datcom to mine. Then, she dashed through the rain to her stoop.

I watched through the window as she ran up the stairs covering her head with her coat. She quickly made it inside of the building's landing, but not before turning to see me one last time. She would only see the car's tinted glass. The window would be too dark to see in from the outside, and she would not see me looking back at her.

Eddie started Penelope back down the street, and through the walls of pouring rain. I sat looking out the window with my Datcom in my hand.

I flipped it open. Inside was a message. "Lexxi" was the name of the sender, along with a Datcom number.

I immediately flipped my Datcom closed along with her message. I didn't know what I was thinking, but I knew not to be thinking it. Eddie rolled the privacy shield all the way down and smirked, not saying anything, and so I said nothing in return.

Instead, I watched the rain shower the city around us.

I played with my Datcom as we made our way through the streets of the slums. Flipping it open and closing it, but really, I was staring out the window watching the looming rain; this rain that never stops.

The slums were not at all what I was used to; having been built during the *Migration*. I grew up in Central D, a place mostly occupied by Paragon citizen housing. Central D is a part of the city, but not like the slums were a part of the city.

Central D connected to the core of the city; going down through all its levels. It wasn't made from the same material that the slums were. They were brick and mortar, just like any pre-migration city was built. I'm not sure if anyone, even Krill, really knew what Central D was made from. The roads were not like the slums, not paved or cobbled, but smooth and seamlessly fabricated. It's more aesthetically pleasing and solid. Technology in the Central District was more vibrant and current.

Here, it even seems that everything has more power flowing to it, as well. Everything worked and nothing was out of place. The people were more sophisticated, and easier to placate. The crime rate was lower in Central D, but of course, that is due to the overwhelming influence that Paragon has there.

It wasn't like the slums at all, really. Which could be why I couldn't believe I found her there. She didn't seem like the type to live in the slums. That part of the city was more run-down and anachronistic; corner bars everywhere, all of the punks, the goons, and thugs. It all seemed barbaric and out of date comparatively.

The slums were far bigger than Central D, which made it harder for them to conform. The technology there was old and pre-revelation. The people are poor, and when one of them did get ahead, someone else always came along and brought them back down. It's not clean. It's not well lit. It even seemed to rain harder there. The dark alleys were filled with trash, and the skyline was haunted by the looming overhangs of broken highways. There were sections of the city that the connector roads didn't even go to anymore. The slums had two more levels, but they're all basically the same; wet and dark. Oddly enough, the slums had a strange appeal, like living in a memory. A sometimes darkly lit, but well-hued memory.

While I was lost in thought, I hadn't noticed Eddie looking at me. He had been waiting for me to say something. I could see his brows were curious. I guess he could tell I was having an unusual day. I shrugged at him and continued staring out the window, watching the rain. He evidently wanted to break the silence.

"Well, that's a new one...You sure do work fast, too. You were only in there for a couple of minutes. I didn't know Club Kelp had a two for one." Eddie joked, but his morbid attempts at humor always unnerved me. We were friends, but I could never tell the amount of cynicism he held for my position in the company. I didn't want him asking any unnecessary questions, so I slid my Datcom back into my jacket pocket. I never knew what he reported back to Marcus.

"I don't understand, Eddie. I was only doing that girl a favor by helping her out of the rain." I replied unenthusiastically, but he probably didn't care either way, really, but Eddie liked to keep me at an arms' distance.

"You can't fool me, Alpha! I saw her send the datcom message. So what's the deal, man? Are you going to Com her or what?" He asked with a little too much excitement. I had forgotten that the privacy shield was down when she gave me her information. It was probably safe to confide in Eddie. It seemed he was genuinely excited about the event; even though things like that happened to him all the time.

"And tell her what, Eddie?" I paused, "I work for the city. I'm in charge of deletion. Paragon uses me to eliminate the criminal element...permanently." I sighed, "I don't think it would go over very well. Besides, there was something about her though, wasn't there?" Atleast, I had noticed something about her that was different. I could only sit back and admit everything I just told Eddie to myself. I was Paragon's tool.

Eddie's brow lightened in the mirror reflecting back at me, almost like he was disappointed, and he let out a low-disapproving sigh back.

"You never know, Alpha. Maybe she'd be into it." His relaxed tone was sarcastic, but at the same time joyful. All the same, it irritated me. His sarcasm, for some reason, had always hit a nerve. I couldn't understand why this time so much.

What was it about her? What was it about Lexxi that made me feel so uneasy? I was done with the conversation, so I hit the button to put the privacy shield back into place. It rolled up, and for the moment I was done thinking about it. Instead, I just wanted to watch the rain and the city pass by on our way back to Paragon and back to Central D. The rain pounded endlessly on the metal roof of the car as we crossed the Boundary Bridge; one of the many overpasses that connected the rest of the city to Central D. It was the only one where you could get a full view of the entire city.

It was always dark, but from the Boundary Bridge you could see all of its skyline. It was a massive spider-web of roads leading from one level to the next. Some through other structures, some through old abandoned buildings, but all intertwining into itself making a massive twisted labyrinth of architecture .

Professor Krill once told me that it was more than sixteen miles in diameter; A city under a cloud of rain, and above that, shielded by the large dome. A snow-globe. It had been so long since the war, none of the civilians really remembered exactly how we all came to be in the city, and all we really knew was that we couldn't leave.

The rest of the world had been destroyed or was uninhabitable because of the scars from the war.

Paragon training told us that no one was allowed to leave, under penalty of Paragon law. Those who tried were deleted, or they would make it outside where the contamination would kill them anyway. Some people just couldn't take it in here, but it didn't matter, there was no place else to go. At the center of Central D was the tallest building in the city; the Paragon Office Complex.

It employed more than twenty-two thousand members of the city's population. People who worked for Paragon were considered Citizens, and only citizens were allowed to live in Central D. Living in Central D is considered a blessing. You would be given access to clean water, air, and a regiment of non-synthesized foods and goods as rations.

Central D was the smallest part of the city, but it bustled. Mainly because being a citizen was usually safer than living in the slums. There was a Shopping district where you could find fresh recycled clothes, the Entertainment district including the Mental Park Arcade and the Stardust Theater, and then there was the Drain.

The Drain is what they called the lower levels of Central D, and where the only exit from the city still remains. It was well guarded. The Ganymede is also in the Drain. The Ganymede is a hang-out for Paragon employees, and it's one of the classier places usually filled with customers. Probably because it's cleaner than anything you'd find in the slums. The only location in Central D that allows access to non-citizens is the Stardust Theater, at the edge of the entertainment district, which borders the boundary bridge.

The Stardust is a giant amphitheater that holds concerts almost every week, now that music has become popular again. It can easily fit almost everyone inside the city into it, and every so often, that actually happens; usually when there's someone big playing it, and there's only one really big act right now.

Eddie tapped on the privacy shield and I hadn't realized it, but I was still holding my Datcom. I slid it back into my pocket and lowered the glass.

"What Eddie? I'm done talking about the girl." I growled out through my teeth a little, but that didn't alarm Eddie like it would someone else. He was pretty used to my temperament, and on very rare occasions, my lack of one.

"Incoming transmission, bossman." His sarcasm coursed through the statement as he held up his datcom and shook it. I don't know how I didn't notice mine alert in my front pocket, but we were apparently being summoned.

"Just put it on the speaker, Eddie." I replied calmly.

Remy didn't generally transmit unless Marcus wanted us to come in directly. Eddie threw his datcom on the front dash, and Remy's voice came out loud and clear.

"Did you finish the Zane Blanc job?" His familiar high pitched tone questioned. He didn't usually ask . Apparently Eddie hadn't sent in the report yet. He typically did that before I even got the job done. It wouldn't make sense that they hadn't heard from him yet.

"Job's done." I told Remy from the back seat.

"Oh?" His replies were always vague and effeminate.

"Found him in Club Kelp, half an hour ago." I kept my tone professional. Remy reported directly to Marcus and he would detail any insolent behavior, even at him.

"In that case, come to the office, Marcus has called a meeting of all of the top operatives." He shot back. Remy had seemed almost as surprised as I did by not getting the confirmation report, but that wouldn't be enough for Marcus to call a meeting of the top operatives. It would seem that a big job is coming up; something important.

"We're on our way." Eddie was never enthusiastic about executive meetings. He always seemed a little out of place. He was more of a grifter than anything else, and meetings upstairs meant more hits; mostly, top priority hits. He felt as good about them, as I had started to lately.

"Remy out." The datcom ended transmission as we entered Central D. Eddie reached onto the dash, and put it back into his pocket.

"What do you think this is all about?" His eyes glanced back at me, but I wasn't paying any attention to him.

"Who knows, probably just another assignment. It's always another assignment." I muttered back so low that he could probably only make out the last part.

I continued to stare out of the window watching the entertainment district pass by. I noticed the Stardust marquee, Estelle Hart would be singing this weekend.

"Why hadn't you reported on the Zane Blanc job?" I suddenly remembered to ask. His eyes narrowed and twitched in the rear view mirror like he was caught off-guard by the question. Could he have known how close I'd come to letting Zane go? His hesitation only made him seem more suspicious.

"You know, I just wanted to make sure you got him before I said anything to headquarters." Ordinarily, he would report the completed assignment as we were pulling up to the door.

"Since when?" I don't know if I felt betrayed, or if he thought I wasn't doing as good of a job as before.

"Well, he might not have been in there, you know?" He wasn't making sense. We knew he was in there.

"His datcom locator was there." I stated. Eddie turned Penelope onto another street, and used the motion to give him a moment to pause. I could almost hear his heartbeat speeding up.

"That wouldn't necessarily mean he was..." I could feel the evasion in his words, but I wasn't going to make anything of it. Not yet. There would be a time and place to question Eddie's motives. Eddie being suspicious of me wouldn't be a good thing. We've worked closely together for the last five years, and we made a good team.

Typically, he was only the sideman on most projects, but on a rare occasion, I took advantage of his people skills. Eddie knew everyone in the city, and everyone, somehow or another, owed Eddie for something. His popularity worked out for me, more than once.

I knew Eddie for as long as I could remember. We practically grew up together in Central D. We were both drafted into Paragon around the same time, and we've managed to keep an eye on each other. As far as things go in this city, he's the closest I've had to a friend, and five years ago, we became partners in Section Seven.

For years, I had been steadily working my way up in Paragon. So was Eddie, but I had something that they were extremely interested in; a lack of conscience and exceptional aim. Having an insufficient moral aptitude had pretty much become my trademark, and Paragon loved to exploit it. It moved me up the ranks faster. Eddie, on the other hand, developed something completely different; a drug addiction.

In his defense, it's not uncommon. The use of Dox-4, or its street name *Uphorium,* was a bad habit a lot of the people in the city shared; whether you were from Central D or the Slums. In small doses it was a mild sedative, but when abused, it put the user in an almost catatonic euphoric state; hints the name. Personally, I wasn't a fan of anything that dulled my senses, so I'd never tried it.

It doesn't affect Eddie's work, though.

Even with the addiction, we still cleared the most open assignments of the Paragon elite teams. This had made his life very comfortable. Eddie was given Penelope, his beloved coal black sedan, as a gift from the organization after he proved his devotion to Section Seven by capturing a rogue citizen in the slums selling Uphorium to street punks. It was only ironic that it was also the assignment that got him his habit.

Before I had noticed, we were at the plaza square; the center of Central D and the city. The Paragon office was a gigantic set of towers that were only connected in the middle by the overpass on the thirteenth floor. Every floor below twenty six was used for a variety of normal day to day city planning activities, and every floor above that was for executives only.

I followed Eddie up the wide set of stairs leading to the elaborately over-decorated front door. We were greeted by Remy; a tiny man in an over-priced retailored suit, dark tinted glasses, and a short cropped haircut. Remy's attitude was always a little more adherent than I liked, and he enjoyed his job a little, too much. He was Marcus' receptionist, secretary, assistant, or whatever he was called on to be for Marcus at that moment, but Marcus had everyone at his fingertips, which made Remy a little redundant.

"Marcus is upstairs in his office." Remy's teeth flickered perfectly white in the fluorescence, and I hated the grin on the little sycophant's face. It would almost seem sinister if I thought him to be more intelligent.

He waved us toward the elevators. I was always pretty sure by his silence that he understood how Eddie and I felt about his creepy adoration for Marcus and Paragon and him altogether.

The elevator doors opened, and we stepped in, and out of his sight. Marcus' office was on the second to top floor, fifty-nine. A floor that overlooked the entire city, and was the highest up I've ever been. To say that the Paragon office was tall was an understatement. It was, at least, twice as high as its nearest competition.

The doors beeped open, and we were on our way down the familiar long hallway leading to the very edge of the building; where Marcus' office sat. I followed Eddie through the dimly lit doorway.

"Come in, Eddie...Alpha." Marcus' voice boomed in the ill lit room. The only light came from the glow of the *holoscreen* in front of Marcus on his desk. From this side the images were reversed, but it seemed like he was looking at concert posters.

Only seconds passed before the wall behind Marcus opened revealing the glass and city behind him; lighting up the room. Marcus sat in his chair, wearing his black on red suit, with his matching dark red-tinted glasses. His blond hair was smoothed down and back, and he spoke through his perfect silvery glossed teeth. As we walked into the oversized office, Eddie was looking around for the others. I had already noticed their absence. Customarily, a meeting like this would involve all of the elite executives.

"Looks like we're early." Eddie spoke softly, as if it were intended only for me. I could hear the worry in his voice. As we neared Marcus' desk and the holoscreen, I could tell the images were of Estelle and her latest concert flier for the Stardust this weekend. I had just seen it moments earlier one the ride over. The slogan *'Hope for the Future'* was written plainly in bold letters across the top, and below was a close-up of her on stage wearing an old style ear-set microphone that gave it some distant vintage appeal. I had heard her music, and it wasn't coincidental that her slogan also matched her title song, and was the message she sent to the people with her music; a message that people were responding to.

"No, Eddie. You are right on time. Ryne will be joining us momentarily, but for now we can go ahead and get started." Marcus' voice was low and affirming, but there was something hidden in his tone. With one hand he spun the holoscreen around to face us and enlarged the image on the screen.

"What's this, Marcus? You want to go to a concert?" Eddie pretended he didn't understand, but unfortunately I could see, too well, what Marcus' plans were.

"I take it you know who this girl is?" Marcus' arms crossed in front of him, and he looked at both of us as if he already knew the answer, but Eddie was quicker to reply than I was.

"Yeah, that's Estelle Hart, a singer from the slums. She's really hot right now." The way Eddie spoke was as if he were one of her fans. I nudged his shoulder to halt his ensuing excitement, because I knew Marcus wouldn't be as excited.

"What?" He gave me a quick undeterred glance. I didn't turn my head in acknowledgement, but I could see his questioning gaze in my peripheral vision. I only knew that his enthusiasm over our next target would be inappropriate in Marcus' eyes, but it only confirmed that he didn't understand our situation, yet. Marcus had leaned forward and put his arms back on his desk. The holoscreen in front of us dimmed and became more translucent. Marcus held out his hand gesturing toward the image of Estelle on the screen.

"This girl and all her aspirations would be a detriment to the authority of Paragon if she is allowed to continue." Marcus always had a way of making his opinions seem like facts.

"She's just a singer." I was nonchalant to hide my assumptions about our newly acquired hit, but it was to no avail. My assumption would be validated.

"Just a singer?" Marcus moaned as he leaned forward over his desk.

"Her songs give a new 'hope' to overthrow the authority of this city! The very people we control, and keep in order. Her lyrics will incite riots, and the people will push against Paragon's rule." He coughed, but it didn't break his totalitarian tone as he ranted. "Paragon has controlled this city ever since it was first established, and I'll be damned if I let a singer bring down this organization. Without Paragon, this city will crumble into chaos!"

Marcus was always absolute. I could imagine him looking over this assignment earlier and coming to this conclusion, but it was still fearfully arrogant to think that one person could undermine such an operation as the Paragon Corporation. It was Marcus' job to make sure things like that were never able to happen. He had recently been given control of Paragon by its former president and founder, Killian Stoddard, and in his freshness to his role had been overreacting to every threat that could be made to the city or the company.

"Do you really think that one person could get the people of the city to rise against Paragon, and if so, why would they?" Eddie's voice was resistant, but he was starting to get the idea, as Marcus's hand slammed against his desk, and his voice became even lower and more intense.

"This one singer could ruin everything we've worked so hard for. She could destroy Paragon, the city, and all of humanity." Marcus' logic made an odd sense. There had always been resistance to Paragon, but ever since *The Revelation* it had always been this way.

"So, what do you need us for?" Eddie was always naïve when it came to women in the workplace. He treated them like flowers, or fragile ornaments to be decorated with.

"Isn't it obvious?" Marcus leaned back in his chair returning his hands to their previously folded position. His teeth gleamed as the smile stretched his face devilishly. He always enjoyed this part of his position a little too much. It is one thing to be forced to delete someone out of necessity but it was another thing to take pleasure in it, and this wasn't the first time I had seen it from him.

"You mean, she's a mark!?" Eddie's surprise was quite genuine despite the lack of mine.

"Eddie, you haven't been listening?" Marcus flossed his tongue across his lips to moisten them, "We can't have the population knowing it was Paragon. Her fame has given her a celebrity status unlike anything else in the city, and if the civilians knew Paragon deleted her, there would be riots in Central D. If the people in the outskirts knew, they'd try to collapse the bridges again, but if she brings them both together with her music...they'll tear this city apart." Marcus' logic was irrefutable to us. If the city had thought, for one second, that their advocate of hope was extinguished by Paragon; they would undoubtedly take it upon themselves to make sure that Paragon would see its end, and without Paragon.

That would throw the city back into chaos.

After the *Revelation*, the population was in shambles and Paragon leaders, along with Killian Stoddard, established a new order within the people. It wasn't until later that the company took liberties with that newfound power.

"But..." I could barely nudge Eddie before he could finish his sentence, and I knew what he was thinking. Eddie had a soft spot when it came to females, and he wouldn't see the same necessity that Marcus had. Defying Marcus would only lead us to *deletion* ourselves. Not that the average lifespan of a civilian was very long in any case, but for now, we would only follow orders. Marcus was peering at us through the holoscreen, and I could tell he wasn't happy with all the questioning Eddie was doing about the new assignment. Eddie also noticed, and cleared his throat, posturing himself into diligence.

"You can count on us." Eddie knew what I meant. I didn't always like it any more than he did, but we would have time to discuss it later at the Ganymede. The assignment didn't have to be done quickly. We had until the concert. We had time.

"See Remy outside for a complete dossier on this assignment, and in the meantime, keep up the good work with the open assignments." Marcus was pleased enough with our current work that he wasn't going to let a little defiance in Eddie's previous tone bother him.

As far as elite executives went, Eddie and I had made a niche of cleaning up the day to day garbage that kept the city worse off; garbage like Zane Blanc.

I used my tasks, like that one, to keep my priorities in check when it came to the bigger, more disputable jobs. People had always tried to take advantage of Paragon and use its power for their own means; taking what they could from the company to try to undermine its supremacy. It was just the way things went. There was no real form of government and no bureaucracy, and it just kept the city breeding Zane Blanc's.

Marcus knew that, and I'm sure his decision to eliminate Estelle Hart was based on that fact, but I've never been able to quite believe his motives were as pure as he'd like them to be perceived, but I was never sure why.

Eddie and I left his office, and took the walk down the long corridor back to the elevator. We weren't half way down the hall when the elevator dinged, and Ryne stepped out. He stood a little better than six foot tall with multi-colored blonde and black hair that stood in a mess above his scarred and scruffy face. His torso was draped in taggers, shockers, and knives. He looked like a pre-Revelation mercenary for the Southland Territories, or at least tried to appear as one; to seem more intimidating, I assumed. His eyes never met ours as he passed us on his way to Marcus' office, but Eddie always looked hard into Ryne's with some weird half-daunting smirk on his face.

I never asked why Eddie didn't like Ryne, but to me, he was just another one of us; a Section Seven member. Although he had his own unit, they rarely came into Paragon. As I understood it, they all held up in different buildings in the slums, in case they were suddenly needed on an open assignment.

Ryne and his team specialized in capture, and I always assumed that was why he had the scars. Sometimes it was necessary to keep someone alive long enough to find out how they planned to undermine Paragon, and Ryne's team was best at that.

'*Interrogation*' they called it, but from what I've seen, it leaned more to the side of torture and made what I did seem almost humane. Clients didn't usually go along cooperatively, and I guessed those are the ones that left their mark upon Ryne. I could only assume that was the reason for his harsh and distant demeanor.

Remy greeted us at the bottom of the elevator with his creepy devotion unbroken. He held holopackets in his hands, which contained the dossier for the Estelle Hart assignment. As he approached with an odd delight, he held them out for each of us to take one. I took it, tucked mine into my pocket and carried on, but worry was written across Eddie's face as he inserted it into his Datcom. The packet was unusually extensive with pages of information; far more than any typical job.

"You think you've done enough recon on this, Remy?" There was a harshness in Eddie's normal sarcasm, but it only spread Remy's grin wider.

Estelle was a very beautiful woman; the entire city knew it and was even proud of the fact. She was tall and blonde with very symmetrical features. Every inch of her was perfect by definition, and it easily stood her apart from the other entertainers; most of them being women also, but she was most beautiful in the eyes of the city.

Apparently Remy was amongst her admirers as well, but I had never thought about her as any kind of symbol, nor had I found myself amongst the drooling masses that followed her every step. Remy's pause at Eddie's question was needlessly long before letting out his signature eerie chuckle, "This one was a very interesting subject."

You could almost feel the intensity in Remy's eyes. Even behind the dark glass that shielded them, they beamed as he grinned at Eddie and the images of Estelle.

"Interesting, huh?" Eddie's sarcasm returned to normal as he flicked through section after section of images. Remy's grin curled out into a smile, and Eddie looked up at him.

"You are one creepy bastard, Remy." Eddie continued scrolling past countless unneeded images, one after the next.

"I'll let you two have fun with the pretty pictures." As twisted as Remy seemed in saying it, Eddie was enjoying the photos just as much, and it appeared to be a good time to excuse myself, so I discreetly began to walk away from the two.

"You're going to com Ms. Pretty Dress, huh?" Eddie's eyes slanted as he turned his attention to me. Normally I would return his sarcasm with some harsh comment, but I didn't want to make more of a scene than needed. Where I was going wasn't technically allowed.

"Yeah Sure...I'll be back in a few minutes." I tried to keep my direction ambiguous as I opened the stairwell access.

"Yeah, yeah. Meet me out front. We've got a few other assignments that we can clear up today." Eddie couldn't help but slip a grin at his false hopes in my social uptick, but what he wouldn't know couldn't hurt him.

"Yeah, meet you at Penelope." I nodded and walked around the corner, out of sight, deeper into the stairwell. Where I was going was only one floor down in the first basement; a place where retirees work, if you were lucky enough to see an age that would allow it.

Normally visiting a retired citizen was perfectly fine, but for whatever reason, Krill wasn't allowed to have visitors. I've never known the conditions, but apparently, his was a forced retirement. Dorian Krill used to be one of Paragon's elite scientists specializing in genetics and human growth; although, his field of study was much more expansive than just that.

I held my *wristport* up to the scanner and the door unlocked. I was greeted by a tiny robot that Professor Krill had built to keep him company. It was a clumsy little thing that barely walked, but it could talk and play chess; which kept Krill busy, for the most part.

"Hello Socrates." I nodded to the little motorized thing as I entered.

"Hello Mister Vincent Alpha." Its mechanical voice was always cheerful as it pronounced my full name upon greeting me, but no one else has ever used my full name; just it and Krill.

"Alpha! Is that you?" The old man's voice was low and weak, but excited none-the-less. The short, white-haired man came out from behind a set of metal shelves which separated the room into halves. His face beamed with enthusiasm.

Krill was the only person in the city that I could talk to like I was a human being, and not just a soldier for Paragon. He was the closest thing I'd had to a family. He was still working for Paragon when I was first promoted to Section Seven, and had always treated me like I was more of a son or pupil than a co-worker. He always tested my strategies and would lecture me on philosophies.

"Krill, how have you been?" I asked, genuinely excited to hear his response, but Krill shrugged, and his smile turned to detest.

It wasn't long after my promotion that he was forced into retirement, and soon after that he was locked down in the basement. I've always managed to stay in contact with him despite executive orders, but now he was all but a forgotten relic in a library of Paragon's history. I could only assume he wasn't happy about it, but at least he was allowed to still tinker down here in the basement.

"Same ole stuff, Alpha. Just an old man playing with his toys." The smile soon returned to his face as he inspected me, just as he always did, whenever he saw me. It was as if he hadn't seen me in years. I've always blamed it on his age. He had just turned fifty-four this past October.

"How's the head hunting business?" He laughed.

He had never enjoyed what I did for Paragon. He had always claimed I was meant for more, but I could never understand what he meant by that. He looked down to find the holopacket in my pocket that contained the Estelle job.

"What's this?" He snatched the dossier from my coat and inserted it into Socrates, who promptly began to display the images..

"A new assignment?" He asked., and I felt slightly ashamed, even though we both knew it could be nothing else. I guess he had hoped for some sort of gift.

"Anyone interesting this time? Are you bringing down another Uphorium cartel? Disgruntled slum-punk perhaps?" He queried again as the old bot projected the first image of Estelle.

"Actually, it's Estelle Hart." As I said it, his face dropped, and I instantly understood Eddie's hesitation about this assignment.

"Estelle Hart!" His old brows furrowed down into the top of his nose, "Marcus! That no good son of a Mutate!" Krill fumed as he prompted the next image.

"A job's a job, old man. It has to be done. Apparently, she is under suspicion of treasonous actions." I tried to explain, but even I knew it sounded like a lousy cover story. Krill paced, and I watched as he looked over the contents the little robot displayed for him, "So it's treason now! To promote peace and hope for this city? Marcus has truly lost his mind!" The anger from his voice was piercing.

His hand rose to his chin as he turned from me. His voice had calmed to a strange low. "You can't seriously be thinking about doing this, Alpha?"

I hadn't thought about it. I would just comply. To me, it was just orders, and following orders was what I did.

"I have to." I explained. It was what I believed.

Krill spun, and his angered tone returned, "You most certainly do not! You do this, and you will be the monster they've always wanted you to be."

His finger wafted at me like I was some child for scolding, but I didn't understand his implications.

"What does that even mean, Dorian?" I asked, feeling like I had disappointed him, but I didn't understand why. The way he looked at me made me feel small and worthless.

"If you kill Estelle Hart, you are no better than Marcus; ha! You'd be worse. You would be nothing more than his finger puppet. Is that what you want? You want to be reduced to nothing, and not have even a shred of humanity? It's bad enough that he's abused you for as long as he has." Krill seethed out his diatribe, and I had never seen him as worked up before.

It was a little humorous. He was ranting like a lunatic, and not making much sense of anything.

"She's just a singer." I tried to interject to calm him. There had been plenty. Estelle Hart wouldn't be last.

"Just a singer? Alpha, surely you see more than what's only in front of your face. Estelle is the embodiment of the human condition. Love, Peace, Hope, Dreams. She teaches people that there is still good inside of all of us, and that this damned city has killed that yet!" He continued his rave, before coming to a pause as he heaved huff after huff, before catching his breath.

"Maybe I've been wrong about you all along." He said low and to himself.

I didn't understand what he meant about being wrong about me, but Letting Estelle Hart continue to spread her message would eventually cause another uprising. Chaos would continue to threaten Paragon's Code.

I couldn't let the errant ramblings of a derelict old man turn me against the city.

"I have a job to do." I turned and began to walk back out of the tiny, what had suddenly become overcrowded, room.

"Fine, you do your job, Alpha, but don't think for one second..." His words trailed off the further away I became, and soon I was back at the top of the stairwell. I walked toward the elaborate front door feeling confused by the lecture I had just been given. I pulled out my datcom along the way, trying to clear my head.

"Lexxia." I spoke the name into the device, and now was as good a time as any to find out more about...her.

It was five years ago when they first brought *that thing* into Section Seven. They even promoted that worthless grifter, Eddie, to watch over *it*.

It was embarrassing to be replaced by that science experiment monster, and I couldn't believe Marcus had been able to convince Krill to even let him use *it*, but without Killian in the picture, Marcus had total control of Paragon.

Supposedly, Killian was still upstairs watching everything, but by now he was so old that he couldn't really do anything. He no longer had any real power in Paragon, and I was just an old soldier; I just followed my orders. That was all I knew, and the chain of command had recently changed. I would have to gain Marcus' respect just as I had Killian's before.

Marcus had once been the leader of Section Seven, but was pulled out to serve directly under Killian.

It made his ego intolerable, but I was glad to have been given his old position. It allowed me to create my own team, and head up all the Section Seven operations. I felt I had finally obtained some control in a city without any.

When Marcus brought *it* into Section Seven, he segregated the team. I was still in charge of my unit, but Alpha and Eddie would do the more intimate assignments. My team was relegated to search and capture. I didn't mind at the time. We did our jobs, and they did theirs. Until four years ago, when the Xack Lutz job was ordered. *It* was assigned to my team temporarily, but only because if the assignment was given directly to Alpha, Marcus knew that I would do everything in my power to stop *that thing* from succeeding in killing my brother.

If Marcus had sent a deletion order out on my brother, Xack, I would have had no choice but to end his little toy monster, and Marcus would never take that chance. It seemed Xack had been in on the bombing of *the Far Bridge*. It was only one of the bridges that connected Central D to the Slums.

At the time, a group of anti-Paragon activists had a plan to completely separate the city by destroying its' bridge system, and my brother, being raised some-what of a hand-me-down demolitionist by our father, was the bomb man. Needless to say, Paragon learned about the plan, and Alpha was sent to clean up the activists, one by one, after the Far Bridge was destroyed. Alpha was to delete all of them, but one, my brother Xack.

I remember the day as clear as the glass that surrounds this city. It was relatively slow that day, which should have been a good indicator that the city was up to something. Alpha and Eddie were out clearing open assignments, one after another, as they always had.

I hated *it* for being so good at doing them.

We had just bagged some *Uphorium* user, and were bringing him into the detox unit over at the central treatment center when the Far Bridge suddenly erupted into flames. If the boom that echoed through the city wasn't enough, Section Seven was immediately notified over the datcom system of the terrorist activity. I let Griff and the *junker* out of the truck and left them back at the center while the rest of our team made haste to the site.

It was already there.

The activists were dispersing into different alleys throughout the streets of the slums. Eddie hung back while Alpha ran towards the flaming bridge. It had begun to crumble and fall down towards the lower levels. My truck raced up an adjacent bridge to a level higher up. We all stared in disbelief when Alpha jumped at the last moment, and cleared what had to be thirty feet of the collapsing bridge. Then, quickly ran off into an alleyway where one of the activists had since retreated. It was a split-second before Alpha was out of sight.

Eddie pulled his black sedan back away from the bridge, and turned back down the street, trying to keep up with Alpha. He circled around, coming up the bridge that we were using, and it set him even further behind us.

"Did you see that?" Ox gulped with a hint of penetrating fear. His eyes were bugged wide.

"He jumped the bridge! Tell me I wasn't the only one who saw that." He clutched at the window's seal, almost pressing his nose against the glass as he peered through.

"Shut up Ox." I wasn't about to let him make a spectacle out of *that thing*. It wasn't just my distaste for Alpha, but also the fact that *it* shouldn't be showing off like that. At the time, I considered the heightened circumstances, and tried not to let it bother me; especially knowing that my brother was a priority target.

Knowing Xack, it wouldn't be long before the next bomb would ignite. He never was one to waste time on a job. We still had that in common. I pressed the accelerator harder to the floor. I couldn't let Alpha get to him before I did. Surely, Marcus would have given Alpha a contingency plan if I failed to bring Xack back to Paragon. As we crossed the stretch of overpass, I could see the canisters under the Boundary Bridge. It was going to be their next target.

Apparently, Alpha's spectacle wasn't unnoticed by them, either, and it had bought us some time to get to the bridge before they did.

I cut the wheel hard down the *Main* into the Slums. It didn't take another minute to get to the bridge.

"Countess be damned...Look at that!" All three of us; Ox, Ramone, and myself looked in the direction of Ox's excited extended right hand. Alpha was jumping from the rooftops of the buildings. One of the activists fell from an old fire escape that was about three stories up. His face crushed against the railing on the way down, the metal mangling his body, and the blood shot out of him as he smacked against the pavement. It didn't slow Alpha, though. In a bound, he was across to the next rooftop where another one of the renegades was making his getaway. Alpha was fast, so fast *it* was keeping pace with us in the truck.

Alpha's shocker was pulled from its holster, and three charges sounded as we rounded the corner to the Boundary Bridge. The truck raced to the bridge, until I stamped the brake and my team barreled out of the doors with a quickness. We were all startled at the crashing sound that came from behind us. Ox's mouth hung wide as he turned.

It was Alpha.

It had jumped down onto the street behind us from what must have been forty feet up. Alpha's eyes were hidden behind the dark tint of *its* glasses, but *its* brows were livid and narrow. Alpha only nodded to me, but never said a word. I turned back around to see Xack running for the bridge and the canisters.

"Xack! Stop!" My voice was harsh and desperate, and Xack did not comply. The sound of a charge came from behind us and Xack paused, mid-stride, and tumbled to the ground. I pulled my shocker, and turned to Alpha.

"You son-of-muta..." I stopped the words when I noticed Alpha's shocker pointed at the pavement. Then, I turned back around to see my brother stumbling to his feet and continuing toward the bridge. Was *that thing* trying to help me by buying me some more time?

"Xack, stop! Or the next time, you don't get back up." I growled through my teeth unappreciative of both attempts. Xack's hands went up in the air. He had stopped only steps away from the bridge.

"I'm not the Evil one here, Ryne." Xack's eyes were tortured and furious as the words crept from his lips. I waved Ramone and Ox to back-off as I stepped towards my brother.

"What the hell is wrong with you? Are you trying to get yourself killed?" I yelled as I started to holster my Shocker. Xack whipped his long black hair to the side; a bad habit that had made him seem smug.

"Dead or alive, it's all the same under Paragon's fist, brother." He responded, as the sweat rolled off of his forehead in beads. He knew my orders. He had always understood what I did for the city, and he had always hated it. He had never understood the way of order, or what it meant to be a soldier.

"I can't let you do this! Did you honestly think that destroying the bridges and disconnecting the city would make things right?" I pleaded with him. Xack took one step backwards for every one that I took forward, and it was a slow chase to the canisters.

"It would give the slums a chance to grow; it would keep you and your freaks out, if even just for one day of peace!" He cried out as he made distance between us. I wasn't ashamed of what I did, or who I worked for. Not until that day. There weren't any sides, and no perfect depiction of right and wrong. Paragon hadn't been the 'bad guy'. The city and the last handful of humanity were just trying to cope with the loss of the world. The Earth still had a fresh wound, and it was seething. To my brother, however; Paragon was the perfect evil.

"Just come with me, Xack, We'll get this worked out." I tried again, but the truth was that the defiance of Paragon law, and acts of terrorism against the city held a sentence of immediate deletion. I just needed to get him away from the explosives.

"No! I'll never be Paragon's pawn." Xack had always been dramatic, and when I was drafted by Paragon he took it upon himself to deem me weak-willed; a slave to order. I would have to appeal to his nostalgia.

"What about dad? He wouldn't want you to throw your life away." I thought quickly, hoping that our shared connection to our father would calm him down.

His brows narrowed, and I had hit the wrong nerve. We had also been split when it came to our father, each having been given different sides of the man during our childhood. Xack's hand fell downward, and he feigned a dash towards the canisters. I quickly pulled my shocker back on him.

"I'm not the one pulling the trigger, Ryne. Maybe you should be the one who's thinking about our father, and his last wishes." He said with the same cocky smile that he had always used to provoke me in our youths. The rain beat down on us in the silence that ensued, and the city never seemed darker. He had always blamed me for the way our father died.

"You don't have to do this, Xack." I cried out through the drops. All hope was lost in my voice, and the words hardly formed as they escaped, but Xack's anger kept his words vibrant.

"That's where you're wrong. I am the only one who can do this. You've already lost yourself to Paragon." He growled through his toothy grin, "See you in hell, brother."

Xack turned to run down the bridge again. I dropped my aim, and began to chase after him. All he had to do was light one of the barrels and the bridge would ignite. We both knew it; me and Alpha. I raised my shocker again to Xack, but my hesitation had cost us everything. He was too far ahead for me to make a running shot. That's when I heard the second charge fire.

Xack doubled over only inches from the containers, and my knees hit the wet pavement. I knew where the shot came from. I knew *it* had killed my brother, but at that moment, I could only be grateful that I didn't have to do it myself.

I got to my feet again, and when I looked back, Alpha was gone. Ramone and Ox were just staring into the rain as I began to walk back to them.

"Clean up the canisters, and make sure they can't be reused." My tone was dead and callous, and they nodded understandingly as they got to work. I headed back to the truck to turn in the assignment. Every time I saw the broken overhangs of the disconnected Far Bridge, I thought of my brother. I remember my father's wishes and the memories that haunt me like a waking nightmare. It was the only thing I ever thought about, whenever I saw Alpha. How I could be so helpless, and *it* could be so exact.

Alpha's the reason that Eddie gives me that stupid smirk of his. Eddie knows that I hate Alpha, and at the same time, owe *that thing* everything. Knowing that gives Eddie some kind of sick pleasure. I opened the door to Marcus' office where he sat behind his desk awaiting my arrival.

"Come in Ryne, you're just the guy I've wanted to see." Marcus said in an overly professional tone, not that I minded.

Ever since that day, everything had always just been business.

"Have a seat." He commanded, gesturing to a chair in front of his desk. Under normal circumstances he didn't offer a 'seat' to anyone.

"No thanks, I'll stand." I didn't like to waste time, and Marcus tended to get long-winded if you gave him a chance to talk.

"Still the hard-ass as usual, Ryne?" He asked playfully, not nearly as upset by the defiance as he would be normally. Something was going on. Ever since his promotion, Marcus used his power to test people; myself included. I liked to let him know that I didn't like that.

"If I weren't, you wouldn't need me." I said in implied obedience, trying to ingratiate myself to him. He appreciated traits in others that he saw in himself, and Marcus always tried to come off stronger than he actually was.

"A very good point." He paused in some sort of inner delight. "Let me show you why you're here."

Marcus' lips pressed and curled at the edges as if he wanted to smile at my last comment. Obedience was the easiest way to make Marcus happy, because it played well to his oversized self-image. He waved his hand over his desk, and the Holoscreen projected above.

On it were some concert posters, and various pictures of the singer Estelle Hart. I wasn't a fan, but I felt like I knew everything about her, just from how much the people were talking in the city.

The slum residents and civilians alike, were always gossiping about Estelle, and the people couldn't get enough of her. She was on posters all throughout the city, and other than Paragon, she was the most iconic thing in the city, and it made sense that Marcus would want her eliminated. Her songs made people think about change, and also, that Paragon was the reason for how bad it had become under the dome. Most of the population didn't like the fact that one power controlled their every move, or how they lived, what they ate, and literally almost everything. For Paragon to continue, she would have to go away sooner or later, or the people of the slums would eventually rise against the civilian population.

I understood, without a word, why Marcus would show me this.

"Estelle, huh…" I just nodded to him. His face was dark behind the holoscreen, "I think I understand." Not that I liked it. She was just one silly girl whose anti-Paragon propaganda cut a little too close to the heart of the city.

"I knew you would, Ryne." His hands laid on the table as he leaned back in his chair.

"Isn't Alpha your 'go to' guy on this type of thing, though?" I questioned for a moment. It always was supposed to be what *that thing* did. It deleted people, so we didn't have to. So that no human had to kill another human, ever again. I wasn't really sure why I was even being briefed on this.

"Yes, I've already assigned her deletion to Alpha and Eddie, what I need you for is a little more...creative." His pause was elusive, and his teeth showed through his smile, gleaming and silver; however, his trademark sinister grin was wasted on me. I've never found it as intimidating as he wanted it to be; just cheesy.

"Yeah? And what's that, then?" I shrugged unconcerned. I never liked his idea of *creative*. He leaned forward to the holoscreen, and it dimmed as his glare caught me.

"I just need you to make sure the job gets done." He said with a weird sinister stare. His inflections held doubt, and some kind of hidden agenda. He never needed to 'make sure' before with Alpha, and it concerned me why he would now. Alpha always finished his assignments, and many more that weren't assigned.

"Since when did Alpha need any more looking after? He always finishes his assignments." I assured, but Marcus didn't give away anything. He never had. Everything he said was part of some elaborate plan that only he could see in its entirety.

"Yes, he does...for now." He said vaguely. He was always vague, and it was annoying. He would only fill you in on pieces of the puzzle, a little at a time. It made me wonder if he ever knew, really, what he was doing.

"What's that supposed to mean?" I asked curiously. I had to admit, the idea of getting rid of Alpha intrigued me. It just never seemed likely.

The *thing* was practically superhuman or something; if it were even human at all. By the way Marcus acted, it seemed like something was wrong with it. Was it malfunctioning?

"There's been nothing major, as of yet, but Eddie's reports have been a little disconcerting, scientifically speaking." He said shifting his glasses down his nose to show his eyes. Marcus didn't hesitate to remind people of his intellect; always peppering up his vocabulary.

"Is it slowing down or something?" I always hoped that they had found some defect in Alpha that would make it easier to eliminate at some point.

"Oh, no, nothing like that. He just seems to be having some...Moral insecurities. It's actually very technical and unexpected." Marcus slithered out.

This was the first I'd heard of Alpha even having feelings, let alone morals. I didn't realize that it was capable of more than replicating human function. It could walk and talk like any other person, but it never really seemed like there was a real thought in *its* head.

"You mean, it feels?" I asked, confused. This was all news to me. Marcus laughed maniacally behind heavy breaths for a brief moment. It was a very awkward laugh, but it didn't convince me I had been fooled by their little puppet.

"Yes Ryne, he feels. He breathes. He makes friends, and he is capable of being the perfect human, and that's exactly what I am afraid of...He wasn't supposed to do any of it!"

Marcus' voice had become playfully sarcastic and a bit irate, as if he were lecturing an ignorant child.

"But, why?" I didn't understand why they would need to make it *feel* things, but I could see the benefit. It would allow it to incorporate itself into our society better.

"If he suddenly decides that this assignment is too much, and that he can't delete Estelle...it would mean disaster for Paragon." Marcus' tone had completely changed as his hand wafted through the holoscreen. If Alpha was gaining emotions and he wasn't supposed to, only one person could be responsible.

"You think that Krill might have something to do with it?" I assumed and it was more than obvious that Marcus already knew the answer. The only other person on the Alpha project was the professor, and it was his life's work. Marcus had stolen it from him in the twilight of its conception.

"He has everything to do with it!" Marcus growled as his fist piled into his desk.

I knew that Krill and Marcus had worked together to create that *thing*, and that Marcus was the one who confined Krill to retirement, but more than that, I never had really understood.

"Krill would have had Alpha become a street cleaner or window washer! He would have never used him for what he was needed for, as I have! I wouldn't put it past that old cog to have crossed me in some way." His ranting had become tyrannical; another side of Marcus that I never cared for.

"I see." I played along. I knew that was the best way to expedite whatever speech was about to come.

"When I was appointed to the project, the prototype was almost finished! Killian was the one who wanted to try to make people resistant to the atmosphere outside the city. He knew the reason we were having so many control issues was because of overpopulation and confinement." Marcus seethed in explanation, "Alpha was made to be able to read and stabilize the conditions outside, but I had a better use for him!"

His hand shot forward, pointing his index finger at me, "If the people of the city stopped fighting with themselves then we could survive in here! If humanity's evil was gone, we could start to heal, and so I suggested that Alpha be used the way he is now!" He smacked the desk with an open palm to accentuate his flourish, "To wash the city clean of the vile that this evil spreads!"

"No human should have taken another human's life ever again!" He preached, as he had so many times before, seemingly lost in his story. It seemed like a horror story he used to justify his actions to me.

"Krill was furious when I took him off the project!" Marcus continued, "He had developed a paternity complex with Alpha, and it was blinding his judgment. That's why he is in the basement playing with his robots and nonsense." He mumbled in obvious disdain of the professor's intellectual prowess.

"He couldn't see the immediate good for the people!" His voice rose again. "If we didn't use Alpha this way, we would have more incidents like the one at the Far Bridge."

The memory was still painful, but Marcus had made his point with me. The idea wasn't lost on me that Marcus and Krill had created a monster that they had let loose in the city. Especially, if Marcus thought that he was losing control of it.

"So, it knows what it is then?" I asked, wondering about the implications of it having awareness. I couldn't imagine what it would be like to know that you weren't human; to know that you were created, and not born.

"Of course not!" Marcus laughed, and by how sudden he said it, I could tell the idea of Alpha realizing his potential was far more frightening to Marcus than anything else, even Estelle.

"That must never happen." He commanded absolutely, "However, he may start to piece things together, and if that happens...I want you to be there. It will be up to you then, to delete him."

The thought sent shudders down my spine. Could I even do that? Could it even be killed? I've known that I was the best soldier in Paragon for the years I've been a citizen, but I'd never seen anyone or anything do what that *thing* was capable of.

"Ryne, you've been with us a long time. Paragon will be in your debt for this." A debt he held to no one, but in any case, I would follow orders. It was how I lived.

"You can count on me, Marcus." For as much as I could possibly do, I thought. I did owe Paragon for allowing me citizenship, and the ability to work my way through the ranks when the rest of my family had already died. Marcus offered my brother the same opportunity, but when he refused, his life ended at the hands of that monster. I would not let my fate be the same.

"In the meantime, I need you to do surveillance on Eddie and Alpha." He said nonchalantly as if they were normal orders, "Check out Eddie, and see if he's still going to be a viable failsafe. He's seemingly growing more and more sympathetic to Alpha's *condition*."

I didn't have a problem with taking Eddie down a couple of notches, and if Alpha deviating from protocol was being allowed by Eddie, he would be responsible for whatever Alpha did. Leashing a beast to the hands of an infant was never a good idea, and now I was going to have to play 'clean-up crew' for the babysitter. Just another day in this hellish bastion. At least, I thought I might get a chance to wipe that smirk he had right into the wall.

"Not a problem, Marcus. I never did trust that grifter piece of garbage." It was true. I never had.

It wasn't just that he was raised a citizen but chose to hang out in the slums, or the fact that he was a drug addicted fool. It was more that he was equal to me in Paragon, when I thought he shouldn't be; when he hadn't earned it, like I had.

"Remy will fill you in with any needed intel…take care Ryne." Marcus quickly dismissed me with a flutter of his hand, and I turned to make my way out his office.

On my way out, I could hear his chair spin behind me so he would look out of the massive windows that viewed the gloomy city down below.

When I reached the bottom floor, Remy was waiting for me with a holopacket in his hand.

"They're already back in the slums." He stated plainly with a wide toothless smile. I knew he meant Alpha and Eddie. Remy's inferiority complex was the most obvious thing about him, so he liked to rub in what he could, whenever he got the chance. "You might be able to catch them if you hurry."

He was having way too much fun with his job, and it showed in his voice. He seemed more pleased than anyone that Alpha was being investigated.

"I'll have Griff keep an eye out for them." I wasn't in any hurry. The whole thing gave me a stomach ache, and I wasn't in the mood to eat any of Remy's crap. I snatched the packet from his hands, and made my way past him.

The rain wasn't letting up, as if it ever had. When I reached my truck, I turned on my datcom and punched in Griff's digits.

"Yo boss, how was the big meeting?" He quickly answered in his own excited way. He was always eager to serve my unit, and always ready for new orders, but I had never liked the responsibility that came with my role as a commander; a sacrifice I made for the amount of freedom I had. I wasn't what you might call a people person, and Griff being needy was something I tried to just put up with.

"Can the 'boss' crap, Griff. I need you to do me a favor and keep an eye out for our buddies, Eddie and Alpha. They should be heading your way." I commanded, hoping we could cut them off, and put a tail on them somewhere in the slums.

"Yeah, uhm...They're actually across the street at Vics, but they're just standing around or something." His reply sounded surprised. They didn't waste any time getting back to work. It made Marcus' paranoia seem a little far-fetched.

"Vic's?" I wasn't familiar with every hole in the slums. There was a lot more to it, way too many corners and alleys for any one person to remember.

"Yeah, there's an old open assignment on the owner, apparently he owes some creds or something." Griff answered with some foreknowledge of what they were doing, which was always a usual thing he did. Recon.

All I could think was that an open-assignment was left incomplete, and a member of my crew was in the building across the street. That was unacceptable.

"And you didn't think to take care of it?" I growled through the little electronic device. A good job was about five minutes long. Most of them completed in the duration of this com.

"Nah, I've been waiting right here, like you said; besides, it isn't an open-ended case or anything. So, not our gig." He replied with a kind of professional absence. He might have been right, but he always acted like a moron; always trying too hard to make people happy with him, but he could take orders. He just couldn't give them to himself.

"Damnit Griff, you could learn some initiative. Stay where you are, I'll be there in a few minutes." I ended the conversation by throwing the datcom on the passenger seat.

Another assignment my flunkies let them beat us to. It wasn't any wonder we looked like fools by comparison, but Griff was a good kid; an ex-shock ball player. He once held the record for *longest hold* in a single game, but when he blew out his knees it ended his career. That's when he found himself here with me. Ox, well, he holds true to his name. Not a bright guy, but he makes up for it in brute strength; toughest guy I know. Then there's Ramone. He's a gangly little guy, who was more wiry than tough. He's our chaser. He hasn't let one client ever get away, and he's glad to be here. He wouldn't have become a citizen if I hadn't found him eight years ago on the run from Paragon. It took me two weeks to bring him in, and I instantly recommended that he was assigned to me.

A few minutes later, I pulled the truck around to the back of the building that Griff was holed up in. I killed the engine and coasted into park behind the structure, so Alpha and Eddie wouldn't know that they were being watched. When I walked inside, Griff was peering out of the window at them without discretion, "Get away from the window, stupid." I snarled at Griff.

"They're not even watching, Boss. They've been in a pretty heated conversation for a few minutes now." His defiance wasn't purposeful, but it irritated me none-the-less.

"I said, cut it out with the 'boss' crap." but he never listened. I think he liked the whole chain of command, but I never wanted to be above anyone. I just didn't like the idea of being below everyone. I wanted to be my own man.

"You think he's gonna use any of his '*powers*' on this one?" Griff asked. He was almost as bad as Ox when it came to Alpha. They both had begun to admire him since that day at the Far Bridge, but Griff had only heard the story from Ox, who had seen it all first hand. He had never actually seen Alpha do anything out of the ordinary, but he made it well known that he wanted to.

"He's just a man, Griff. Besides I don't think it would take powers to take down Vic. He's practically an old man now." I said, making the observation. Thirty-nine was old in this city. You would only see it if you were good and didn't step on Paragon's toes, or if the left-over contamination sickness didn't claim you; although, that was becoming more rare.

Still the slums were as prolific as rats, and the population actually increased instead of declining, like predicted.

"Does it usually take them this long? What are they doing?" Griff huffed out. I walked over to the window to take a glance for myself. Then, I walked back to the center of the room and took a seat on the old dusty couch. It sat almost alone, except for the rickety little table leaning next to it.

"They're waiting." I told him calmly. He was always too anxious, and just wanted to get a job over with. Probably, because he was always just the muscle.

"Waiting? For what?" He was like a child; always asking questions that didn't need answers.

"The store to clear out. It wouldn't make sense for them to delete everyone in the store." and like a child, you can't help but indulge them to please your own ego.

"Ah, gotcha. So, what was the big important meeting about? Watching them? They do something?" I crossed my arms at his astute deduction. I didn't like our mission. Every passing second made it seem more and more unnecessary.

"That's what we have to find out. They got an assignment and we've got to make sure they do it, or we have to." It didn't even sound right saying it.

"Oh, what's the assignment?" Griff didn't even flinch at the comment, not like I did. He was all team, and that apparently didn't include Alpha and Eddie.

"Estelle Hart." Her name came out sounding like I was chewing gravel. I assumed Griff wouldn't like hearing it.

"What!? What has she done?" He said with a little too much excitement. It would figure that he was a fan. He was used to the spotlight, too. He probably even thought, at one time, that he could be with a girl like her. Hell, he probably even could have.

"She's under suspicion of conspiracy." It sounded ridiculous and logical at the same time. On a basic human level, she had done nothing wrong, but she would be a victim of the era that she lived in. Another Section Seven secret.

"Oh wow, she never seemed like the type. She was always real nice when I met her." he said casually, and If I were drinking something, it would have shot out of my mouth and nose at the statement. Instead, I just glared at him in disbelief.

"Yeah, she really liked Shockball." He smiled at his memory, "She sang at a couple of our games when I was with *the Elites*. I thought her songs were inspiring. You know, made you want to be a good person and all that."

It was true. I hadn't listened, but her music did seem to calm people, and made them want to make a better effort to be better people.

"Sometimes you can never tell with people, Griff." I tried to stay nonchalant about how flattering he was of her. I didn't want him to realize that the treason was because of all the things he just described about her.

"Yeah, it's a shame really." He said abruptly. I didn't expect him to take it so well after hearing him adore her, but it was better off that he did.

"Oh, they're going in." Griff redirected our attention back outside, and I walked to the window and glanced out around him. A person had just walked out of the store, and the door was closing behind Eddie as he entered, but Alpha remained outside. That didn't seem right to me. Alpha looked around, and, for almost a second, I thought I saw him look right at us. We both ducked to the sides of the window. When we looked back out, he was gone with only the market's door closing behind him.

Only a moment passed before the market's window and glass door flashed a brilliant white. Then, Alpha walked back out, followed by Eddie who was eating something from a foil wrapper. We watched them continue to stand around talking outside of the store for a moment before Eddie tossed his car keys to Alpha. Alpha sat down inside the sleek black sedan, and Eddie leaned down to say something to him through the window. Soon after, the car rolled away out of our sight.

Eddie stood in front of Vic's market smoking his gasper for a few minutes. Then, he pulled a flask and a vile from his inside coat pocket. He poured the vile of Uphorium into the flask. Uphorium was a powder drug, and was only potent when mixed with synthohol.

He was doxing.

He shook the flask with his hand like a centrifuge; mixing his mind-numbers before he took a big gulp. He let out a sigh and shook as his drugs set in. Then, he returned the flask back to his pocket and tossed the vile onto the watery street. When his hand reemerged from his jacket, it was holding his datcom.

"He let Alpha take his car? Where do you think he's going?" Griff puffed out. Griff was more shocked by Alpha taking the car than Eddie's random public drug use, but he was right to be. It was strange for Eddie to let anyone drive *Penelope*, and even more curious that he would let Alpha out of his sight.

I didn't respond to Griff. I was more interested as to who Eddie would be calling on his datcom. That would have a better chance of answering Griff's question, but before my thought had finished, my datcom started humming in my pocket.

"Ooh, that's freaky." Griff stated, and then I pulled my datcom and saw that it was, indeed, Eddie. Had they seen us watching them? Is that why Alpha took off in Eddie's car? Was Eddie protecting him?

I answered the com reluctantly, "It's Ryne." I tried to feign ignorance in my gruff answering manner.

"Hey Ryne, what's up buddy? It's Eddie." The familiar voice came through. It was awkward for Eddie to com me. We didn't have the strongest friendship, to say the least, and he only called when it was business, or he needed something important.

"Yeah, what is it?" I was trying to be indifferent by being my usual self. This was an uncomfortable situation.

"Ah...Yeah, so I was wondering if you were in the area." He asked, sounding coy in his demeanor. Was this the setup? If he knew I was watching, then he knew I was in the area, but how would I know where he was if I wasn't watching him.

"Which area is that, Eddie?" I asked, playing it off like I didn't know. Before your datcom could broadcast your location, there had to be an assignment out on you, or you'd have to willingly give your coordinates.

"Oh, yeah...sorry about that..." He said unconcerned, and then there was a pause. When I looked outside I saw him pull his datcom from his ear, and mash his finger into some of the keys. He stared at it for a moment, waiting for something to happen. Then, my datcom buzzed again against my head, and I pulled it away and looked at it confused.

Incoming Message
ASSMNT: *Vic Harden*
Location: Sector 9 – Vic's Market – Main
Details: **COMPLETE**

I put the datcom back to my ear, and my confusion was replaced with annoyance. He was just being smug and showing off. I could hear the laughter coming through the other end of the transmission. Although this could have been his way of indicating that he knew I was there, chances were, knowing him, he was just bragging.

"I'm at Vic's Market. I forgot to send that in again, sorry. Listen, I could use a ride back to Central if you or any of your cronies are near here." He chuckled, and he was putting an awful lot of faith in me not asking any questions, but that was the way Eddie was; used to getting his way.

"Where's your car, Eddie?" I had to ask. He was never without Penelope. I was going to make him tell me why he was without it now, not that I didn't already know, but I wanted to see how well he could lie.

"Oh that, yeah... Alpha took it. He was wanting a little alone time, and I thought it would be a good reward for working so hard, ya know." Eddie laughed again, but he didn't lie. He was a plain idiot, really. He really did think that creature they made was an actual person.

"You sure that thing should get *alone time*?" I questioned back. Who knew how it would malfunction next? If it was becoming aware, what was to stop it from getting angry? If it were angry, who knew what it could do. Until fifteen minutes ago, I didn't think it could feel anything.

"Everyone one needs some downtime now and then, Ryne. Even Alpha." He mused. He was hiding something, but I wasn't sure if it was Alpha or his drug habit. He really shouldn't have driven if he was *stargazing*. His words were too relaxed, even now, and his speech gave away the drugs setting in his system.

He had given me a way to get closer, and that was really all that mattered, "Yeah sure, Eddie. I'll come pick you up in a few minutes."

Maybe, I could get something out of him while I had him in the truck. I would have to convince him to tell me more about Alpha's behavior.

"By the countess, be blessed. Eddie out!" He called out in naive enthusiasm, and then the datcom clicked, closing transmission. I slid it back into its compartment on my vest.

"I'll be back later, Griff. Clean up Vic and the shop while I'm gone." I commanded the large man next to me. Griff would be of better use doing the routine detail work. He'd seen it enough that it had started to bother him less, and he was becoming a loyal soldier.

"Will do, boss." He replied in obedience. It was hopeless. He was never going to get it, but I wasn't going to tell him again, not now. I started making my way back out of the rear entrance; to my truck.

"Oh, and Griff...Remember, initiative." I nodded a finger back his way as I left. He posed an awkward and stoic salute out of my peripheral vision.

"Initiative, gotcha, bos..." He stuttered. He was reliable when I needed him, but otherwise, he and Ox had their own category when it came to intelligence.

The door closed behind me.

I started up the truck and pulled out onto the street, driving away from the corner where Eddie stood. I would go three blocks down, and circle back to allow some time to pass.

Then, the rain was beating down around the truck as I pulled to the curb. Eddie ran out from under Vic's awning and quickly opened the door; climbing into the cab. He seemed comfortable as he adjusted in the upholstery, and shook his wet hair onto the floorboards. His eyes never met mine when he got in, but that stupid grin wouldn't leave his face. He was as proud as ever, and his motives still lingered in the back of my mind.

"Beat your boys to the Vic job, huh?" He sneered out from his near-perfect teeth. His attitude was about as much as I could stand. There was just something about him. He was that one person in the world that it was easy to hate. His appearance alone disgusted me.

"Can it Eddie, it wasn't that open-ended. Seems like you guys like doing your job, so my guys figured you could use the practice." I shot out in sharp retort. His grin turned into a full-bellied laugh at my comment.

"That's funny, Ryne...I never knew you were such a joke man." He laughed out loud. I wasn't. Sure, Alpha wasn't in any league that either of us could even see, but Eddie could take some notes. He always seemed a little out of place in Section Seven; a team of elite adjudication operatives.

"So, I take it Marcus filled you in on the Estelle job, huh?" He asked unprovoked. He was clever, I had to give him that. When it came to acquiring information, Eddie was a master manipulator.

I didn't know if he was implying that he knew the extent of my assignment, or if he only thought my assignment was the same as his. I couldn't give him much.

"Yeah, something like that." I said plainly.

You can't read a blank slate. If he did know that my assignment included them, he wouldn't have me confirm it for him.

"What's your take on it?" He asked, and I could tell he was fishing. I assumed that he meant her deletion, but who knew with him. He twitched in the seat next to mine. The Dox was setting in hard, now. His grin was ear to ear as he watched the lights pass us through the windshield.

"What do you mean, Eddie?" I kept it simple because I couldn't tell if he could handle more than simple just then. His neck twisted his head around to watch the different street lights race by, and then to me. He was lucid, but somewhere else. He didn't seem concerned with me at all.

"Do you think she's as big a threat as Marcus claims?" He managed to ask, but his eyes were lost behind his tinted glasses. It was a good question. The investigation that prompted the assignment was swift and deliberate. It closely associated her with known activists, and assumed they were using her music to cause public tension.

"Maybe. Her songs do incite the people." I said, trying to make sense of it to him the way Marcus had made it make sense to me.

If the population rebels again, who knows how much damage it could cause? Humanity had been fighting for so long, each fight could be the last. There was only one problem.

"I guess, but they're not violent. I mean, she doesn't seem like this huge menace to Paragon that Marcus is making her out to be, you know." He muttered out in protest.

Could the Dox be making him speak his thoughts, or could this be what Marcus meant by assigning me to this case? His dosed up brain had rotted, and it had influenced Alpha's, that *thing's,* perception.

"You and that monster getting cold feet, Eddie?" I asked, feeling more smug, and he knew how I really felt about Alpha. So, I let the words come out a little harsher than I could have.

"Nah, I just think it's a waste of something pretty to look at." He grinned at his last remark. His eyes stayed fixed off in some other place, when suddenly; he pulled his attention back to the car and the surroundings, the rain, and me.

"Are you going to Ganymede tonight?" He asked as plain as day, but I didn't understand. The bar? He knew I wasn't really the type to be social, and the question caught me off guard with its speed.

"Huh?" I huffed. He instantly seemed more alert; looking around and talking like any other normal person would, now.

"You know, get some drinks, and play nice with the rest of the citizens, maybe even take turns getting rejected by the cute new girl they got serving there now. Life man, you gotta live it." He grinned out, placing his hands behind his head resting it back. It wasn't like Eddie to want to spend his free time with me, but he did like The Ganymede. He was notorious there, but I didn't understand this new rapport that he seemed to think we had. All of this chatter because of a lift back to the office? Something was up. I wasn't the type of person that danced around this kind of crap, and so I didn't.

"What gives, Eddie? I know you don't exactly like me. What's with wanting to get all chummy now? I'm not exactly the buddy-buddy type." I snarled. It was never wise to let your guard down around Eddie. That was when a hug could turn into a heart-attack. It was the way he worked; all smiles.

"I know, but it'd be nice to bury the hatchet, don't ya think? It's not that I don't like ya, Ryne. I just take some odd pleasure in watching Alpha tie your boys up. It's more because of him than your boys, though. You'd have to get to know him. He's actually an alright guy." He declared, his whimsy beginning to return to his speech. He laughed intermittently through what, I could only guess, was his way of apologizing mixed with a sales pitch. It pissed me off even more to have him confirm the fact that watching us fail gave him pleasure.

"He's not a guy." I shot back. He was a twisted experiment; something the professor and Marcus cooked up in some weird lab in the Drain one night, to try to save humanity or something, and look at it now.

"He *is* more than you'd think, and besides I'm flying solo tonight and I hate to drink alone." He said it all very matter-of-factly.

So, Alpha wasn't coming back until later. It wasn't like Eddie to give up information like that so easily. He was, most likely, still feeling the effects of the dox.

"Why would I?" I said with a false reluctance in my voice that would keep Eddie persistent. It was going to make following him much easier.

"Oh c'mon, it'll be fun. First round on me." He insisted, taking the bait. I didn't like the idea of socializing with Eddie, but it would be a good opportunity to do some recon on their relationship. They didn't really have any oversight, except for Marcus, who had Eddie report everything directly back to him. Even then, he gave them a wide berth when everything was going smoothly.

"Fine, yeah, sure. Ganymede. What time?" I inconspicuously agreed. It wasn't safe for that *thing* to be running around the city unchecked. Eddie wasn't stable. I've seen worse users, but he was pretty bad. He definitely had the addiction.

"I'm heading there right after I handle some assignment stuff at the office." He stated in a dejected response. He didn't seem enthusiastic about going back to the main building.

"Don't you need Alpha for that?" I asked, trying to make my exterior appear more relaxed, now that I had agreed to meet him later. If he wanted to pretend we were friends, I would let him, for now.

"Nah, he'll catch up quick." He joked. Before I had realized it, we were crossing the Boundary Bridge. The chat with Eddie had made the drive feel shorter somehow. It had kept my attention split, and I had lost my perception of time.

"Just let me out at the front office, I'll meet you in the Drain in a bit." He remarked looking out to the roadside. I pulled up to a wide set of stairs in front of the office building. Eddie opened the door, and barreled out of the seat plashing his feet onto the sidewalk. The rain poured around the truck and he started to shut the door behind him.

"Her name is Reimi." I said it directly, as I looked through the open side of the cab. He turned back to look at me with a puzzled look on his face.

"The new girl. Her name is Reimi." I added, hoping the realization would strike some jealous nerve, but I didn't go to the Drain to socialize, or the Ganymede for women.

"Ryne, you scoundrel. I didn't know you kept up with the ladies so well." He chuckled as he shut the door and continued up the stairs. I wasn't a regular at Ganymede, but Griff, Ox and Ramone had kept me going back on the occasional synth-filled off-night.

Reime wasn't easy to miss either. She had red hair and a cute face, not to mention, she was probably the sweetest person in the place. She wasn't like the snobby servers who took their citizenship for granted, and only wanted creds. I think I liked most that she took the time to enjoy the job, and did it smiling.

I decided to wait for Eddie in the Drain. It was down a level from the surface sector of Central D, and it was where the Ganymede was located. I wasn't really popular amongst the citizens, and I never tried to be. They saw me for what I was; a glorified bounty hunter, and that kept most of them distant and scared. I pulled the truck into the small parking zone next to the bar. There were more cars in the lot than I had expected, and there were people coming and going through the neon entrance. They all smiled as they hid under their coat hoods from the rain. They raced to and from their cars, and they were happy. It wasn't unusual for this place. They were citizens, and they had worked hard for their happiness, and the Ganymede gave them a place to be with each other.

I walked in.

Most of the room was well lit over the dance floor, and it was busy for the time of night. People were dancing, and the music was unusually loud. The waitresses were moving quickly from table to table taking orders and carrying drinks.

I made my way to an empty table in a dimly lit corner. I knew it was Reime's section of the club. I pulled a gasper from my pocket and pressed it between my lips under my mustache. I lit it and inhaled, and through the smoke I could make out Reime's slender figure approaching.

"What can I get for you tonight, honey?" Her sweet canary-like voice resonated across the table. She was a pretty girl, an average citizen, but she never seemed to mind me. Not like the other citizens.

"Just a synth-ale, for now." I stated, trying my best not to sound too guttural or intimidating. She winked and walked away. Her perfume wafted over to me in a low amount, but it was intoxicating. Eddie would be a fool to think he was classy enough for her; she was way out of mine and his league. That's when he came through the door, strutting like he was made of creds. He'd even changed his jacket since I had dropped him off. He might as well have been blowing kisses at all the girls as he walked by. He, eventually, sat down across from me at the table; laying a relaxed arm across an adjacent chair.

"You came early. Are you trying to beat me to *ole' red* over there?" He smirked as he gestured to Reime, but I didn't want to respond. His attitude about her was boisterous and low class; the kind of crap you'd find in a slum dive. Then he reached over, slapped me on the arm and laughed.

I didn't like this. He pulled out a gasper of his own, and Reime returned to take his order. It didn't help that she was blushing as they made eye contact.

"What can I get you tonight, Eddie?" She said, in that small canary voice, only this time, it held a hint of adoration.

"You know what Eddie likes. You just bring me the usual." He soothed out like it was a regular Tuesday. The grin never left his face.

She giggled, turned, and began walking towards the vendor as his hand hit her right buttock, sending her that much faster. He pulled a drag of his smoke, and twitched his eyebrows up and down at me.

"She's cute, huh?" He said as kept grinning.

"I guess, for a redhead." I turned from him to break the conversation quickly. I was almost ready to deck him, but since she didn't seem to mind so much, it would have only made me look bad.

"Ooh, that kind of sets a bad mood, doesn't it?" He said off-topic as he nodded to the air, to nothing. I didn't understand what he meant, and it made him more annoying.

"What does?" I groaned. I turned back to him, expecting him to razz me for my egress from his last remarks.

"The song that's playing; it hits a little too close to home right now, and I come here to get away from work." He said, thick with sarcasm, as he peppered his gasper around the ash cleaner.

I listened to the music, but it was tapering out of a chorus.

'look deep into the shadow
To find the light of tomorrow
It's been way too long now
That we've seen this sorrow
And with you, it can end forever
Just believe, hope for the future,
Is all I see.'

It was Estelle's new song *'Hope for the future'*. I had to admit that it had an elegant sound that was different from the other drab that was being played these days. It had the feel of a different era to it, like something ancient.

"I didn't even notice." I remarked, and it was true. It had just faded into background noise in the busy establishment, and my own social reluctance had distanced me from trends and culture.

"How could you not? It's such a good song." Eddied insisted, but music just wasn't something I kept up with. Other people supplemented their lives with gossip and entertainment, but mine had always been about Paragon.

"Yeah, shame." I noted, putting a damper on his enthusiasm. I thought back to the conversation I had with Griff earlier, and how tame he had said the same words. Eddie sat across from me, listening to the song, when Reime came back with his drink; a tall green girly looking thing with some kind of fruit peel in it.

"Hey honey, we need a woman's opinion, you got a second?" The words came out smooth for him, and he made talking to this gorgeous woman look effortless; just as if he were talking to me. Reime looked around for a moment to check on her other tables, but then turned back to him, all smiles, and nodded.

"You like this song?" He asked, and her eyes lit up like they were filled with sparkles.

"Oh yeah, it's Estelle! She's the most awesome singer ever! She's my idol…I mean, not that I'm as good-looking as her, but you know, I…uhm…yeah, I like it," She giggled, and her face beamed with happiness, as she blushed at her rambling worship of Estelle.

"Oh c'mon now, you're twice as pretty as she is. Look at you! What's she got on you? I've heard reds have more fire, anyway." He sang out praising her, and then he wrapped his arm around her waist and pulled her closer to him. She blushed again, and ran her finger down his nose as she let out a quiet private sounding little giggle.

"You're a real bad boy, Eddie." She hummed to him, and it was then that I thought about crossing the table and ripping out his throat. Before I could, a customer called for her, and he released Reime so that she could return to her work. I leaned my elbows onto the table, and lifted the glass to my mouth trying to hide my disgust with the little bastard as he just watched her prance to her next table. When she was out of sight, he let out a sigh of longing that made it even worse, and again I wanted to kill him. I placed my glass back on the table, and leaned back in my chair to hide in the shadow of the corner. I rapped my fingers on the table in front of me, impatiently.

"So, what's the deal Eddie? You didn't just want me to come out to watch you schmooze all over Reime." It was almost a snarl as it left my mouth.

"Thank the countess you said her name again, I had totally forgotten it. You're handy, you know that, Ryne?" He paused while his grin set in, but then his eyes tightened, "But you're right. That's not why I asked you to come here tonight. I've got something I want to talk to you about."

He paused, and took a sip of the disgusting drink, and a drag from his gasper. "I need your opinion on something, before I report it back to Marcus. You know, to see if I'd be wasting his time."

He instantly had my full attention. This wasn't about earlier today at Vic's. Something else *was* going on, just as I had suspected. He hesitated, and pulled the vile out of his jacket. He poured it into the tall fruity drink, and then held the vile out to me.

"Want some?" he asked, but I objected by throwing a hand out to usher it back at him.

"Are you still dealing with that slum creep, Hilder?" I asked. We all knew about Eddie's habit, but we all looked the other way, too. I had even crossed paths with the dox dealer who supplied him.

"Nah, this is the good stuff." His grin reemerged.

"You shouldn't be taking that shit. You know I could haul you into detox right now, if I were so inclined." I leaned forward from the darkness, to show him I was serious. To let him see the intent in my eyes. I wanted to do it, and if I thought nothing worse could come of it, I would have hauled him in already.

"Lighten up, it's just a little fun now and then." He mused, blowing off my intent. He swirled his drink in front of him, and swallowed it all in a single pour. Then, he began the aftershocks of minor ridiculous looking shakes and head spasms, and then quickly settled.

"I'm more concerned about my car; Alpha should have been back by now." He said plainly, and the blankness started to consume his vision. It was almost as though he were looking through me. Who knew what he saw when he doxed, it was usually different for everyone.

"Yeah, about that. You wouldn't tell me where he went earlier." I sternly reminded him.

"He's on a date." He just said it plain and simple. He said it like he was talking about a childhood friend, or any other random person.

"A date! That *thing* can date?" My voice raised and I flinched in shock. I never thought that *thing* would want to mate, or even if it looked at women. It was absurd. Was it even possible?

A date? It just sounded so ordinary.

"Yeah, a date. Come on, Ryne. Alpha is a man like you or me, and besides it's just some dress he picked up in the rain this morning after the Zane Blanc job." He answered nonchalantly in an effort to calm the conversation. Eddie seemed way too light-hearted about Alpha's actions. He had stopped seeing Alpha for what it truly was.

It wasn't a man like me or Eddie. It wasn't even technically human, and Eddie was under strict orders to report all odd behavior back to Marcus.

"Eddie, I don't think Marcus will be happy to know that Alpha has developed a social life. *It* wasn't supposed to feel. That was the point. It took the shame away." I declared, remembering what I was told in the beginning. When they first briefed me on the *Alpha* project. Eddie began staring at the lights above us, and grinning at nothing.

"The guy is all work and no play. I think it is good for him." He slurred in his relaxed speech. He didn't fully comprehend the context of what was happening. He had become its friend; its *'buddy'*; how novel. Someone would have to tell Marcus about this.

"Well, we had better hope *it* keeps doing *its* job." My voice became rough again, as I lectured the doxed fool in front of me. This wasn't good news, and I didn't plan on playing pals with Eddie anymore. I finished my synth, and plowed the glass back down to the table. Then, I stood up; throwing down a few creds.

"That's for Reime, make sure she gets it." I demanded as I walked off, but I could still hear Eddie murmuring to himself, mockingly.

"He'll still do his job. He better still do his job." I could hear him assure himself. He would undoubtedly be the one to pay the worst price for Alpha's failure.

I'm sure he knew that, too.

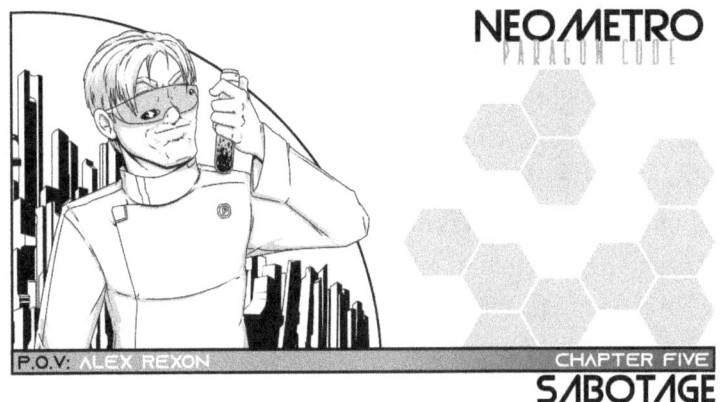

It was Tuesday, and I was in Krill's laboratory on the retirement floor.

He lectured me on molecular genetics, atomic base, and compound proteins. I took notes and paid attention while he messed around on his antiquated computer system. It was ancient in comparison to the things we had on the floors below, only having a first-gen *liquiglass* screen. I didn't see how he could get any work done on it, but he was probably more adept with that technology, than I was with mine. I couldn't really see what he was working on, and he didn't include it in his teaching regiment. I could only make out the bold text at the top of the monitor which read *'BETA system'*. It didn't make any sense to me at the time, and I wouldn't bother to interrupt him as he prattled on about transmuting molecular composition.

His voice was exact and scientific during his lectures, but he never turned to look at me. He just expected me to take notes, and I was alright with that. He seemed like any disgruntled old man, but his genius was renowned in Paragon. His father, Adrian Krill, had helped configure the Dome to support human life, and that was how I guessed the Professor had managed to maintain in retirement instead of being shuffled off by Paragon after Marcus took over.

"... forcing the chromosomes of one altered species to become dominant; then when fused to that of another, creates a whole new strain of hybrid artificial DNA." The old man purged, and my eyes glazed over for a moment, "Are you paying attention Alex?"

Another holoscreen projected his teachings in front of me. He had made a mess of it with different equations and solutions. I copied everything in my notes. It would all be useful.

"Yes, but I don't understand. You mean that changing the base of one chromosome can cause it to believe that it isn't from that species? And yet, still live inside the same species by sharing its prior alleles?" I asked, hoping to still be on the same page as the old man. I understood most of what Krill taught to me, but he had experience in fields I had never heard of. I kept up well in molecular physics and anatomy, and sometimes I even felt like I impressed him with my ability to do so; not that Krill ever really seemed impressed.

"Ha, you are starting to get it." He said with a grin.

Actually, I had no clue how to achieve what he was suggesting, but he had worked far more with the gene encoder than anyone. I assumed it was some theory he had successfully brought to life. He didn't mind sharing that kind of stuff; even though it was usually still classified. I was only *allowed* to work with him, so that I could eventually replace him on the new lab team. Marcus had re-opened the Proto-Human Sciences Division. I couldn't tell Krill, but that was six months ago.

Marcus had worked alongside Krill when Alpha was created, but he wasn't as capable as the professor. He was having me leak information back to him via these little lectures. I sometimes felt bad for doing it. Krill and I had become friends in the short time we had been studying together. We were solving problems for each other, and playing chess when Socrates wasn't using the board to play against itself.

Krill kept spouting out information about genetic crossovers and programming artificial DNA, when I heard Socrates behind me.

"Good afternoon Mr. Marcus Creed." The little mechanical voice pronounced every syllable accurately as the door slid shut behind Marcus. Krill jumped up and rounded the metal shelves that separated his computer desk from the rest of the room.

"Well, if it isn't the magistrate that condemned the philosopher. The king that chopped off the hand of the artist; Marcus Creed, to what do I owe the pleasure?" Krill's voice was hateful and sarcastic, but he had made his point with the inflection; the words were just added insult.

Marcus looked around the room, and eyed me carefully.

"Well professor it seems you've been making good use of your retirement." Marcus' lips pursed out the words as he spoke. Then, Marcus picked up Socrates between his index finger and thumb and watched the tiny machine wiggle for safety. A grin passed over Marcus as he watched the little mechanism squirm.

"I do as much as I can, or should I say...am allowed." The old man gruffed out, and his brow settled lower. Krill hated Marcus, and it was evident. Marcus started to walk slowly around the room, picking up small parts of old machines with his free hand, and bounced Socrates in the other.

"Well, maybe after hearing about what's going on with your prototype, you will feel lucky that you are still able to tinker around down here, at all." The last of the words came out slow and diabolic. Marcus was after something, and his subtle threats were his way of getting information. I didn't like the way Marcus used fear to get what he wanted. Krill watched Marcus closer now, scrutinizing his face for any signs that would give away his hidden motives. It looked like a match of wits between two classic opponents.

"What's happening with Alpha?" The professor growled out. Krill's voice was low and discerning as if the question was a demand instead of curiosity.

"Well, old man, maybe that's something I should be asking you." Marcus' voice came out low, but building in volume as at his next demand, "Is he supposed to not want to do his job?"

The anger that came from Marcus was completely abrupt and unexpected. Marcus was almost bent over the top of Krill, looking down at him through his red tinted glasses; his grip crushing Socrates in his right hand.

"What do you mean?" Krill's eyebrows danced back and forth as if they were fighting back against his attacker.

"I mean, the data shows anomalies in his neural system, and now I'm getting reports from Eddie and Ryne that there's been performance inconsistencies. You have sabotaged the project, haven't you? You old crone!" Marcus shouted out, ascending to the heights of his fabricated outrage.

In that moment of rage, Marcus threw the little robot against the wall, shattering it to pieces. Its little motors hummed to as stop as it shutdown. Krill had not looked scared, and it was sure to have angered Marcus even more to not get the response he was looking for from his act of violence; instead, Krill chuckled a little at Marcus' attempt at fury.

"You mean, he doesn't want to *kill* anymore." Krill laughed again, almost as if he was the victor in their little game of wits.

"What have you done?!" The slick blonde-haired executive seethed and then Marcus grabbed Krill by the collar of his lab coat, but the smile on Krill's face didn't leave with the threat. It merely intensified.

"You know Marcus; a child will only obey long enough to decide for itself what it thinks. If Alpha is starting to show signs of compassion, then there is nothing wrong with my design. Our compassion is what gives us our humanity. I was designing a human being wasn't I? Well, I would call what you are describing as a success." The old man ended with another pop of a laugh. Krill's words seemed to eat at Marcus as they came out, and he slowly pulled his coat from Marcus' grasp; almost condescendingly patting his collar back into place. Krill obviously thought very little in regards to Marcus' humanity, and it pleased him to hear that Alpha wasn't just a commercial killer, like Marcus had wanted.

"Then what use is it to me if it doesn't do its assignments." Marcus' voice became low, and in his words hid another threat, but not to Krill, now. Marcus had never called Alpha an "it" before. That was more like how Ryne spoke of Alpha; disposable. Marcus had always seemed to think much more than that of Alpha, but apparently without his will infused into him; that would end. Krill's lightheartedness ceased quickly, and his brows furrowed back down above his deep old eyes.

"I did not create a puppet. I made a masterpiece. My work was tainted when you pulled me off my project!" The old man said stern and cold.

"You trapped me down here in this fancy prison you call retirement. Then, you turn my boy into some high-class thug, and now you come to me when you can't get him to do what you want! HA! You'll find no help from me." Krill was now giving Marcus the lecture.

I could barely watch them going at it without feeling slightly withdrawn. It was as if I wasn't there, and two old rivals were taunting each other in a foreign tongue, known only by them. They began staring at each other, silently.

Neither spoke nor budged, and suddenly without any reason, Marcus started a hollow laugh that began to increase as some unknown thought sprawled across his face. It was evil. Like somehow, Krill had instantly become insignificant.

"Help?" Marcus' laugh became even more crazed as he continued, "I didn't come here for your help. That's the last thing I need! You've already helped enough!"

His eyes slid to view me at his peripheral, and then back to Krill, "Alpha won't be a problem anymore, as a matter of fact, I'll just replace him." His laugh smoldered into a chuckle as he tried to bury it completely.

"What does that even mean? Just how do you think you are going to do that?" The old man questioned Marcus' confidence. Krill's eyes were wide, but the wrinkles around them made it look like he was almost squinting. Then, Marcus' evil laugh started to bubble up again, as he watched the clueless old man struggle to grasp the entirety of what had been happening behind his back in the previous months.

This is what Marcus wanted; the win. For once, just to have an advantage over the professor and his genius; to have something that Krill couldn't know, and it was then that my stomach jumped into my chest.

I was to be the pawn that checked the old man.

"I took your design back down to the basics, and streamlined it. What you wouldn't do I have now done myself, with a little help from other very skilled geneticists." Marcus explained. My head lowered as I had hoped it would not have been like this. I knew I was being used, but not like this. Marcus was taking pleasure at Krill's ignorance of me, and the theft of his ideas and methods.

"You did what? Who helped who? Who did what?" Krill's excitement flared like a mouse caught in a trap. The words shot out like flashes cutting through the tension-filled room.

"You did, old man." Marcus sneered, and my head sunk even lower. I was ashamed, and I deserved to be.

"What! I did no such thing." Krill demanded, and his faith in me wouldn't let him see what had happened. His faith in me kept me innocent in his mind, and that was how he was defeated; he had trusted me.

"Oh, you didn't know you were, that's true!" Marcus said snidely looking in my direction. Then, Krill looked at me with sudden realization, and his anger and attention turned towards me in slow motion. His eyes held fire as he gazed angrily into me.

"You! You little bastard. I took you in! I was teaching you everything, and you do this...do you realize what you have done?" Krill yelled as he approached me, clinching his leathery old fists.

Marcus only began his tyrant's laugh once more; obviously pleased with how well his plan had worked. "There's no reason to take it out on him. It's all already done." Marcus proclaimed, and then turned to me. "Alex, Go back to the lab downstairs." He said more stern than necessary, in an apparent show of authority. I gladly began to rush my way out of Krill's little junk-filled room to anywhere that I could get away from the shame I was feeling.

As I passed Marcus, the doors slid open.

"Soon, I'll have new soldiers; ones that *will* obey my commands. The Alpha Program is officially terminated." The laughter from Marcus erupted louder as he followed me out of the room, "See you later, old cog."

The doors slid closed behind us, leaving Krill fuming in the tiny room. Marcus followed me down the corridor to the lab on the floor below.

There were four floors below this one. The three directly below had been turned into a huge laboratory that held more than enough of Paragon's scary secrets, but the one furthest down was the biggest mystery. It had been locked with a restricted entrance ever since the first inhabitants. Nobody but Marcus, Krill, and Killian Stoddard knew what was down there. Some say it was the machine that powered the city, others would claim it was the remains of the dead society that lived in the dome before us. Yet, once you stepped off the elevator to that floor, it went nowhere, and you could only go back up.

The lift doors closed once we were inside, and Marcus pressed the button to take us down. He still seemed quite satisfied.

"Good work, Alex. It won't be much longer now." He soothed as his hand landed on my shoulder from behind. He was pleased with my performance, but I couldn't say the same.

"Thank you, sir." It burned when it came out. I didn't mean it. I didn't want congratulations. I wanted atonement.

The lift sounded as it opened to the first part of the huge lab, and we exited. The path led down a small set of steps that opened into a massive room filled with sleek white machinery. More stairs connected each side of the landing that led up to the catwalks, and the hibernation pods that lined the walls below; all of them vacant but three.

This was where I worked. It would be a nightmare if seen by anyone from outside, and now, it was to me as well. Fog covered the floor of the unnaturally cool room, and scientists wearing masks and full body suits paced around from instrument to pod. They checked statuses and made sure Marcus' new little monsters would be produced.

Marcus stopped and placed his hands on the railing next to the steps, and leaned over watching his plans come to fruition. The grin still hadn't left his face.

"That should do with Krill's little legacy." He muttered it to himself victoriously.

"It will still be three more days before the samples are ready for testing, Marcus." I had stated it casually to try to tone down his ego a bit.

"Oh, there will be no testing Alex. I need them awake and operational before the concert." He insisted. I wasn't privy to all of Marcus' plans. I assumed they were taking Alpha's place in Paragon, to be used in the same capacity; city clean-up and keeping humanity's moral conscience intact.

"But if we don't run the tests they could come out corrupted or incomplete. It could cause physical damage to their epidermal coating, neural relay systems, or who knows what else." I declared, hoping any defects may sway his need to push the project forward too quickly. It was irrational to not complete all of the work needed to make the new subjects as perfect as possible. I was starting to see why the professor and Marcus were at odds, especially from a scientific standpoint.

"You forget that I've done this before! They will be fine, and besides, my faith in the previous plan has been wavering lately." He wafted his head around in uncertainty.

"This should fix all that. In the meantime, I will just have to have Ryne dispose of the professor." Marcus finished in a sinister voice that shocked me.

"You are going to have Krill deleted? Wouldn't that upset Mr. Stoddard?" I asked, appalled at the idea. Killian and Adrian Krill, Dorian's father, were friends before the Migration, working in Paragon together.

When Adrian was killed in the first riots, Killian took responsibility for Dorian, and gave him his place in the company.

"What that old fool doesn't know, Alex. He left Paragon a long time ago. He doesn't even pay attention any more. Don't get soft on me." Marcus sneered. My eyes widened. I realized in that moment, that he had already planned all of this long before anyone could have put a stop to it.

"I'll be in my office. Make sure these three are ready. You have twenty-four hours. No more." Marcus sniffed and turned away from the railing.

"But..." Before I could object, he was already back in the lift, and on his way up. I couldn't help but feel uneasy about everything that had transpired, and I was going to have to deal with having the blood of my mentor on my hands, as well as the death of his dreams. I walked around the floor trying to think of a way out of it all. My first thought was to sabotage the three specimens and end Marcus' plans, but there would be witnesses, and I couldn't get it done without being stopped in the middle of doing it.

It wouldn't change anything. Marcus would just start over, and I would be added to the list of assignments for Ryne. I paced and paced the floor thinking, and looking into the tubes that held the newly formed and almost fully grown Protosapien men. All I would have to do is put a tiny crack in the glass of each chamber. Without a fully-formed immune system, they would die of contamination in days.

Their bodies hadn't grown into their outside epidermis, and they were still semi-translucent as the lights from above shined through the thick glass pods that encased them.

There had to be a better way. I would have to find a different way to atone. As I looked at the innocent men, knowing what they would become, I still couldn't bring myself to destroy them. I would have to move Krill, and hide him somewhere.

The Slums. I would have to find a way to hide Krill in an abandoned building in the Slums, but I doubted if he would even talk to me. He would probably even try to strangle me on sight after what I had done to him. I would deserve it, maybe worse. It didn't matter. The more time I sat and thought there would only be more time that Marcus had to contact Ryne. Where Krill was; he'd be an easy target. I had to act quickly, so I entered the lift and headed back to the floor above. For now, Marcus' Protosapiens would be completed. I could only hope that his impatience would damage them in some way.

The door slid open to Krill's room as I swiped my wristport. He was still in a fuming march around the little room. His hand rubbed his chin, and you could see his thoughts were swirling. He looked up to me as I walked in, and stopped in his place. His eyes burned holes through me, causing me to pause mid-step, but then they relaxed in defeat; almost as if tears would emerge at any second.

I didn't need any acknowledgement to get my feet moving again. Time was of the essence. I grabbed a box and started putting some of his tools in it. His eyes became curious as he watched me.

"And, what's this Alex?" His voice shook with the question. He may have thought I had returned for more betrayal.

"We have to go, Dorian. You have to leave. The quicker the better." I said, plain and simple.

He walked over to the mangled robot on the floor, picked it up and held it affectionately in his hands.

"I'm not going anywhere." His voice came out broken. It seemed that Marcus' plan had not only defeated Krill, but deleted his spirit as well, "There's nothing more I can do." He carried the little robot as he crossed the room towards me.

"Come on, old man. There's always more." I said as I stopped packing the box, and turned to assure him. We didn't have time for him to give up. He had to leave, now.

"Not this time, Alex. Time..." He let out an awkward little laugh as he gazed at the robot, dead in his hand. "If only there had been more of it. It wouldn't have to be like this."

He walked around looking at Socrates, but never at me. It was killing me to watch him suffer, but it was needless. If he didn't act, Marcus would win. He would lose everything he'd ever worked for. I had to get him moving, and as I watched him pine for the loss of his robotic counterpart, I realized that he would also lose Alpha; his artificial son.

"Marcus isn't just going to delete you, Krill. He is going to delete Alpha, and probably me too!" I pleaded with his compassion.

It is what makes us human, the professor had said. I would have to hold him to it, and count on him to be what I knew him as; the most compassionate person I'd ever known.

It worked quickly. Alpha had an effect on Krill, and he snapped out of his melancholy state at the thought. His eyes burned with the same anger they had when Marcus had been in the room.

"We have to warn him...How long until Marcus' new Protosapiens are ready?" He shot out and new life had sprouted in his step. He grabbed the half-packed box I had started.

"He is going to wake them up tomorrow. You pack, quickly. I'm going to find us a way out of here." I noted, hastening the professor even further.

Alpha didn't remain in the building, but Eddie had been there all afternoon. It was strange for Alpha to not be with Eddie, but I had inferred from Marcus' rant earlier why he wasn't. I would have to hope that getting to Eddie would do for now.

Krill dropped Socrates into the box I was packing for him.

"Go. Hurry." Krill shot out quickly ushering me out of the room with a waft of his hand, and then he disappeared around the metal shelves.

I made my way out the door in a panic, hoping I was about to do the right thing.

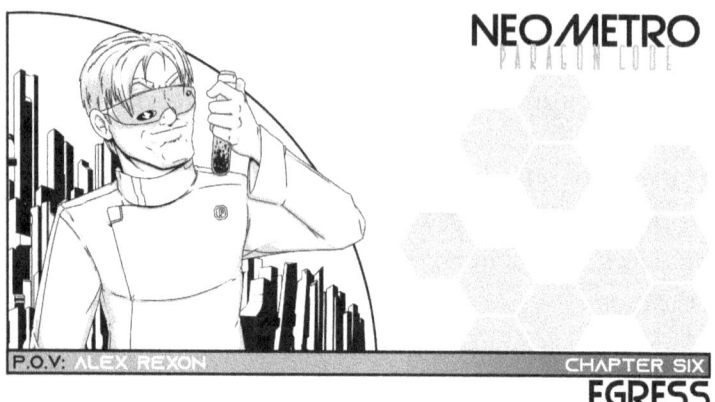

I knew that Eddie shared an office with Alpha, and that it wasn't necessary.

Alpha was always on the training level and Eddie was hardly ever at the Paragon main building. It was only by chance that I saw him entering the lobby earlier that day. Their office was on the twenty-fifth floor, and it would take a minute in the lift to get me there. I just kept hoping that we would have enough time.

The lift seemed to take forever. I tapped my foot watching each floor pass by on the way up; hoping it wouldn't stop. I hoped that no one, besides me, needed to use the lift at this very moment. I couldn't be seen by anyone. Marcus couldn't know I was undermining his victory.

It would ruin everything.

Then, the indicator light dinged, and I hurried to the small office at the edge of the building. Eddie still sat in his chair looking at a holopacket, and picking at his teeth with the stem of his glasses. It was a holopacket dossier on the job he was working with Alpha. I shut the door quickly behind me as quietly as I could. The click of the door lock alerted him, and he quickly pulled his face up to see me.

"Alex, what's up, buddy? Besides you. Shouldn't you be in the basement?" He joked. His greeting smile was a mere courtesy, as his left hand wiped the holopacket closed to quickly hide the assignment. His swiftness dislodged a data chip from the packet, and my expression must have looked panicked, because he picked up on there being a problem without me saying anything.

"What's going on, Alex?" His eyes narrowed. The question was direct. As if he already suspected that it had something to do with Alpha. They had always seemed like they had more than just a working relationship. When they were together, they seemed more like friends, really.

"Where is Alpha, right now?" I stammered out quickly. A lot of questions would waste valuable time that we didn't have, and this was the most important one.

"I haven't a clue." He mused in protest. This wasn't good. Eddie was usually never far from Alpha, and he was never unaware of his location.

"Isn't that a little odd, Eddie?" I asked nervously. Eddie's office had glass walls, and I was in plain sight. My legs shook, enough that I could feel my pants brushing against them. I could tell Eddie had noticed that, too.

"Stop dancing with me Alex, what's going on?" Eddie's voice rose in a curious anger as he repeated his question. He was apparently more worried than he liked to let on. Usually, Eddie's demeanor was calm and relaxed, but Alpha's absence seemed to trigger an alarm that I wasn't aware of.

"Alpha is in danger." When I said it, it came out as fast as my lips could move. I was quick and to the point.

"What?" His voice heightened again, as if the statement was some absurdity that wasn't understandable, but with as much information as Eddie lacked, I could see why he would think I was being ridiculous. It wasn't like Eddie was unaware of Alpha's physiology. He knew Alpha was more than human, but that never seemed to matter to him.

"Marcus." I shot out in haste, "He wants to delete Alpha, and replace him with his new proto sapien soldiers." I explained. I didn't know what else to call them. 'Soldier' seemed like an archaic word to use to describe them, but knowing their intended use, it was the only appropriate one that I could conceive of.

"Wait...what?" Eddie's face snapped wide in disbelief. He was completely caught off-guard, to the point that his head shook the question out.

"Marcus wants to…" I started to repeat, but he cut me off by raising his hand, before I could finish.

"When did Marcus make the new ones?" He asked, appalled by the notion. I could imagine how it sounded. Only Marcus and the team of scientists in the basement knew of him reopening the program, and it still was a terrifying fact to anyone who really understood what it meant.

"Six months ago. They're going to hit the streets tomorrow. We need to hurry." I urged. Eddie walked over to the rack where his coat and hood hung, and draped them across his forearm. He grabbed his fedora from its specific position on his desk, and pulled it onto his head.

"Sorry, Alex…you're on your own" He stated in a pause between strides. "I've been trying to get Alpha on coms, but there's been no answer. It's weird, too. It's like he dropped right off the grid. His locator won't even find him." He explained, and it was weird indeed. The locator matrix system was built by Paragon and placed throughout the city after the riots. Supposedly, there wasn't a place under the glass where Paragon couldn't find someone. They were linked to the datcoms, and each individual had a distinct signal identifier that routed back to central.

"We need Penelope." I declared thinking out loud. My only hope now was getting Krill out, fast. Penelope was the fastest car in the city. I had worked on her myself when she was commissioned for Eddie. The city didn't have many vehicles at first, but after time and some shared ingenuity, they were becoming more and more common.

"Alpha still has her." He said with a slight laugh to himself. Now, his nonchalance now made him sound more like the typical Eddie, but there was still a hint of worry in his speech.

He strode passed me to the door, but hesitated as I spoke.

"I have to get out of here." It was a panicked whisper that came out in a rasp. I felt like everyone heard it, even though there was no one around. I grabbed Eddie's sleeve with a tight grip to pull him to a complete stop.

He was supposed to be helping me.

I wasn't usually a physical person, but the situation worsened with every next sentence. It was an extreme gesture, and it hadn't been lost on him.

"You can take one of the old surveillance vans in the garage." he stated calmly as he pulled my hand free of his sleeve. Then, he walked back over to his desk.

"Ok, that will have to work. Just pull it around back to the basement stairs exit as soon as you can. I need to get to the slums, quick." I explained, hoping he'd be forced to do as I had asked. Then, he paused, understanding that he would have to be involved.

"Wait a second, do you think you know where Alpha is?" He asked, visually perplexed. Something about the slums made him change his attitude again. He was reading into something I had said, the downfall of being a grifter; you're always looking for some hidden double meaning when people talk.

"No, unfortunately not. I need to find him too, but right now I have to get Krill out of the building and somewhere safe." I stated, hoping Eddie would understand. He and Krill didn't really see eye to eye, but I could tell the old man liked Eddie enough. If not for just the fact that Eddie treated Alpha like any other person, he also seemed to have befriended his artificial son, too.

"The old man's in trouble, too?" I could see him putting it all together in his mind. The coming fight for the city, and his inevitable chore of picking a side. I had picked mine. I had faith in Krill.

"We all are, Eddie." I insisted. Eddie pulled some keys from the drawer of his desk, and stood wrapping his coat around him and looping his arms through the sleeves. Then, once he had finished, he stood looking at me impatiently.

"Well...Let's get moving." He gestured to the door, and I just nodded. We exited his office as inconspicuously as possible, and headed back to the lift. Luckily, no one stopped us on the way down, and I hid behind the side panel.

I nodded to Eddie as he exited into the lobby. No one would question his coming and going, so I continued down to Krill's lab where he had been packing feverishly. I took the stairs exit to the basement at the other end of the corridor from the lift, and the floor was relatively unoccupied. So, with any luck, getting the professor out unnoticed wouldn't be a problem.

I used my wristcom to access the professor's room, and quickly entered.

"Well, come on, this is almost everything." Krill said abruptly without introduction. Then, the professor jabbed a box into my chest. We loaded his equipment onto one of the rolling tables from his lab, and quickly made our way to the exit door. Eddie was waiting with an over-sized surveillance vehicle. It was running with him in the driver's seat, so I opened the utility doors. Krill grabbed a box, jumped in crawling towards the front, and I tossed the rest of the stuff in hastily. Then I jumped in, and closed the doors behind me. Eddie took off down the street towards the Boundary Bridge, and the professor and I watched as the base of the Paragon building left sight behind illuminated storefronts and vacant buildings.

"Okay, Alex, What's this all about? How bad is it?" He questioned. Eddie's voice was still serious, and I still didn't understand why he had even helped up to this point.

"It's Marcus!" Krill demanded angrily. His face protruded from an opening between the front seats. His eyebrows wafted up and down as he spoke.

"Yeah, Yeah I figured that much out already, Old Man." Eddie's eyes were fixed on the road as his hands clutched the wheel. The truck sped down the Main.

"How could you turn on Alpha so easily?" I demanded.

The words weren't as strong as I wanted them to be, but it was what was on my mind. From what I understood Eddie and Alpha had been working together for a long time, surely they had formed some kind of bond that would keep Eddie from alerting Marcus to any abnormalities with Alpha.

"What? What the hell are you even talking about?" Eddie shot back with an obvious ignorance that told me that he might not have been the one that had alerted Marcus. The emotions in the truck were running high between Krill's anger and Eddie's intense driving. We were probably going too fast out of Central D and making a scene, but I couldn't see over the mounds of equipment boxes that littered the back of the truck.

"Marcus said that you reported back to him on Alpha's indecisions." I declared assumingly, using the only information I had from Marcus' conversation with the professor earlier.

"I haven't told Marcus anything that's been going on! Never have!" He yelled out in offense. Silence overtook the cab as both Eddie and Krill stewed, but suddenly a look of alarmed realization swept across Eddie, "Ryne...that son of a mutate."

Eddie's palm slapped the steering wheel.

"What?" Krill and I both echoed each other.

"I talked to Ryne last night. I told him about Alpha's date. The date he never came back from." Eddie solemnly explained.

Krill's eyes widened to a squint, which for him, was pretty wide.

"A date?" Krill's voice suddenly became polar opposite from its previous tone. It seemed like he had become excited for Alpha, but Eddie disregarded his enthusiasm for the sake of driving.

"Yeah, old man...He went on a date, but he hasn't returned, and he's got my car!" Eddie noted sarcastically.

When we entered the Slums, I felt a wave of calmness come over me. We had made it out of Central D, and we were essentially safe for the time being. We passed store after store, and clubs heading further and further into the slums. That's when I realized I didn't know where we were going. Everyone else in the cab seemed content in silence. The professor contemplated Alpha's situation, and Eddie was lost in thought of his own. I could only assume it was frustration at Ryne. I watched the buildings pass from the back windows as we descended into the lower levels.

I hadn't been in the slums since I was a kid. My father had become a citizen when I was four, and my family moved to Central D for him to work in the Paragon office complex. I went to school in Central D too, and even there, no one had been to the Slums unless they came from there with their parents, like me and my brother. We would always wonder what was out there in the skirts, and we were told stories about how dirty it was. Growing up in Central D, I had lost most of my memories of the Slums. It was refreshing to get away from Central D and Paragon. I still didn't have any idea where I could hide the professor, but I had a feeling Eddie knew where we were going.

"Does anyone have a plan?" Eddie's question was more relaxed than it should have been. It would seem as though he didn't grasp the danger that we were in.

"First, we find a place to go." I was quick to say it. Saving Krill was my ultimate priority. It was all my fault that we were in this truck in the first place.

"I have a plan." Krill said it under his breath, not that he seemed like he was trying to hide his words, but more that he was assuring himself.

"I know a place." Eddie said to me, ignoring the Professor's statement. "The doc will be safe there. It's more than out of the way, and it's been abandoned since the far bridge incident." He noted, before letting out a sigh, "Now, tell me exactly how much trouble Alpha is in. I know he didn't come back last night, but is Marcus really going to go after him because of one stupid date?"

Eddie's eyes stay fixed on his secret destination. We would just have to trust that the Dox hadn't made Eddie's judgment completely negotiable.

"The rules are different for Alpha. They always have been." Krill said abruptly, pulling my attention back to him.

"Marcus never wanted Alpha to live a completely human life. He just wanted a drone for Paragon, but I couldn't willingly condemn any man to know only servitude." Krill was grim as he reflected on his mistakes of the past.

"Well you did a real bang up job, doc. Alpha is really something from what I've seen, but he ain't no man." Eddie remarked. Krill gave a small chuckle at Eddie's ignorance of Alpha's full capability. Only he knew what level Alpha really operated at, and what his range was.

"Alpha can do much more than anyone knows. Even me. I'm actually a little surprised that this hasn't happened sooner." He smiled with a certain amount of pride.

Sooner? Did Krill really know that Alpha would become aware? Did he disobey Marcus' orders and make Alpha sentient?

"What does that mean, sooner?" I asked the professor, trying to make my way into the conversation.

"When I designed Alpha, I did so with the idea that he would live outside of the dome, where the conditions would kill even the strongest man." Krill became intense, but then suddenly relaxed his tone again, "You see, unlike you and me, he can't even get sick. I'm not sure anything can hurt Alpha, really. So, I wouldn't be worried about him so much." Krill seemed assured that Alpha wasn't in any danger, but if Marcus believed that Alpha could be killed, then there was the probability. The new test samples were nearly completed, and Marcus wouldn't waste any time.

"But, what about the new Proto Sapiens that Marcus has created?" My voice propelled itself through the van to be heard, and the question turned Krill's happiness back into frustration.

"Well, that's another story entirely! Not that I doubt that Marcus was paying attention when I created Alpha, or that he has had access to all my work on the matter..." The old man's eyes twisted in their sockets towards me, "But I didn't oversee their creation. There's no telling what kind of horrible monsters he has constructed."

I knew what kind of monsters, and Krill was right. Marcus had access to all of the professor's research. The new subjects would be in the same vein as Alpha, almost identical genomes.

"They could kill, Alpha." My voice was low again and unsure. I knew he didn't want to hear it, but I created the new specimens, and I knew what they were capable of. They were based mostly on Krill's original design.

"Are you sure about that, Alex?" Eddie's voice boomed as he re-entered the conversation.

"They are of the same design as Alpha, and there are three of them, but they are different in many ways." I tried to explain my statement, and reassure them both at the same time. I didn't know what Alpha was capable of from seeing him in the field, only the stories I've heard, which have been elaborate. I only understood from a scientific standpoint.

"How so, Alex?" Krill demanded. He knew of my involvement in their creation, now. His anger about the hand I played hadn't calmed very much.

"Well, Marcus instructed us to remove their hypothalamus and a lot of the other nerves that would give them any reason to object to his control, but their physical make-up is almost entirely the same." I explained. Removing the hypothalamus would, in theory, remove the need for the specimen to form emotional attachments, or bonds to people or memories. They would, in effect, serve with mindless obedience to whom they were told, once programmed.

"That would leave them with only their baser thought functions." Krill told me with some condescendence in his voice. I could tell he completely objected to my work.

"Yes sir, perfect killers." The words made my skin crawl, but it was the truth. They would never grow, get sick, tired, or sidetracked. They would only do what they were told.

"You have to go back, Alex." The professor demanded.

"What?" Eddie looked to Krill in amazement.

"Marcus will order them to delete Alpha on sight." Krill proposed, and he was right.

I would have to sabotage the project. I had already thought about it before, and now that Krill would be safe it would be easier to do. I wouldn't even have to destroy them, I could just make sure they didn't get a chance to complete their final incubation cycles.

"Maybe not, if he doesn't know I'm gone. He was in his office when we left, and I don't think he suspects any of this. He was a little too happy with the thought of crushing your legacy doctor, no offense." I said despite knowing he would take some. He obviously hated Marcus, and knowing that Marcus had driven him out of his home, after forcing him into retirement and then trying to kill him, wouldn't have helped with that.

"This is crazy. First you make some kind of techno-organic super-human, and now there's going to be three more of them!" Eddie said, sounding astounded at it all, "And, and it's all for humanity's sake, to save us from the results of the last wars, only now it's become nothing more than this little war between you and Marcus. People." An undeniable smirk had pulled at Eddie's cheek at the rant. Krill and I both looked at Eddie in wonderment. My only thought was that he'd been on Dox for far too long. There was no way he could be taking everything so lightly, but he was, despite the fear and panic that filled the truck just moments ago.

"We're here." Eddie popped out from behind the smirk, and the truck pulled to a halt outside of an old building that was torn and shabby. There wasn't any risk of getting Krill's equipment wet because the building was on the lowest level of the slums, and the rain didn't really make it down this far. I popped open the utility doors and started pulling out some of the boxes. This wasn't the nicest part of town, but it was empty. No one would ever suspect to find Krill here, or even look. It was perfect.

It didn't take long to get his equipment into the small building. The door creaked as we entered, and the dust flew up from the floor. It was as empty as the city that surrounded it. I put the boxes in the middle of the floor.

"It's not much, but it will have to do." Eddie said, smacking the dust from a pillow that was sitting on an old chair.

Krill walked around. In the back was a small room that looked almost surgical. It had white tile walls and the floor was the same. There was some kind of steel plating against one of them, and a rack that hung from it; underneath was a sink. A kitchen, I assumed.

"Actually, this is perfect." Krill said deviously, and I didn't understand what he was thinking about. To me it looked like any other disheveled building.

"There's a bar up one level called 'The Zigg'. It's not too far away, and it's usually pretty empty. You should be fine there, too, if you need something to eat, make sure Darby makes it." Eddie pointed upward with a smile on his face.

I could tell he was thinking about how funny it would be to see the old man in a bar. People didn't live as long as Krill did in the Slums. He would stick out like a sore thumb on the upper levels, but I didn't see how anyone could live down here.

"I'll try to get you some furniture soon, old man." Eddie walked from tiny room to room, checking the windows and doors.

"That reminds me. Alex, I need you to try to get me some equipment from the Paragon labs." Krill said it while looking around the room, as if he were already working out where he was going to put his tools.

"What?" I was already terrified of going back, but now he wanted me to smuggle out equipment, too.

"Just some odds and ends. I want to repair Socrates. I will need some company if I am going to be here all alone, right." He posed dubiously, but the thought was sincere. It wouldn't be too hard to get whatever he wanted. Paragon didn't keep inventory, but worked on a very advanced honor system.

I say advanced, because you never know, who or what, would be leveraged against you to find the truth about anything. I would just need to employ some stealth to achieve what the professor desired.

"Also, I want you to delete my work from the Database Mainframe before Marcus realizes anything and creates a backup. There's no need in helping him anymore than we already have." He said, accenting the 'we'. I could tell there was a stab for me in his statement, but a stab I had earned.

"Yes sir." I said obediently, as I would to Marcus, but Krill just smiled at my obedience; not like Marcus would have. It was friendlier and held a hint of hidden truth. He walked over and put his hand on my shoulder as if he had forgiven me for having wronged him so much. It brought back the shame I had felt in his lab at Paragon, when I saw the defeat on his face, and my head fell slightly.

"Don't worry, when you're done, I want you to get out of there. You can do better than being just another one of Paragon's assets, too, my boy." He smiled, trying to smooth over the shame he saw washed across my face.

I just wanted to plead apologetically to him for deceiving him for Marcus, but the look in his eyes had already given me the forgiveness I longed for. He was as remarkable as I had always thought of him.

"I hate to break up your little moment, guys, but if you're going back, it is best that you not be missed, remember?" Eddie called out from outside of the building. I glanced out at the truck, and then back to Krill, before I started to make my way through the old noisy door.

"I'll get you the equipment as soon as I can." I nodded crossing the threshold, and my glasses slid down my nose a bit, forcing me to push them back up.

"That's fine, go." Krill ushered me out to the truck with that same forgiving smile never leaving his face. I jumped into the passenger side of the truck, Eddie started it up, and we were on our way back to Paragon. The buildings and stores passed slower on our way back, but it was mostly due to how anxious I was about returning, and the job ahead of me. It wouldn't be easy to fool Marcus, and I wasn't sure how much good it would do. The proto sapiens were already mostly complete. They would still be as strong as Alpha, and I didn't have the same hopeful devotion to him as Krill did.

"You know this would be faster if I had my Penelope." Eddie muttered, still a bit upset about the absence of his precious automobile. "You sure it's going to be safe for you to go back?" He looked over to me with one eye wider than the other. He didn't think I could pull it off, but I had to. It was up to me to make things right, now.

"I'll be fine." I hoped, but I wasn't going to be a pessimist now. It was far too late for that. I couldn't fail. I had made Krill safe, but I had far from atoned for what I'd done that could still destroy his work; his son, Alpha. We sat motionless on our way back to the Boundary Bridge, the only movement from either of us being Eddie's steering, but even then, he had perfected that to mere minor adjustments to the wheel. The city passed, and the bridge only opened it up wider into view.

It was indeed an impressive sight to behold. Then, Eddie's datcom sounded in his pocket. He pulled it out, and a smile came across his face.

"Finally." He calmly said it to himself, and then punched a button to receive the transmission.

"Hey lady's man, long time no see...where's my car?" He said, eyeing over to me again with a cocked brow. It was Alpha. Eddie's voice was sarcastic when he spoke to him, but it wasn't like disrespect. It was more like friendly banter.

"I take it you sealed the deal, or you'd have been back by now?" His sarcasm had become curious now, but Alpha's response seemed to alarm him. Eddie's neck straightened up, and his tone leveled. I tried, but I couldn't make out Alpha on the other end of the conversation. "Well, there's been a lot going on in your absence. I don't think you should go back to the office, right now. Meet me at Club Kelp in an hour."

There was another brief pause and I anxiously anticipated the com's end, so that Eddie could relay what was said.

"Fine, fine. I just need a drink. I don't care where we get it. I have to take care of something first, but I'll meet you there." He then ended the datcom transmission and looked over to me.

"He's still not supposed to know, right?" He asked in earnest, but I was confused. He was the most serious I've ever seen, but I didn't understand what he was talking about.

"Know what?" I asked. Eddie was scratching his hair around his hat like he was trying to use the friction to get his brain started, and I had no idea what he was implying.

"What he is." He said in a dead calm.

What he was? He was a genetic prototype human experiment designed by Krill and used by Marcus to kill what he considered degenerates and human trash in an effort to cleanse the city of his version of evil. I had never thought to ask.

"I don't know...Does he know?" I answered questioningly. This was a curious conflict. I didn't really know if it would help or hurt if Alpha were to know he wasn't technically human. Marcus didn't want him to, because he feared Alpha's enlightenment, but Krill kept it from him because he wanted Alpha to lead a normal human life.

"You know, I'm going to say 'no', since he sounded upset." Eddie answered, and I found it interesting. I thought having the secret kept from him would hurt the most.

"Why would you say that? Wouldn't you think knowing would upset him, too?" At least, I thought that it would. To think you were normal one minute, only to find that you weren't even human the next, and that your childhood memories were fake, would probably be upsetting to me

Eddie laughed at the comment, and I glared at him obtusely misunderstanding what I had missed.

"It's a different kind of upset." He remarked, but I had missed something that had transpired on the com.

"What?" I asked, again. This had become some kind of game to Eddie. His smiles and laughter were at me and my lack of understanding.

"I'll tell you later, for now, I would guess the doc would still want to keep it from him." Eddie observed, and I had to agree. He was probably right. The professor just didn't see Alpha as different. He saw him as his lineage; his successor, and in some ways, his child.

"Probably. Krill wants him to have a normal life. I never thought it was possible, but I guess it has been working." I admitted in disbelief. In the time that Alpha had been with Paragon, he had developed friendships with Eddie and Krill, and he was even liked by most of the civilians, even though he was standoffish and antisocial.

"Yeah, something like that." he said with a grin.

Eddie's eyes refocused on the road ahead. We were already almost back at the office. Eddie dropped me off at the side entrance to the lab, so I could sneak back in, not that it mattered.

Marcus never came back to the lab that day. I checked on the three new proto sapiens in their containment chambers, but there would be nothing I could do at this point to greatly decrease Marcus' success in finishing the monsters. The other scientists had left for the day, and the three specimens were in stasis; suspended in their tubes. Their bodies would still naturally continue to form. They already looked almost human with the exception of their chalky white skin. Each of their facial features were different from the others, as they had each been pulled randomly from the DNA of an unknowing Paragon citizen; a citizen that would unexpectedly disappear or become deleted. Their blue veins could be seen through the surface of the white skin making them look even more eerie suspended in the glass tubes. They looked like they could wake up at any moment, and that thought horrified me.

I could no longer feel any accomplishment in my work; I could only stare at my reflection in the glass in front of me, and feel shame at the face that stared back. I would have to do whatever I could to make amends. I wanted to smash each chamber and delete the three inside. I found a heavy surgical tool on the stand beside the tubes. It would mean my deletion, but Krill was safe for now. Marcus wouldn't be able to find him, so what was the difference?

My life in atonement sounded good, but as I raised my hand to bring the tool down into the glass; I couldn't do it. I was selfish. I didn't want to die, not today. Today, I would rely on whatever plan the professor had.

I gathered up the equipment that Krill had asked for, and went down to his office to delete the files from his computer and the database mainframe. The old screen hummed as I peered into it. There was only one file on the old drive. It didn't take long to delete. Now that the lab workers had left, I was also free to leave without being under Marcus' scrutiny. So I headed back to the abandoned building in the lower slums.

To my surprise, Krill had already managed to furnish the place with a few chairs, and even found a steel table for the white room in the back. Krill was asleep in one of the chairs as I entered, but awoke abruptly as I came in.

"It's just me, Dorian." I whispered, to not alarm him any further. He shuffled in the chair, but his eyes were heavy squints as he watched me. I set the supplies on the floor against a wall, and began to sit in one of the chairs that Krill had made look so comfortable.

"Wait!" Krill's determined voice leaped from his body before I could park myself in the chair. I cringed and paused. He sprang up from his chair eyeing me, or so I thought. Then, his hand reached out past me, grabbing for something on the chair.

A hair. A long, brown hair.

He pulled the hair from the fabric of the chair and a delighted grin came across his face.

"This is perfect." he stated ominously. He walked around the small room staring at the hair; holding it to the light and inspecting it thoroughly. He didn't say anything else about it, but I could tell there was something brewing in him because of the discovery. He pulled a data chip from his pocket, and tossed it up and down in his hand a few times, as he let out a delighted little laugh.

"Just perfect." he repeated even happier. This time was enough to pique my curiosity.

"Professor?" I questioned without asking. He turned and looked at me with the little grin dancing on his face. "What is it, Krill?" I clarified. He spun the hair around between the tips of his thumb and forefinger, eyeing it delicately, and holding it up for me to see.

"A solution, my boy. All is not lost." His face was filled with amusement, but I didn't understand what he meant. He didn't seem like he wanted to explain anything to me either.

"Is it going to save Alpha?" I questioned, but Krill just smiled. His cheeks were a bright rosy hue.

"I believe it might." The old man hiccupped, and then I realized he was acting a little too happy. He was drunk.

"Have you been drinking, professor?" It demanded in shock. Had he left and went to the bar that Eddie had told him about in the short time I had been gone?

"Drunk is when you don't see straight!" he exclaimed with a glare at me, "I'm just a little abbreviated at the moment. I haven't had synth-ale in almost six years, but I could always hold my own." He hiccupped again. "Inebriated!" He laughed, "I've always been this short."

I instinctively walked to him trying to aid him back to his chair, but he shrugged my arm away from him.

"I'm fine!" he protested. Then, he looked back at the disk and the hair in his hands, "Better than fine." He mumbled out. His speech had become breathy and slow.

"Maybe you should just sit for a second, professor." I said coaxingly, so that the old man returned to his chair. He put the contents of his hand on the small table that sat beside him. Soon he was fast asleep again, with the grin still on his face. I decided that sleeping wasn't such a bad idea either. It had been a long day, and tomorrow was going to be worse. I would have to go back to Paragon, to Marcus, and to the three monsters I had helped him create.

Tomorrow, I would have to wake them up.

He sat in the seat across from me in the black sedan, as we rolled downed the Main.

I hadn't been able to get the best look at him outside in the rain. Now that we were in his car, I could tell that he was as handsome as I presumed from the voice that came from behind me, or maybe it was the quick glance I took before I felt too nervous to look at him.

He was absolutely gorgeous. His jawline was impressive from the side. It was cut long and ended sloping downward to his perfect stubbled chin. I couldn't tell what color eyes he had; they were hidden behind the tint of the glasses he wore. He had medium length black hair that stuck up in tufts. The rain had pushed a few of them down, looping them onto his forehead. It wasn't usual for a man in the slums to be wearing the extravagant coat that seemed to fit him so perfectly. I had to assume he was from Central D, and it made me even more nervous. He was a citizen, and I wasn't.

He was very still, and very quiet. It was unnerving. Who was this kind man? I had never known anyone like him. He was staring out the window watching the rain, and he looked very stoic with his hands in his lap. I guessed he hadn't noticed me looking at him so much. He hadn't even glanced at me. Of course, I was trying not to look, so I stared out of my window at the rain, as well. Occasionally, I would peek back at him.

The rain marked the seconds that passed in silence; battering the car as it went down the road, until finally, I noticed him turn to look at me. Instincts took over and I turned to look at him at the same time. Our eyes met, and for the moment it almost seemed as if I could see his eyes widen behind the dark glasses. He was a beautiful creature.

I couldn't help but blush, and we both turned away from each other. It seemed he was almost as nervous about our chance meeting as I was. There was a pause as we went under an overpass. Then, the rain continued to dance on the roof of the car. It made me more comfortable to know that he was as shy as I was, but he was playing a game of silence. It only made him more mysterious to me.

The tall, dark, and mysterious type...how cliché, but it was true; he had gotten my attention. The shyness only made him seem more kind. 'How could a mean man be so shy?' I asked myself. The silence was maddening.

"Coat and tie guy, huh? You must be someone important." I said presumptively. I was sure it sounded stupid. I wasn't the flirty type, but for him, I was going to try with some awful observational comment.

I couldn't think of anything smoother? Jeez, I couldn't believe he hadn't started laughing at me yet.

"Not really." He said not turning to look at me.

It only made me feel even more dull, but for some reason I couldn't help the questions that were bubbling inside of me. I wanted to know him. I didn't know why. It was obvious that he didn't care to know me. He wouldn't even look at me, but I couldn't stop the words that wanted to come from my mouth. I had opened a door that didn't want to shut.

"So, do you always pick strange girls up off the streets?" I questioned why I was asking, before I could even finish the question. I wasn't thinking that, it just came out, and it came out sarcastic. I really didn't want to barrage him with silly accusations after he was being so nice by giving me a ride home, but my lips moved and I had no control, and then an awkward and cute smirk curled the edge of his mouth. It was adorable.

"Are you a strange girl?" he shot back quickly.

Yes. I am now.

I didn't even notice at first that my eyebrows had slanted. I was shocked that he even gave credit to the ridiculous question. I couldn't stop the hasty and impromptu answer.

"No!" I gasped out. I was sure I sounded angry, so I tried to quickly recompose myself, but I'm sure the smile looked tangled on my face, and then my mouth started leaving my brain behind again.

"Let me guess, a guy like you doesn't need to, right?" I accused him. I had no right, but it was like someone had cursed my tongue, and the first thing I thought came out of my mouth. It was horrible and terrifying.

He looked at me with a puzzled look. He couldn't believe the things I was saying either, but that didn't stop me from finishing the rant, "Nice car, expensive coat, handsome; I bet you have women just falling into your lap." I was flirting. I didn't realize that I was doing it until I felt the sly smirk pull at the side of my mouth as I finished berating him.

"Not really." This time he said it with a surprised look on his face, and not at all with the same distance as before. I could only giggle at his lack of response. Apparently, he didn't flirt either. He just sat there smiling his perfect smile.

"You're not really the talkative type are you?" I asked innocently, but I was ready this time. It didn't take him a moment to think about it. We both already knew what his answer would be.

"Not..." he started to say, but I didn't let him get it out.

"Not Really!" I burst out, cutting him off. I couldn't help how hard it had made me laugh. He had made it so easy, and it was the cutest moment. I covered my mouth so that he couldn't see how hard I was laughing, as if he couldn't hear me, but he just kept smiling. It tugged at the sides of his mouth, pulling his well-formed cheeks up and under his glasses.

"I'm just not really that interesting. So I don't have much to say about myself." He said seemingly honestly, but I knew it was all lies. He was nothing but interesting.

He was playing back now. It made me blush, and I couldn't stop giggling; however, I did stop when I glanced out of the window and saw the familiar setting outside. The ride would soon be over. I was almost home, and my apartment was coming up quickly on the right. I didn't want to be a nuisance by making him turn around if he'd missed it because I wasn't paying attention, so I tapped my fingers on the glass that separated us from the driver. It rolled down as the driver leaned an ear back to hear me. I couldn't see how he could hear anything with those sideburns in the way.

"This is my stop, right up there on the right." I said throwing out my hand, and I pointed a finger to the building that was quickly approaching. It looked like he understood where I was aiming, so I leaned back to the seat. I wasn't about to end this without a chance of him returning into my life. There was something very special about him, and I could feel it. I desperately wanted to make sure I saw him again.

I couldn't find my lightpen. I always kept a lightpen on me in case I needed to send something that I randomly thought. It was a habit I had since I was a little girl, and my lightpen was always in my side pocket, but it wasn't there. It had to be there. I couldn't feel it in my coat. Had I left it at the bar? No, Estelle gave me that lightpen. I couldn't lose it. "Ah Ha!" I exclaimed aloud, not meaning to.

I found it, inside my coat pocket lying down; the sneaky little thing, trying to hide from me when I needed it the most. I hadn't realized it, until I had finished scribbling mine into my com, but we hadn't even exchanged names. It didn't matter. Chances were that he wouldn't even dial my datcom. Why would he? He was a citizen and I wasn't, but I wasn't going to give up on him without some effort. I looked at my com and started to swipe the lightpen to send my info, then pulled the door handle to pop it open.

Drops of rain assaulted my leg through the cracked door, and I stepped out. I turned back and looked at him, swiping the lightpen across my com. My information was sent. He knew me now.

"Well, I'm intrigued Mr. Mysterious. Com me." I tried to smile, but I'm sure it was filled with doubt. I closed the door, and took the opportunity to leave without getting his reaction. It would be the least I could do for myself if he did reject me. At least, I wouldn't have to see it immediately. I could suffer in waiting without knowing if he was or wasn't going to com me, but I couldn't handle it if he looked up and his face said '*no*'.

I made it to the steps before I realized that, if he didn't com me, I may never see him again, and I couldn't stop my body's impulse to turn back; to look at him once more. When I did, I couldn't see through the tinted windows of the car, and then it pulled away from the curb, and made its way through the rain and down the street. I buzzed myself in, through the door of the old building, and dripped up the two flights of stairs that lead to the apartment, where I was graciously allowed to live.

I didn't have a job. I was recently fired from the Hidden Palace, a seedy ration vendor, for having too much pride to let my boss get handsy with me, like he did with all the new girls. So, My best friend had let me live with her.

She was becoming more and more famous in the city, and she didn't really have to worry about credits; not that she would ever move to another building. She said she loved this old one. Estelle even thought that she had a chance at becoming a citizen, because of how well her music was doing, but I didn't really think it worked like that. It didn't matter; everyone in the Slums loved her like she was better than just any citizen, and it wasn't hard to do so. She was absolutely the most beautiful and talented woman in the city, and probably one of the nicest, too.

She was exceptionally classy, comparatively, and that was happily rubbing off on me, as well. She let me stay for free, as long as I cleaned up after myself, and most of the time, her too. That wasn't hard, she was never there unless she was getting ready for a show, or sleeping. She spent most of her time rehearsing, or playing gigs at the local clubs.

I unlocked the door, and walked into my apartment. I shook the drops off at the door, and hung up my coat on the rack next to it.

"Hey Ess? I'm home!" I shouted. I could hear her banging around in the bathroom towards the back of the apartment, so I knew she hadn't left, yet. I was always excited to see Estelle, but now especially, so I could tell her about my 'mister mysterious', and the fresh fantasy car ride.

She came quickly from the bathroom with one large towel wrapped around her body, and another curled on top of her head, sponging up her wet hair. She went directly into her bedroom without acknowledging me, at first. She looked like she was in a hurry scampering about the place looking for her accessories. When she returned to the hallway, her smile sparkled at me, as she hung her head to one side, putting in her extravagant looking earring.

"Hey Lexxi, how was your day?" She asked with all her teeth. Her voice was raspier than any normal woman, but it fit her. It made her seem strong, but I assumed it was from constantly straining her vocal chords.

"Amazing!" I couldn't help but glow in response to her question. I'm sure I looked like I could float up from where I stood, I was so happy. She could apparently tell, because her eyes lit up, and her smile turned into a wanting smirk.

"Really? Well, tell me all about it then." She beamed out brilliantly smooth. She finished putting the other earring in, walked into the open main room, and over to the couch, sitting to hear the story. She crossed her legs and propped her head on her hand. Her eyes coaxed me into a giggle.

"You wouldn't believe me if I told you." I said. I didn't know why I was being coy with her. I told her everything anyway, and this didn't make me uncomfortable. I just didn't know how to put it into words.

"Oh, come on...Who is he?" She asked coyly.

She knew! I must have been transparent as a ghost, because she could see right through my timid demeanor. I guess it wouldn't have taken much, really.

"I don't know his name." I confessed. Thinking about him tied my tongue in knots, and I couldn't find the words to describe the incident.

"What? You didn't." She mused. An appalled look crossed her face as she had, apparently, conceived the wrong idea about my flustered composure.

"No! Nothing like that...geez, you know me better than that, don't you?" I reassured her in an appalled manner. I didn't date. She knew that. Me and Men never really worked out, and so I had stopped trying and just stuck to myself.

"Well, then what?" She crossed her arms. She had become impatient with my story-telling abilities, and gave me a look that told me to get to the point I was desperately wanting to make.

"Well, it was just a guy who gave me a ride home..." I didn't know where to begin, so I figured the beginning would be the best place to start, "...I was down below, at the Zigg earlier, totally getting drenched because I forgot my cover, and this guy suddenly appeared and opened an umbrella for me."

Estelle looked at me, very intrigued. Kindness was something this city was running out of, and she was a constant skeptic. I paused to get her reaction, but she didn't say anything, merely ushered me to continue.

"Then, he offered me a ride home, but it wasn't weird or anything. There was something about him that made me trust him. So I got in the car with him." I explained. She made a horrible face at me as I finished the sentence. I knew it was because I had gotten into some strange man's car, and she didn't approve of that kind of behavior. She was very protective. If I had let her say anything it would have just been 'You know better', so I continued before she could.

"After we got in the car he was just really shy. It was cute, but he was really handsome. He even had a guy that drove, so we just sat in the back seat." I giggled at my memory as I retold it. Estelle's hands flipped around in the air as she uncrossed her arms.

"Wait, wait, wait..." She exalted. She interrupted me with a disturbed and questioning look on her face, as if she knew something I hadn't.

"Was he wearing a coat and tie?" She asked with a cocked brow. Her guessing that detail was a little freaky. Estelle was always really perceptive, and sometimes it was almost like she could see into your mind.

"Yes?" I said, puzzled by her unknown knowledge. I didn't understand how she knew that, or why that fact would be important enough to upset her, but it had. Her face became lit with silent anger. Her eyes closed as her brows twitched and furrowed.

"Why?" I continued my ask. I still didn't understand, and it seemed that my naivety only upset her more.

"He's one of those corporate slimes; working for Paragon, doing whatever they ask of him! No one else in the city can afford that kind of decadence." She demanded. It was cute that she worried so much about it, but her level of anger seemed uncalled for. She never cared for Paragon, despite wanting to be a citizen. She claimed that they were a 'tyrannous company' that had 'corrupted humanity' and 'trapped it in a snow globe'.

I had heard the spiel a hundred times or more; every time she saw a sign or poster with their logo on it.

"Oh come on, Ess. You know I just love how you worry about me." I said with a little sarcasm, letting my tone become playful to try and calm her, but it only made things worse. I froze as her eyes scorched through me.

"There will be a lot to worry about, with you messing around with a guy like that, I'm sure!." She blurted in detest. I couldn't help but reflect on exactly what type of guy he was, and for a moment, I had gotten lost in my thoughts of him. I quickly pulled my attention back to our conversation.

"Well, I don't think so. He didn't seem bad to me." I tried to deflect her opinion with my own experience. I wasn't trying to contradict her to hurt her, but only because I didn't get the feeling that she understood him. She hadn't met him. She didn't know what had happened. She didn't see how kind he was, or the shyness that made him seem so endearing.

"Maybe not everyone from Paragon is the same...You know, maybe some of them are good people that just can't help who they work for." I explained.

It didn't sway her. She stood up from the couch and adjusted her towels. She huffed as she began back into the hallway, and I could hear her mumble, *'Naïve girl'*, under her breath. She was not as pleased with my news as I was.

A few moments passed, and she didn't say anything to me as she rummaged around in her room. She had a rehearsal tonight for her big concert at the Stardust on Saturday. She was going to be rehearsing all week. Whenever anyone played the Stardust it was a big event. Most of the time it was only used for shock ball tournaments. The rummaging stopped and Estelle poked her head out of the room.

"Are you coming to rehearsal tonight?" She asked in a new tone. Her voice had mellowed and she had returned to her cheery upbeat self. It was enough to make my smile return as well.

"Of Course!" I replied with a beaming grin that hid my previous feelings of conflict. I always loved going to her rehearsals. She was a magnificent performer with the most stunning voice I had ever heard. If I didn't love her so much, I would have been envious; not that every other girl in New Axis wasn't already. She smiled and pulled her head back into the room. When I sat down in the chair, I heard her scamper into the bathroom, and a flurry of tiny noises filled the air; brushing, spraying, and the twisting of tiny little caps on lipstick and eyeliner bottles.

"That dress looks great on you, Lexxi!" She shouted out from the tiny bathroom.

I had forgotten I had borrowed it from her earlier that day, but she never did mind when I took her clothes. She had more than enough, and she hardly wore the same things more than once. I looked down at the shimmering blue piece I had taken from her, and it did fit me well. Even though I found Estelle to be a league above me, we did wear the same size clothes, and I was happy with how nice the little blue dress contoured me.

"Thanks, Ess. I found it in the back of your closet." I called back to her.

"Oh? I didn't even recognize it." She called back, musingly. She had known better than to think that I would be able to afford anything as nice, but it was her way of lightening the mood that filled the previous conversation.

I sat soaking in the chair waiting the eternity it took for her to be done, so that I could use our only bathroom. Estelle took hours to get ready and I had interrupted her in the middle of it, so I turned on an old datacast while I waited. Then, all the little noises from the back stopped, and Estelle reemerged down the hallway and into the room where I sat. When she appeared, she was a vision of beauty and radiance; stunning in a white dress that flowed down just past the arch of her knee with straps that crossed her chest to her back. Her hair was pinned in at the sides, pulling it back into long curls that swept across her face and shoulders.

She was always a good judge of how to do her make-up just right. It barely lightened her perfect skin around her cheeks, and her eyes dazzled in the delicate black accents of the eyeliner.

"Well, how do I look?" She said twisting, making the white dress follow her elegant movements. I never ceased to be amazed when I saw her all done up. She didn't look like she belonged in this dark dreary city, but more like she was that of a being sent from another plane of existence. I didn't realize my gaping mouth as I gazed upon her, and the jealousy I so rarely felt, crept in. I quickly pursed my lips, and shrugged the jealous feeling. I slowly started to clap my hands, in giddy approval, as my lips curled into a smile that pulled up my cheeks.

"If that's what you are wearing to the concert Saturday, you will be absolutely gorgeous." I assured her in an overly giddy response. Estelle's eyes cracked at my approval, and a similar smile stretched her face.

"Awe, thank you." She beamed out, and began to walk back to the bathroom, but she paused as my datcom started buzzing. I had sat it on the counter in the dining room. I quickly scampered over to it, and looked at the number.

Unrecognized

Normally, the datcoms would identify whoever com'd no matter who they were. It was all part of a system that had been put in place when the city was first designed. I was puzzled at first, and Estelle had returned to the room without ever making it back down the hallway. She looked at me quizzically. I could only shrug as I pressed the button to accept the transmission.

"Hello?" I spoke softly in hesitation. My voice trembled in the mystery, but nothing came from the other end of the line. I waited another moment for a response, but there was nothing.

"Hello? Is anyone there?" I repeated a little louder, but I sounded even more shaken the second time I asked. Then, I heard a man clearing his throat from the other end of the line, and relief took hold when I heard his soothing voice.

"Lexxi?" He asked awkwardly. He sounded nervous, and immediately I entered the weird flirty manner that I had begun earlier in the car. It was him; my mystery *'bad'* guy from the *'evil'* corporation.

"This is her..." I soothed with a playful inflection. I had never dreamed that he would com me, especially so soon. What did it mean? I would have time to ponder that later.

"It's Vincent Alpha, from the car ride earlier." He said it clear and plainly. Now he sounded assured, settled; like he was doing business. I didn't like it. I wanted him to be the playful and shy person from earlier. I would play coy to try and re-conjure that man.

"So, mister mysterious has a name?" I asked rhetorically, trying to evoke a response. It was all childish looking from Estelles point of view, I was sure. His throat cleared again, and I could almost feel the tension coming through the datcom. He was still nervous.

"Yes, sorry about that. I never properly introduced myself. I'm bad at that. I was hoping to make it up to you, as I have been thinking about our meeting. I would like to meet you again. " he said calmly, and it was a little charming how official he was trying to be, but I could feel my cheeks getting warm as he spoke.

"You would?" I asked in a voice I didn't know.

"Yes. Very much. I will come get you." He explained in a way that sounded both utterly alluring and terrifying at the same time. I could feel Estelle's eyes burning through me again from behind. It was almost enough to end my innocent smile, but I wasn't going to let it; however, it did remind me that I had promised to come to her rehearsal later, and now I felt torn. I had seen her sing hundreds of times, but I knew she would want me there. A sudden wave of defeat overtook my tone, "Actually, I'm supposed to go see my roommate tonight..." I looked back at Estelle, who was still glaring in anticipation at me. Then, she suddenly threw her hands up with a huff, shaking her head, until waving me off to let me know in our own language that I was released from my obligation to go to her rehearsal. "...But I don't think she will mind if I reschedule." I said smiling back at Ess with gratitude.

A sigh of relief came through the phone and another dejected one from the direction of Estelle, who had found a seat to slump down into as she hung her head. A piece of her dress caught the chair as she slid down in it, and a tearing noise sounded. She picked up the edge of her dress and stared at it in disappointment, huffed, threw it back down, and braced her hand upon her forehead to stew.

"O.k. I am on my way to your apartment." The voice on the other end explained, and I gasped a little as it brought my attention back to my datcom.

"Right now?" I asked in a squeak.

"Yes." he shot back in a clear assured tone with a professional demeanor. I'm sure it made him more comfortable.

I looked down at my dress, and the tangled mess of hair that hung below my chin and matted to my chest. I was still soaked from my trip in the rain earlier.

"But, I need a little more time." I replied reluctantly. I giggled. I didn't know why.

"O.k." he said, and before I was able to respond, the datcom ended transmission. I was all smiles, despite the need to rush to change. I leaned back in elation contemplating seeing him again when I could feel Estelle turning me towards her with her eyes. Her face spelled disappointment in big bold letters.

"So, you're not coming tonight, then?" Her tone was small and thwarted. I glanced at her confused, and she looked upset but was trying to hide it.

"I thought that's what you wanted me to do? You know, when you gestured with your hands for me to go with him?" I said mimicking the same gesture she had given me only moments before, but she sighed and rolled her eyes at me.

"No. I meant exactly the opposite." She argued, repeating the gesture again. Only this time she did it with a sarcastic look on her face that I didn't catch the first time, and I understood where I had gotten confused.

"Why would I have advocated you going out with some corporate sleaze?" She huffed again at the thought of him working for Paragon. "Where is he taking you anyway?" She demanded. She was obviously disappointed in me.

"Actually, I don't know. I didn't think to ask." I said with a giggle as I realized we hadn't really planned anything; only to meet each other again. I floated in the memory of the short com, but Estelle only scowled deeper at me. I didn't care, though. She didn't understand. She hadn't met him, she couldn't see what I saw in him, and she was starting to get fed up with me.

"What? You don't know? This guy sounds like something else!" The ridicule bled out in her statement, but again it had no effect on me.

Estelle stood back up still glaring at me.

"Oh come one, Ess. He's just a guy, innocent and shy." I soothed out. I could tell right away that my words had triggered a reaction in her, different from the one I was looking for.

Her hands jutted down to her sides, and her shoulders seemed to rear. Her eyes became fiery and penetrating.

"No one from Paragon is innocent." She huffed as she watched my smile fade with her anger. I never did understand her hatred of Paragon, and it was something she didn't like to talk about. I had the feeling something had happened in the past that made her feel that way, but she never did reveal to me what it was exactly.

Her shoulders relaxed as she studied my blank expression, and she could tell that she was hurting me with her blind judgment and contempt of my desires. She smiled hesitantly.

"I just want you to be careful, Lexxi. Just remember to do that, for me. You know where I will be tonight. Don't forget to com me if you need me, and I'll be right there, with Benny." She ended sternly. Benny was her bodyguard at performances; a big mean and ugly guy I never understood how she knew. My smile had returned. I knew she didn't approve, but I was happy enough to know that she understood how much it meant to me. It didn't make sense, and I knew that. How could she understand? I had only just met Vincent Alpha.

'Vincent Alpha'

I had just found out his name. I was so distracted by Estelle, and the emotions I was feeling to even think about it. It was a funny name, but it did have a strong sound. He was already special to me, but I didn't know why. I didn't understand how someone I had only met for just a few minutes could have impacted me so much, but he did.

Estelle walked over to the door and grabbed her coat. I was lost in thought and didn't even realize she was still watching me. She seemed like she was unnerved by my feelings.

"Remember, *be careful*." She repeated, interrupting my thoughts, and I looked back up into her eyes. They were now yielding and filled with worry. I tried to give her a reassuring smile.

"I will, don't worry. Have a great show tonight!" I shot back upbeat and cheery to help ease her worry. She smiled back at me and opened the door.

"I'll be back late, as usual. Have fun on your... date." She sounded like she almost choked on the last word, but she never broke the smile. She walked out, closing the door behind her and I realized I still had to clean up and get ready, or I would have to go already soaking wet. That wouldn't do.

I made my way to the back of the apartment, and up the stairs to Estelle's room, wondering what else she might have in her closet.

The time passed in a hurry as I dried off and changed clothes. I borrowed another one of Estelle's outfits, only this time I decided to go with one of her pastel sundresses. It was weird to call it that, it was never sunny. The city was covered entirely in a thin layer of clouds and rain.

It never stopped raining.

The time went by so quickly that I hadn't realized how much so, when I heard the door chime from the bathroom. I rushed to the door's intercom, and composed myself by running my fingers through the thicks of my hair, trying to untangle the ends. Then, I pressed the button on the com.

"Mister Mysterious?" I asked playfully through the electronic system. I almost thought it was ridiculous that I had already given him a pet name, but it was how I had remembered him; shrouded in dark clothes, dark glasses, and his black hair.

It only added to the fact that I had no clue what he did. It was only an assumption that he worked for Paragon, but Estelle usually knew what she was talking about when it came to those kinds of things. She was a very good judge of character.

I heard him release a small chuckle through the speaker, and he didn't have to say anything for me to recognize it was him. I remembered, all too perfectly, the sound of his voice, even when it was just a small laugh.

"I'll be right down!" I giggled, releasing the button.

The door closed behind me, and I took the stairs down in just a few bounds. I didn't realize just how quick I had made it to the bottom door in my excitement. Before I opened it, I tried to compose myself again. I opened the door and there he stood, the same way I had left him earlier. Same black coat, glasses, and the rain had even matted his hair in the same way it had looked in the car. Only now, the building's awning was his only shelter.

His face was illuminated with the flawless smile it held. Without a word, he held out his hand for me to take. I blushed and quickly took it. He led me down the stairs to the same black sedan that was parked on the curb in front of the building. Then, he opened the passenger side door for me to get in, and I looked over to him questioningly.

"No driver this time?" I asked with a smirk. He laughed, but only a little. I guess I looked odd asking such a presumptuous question.

"I thought we might have some privacy." He said, smooth and pleasant. I entered the car with him closing the door behind me. He got in on his side, but he didn't look natural behind the wheel. The car roared to life as he pressed the ignition button, and we started down the rainy street.

He was silent. His silence made me a little uncomfortable, but it looked like he was concentrating on his driving. He didn't turn to look at me, but instead stared straight out of the windshield watching the road, and adjusting for every minor divot in the street.

"So..." I started, hoping to break the silence, "Where were we going?" I remembered back to Estelles words of caution and her shock at our lack of destination. It was the first time he turned to look at me. His face held a puzzled expression as he let out a sigh.

"Well..." He panted out a laugh, "I don't really know. I've never tried to do something like this." He smiled, but now I was confused.

"What kind of thing are you talking about?" I asked, studying his face to anticipate his response, but it was stoic and firm other than his smile.

"Meeting people. That's more like a thing Eddie does. I don't meet many people." He assured me, and it was a relief. He seemed as innocent as I thought, and Estelle was wrong about him; I told myself.

"The driver?" I prodded, hoping he would reward me with more insight into his world.

"Yes." He said directly. Then, the silence continued. He sat poised at the wheel, turning it ever so slightly at every imperfection in the road.

"You can relax. We can just drive if you want. Are you always so tense?" I teased playfully as I watched him. He turned to look at me, and let his shoulders slide down ever-so slightly. He looked less comfortable like that. As if he knew I was thinking it, he pulled them back up against the seat. I couldn't help but to laugh as I watched him.

"Yes." He responded to the latter part of my query, and I started to laugh harder. A small grin jutted out from the side of his face. The city passed as we followed the Main through the Slums, and I watched as the familiar places appeared and disappeared. He seemed like he was becoming more comfortable the further away from Central D we became, and it reminded me of my favorite place in the city.

The outskirts.

No one ever went to the outskirts of the city. It was completely unpopulated and worn down. It was the only place where you could actually see the glass dome that encased the city, but with a little help from Paragon, the people had become disenchanted by it, too. I never had.

It had always amazed me; even though everyone in the slums thought it was haunted because of the rickety old buildings there. It was where the first population had lived in the city's beginning.

A lot didn't live through the first decade due to the contamination, and the survivors pushed forward into the city where they went to repopulate, in Central D, and the newly formed districts; now known as the Slums. The outskirts were different from the rest of the city, in the fact that it didn't rain there. Well, at least not in the part I knew how to get to, and there was grass; something that no one in the city usually gets to see. It gave them even more reason to fear it.

Green wasn't a familiar color; especially the green of living things. It would be the perfect place to take him. It would be quiet, and we would be alone.

"I guess, I do know somewhere we could go." I managed out in a mousy tone that held the hint of my hidden excitement. He turned to me slowly, and smiled revealing his perfectly white gleaming teeth. It was an innocent smile that made me blush, because it was filled with such relief.

"Really? Where is that?" He sounded calm, but I could tell he was happy that he didn't have to come up with the day's events. We passed the old Escapade's venue, and around the corner would be the ramp to the lower levels. It would take us to the outskirts.

"Take a right here...It's amazing." I pointed to the old broken intersection and the car turned carefully as we began gliding down the ramp. In just a few blocks we would see the old decrepit sign Paragon had put up more than half a century ago to keep people out. The rain beat down on the car as we traveled down the old avenue. The windshield flooded as the water flowed down it, thick and even.

"Rain." He started and ended with a sigh of dejection.

It hadn't ever stopped raining in the city; not even for a single day. They said in the beginning that it didn't rain as much, but I could barely remember a day without it. He apparently didn't care for it either, and it made me happy that I would be surprising him in only a few moments.

"It's ok, it won't be raining where we are going." I assured him with a smile.

"Huh?" His eyebrows pulled up over the rims of his dark glasses. I had piqued his curiosity. I giggled again at my secret.

"Take the next curve." The road split. One way led to another of the lower levels, and the other passed the old sign and onward to a small cracked barricade. He began looking around outside as we came closer to the small concrete barrier. It had become sparse with buildings. There was almost absolutely no sign of civilization here.

"I don't think I've ever been to this part of the city." he stated in awe. He was full of wonderment at the age of everything, and as I looked around all I could feel was the sense of freedom that this place gave off.

"It's ok. I don't think very many people come here. Actually, I might be the only one." I assured him. The car continued forward until the rain ended, as if we had passed under a curtain. A perfect line; on one side the rain pressured down violently, and on ours, nothing but clean air.

"What is this place?" The amazement showed on his face. He spoke very slowly, and I cracked open my door and stepped out. I smiled back at him and waved him out of the car with a hand.

"Come on, I'll show you." I urged. I couldn't help but continue to smile as he got out of the car and looked up. The slope of the glass dome was clear overhead, and the afternoon sun was setting in the distance over the tall grass beyond the barricade; something that was never seen anywhere else in the city. Even though I had seen it before, it stunned me every time. He walked slowly to meet me in front of the car, looking at the dome, and the sky he had never seen.

"Isn't it beautiful?" I asked rhetorically.

I didn't look to see his response. The sun held my gaze firmly. Its spreading hues of oranges and yellows painted the outside sky, with purples that faded into the dark blue of the night that was coming. We crossed the small concrete blockade, and he stepped into the tall grass that waded about his waste. He reached out with one hand and brushed it across the green field. The grass danced below his fingertips.

"Grass? Isn't this green plant called grass?" He asked, amused. A weird smile emptied the rest of his face, and I beamed at his bewilderment. We continued through the tall grass, and eventually came to my spot. It was a dirt hill that met the very edge of the dome; its curvature burying deep into the ground in front of us.

The red scorched and dead earth outside showed through clearly. Its dust blew violently, but it looked very serene from this side of the glass. I took my normal seat on top of the mound of brown dirt that had built up. He followed it until his hand could touch the smooth surface of the glass. I had the same response the first time I had come here. I watched him as he ran his hand along the glass dome, and up to a thin crack that had been there as long as I could remember. This place had always had a way of making me feel at ease with the world, and it would seem to be working its magic on him, too. His demeanor had completely changed, and the hard cold that surrounded him started to thaw.

His face was lit with mystification as he scanned around the hill, the grass, the glass dome, and then back to me as I watched him. Our eyes met again, only this time it was not awkward, and there was no need for me to blush at his amusement.

He captivated me. Only minutes ago in the fancy black sedan he was almost impenetrable, but now his face showed more emotion than I had ever seen from him, or had imagined possible. He seemed more alive. His smile was wider still, and he laughed enthusiastically as he gazed at me from the edge of the city's wall.

"This is amazing. I've never actually seen the dome this close before." He called out. His face was filled with the joy of a small child, and I couldn't help but to giggle at his innocence.

"It's the only place you can! I don't think Paragon likes for people to come here, though...not that they would." I observed. He walked over to me with a puzzled look, and sat down beside me on the top of the hill.

His palms hit the dusty ground, and he reacted oddly, looking at the dirt, before dusting off his hands. Then, the smile returned to his face as the chalky brown mist filled the air in front of him.

"Why wouldn't anyone want to see this place?" He asked, but it was more of a statement. I smiled back at him without an answer. I didn't know. Why wouldn't anyone want to see this? It was paradise by comparison, especially with him here. I didn't understand how it was happening so fast, but my defenses were all destroyed by him. It was as if he was a warlock, and I was under his spell.

My lips couldn't relax as I looked at him. I could feel the pain in my cheeks from the grins, smirks, and smiles that had rampaged across my face in the past hours since we'd met. He looked at me the same. It was reassuring, if not something more. It was a haven. Almost as if his presence was a place that I could feel safe in; like this hill.

"How did you find this place?" His voice was now balanced and calm as he asked, but the lighthearted tones still lingered around his words. It made me feel even more relaxed in his company.

"I started coming here when I was a kid. I found it by accident one day. The sign had been scratched out and battered so much, I couldn't make out the warning from Paragon. I saw the grass and I was amazed; just like you a minute ago." My smile made itself known as I explained.

"No one comes here, and no one knows that I do. Apparently, it is forbidden by Paragon, and the people say that it is haunted because of the green grass and the lack of rain, but I don't see how people could think something so beautiful could be evil. No one knows why it's green here and nowhere else. People seem to fear what they don't understand. So, I guess, the beauty of this place has stayed hidden from the city's eyes, almost like it doesn't even exist." His brow rose as I continued to tell him all about my little paradise.

"Why would Paragon not want people to see this?" He asked, but he understood as much as I did. This was a garden of sorts; an amazing green garden of grass. If he worked for Paragon, he should have known about this place.

"I don't know. You work for them, right?" I took the opportunity to ask, and I didn't want to seem disapproving, but Estelle's attitude towards Paragon came into my head. I didn't have many personal reasons, but I wasn't much of a fan of the corporation, either. I had never met anyone from Paragon, but they were very foreboding in the eyes of the people of the Slums.

He sat silently, staring at the ground as if he were thinking of an answer to some critical question. He almost looked ashamed. His brow had lowered back down below the brim of the dark glasses, and his head hung down to his shoulders.

"Yes." He stated, but it almost came out muted, "I do work for Paragon." His voice stayed low, but began to build as he continued. "...But Marcus tells me all the time that Paragon is the future. That Paragon is fixing the past. I don't understand."

I leaned forward trying to peek behind his glasses at his eyes. To try to see what was going on in his mind.

"You don't understand what?" I asked in defeat. I couldn't read his expressions, but I did understand he was thinking about more than just the dirt hill. His head jerked upward and forward again, and his face was hiding its previous contents as a smirk tried to grow from the left side of his mouth, but died before forming.

"If Paragon knows about this place, I don't understand why we wouldn't be trying to make the rest of the city like this. It's so unreal and amazing." He shot out in a new tone. My eyes reflected in the dark tint of the glasses that hid his real feelings. Just watching him, I had mimicked his distressed look. I quickly recovered my smile when I realized our proximity. Without knowing, we had been inching closer to one another. He didn't seem to notice either, and I used my hand to move some hair from my shoulder to disguise my retreat.

What was happening to me?

I bit my lip in thought; trying to think about anything other than his perfect face full of worry, how supple his lips set, or the way the light reflected from his hair; showing all of its thick curls and loches. I searched desperately for other thoughts, when I realized he had admitted to working for Paragon, and that it seemed to be worrying him at that moment.

"What exactly do you do for Paragon?" I asked again, turning to look away to the sun that had almost set in the thick red dust of the horizon.

An awkward silence surrounded us after the question until a ping sounded from the glass wall a few dozen yards in front of us. Then, a small rock thudded into the ground in front of it.

"That's not really important, anymore. Lately, I've been thinking that I would like to change some things, if I could. Maybe I haven't been living the best life." He soothed out.

I turned back to find him bouncing another small rock in his palm. Had he noticed my retreat? Did I upset him? I tried to act casual, and pretend to myself that I had not known I had purposely moved away from him. My smile returned as I wondered what he meant. Did he not like Paragon? Was I right when I told Estelle that not every person from Paragon was bad?

"Really? What would you change?" I smiled, scanning for a rock of my own.

"I'm not actually sure," He said. "I know I'd like to help the people in the city. I just don't know how, really."

He threw the small rock he was holding, and it thudded into the ground tapping against the first rock, but didn't make it to the glass. I thought it was endearing that he didn't make it as far the second time. I responded with a smirk as I picked up another small rock, and stood up, bouncing it up and down in my hand in the same manner he had.

"Well, that sounds very noble of you." I mused playfully, holding the tiny pebble. Then, I launched it over the distance into the glass. It clanked against the dome and fell to the ground. I smiled encouragingly at him, and he smiled at me in return.

"I just hope you weren't thinking about becoming a Shock Ball player or anything." I teased laughingly, "Not with that weak throw of yours."

His smile turned into a competitive grin as he grabbed another rock and stood up. I laughed again, as he loosened his tie and unbuttoned his coat to give him more range of motion. In the distance was a tattered building, which at one time, could have been a school in the outskirts, but now was a disheveled image of its former self.

He turned to face it. I cocked a brow at him in disbelief of what I knew he would soon attempt. The building was at least two hundred yards away, but it didn't stop him from gearing up for the effort. I barely even saw him draw his arm back before he released the rock into the air. I peered into the distance as it became smaller and smaller in the clear empty sky, and was eventually out of sight. Then, the clatter of wood could be heard after seconds of nothing. My mouth fell in shock, and I turned to him in an even greater amount of disbelief.

He only smiled, and sat back on the top of the dirt hill.

"I don't know...maybe I could play for the Elites." He sang in sly retort.

My gaping mouth only turned into vibrant laughter at the comment. He had been amazingly modest in this little game I thought I was playing with him, but he had let me understand just how out of his league I was. At the sight of the feat, it became hilarious to me that I had even thought I could compete. He was just as I had thought, perfect. The sun had almost completely faded into a thin purple line on the horizon, and it was getting late; not that you would know anywhere else but here. The city would still be full of life. I sat in front of him with my knees curled up under me.

We only looked at each other in silence, as the thin purple line fell below the night sky's reach. The only light came from an old street lamp that stood in the distance. I wanted to look into his eyes. I was tired of wondering what emotions they held behind the dark glass that now only seemed like shadows on his sculpted face. He didn't move as I raised my hand to remove them. Then, pulling them from his face, he showed me a familiar and comforting grin.

"What?" I asked softly, placing the dark glasses on the ground beside me. His eyes were a beautiful light green that contrasted his dark hair. They sparkled as his cheeks pushed up at the edges of them, revealing all the hidden emotions of my quandaries. The way he looked at me was unlike anyone before, and I could feel myself looking at him the same way.

"I'm not sure." He paused, and I continued to stare at his beautiful long-hidden eyes, "I'm not sure what's happening to me."

His eyes burned as they reflected my same longing. I wasn't sure what was happening to me, either. I hadn't known love. I had seen it on old telecasts, but I had never experienced it. Estelle had men all the time, but she never talked of love. This felt powerful. Compelling me to him, as if he were a magnet, and I was his polar opposite being pulled ever closer to him inch by inch. My hand fell on his chest, and he wrapped it with his, holding it close to his heart.

Our eyes were locked, and they pulled us into each other until his lips met mine. They were firm at first, with apprehension, but soon they succumbed, as did mine. The lights of the city behind us seemed to glow brighter as we connected, and their electricity pulsed through my body as I tingled at his slightest touch. His free hand cupped my shoulder and slid down the length of my arm giving me chills.

Our lips embrace didn't give way, when he laid me on my back, and my arm stretched to pull him closer into me. My hand smoothed the wrinkles of his shirt, as it moved around to his back, until stopping at something solid fastened under his arm; something metal.

He pulled away at the slight nudge to the metal object and his hands brushed down his face, as he cupped his chin in them. Then, he pulled them downward, as if to wipe the look off his face. I couldn't stop staring at him. Watching him go through motions and gestures trying to find a way to explain a question I hadn't asked yet, but that he knew I was going to.

"What was that?" I asked almost instinctively.

His head lowered at the question, and his left hand reached quickly under his jacket pulling out a small odd weapon. In a few more quick movements, a charge clip fell from the device. Then, he threw it onto the ground in front of me. I was sure that my face hadn't moved in the entire time that the weapon had made its appearance, and that it only held some sort of astonishment. I stared at the strange device that sat in the dirt only feet from me, but he didn't say anything. I tried, time after time, to recompose myself enough to ask more about it, but I couldn't find the words or the courage.

He just looked at me with some weird guilt that I didn't understand. I knew that some citizens carried a weapon, but I had never seen one before. I thought it was just stories Estelle told me to scare me away from going into Central D on my own. I tried to use that fact to bring me some sort of comfort. Violence was becoming less uncommon. I shouldn't have been acting so appalled. People had become very volatile in the Slums since the uprising, and I could only guess that it was the same in Central D. Paragon would want their citizens protected. That would have to be why he had it. Wouldn't it?

"Why do you...have that?" I gulped, my voice breaking with every syllable.

He still didn't respond, but instead held his gaze, studying my face and its expressions. He looked like he was embarrassed, and despite the metal weapon lying in the dirt, he still looked very harmless and innocent. I didn't know what to make of everything. I tried to think quickly. How should I respond? Was I wrong about him?

I couldn't be; not now.

"Who are you, Vincent Alpha? Really? I have to know." I said, able to calm my voice enough to sound less disparaging, and I pushed the weapon aside. I moved closer to him, peering into his eyes anxiously. My lips pursed and my hand repositioned itself onto his chest. I brushed back my hair, and it fell onto my shoulder.

"Lexxi." His voice said my name smoothly; too smoothly. It was almost eerie, and it was the first time I had heard it come from his lips, "I don't know who I am anymore, but I don't think that I'm a good man."

His fingertips glided over my shoulder, up my neck, and his thumb traced my cheek sending the same chills through my body.

"I want to be." He said looking deeply into my eyes to express his sincerity, but his eyes held an instability in them.

"Any man who has a heart, is a good man. You do have a heart don't you?" I asked, observingly. His hand moved to mine, pressing it ever more firmly against his chest where I could feel the gentle thumping of his heartbeat. It seemed to race at my touch becoming more prevalent with the passing seconds.

"Do you feel anything?" He asked honestly.

I leaned forward nestling my head against his chest, and placed my arm around his waist. I was sure that he was good. He was the best man I had ever met. Before I could begrudge him his past, I had forgiven him for it.

His arm folded over me, and his chin sat on top of my head, buried in my hair. He exhaled and his chest moved my face back and forth with him, as he let out a sigh of relief.

"You are a good man. I know it." I spoke softly to assure him, "I don't care about your past. Any man who would save some poor girl from the rain, and then appreciate this beautiful place with her as much as you have, would have to be." I clenched my arms around his waist hugging him tightly, and he ran his hands along my spine, rubbing me affectionately.

"I can't change my past, but I can change my future." He promised. I raised my head to meet his gaze once again, and pressed my lips to his. The city behind us sparkled like stars in the night sky. Then, I laid my head on his shoulder, and wrapped my arms around his neck.

With my mouth at his ear; I whispered, "Your future is all I care about."

His world is so different from mine, with a past that seemed so troubled, and yet the beat of his heart told me everything I needed to know about him.

That I was sure I already loved him.

The next morning I awoke on the dirt hill on top of his jacket. He was already awake and looking at me as I stirred to consciousness. The bright sun came through the glass behind us, heating the patch of earth where we rested.

He was lost in thought as he watched me, but he seemed happy. A grin crossed his face as I turned over onto my side, propping myself up on an elbow. I smiled back at him eagerly.

"Good morning." My fresh voice sang out full of enthusiasm. He laughed, and I felt very different than I had the day before. All the hesitation had left me, and the only thing I could do was feel the need to be with him. It was strange to be so comfortable around him. I wasn't even this comfortable around Estelle, but with him I felt like I could do anything, be myself, and he would only laugh lovingly at any silly remarks, and smile his perfect smile.

He picked up my free hand in his and held it affectionately. His other hand came from around his back, and placed a wildflower he had found in my hand. It was a small red skimpy-looking thing, but it was beautiful in its own unique way. Unique that it wasn't a garden flower that you would find in the city's florists, but instead like us, it was rare.

"Good morning to you, too." His voice was soothing, just as it had been the previous night. It was a perfect dream that we could both live in; the sun bright in the sky, the grass, and our little dirt hill. The day felt confident with new beginnings, as we lingered into each other's eyes.

"It's beautiful." I said, looking at the flower he had placed in my hand, but he didn't take his gaze from me.

"Almost the most beautiful thing I had ever seen." he whispered in a breathy voice. My heart jumped at the hidden implication that was held in his silky tone. I didn't raise my head back to him, as I tried to hide my blushing cheeks, but then I felt him rustle to his feet. I looked up to find him returning his glasses to his face.

"Is it time to go?" I asked with caution. I didn't want to leave, but I didn't want him to know how desperate I was for his company. I also felt a little disappointed that he wasn't as desperate for mine. I couldn't show him that either. He dusted off his pants and shirt, and put out his hand for me to take.

"Eddie will be furious that I haven't gotten Penelope back to him by now." He laughed through the statement. I'm sure to ease my caution, but it only confused me. Who is Penelope?

"Penelope?" I asked, feeling a bit of jealousy. He laughed, again.

"The car." He explained with a nod. The car had a name? There was nothing usual about him; from his job to his friends with named cars. He was definitely interesting, but I didn't know what to expect next. Would he come back? Would he keep the promise to change from last night? Had I imagined that he felt the same for me? Certainly not.

"Eddie's a friend, right?" I asked again nervously. I had hoped he was. The way he mentioned him, laughingly, made me think he'd have to be. Friends don't get upset at each other.

"He's something like that." He said it uncertainly, but I knew what friendship meant. Estelle had shown me, and anyone who'd let you take their car to have a magical evening would have to be a friend.

"Well, I'm sure he'll understand." I winked. He smiled at me before chuckling, once more, at what I didn't understand.

"You don't know Eddie and his car." He argued, and I shook my head mockingly, and then picked his jacket up from the ground. I hadn't even felt him move me onto it. Now it was covered in dirt. I shook it, as clean as it could get, and folded it over my arm.

"I'll clean it for you. Are you coming back after you take back *Penelope*?" I asked, and the car's name came out in playful sarcasm, but it didn't change the fact that I would be hanging on his answer. He would come back. Wouldn't he?

His head hung down, and he stared at the small weapon that still laid on the dirt hill in front of us. I had forgotten about it, and was too preoccupied to have even noticed it. My eyebrows lowered at the sight of it. I thought about him being a pawn for them, just like Estelle had said. I tried to imagine that he was nothing more than just a corporate sleaze, doing whatever they told him. It infuriated me. How could he let them do that to him? How could he be so easily used by them? He looked frozen, as he stared at the weapon; not moving and not answering.

"Are you going back to Paragon?" I repeated almost furiously, but he still only stared at the ground; at the weapon. Then his voice became dead.

"I have to." he said matter-of-fact. He did not move. He just stared deeper. I could feel the water forming along the lines of my eyes, but the anger I felt would make them dry for the moment.

I didn't want to believe him. I wanted him to make an excuse not to see me again. I wanted this to be his way of throwing me away, to move on to his next girl, but I knew it wasn't the case. We had shared something, and I could tell he felt it too. Paragon had its grip around him, and now I could feel that, as well; in his dead voice and disheartened inaction. My heart was confirming everything Estelle had said. He was a puppet. All the things he had said the night before, he had known the whole time he was trapped by Paragon.

"But, what about everything you said last night? What about wanting to help people, and changing your future?" My voice was stingingly sharp.

I could feel the nails of my fingers digging into the palm of my hands as they clinched, and I'm sure my face reflected that same anger, but he didn't notice. He maintained his gaze at the ground, until he slowly lifted his head to huff.

"I do want everything I said, but..." The calm in his voice made him sound vacant, and it was disgusting.

"But what! If that is what you want, then do it! You don't have to throw away your life being some stupid puppet for Paragon!" I shouted, and the water broke free from my eyes, and a line formed down my cheek. It was almost as if Estelle had jumped into my body and spoke the words for me, and it had upset him. He was no longer dead. His head rose and he met my teary gaze through the dark of his glasses. His brows twitched at the widening of his eyes.

"It's not that simple." His voice burned with a chalky hollow as he looked at me, "What I am...What Paragon has made me, it's..."He paused and looked back to the weapon on the ground and took a deep breath, "It's something that I can't just walk away from. It wouldn't be safe."

I couldn't help but hear the worry behind the explanation, and it was alarming, but I still didn't understand. What had they made him? What did he mean it wouldn't be safe? And then, I realized his vague answer from the night before about his employment with them.

'I'm not a good man.'

I had to know exactly what that meant, because I was starting to believe him.

"What do you do for them, Vincent? What do they make you do!?" I screamed, and each word seemed to crash against him like waves on a rock as he stood, even further now, in front of me. The tears began faster, and I shook as I began backing away from him even more. His hesitation told me everything I never wanted to know. He was a bad man. I could feel it now as I stared into his dark glasses and his quivering brow.

"Tell me what you do for them!" I yelled again, and as I did the tears flew from my cheeks. He stood still and silent, and I could feel him deliberating; his gaze still on the little death-dealer that sat in the dirt. In a sudden movement, he had picked it up and was holding it in his right hand. Then, he looked back at me.

Still silent, he started walking towards me. Although he had not pointed the weapon at me, I was still scared. The look on his face had turned to repulsion, and anxiety started to swell in the back of my throat. I tried to gulp it back down, but I couldn't, nor could I take my eyes off of the hand that held the weapon, as he approached. I was still backing away when I noticed he stopped, but he had still made up some ground between us. He leaned forward and held the weapon out to me in the palm of his hand.

"I am this for them." The sound of his voice rattled me, as it had become harsh and stern. My eyes widened at the weapon that was now only arm's length from me. I didn't really understand what he meant, "This is what they make me do."

He continued, "I am Paragon's weapon."

With the statement, he drew the little device back closer to him, and stared down at it himself. A look of disgust crossed his face, but I was still in shock.

I was starting to understand. All the stories I had heard from Estelle and the people in the slums about Paragon killing the people who disobeyed them were true, and he was how they did it. He was the shadow man. That's what they called him in the slums.

"I've never met anyone I didn't hurt." He explained, still staring at the black metal instrument, "Except for you."

The thought didn't make me feel any safer. He was death, and now I could feel it from him. That cold grip that Paragon had around him was the death, and his aura exuded it. I could feel it choking me, closing my throat as the tears streamed down my face. I didn't want to believe what I was thinking, and I could have been imagining or exacerbating the situation. I did that. I could be doing it now, but I knew I wasn't. The death was all I could see in him now, and it had been there all along.

"You...kill people?" I stammered it out, already knowing the answer. I wanted him to lie. I wanted this to be some sick twisted inside joke that I had not been privileged to. Instead, his free hand grasped at his face covering it from me, and his shoulders lowered. I could hear the slight crunch of his glasses as his hand gripped furiously against them, and tightened around his face.

"I was raised by Paragon to delete people. It's all I've ever known." He growled out.

The shock set in deeper. My speculations were right. My chest felt like it was collapsing in on itself, and the clean air was getting harder to breathe.

"What kind of people?" I squeaked out the question, and my curiosity kept me near him, but a weird instinct told me to get as far away from him as I could.

"Whatever people I am told to." His voice had become hollow, but his despair didn't halt the fear swelling inside of me. Estelle's voice started to ring in my head, in shouts of the evil of Paragon, and the instinct to get further away grew.

Through him, Paragon killed indiscriminately. He was the worst kind of evil, detached.

"I don't believe you! Estelle was right! You are nothing but a horrible pawn for those evil creeps!" I screamed. I hadn't noticed the steps I had taken, in anger, towards him despite the cry in the back of my mind to run. He had not raised his face back to me, until I was only a step away from him. My arm acted without my approval, and my hand smashed into the side of his face. It was like hitting a wall, and he probably didn't feel any pain from it, but the physical damage wasn't the intent.

I fumed in front of him without words. His hand still covered the majority of his face in a sort of crazed disgust, and he did not acknowledge my show of force. I didn't wait any more than seconds before turning to run, but before my feet could pick up, I felt his grip around my arm, and it infuriated me even further.

"No! Do not touch me. You never touch me." I could not control the shrill sound of my demand as it came from me, and I pulled free and continued my departure.

"Lexxi, wait...please." His tone had become painfully harsh. I couldn't help but to stop and turn back at the sound of it. He sounded like a man who had been shot and was calling out for salvation. His wounded pride was all I could see. He had lied, and now he wanted to lie his way out of it. I stood frozen at the sight of him. He started to approach me, and with every step my anger was fueled.

"Stop right there. Whatever it is you want, you can say it from right where you are." I demanded, and he did stop.

He tried to posture himself from his defeated slump, but not to much improvement. As he removed the hand from his face, the glasses beneath cracked and fell to the ground in pieces. His arms dropped to his side, and he tried again to lift his shoulders to appropriate himself. His chin lifted, but his eyes stayed pained and fixed on me. It was as if they wanted to shed tears, but nothing; not a drop came from the agonized gaze. His body was shivering in slight motions, and he seemed anxious to speak. His mouth would open to start a word, and then close with nothing.

"I'm so sorry..." He said in the smallest voice. He turned slightly to not face me directly, and he was looking back at the glass wall that separated the outside world from ours, "I'm not a puppet. I won't be anymore."

I could only see insincerity coming from him now. The night before had been sacred, but now was only a fantasy. I wouldn't get lost in the fairy tale that he had spun out of intimate moments and desires to change.

"Everything you say is a lie. You are a bad man." The hate seethed from my lips, and with each word my retreat furthered.

"No! I promise I'm not. I don't want to be..." He started murmuring gradually trying to force the words out, but they weren't slowing me. My head began to shake in disgust without me even wanting it to, spreading the tears around my cheeks.

"I've never met anyone like you...I had no idea what I was.." He continued, but I had made it to the tall grass. When I felt the thick reeds touch my back, I turned and made a dash for the barrier, and the dismal dark city beyond, leaving him alone on top of the dirt hill.

I couldn't stop the tears from falling, or my legs from carrying me away.

ROTTEN BANANA SPLIT

My tears did not stop like I thought they would the further away from him I became.

I ran past the black sedan that had delivered us through the wall of rain. It was only twelve blocks back to my apartment. Twelve blocks, and I didn't slow my pace or look back once.

I couldn't stop all the thoughts that swam in my head; thoughts of him coming to find me, and what he would do when he did. Would he kill me? How would he do it? Would it be soon? How long would I have to wait for his retribution?

The rain felt like small pin pricks as I dashed through them, each one reminding me of the dreary outcome of my fairytale. Two people locked in a moment, almost seeming destined to find each other. Then, to have that moment destroyed in an instance.

It was madness; the fast feelings and the immediate connection. My heart was in shards, and stabbing me in the chest. I could only tell tears from rain by the frequency of their touch on my shoulders as I ran. I hit the turn back onto the Main in what had been only moments in my mind, and there in the distance was the comforting glow of the steps to my apartment, and the awning that only read "Miserere" in elegant cursive. I didn't waste any time getting inside, and up the stairs that would take me to my refuge. I closed the door behind me, and realized that Estelle had not left yet, but instead, she was in the bathroom starting her normal routine of dressing for her rehearsal.

I didn't want her to see me so upset, but there was no way to help that now. My eyes wouldn't stop the downpour they had begun. I couldn't let go of the memory of the perfect encounter, the perfect evening, and the perfect night. Those memories were only conflicted by the more recent ones of enlightenment, and the cold I felt come off him; the death.

I knew it wouldn't be long before Estelle came from the bathroom and she would see me, so I had to fake a happier mask. For a second I debated on leaving, but I was able to get the tears to stop, and I wiped their remnants from my cheeks. I flashed a smile as she quickly scampered through the door, fully dressed, in another elaborate ensemble. She looked just as stunning as usual. When she saw me, I could tell my deception hadn't worked. My eyes would still be red and puffy, and I'm sure I couldn't completely erase my skewered expression. She immediately marched over to where I sat on the sofa.

I grabbed the nearest pillow and clutched it to my chest. Her daunting shape over me only broke my composure, and my tears began to roll out again. She would think I was in agony, and I was.

"What's happened?" She demanded. Her concern was obvious, but seemed almost hysterical and artificial. She always looked after me, almost like a mother, even though she wasn't much older than me. I couldn't respond to her question, and her tone quickly changed with her own deductions. "It was him wasn't it? That Paragon goon did something to you, didn't he? Did he hurt you?" She demanded again as she tapped her foot and crossed her arms over her chest. I still couldn't talk enough to tell her what had happened. I was ashamed to admit that she was right about him, but I also didn't want her to know how I felt. She was coming up with her own conclusions for the tears, and I couldn't muster up the courage to tell her that they were from disappointment, and not any foul play. "Ooh, I knew this would happen... I've got half a mind to round up Benny and his boys." She exalted. Benny was her bodyguard, but he also ran a small group of left-over rebels against Paragon. So far, they were all mostly talk, but with Estelle's dramatics they would undoubtedly use this to cause a scene; a scene that could get them all killed if they found him.

I could do nothing but clutch the pillow tighter as she rambled on. Images of the day before flickered through my mind, like an old datacast, persisting in making me relive all the lost perfect moments.

I wanted to tell Estelle not to com Benny; not to get them involved; get them killed, but my voice was missing. My eyes peered wide over the top of my pillow, as the flickering images in my mind stopped on him holding his weapon out to me; the little death device gleaming in the sun from outside the glass.

"Lexxi!" Estelle's voice awoke me, and I hadn't noticed that she had sat on the sofa beside me, or that she had put her arm around me. She shook me and I suddenly felt the images stop, and I began gasping for air. I had apparently forgotten how to breathe. The tears still ran down my face, but not as profusely as before, and they had made little rivers over the tops of my cheeks.

"Lexxi, what happened?" Estelle's voice was now soothing and motherly as she held me closer to her. I began to wipe the tear streams from my face, and prepared to gather my voice, but all I could think about was the happiness I had felt the day before.

"It was... so... perfect." I breathed out. I was right to think my voice would be weak. I tried to clear my throat, so that I could explain everything to Estelle, but she was now looking at me almost in shock. Her eyes widened, and her lips pulled in at the edges in doubt.

"What?!" She sounded appalled, "Then why are you crying like this?"

As I tried to think of a way to answer her, my chest grew heavy at what I had come up with. The corners of my eyes started to flare up again, to create the streams of tears, and an overwhelming sadness hit.

He killed people.

It was all that was wrong. He killed people for the evil company that controlled the city. I couldn't imagine how to say it any differently. If it weren't for that, there would be no tears, no sadness, and no cold death surrounding my mental image of him.

I wanted to ignore his stupid job, but I couldn't.

"He... kills people for them." My voice was low and breathy. I slowly turned to look at Estelle, who now had a blank expression on her face. Her mouth hung open slightly in her shock, and her hand slowly gripped me tighter pulling me even closer to her.

Killing wasn't common. It had become taboo. This city had been built on the last breath of humanity. Sometimes, in the slums people became violent, but killing someone would make you an outcast. No one would associate with you. You would almost be better off battling the elements outside, in the contamination sickness ridden Earth.

"He kills people for them?" She repeated, but it was more like a statement than the question she meant to be asking. In her mind it only confirmed her suspicions about Paragon and their ruthless ways. Her eyes filled with her own agenda and my pain seemed to get lost. I don't know why, but I suddenly felt the need to explain to her all the things about him that I fell in love with, but She would march Benny and his men into death for a good cause against Paragon, and I didn't want to be that for them.

I never understood Estelle's dream of martyrdom. I still couldn't stop the tears from coming, but they fell slower as I recomposed.

"You don't understand. He doesn't want to. They make him. It's all he's known. He isn't a bad person. He was trying to explain, but I...I left before he could." I could barely get all of the words out before my realization hit. I hadn't been fair with him. I wouldn't hear him out, and instead I just left him there out of fear. Maybe I could have helped change him, but I lied, too. I lied to him the night before when I told him I didn't care about his past. I had no right to run from him when he was trying to be honest with me, but in my shock I didn't know what else to do. That realization hit me just as hard. What if I could have saved his next victims just by listening? Would what happened from then after be entirely my fault? The tears started to come harder.

"It sounds like you did the right thing." Estelle said as she relaxed a little, and let her hate for Paragon surface.

"I don't feel like I did. I didn't even give him a chance to explain." I sobbed. Estelle released me and stood up. She seemed almost proud that I hadn't let him explain, and she stood over me again with her arms crossed.

"You were right not to. No one from Paragon even deserves a chance. You were right to leave. At least, you're safe now." She said sternly in her conviction against Paragon, but I could look beyond his past; I promised him that I would, but I just didn't know how to, until now.

Estelle paced away back to her bedroom to finish getting ready, and I sat imagining how he felt when I left him. I became torn with the ideas of my love and Estelle's hatred.

"You'll be O.K. It was only one date. Are you coming to rehearsal tonight?" She asked from what now seemed the distant room in the back of the building. It was so easy for her to just look over this, but it was only because of Paragon's involvement. I knew that any other guy, any other situation, she would be more concerned for my feelings.

I hadn't thought she would be home, or I wouldn't have come back to the apartment. Now, it had become clear that it was better that I didn't involve her.

I needed to think for myself. I needed a better place to do that, but going back to my dirt hill wasn't an option. Aside from the recent conflicting memories, he might also still be there. No, I would have to go somewhere else, and the only other place I ever went was the Zigg. So, I grabbed my umbrella from the tin next to the door, ignored Estelle's question, and went back out into the rain. The Zigg wasn't far from my apartment building, only a few blocks, and then down the ramp to the lower levels of the slums. I didn't rush this time, but instead took my time to think about Vincent and my feelings. I couldn't help but mope over how I acted, and how that must have made him feel, and guilt took over.

The Zigg was usually empty except for a few regulars, the tender, Darby, and a waitress, but that day it seemed to have more people. Not many more; just some unfamiliar faces.

My favorite table sat in a corner next to some archaic dusty printed photos of people from before The Shift. A man in a pilot's uniform stood out, and I often wondered what it would have been like to fly through the air; the freedom he must have felt. It was all almost prehistoric now. It was why I liked the place, it was a mosaic of a time long forgotten, and the photos made up for the grim aesthetics. I found it pleasantly comforting. The atmosphere was dull with only the swinging screech of a few lonely ceiling fans making any sound.

I took my seat, and soon after the waitress met me at my table. She was a normal girl, young with an average kind of beauty that had become common in the city. She wore high top boots with a skirt, and a low cut shirt that was only outdone by her streaky blonde and fiery red pigtails.

"What can I get you, dear?" Her tone was pleasant and routine. I had come here many times before, and I usually didn't drink synth, but I would always order something so I didn't seem like a loiterer.

"Just a rotten banana split, please." It was my favorite even though I never drank them. I just liked the name; an oxymoron. It reminded me of the city; something that could be beautiful and happy, but instead was dismal, dark, and decaying. That now seemed to apply to my life, as well.

She didn't say anything in response, only smiled and walked back to the bar at the other side of the room. It wasn't long before she had come back with the green and yellow looking concoction and left again. I stared into the glass watching the colors swirl around themselves, and tried to let my puffy swollen eyes calm.

I had gotten lost inside the drink, because I hadn't noticed the emergence of a man standing in front of my table looking at me over the top of my glass. He wasn't very tall, maybe even only my height, with white hair and glasses that sat above his pudgy nose and thick white mustache. His cheeks looked warm, and a smile crossed his lips.

"Are you o.k., miss?" He asked. He seemed kind and his concern was genuine. No one ever usually talked to me. Sometimes, a duster punk would try, but I always ignored them. This seemed different. He was old, and he didn't look at me like he wanted anything more than to actually know how I was doing. His question sent a single tear down my cheek at my reason for being there. I still wouldn't give him the satisfaction of breaking my seclusion.

"That's a silly question. I'm a mess...I don't think I would be good company right now, old man." I shot out. My acuteness seemed to catch him off guard, and he was aghast at my comment. I heard him gulp as he looked down at himself, as if to check his appearance. Then he started muttering to himself.

"I guess I have let time catch up with me...damn Paragon, I'd been down there way too long." I heard him say to himself. He then turned his attention back to me, but he already had mine with his last statement and his mention of Paragon.

"Guessing from the tears, you are having some sort of man troubles, miss?" He poked, but I ignored his oddly accurate diagnosis, and went right for the answers I wanted. I wiped the tear from the base of my jaw and looked up to him more directly.

"You work for Paragon? Are you a killer, too?" I asked, glaring up at this stranger. I don't know why, but I couldn't control what I was saying to him, this genuinely interrogative person. The old man staggered and smiled back at me in amusement.

"Me?" He questioned, jabbing one of his stubby fingers into his chest, "A killer?" He then began laughing absurdly, "No, young madam, I am Professor Dorian Krill! A brilliant and underestimated scientist..." His tone rose with his boast, but then his face became disheartened, "That has been locked in a basement for the past half-decade." Then, he ended his speech with a hiccup, and sat in the chair across from me. He waved his hand for the waitress, and turned his gaze back to me.

"Why? Who do you know from Paragon?" He asked. I stared back into the swirling yellow-green drink in front of me, not wanting to answer him directly only to not have to say *his* name.

"Just some murderer." I claimed, and I couldn't stop the sobs that began. So, I cupped my face in my hands, and hid them from the old man in front of me, "Just some murderer that I think I might be in love with..."

The waitress set another drink in front of the professor, and collected the empty glass he came with, cocking an eyebrow at me. I barely saw through the cracks in my fingers, and then she walked back. I must have looked pathetic.

"There, there child." The old man soothed as he took a gulp from his new drink, and then set it back onto the table with a pucker of odd satisfaction drawing from his lips, "I just hope it wasn't that Eddie Brinnigin fellow. He's nothing but a drug addicted lady-chasing low-life ..." The old man hiccupped again, "...and he never had an ounce of respect for the ones that he caught."

I knew that name. *Eddie*. Vincent had said it. The owner of the black sedan named "Penelope" was Eddie. Could this babbling old man know Vincent Alpha? The notion grabbed me hard and shook my senses. The old man's squinty eyes widened when the shock sprawled across my face, and my involuntary head shaking started. I was trying to get away to sort out these new feelings that I had developed in the previous day, but it seemed like fate that I would still find his presence here. While lost in that thought, I couldn't manage much of an acknowledgement.

"No...Not Eddie." I answered softly. One of the old man's eyes widened further pushing his bushy brows into a cocked manner. "Vincent Alpha." I uttered in an almost silent whisper, and instantly felt my stomach turn in uneasiness.

Dorian almost spilled his drink, when his shaky hand brought it back down to the table. His face was almost pale, but in an amazement. I found it almost cruel. A small grin jutted from the corner of his mouth pushing his mustache into his rosy cheeks wrinkling one entire side of his face.

"Did you say 'Vincent Alpha'?" He reiterated the name, specifically, as if to make sure he heard me correctly, and all I could do was nod in agreement. The old man pulled his drink up to his mouth with amusement; swallowing almost all of its remnants. Then, he returned the glass back to its resting place.

He turned from me in a happily puzzled manner to wave the waitress back to him for another drink. She acknowledged him, but looked busy doing some cleaning. We sat in silence for what seemed like an eternity, without another exchange of words, studying each other's expressions. He didn't seem willing to freely offer up any information, like I thought he would have when I had mentioned Vincent, but instead acted as if I were the one with the conversational edge. The waitress finally interrupted our standoff by sitting down another drink in front of him and scooping up the empty glass on her retreat. The curiosity was quickly becoming unbearable.

"Do you know Vincent?" I quickly shot out trying to spark more conversation.

"Know him...I'm practically his father...sort of." The old man murmured, keeping his eyes away, as he raised the new drink to his face. This time it was me who was stunned by his answer. Not only did he know Vincent, but he probably knew him better than anyone would.

"You're his...father?!" I stammered out in a rush born of shock. A million thoughts steam-rolled their way through my head at the fact. How could a killer have a father, and be a killer? Maybe Krill didn't know his son as well as I thought he should, or did he not care?

I had thought Vincent said he was raised by Paragon, so could this old man be lying?

"You said before that you 'love' Vincent, ahem, I mean 'Alpha'. Is this true? Tell me, does he love you?" He excitedly asked. The old man sounded like he was trying to put a puzzle together again, but his emphasis on the word 'love' made me start recalling my conversations with Vincent on the dirt hill. My heart started pounding rhythmically, and my stomach turned again. I remembered the look in his eyes, and when he laid the flower in the palm of my hand that next morning. The memory became overwhelming, making my eyelids quiver, tempting new tears to form. I quickly pulled my hands up to cover my face again. Kril's concern for my feelings reminded me of the way Estelle had acted, when I told her. He seemed more curious about them than compassionate. He adjusted his glasses up his nose, taking them from his pudgy cheeks.

"I did better than I thought." He whispered to himself, but not low enough to evade my hearing.

"What?" I demanded. A newfound confusion cleared away my emotional outburst, and I didn't understand what he couldn't have meant by saying that. Was it some weird vicarious response? I wiped my cheeks again, but now it felt like all of the day's tears had begun to cut into my face.

"How much have you had to drink? The strange man hiccupped as punctuation, but the question only baffled me further. Krill talked as though I was behind in the conversation and needed to be hurried along. I didn't know what to make of it. He knew something, but I was too twisted around in the conversation to understand where it was going.

"What?" I repeated, looking at my untouched green and yellow nectar, and then pointed awkwardly in confusion at its fullness. "I only ordered this one, but I wasn't planning on drinking it. I'm too upset." Krill's face lit up at the response and his hand slid across the table to my glass.

"May I?" He said in excitement with a slight nudge of his head to my drink. I could only nod and watch as he picked up the stemmed glass, and swallowed it all at once. He let out a sigh as he put the glass down next to his other empty one.

"Yep, I liked that one, too!" He smiled, looking across the table at me. "Would you be a nice young lady, and help a foolish old man back to his home...I think we might find some answers for you there." I only nodded again.

He moved his chair out from the table, and put some credit coins down next to the newly emptied glasses. It was far more than enough to cover the drinks he had when I was there, and plenty more than any bar tab should ever be. Then, he walked around the table and took hold of the back of my chair to pull it out for me. As I rose he jutted out a folded arm for me to entangle mine in; both rather archaic customs, and it seemed he was a perfect gentleman. I noticed I was slightly taller, as I stood next to him, arm in arm, and we proceeded to the exit.

The waitress stopped us with an acknowledging glance, and he smiled back to her. I could only imagine what she must have been thinking.

"Are you finally leaving, old-timer?" She shot out across the room. He tilted his head to her, and without a word, we left the Zigg.

I popped open my umbrella once we were outside. The rain had managed some harshness now, even down here on the lower levels.

"How far is it, Krill?" I prodded as we stood halfway covered by the bar's awning.

"It's just down the street. I have to warn you...I've only been there since this morning. It's not the nicest place to show a lady." He said, still smiling. He seemed to be getting a kick out of being with me.

"Don't worry though, it's not far." He assured, in acknowledgement of the rain's increase, then stumbled off the sidewalk. Then, he began to lead me down the street, only a couple of blocks, to the abandoned part of the Slums where we found his building. He twisted the lock on the rickety old door and we quickly escaped inside. The room was lit only by a small desk lamp next to a dilapidated set of chairs. The air was still musty and damp from the building's prior vacancy. I couldn't make out a lot of the surroundings, but there seemed to be an odd room in the back with a series of machines, all with small indicator lights that developed their silhouettes.

I helped the old man to one of the chairs, and he plopped down recklessly, sending the chair into an awkward rock that he quickly tried to recover from.

"You said you had answers for me, professor?" I asked cautiously, but mostly because of the dark ominous room. I dusted off the other chair with my hand, before sitting across from him.

"Krill." He returned in an abrupt manner that was seemingly dissatisfied. I didn't understand.

"What?" I asked. He adjusted in the chair, trying to get comfortable.

"My name young lady; it's Krill. Dorian Krill." He stated sternly, repeating his name to me. I couldn't help but to let out a sigh at his coyness. He seemed to be inspecting me with his every breath to make sure of something I wasn't aware of.

"Ok...Krill...Tell me about Vincent, and why did you call him Alpha like that?" I asked, making sure to sound more pleasant this time. He paused for a moment and smiled, then took off the tiny spectacles that laid rest above his nose. He folded his arms over his paunch and cleared his throat.

"Well, you see dear, that's his name 'Vincent Alpha', and the rest is rather difficult to explain." He said with a little chuckle and I'm sure he saw my brow tilt as soon as I felt it myself. Then, I crossed my arms as well, but not in the careful manner he had. Instead I made it clear that I wanted my answers, and didn't want to waste time with trivial formalities. It occurred to me then, exactly how much he was like Vincent; his careful movement, his analyzing eyes, and his detraction from conversation.

"You really are his father, aren't you?" I said questioningly, already knowing my answer. His brow cocked at my slanted remark, and a smile wrenched across his face.

"Not exactly." He soothed out, as he pulled one hand from its hold under his arm to gesture for me to remain calm. I hadn't noticed, but I was leaning towards him, aggressively.

"Not really, not exactly...what is it with you two! Can't either of you give someone a straight answer!" I demanded. The old man's eyes were wide, and I realized the words had pulled me almost out of my seat, and my arms were no longer crossed, but instead, positioned in shaking frustrated fists out in front of me. My frustration quickly collapsed as I saw it, and I returned back to my seat with a sigh. I changed my gaze to the window. I could still feel Krill's eyes studying me, now in astonishment.

"Damn you're a pushy woman...Fine then! He's not even human!" He shouted drunkenly back in response to my aggressive move. I turned back to him trying to lift my jaw, and erase the puzzled look in my eyes.

"I mean, of course, he's human... he's the perfect human...I made him." He hiccuped. His attempt to clue me in was worthless. I still had no idea what he meant by that.

He 'made' him? What exactly does that mean? I lingered on the words for a moment, hesitant to make any wrong speculations. My pause ended with the old man's next hiccup.

"What do you mean...you *made* him?" I asked.

I'm sure the weird look on my face showed him the doubt held in the question, but it only seemed to amuse him.

"...In my lab almost six years ago." he answered with startling ease. An electrifying pulse shot up from my feet, turning me erect, and I couldn't stop myself from pacing around the tiny dark room. A million thoughts raced in my head. Who was this old man? How could he just *create* a person? Was Vincent some kind of robot? How could I fall in love with a robot? There was something terribly wrong about all of this.

Paragon. He said he worked for Paragon. This was all because of them. Did Vincent even feel? Of course not. He's not real. Then why did he act that way? Is he human? Damn you old man, I didn't want to know any of this. Then, Krill started to explain, but I couldn't stay focused on the words. The thoughts in my head kept me frazzled.

"I told you. I am a geneticist, and fifteen years ago I started a project that was supposed to help us get out of this dome. I was to design a flawless human that could withstand the world outside, and then, in time, we would repair the Earth and integrate these 'Protosapiens' into our society, eventually repopulating the world with a stronger race of people." He went on, and my hands felt their way through the thick of my hair.

"This is madness." I said, and It was all I could think of; the lunacy of the doctor's ill explanation. Sure, it answered a few questions, mainly about Paragon, but nothing of Vincent and me.

"Marcus took over the project. He didn't care about the world outside. He was always near-sighted when looking at the future, and the city only fueled his reasoning. All of the chaos that was happening from everyone being trapped inside this place, and the breakdowns in the social strength of us all. It made him look inward, wanting to solve the immediate problem Paragon was facing; the loss of power by its people. Then, he turned my research into a weapon." He explained, and I continued to pace as he rehashed the story.

I was in an eerie denial, which was quickly dissolving, as I listened. He didn't bother trying to comfort me or sugarcoat anything. I guess he already thought of the impact this kind of news could make on someone. So, he was direct. "After Marcus had everything he needed, I was locked away in the basement of the Paragon building, and that's when Alpha was born." He seemed lost in his own tale, not even watching me anymore.

I had paused with him, and was standing in the middle of the room waiting for him to continue, but he didn't seem to want to go on.

"So, he's not real?" I managed to ask, interrupting the new silence. It was all I could think to mutter out, mostly acknowledging that my own voice would still work, but the near-whisper still caught him. He began to laugh a healthy and voluminous laugh.

"He's as real as you and me, dear...only better. He simply lacks our defects, and now that I see he knows how to love, it seems, that's all he lacks...making him essentially perfect by design." He assured me with a satisfaction in his voice that was unmistakable, but it left me with even more questions, and some affirmations.

"Perfect?" I whispered, almost questioning, but to me it was starting to make sense; all the things I had noticed, not only physically, but the purity of his emotions that seemed so indescribable. The way he moved was almost majestic; his strength with the rock and his impeccable sense of duty, and all the little refinements that I didn't have words for.

"Can I ask you something, young lady?" Krill sputtered out. I was lost in my own mind and almost didn't hear him ask. His question caught up to my thoughts, which now settled a bit.

"Lexxi." I shot back without thinking. It seemed a courtesy now to be as frank with him, as he was with me.

"Lexxi, would you please come and sit down with me, again?" He said smiling, and wrinkled an eye as he waved me back into my chair. I slowly returned back to my seat, letting the conversation sink in. The old man propped himself forward in his seat leaning closer to me; the smile still spread across his face.

"Why do you think you 'love' Alpha?" He asked. This question had recently become easier to answer, and I found a way to relax in the chair. I smiled back genuinely at Krill, and felt my grasp on things return.

"Well, besides the fact he kills people...he's essentially perfect." I said with a slight degree of sarcasm in response to what I now found to be a silly question. Krill started his amused laugh at the statement, and I couldn't help but join in with him in light of the recent revelations, but it didn't completely alleviate the shock they held. As my hesitant laugh settled, the old man leaned forward to me and placed one of my hands in his as if to console me.

"You know young lady, within every soul on this Earth there is a desire to do good things." He assured, and the smile widened on his face, forcing his round reddish cheeks up under his eyes again. "Some of us, however, just have the rotten luck of not being taught how to go about doing those things, the right way." His hand patted the top of mine in a strange affection that would come only with family. "This desire can be overwhelming, and you should have faith in Vincent that his desires will prevail." He soothed as he released my hand back to me, and nuzzled back into his chair and relaxed. He seemed almost as if he would fall asleep at any moment, and the grin on his face maintained as he folded his arms back atop one another.

"If I'm right, his desires will flood through him. Being perfect, as he is, makes his desires fill him to the point that he will always achieve; to where you or I would give up, he never will... to where you or I would succumb to evils of the Earth, once he's known good, he never will be evil again... for him, he will feel that instinct in far more abundance." he muttered off to himself, and Krill's eyes began to close as his voice became more somber and quiet with every passing word. "You should give him another chance. It may very well be our only hope."

My eyes were once again peeled at his comments, and again, I was more confused. What did he mean by telling me all of this? Was this why everything was happening so fast? Was Vincent designed not to be flawed with the many inadequacies that would keep other men more guarded by their emotions?

I didn't understand any of this. What did he mean by *'our only hope'*? I couldn't stand all the questions in my head, and now instead of blaming Vincent, I was starting to feel sorry for him, again.

I felt sorry that he was only doing what came natural for him to do; that he was expressing himself as true as he could, as anybody could, and that I wouldn't believe him. I noticed Krill's eyes had become heavy, and it would seem that I wouldn't get much more out of him, before he was peacefully asleep in his chair from his drunken adventure. I didn't even know if I could believe the old man. He seemed honest enough, but that was the least of my worries.

"Does he know?" My small voice questioned, and the old man stirred slightly.

"Know what?" He pushed out the words through his tired lips.

"All of this. Everything you've told me. Does he know what he is?" It was the only question I knew I would need the answer to, before seeing Vincent again.

"Unfortunately, I was never able to tell him any of this. I expected him to figure everything out in time, but Marcus wanted to keep him in the dark as long as he could. I, well, I just wanted him to have a normal life. Keeping everything from him seemed to be the only way to keep life normal for..." Krill trailed off as the sandman took him. The chair rocked as I stood up; the old man stirred slightly, but found his way back to sleep quickly.

I had to find Vincent, and let him know that I had made a mistake by not trusting him. Now, I knew too much, and I couldn't let that go to waste. Even if all I could do was to tell him that I now understood what he was trying to say. The old door made a screech as it opened and closed at my exit. Once again, I was back on the rainy streets of the slums, without a clue as to where I could find Vincent. The rain pelted the top of my umbrella as I made it down the street, and back up the ramp to the main road.

My only thoughts were of Vincent, Paragon, and Central D. That was where I would find him, or so I thought to myself, as I made my way down the Main.

It was a few blocks to the boundary bridge, and soon after I would be in Central D; a place I had limited access to, but I wasn't going to let that stop me. I would find him.

I would tell him everything. I would tell him that I loved him. On the left, I passed Club Kelp, and with it came the déjà vu of our first meeting under the awning. His voice, his smile, and what seemed like fate.

"Hey girlie." A voice came from behind me, but before I could turn to see who it was, a hand folded around my face, and another around my waist, dragging me down an alleyway. I then heard a door open, and then my face found the back seat of a car.

The door shut behind me, and I heard the car roar to life.

"Grab the girl." I commanded.

It was the only option I could see that would give us an edge over that *thing*. If Eddie was right about Alpha's little dating excursion, and it did have feelings; maybe *it* would come for her.

"How are we going to do that, boss? We don't even know who she is, do we?" Griff had a point. All we knew was that she came from the slums, but I knew who would know more about where we could find her. Eddie. That weasel grifter had seen the girl, and he knew who she was. It almost pained me that he would come in handy for once.

"I'll find out where she is. You guys just wait for my cue." I ordered, and Ramone and Griff both nodded in uniformed acknowledgement, but Ox didn't seem very enthusiastic about the plan. He sat silently across the room, looking out of an old tattered and boarded window at the rainy streets.

I wasn't the only one who noticed his stillness. Ramone and Griff were waiting for Ox to say something, but he only sat still staring out of his window. The silence filled the air like a stagnant smell that wouldn't go away and it started to bother Griff, who was still focused on Ox, as Ramone and I began to walk out of the grungy room.

"You think this is such a good idea, Ryne, pissing him off I mean?" Ox suddenly broke out with it, and just like that, the air started to clear with Ox's question, however; he didn't turn from the window.

"His job is to *kill* people, and he's damn good at it. What makes you think he won't *kill* us?" He continued. It wasn't like any of us to use *that* word. We were civilians, and to us, 'kill', was an off-limits turn-of-phrase.

"Grow a pair, Ox." Ramone shot back, without any hesitation. He was always the most overconfident one of the group, and even if he did see the dangers that Ox had; he wouldn't show it. Either way, now was not the time for dissention.

"No, Ox is right." I stated as I shot a glare at Ramone, "I am banking on *it* coming after us for this. It's the whole point of what we're doing." My shocker rested on the table in front of me and Ramone. I grabbed it and cocked it, as if it would further explain to him exactly my intent, "We are going to '*kill*' *it* first." I said the word the same way Ox did, to assure him of what our mission parameters would be.

"No way!" Griff let out in astonished excitement.

"Hells Yeah." Ramone chimed in, with too much enthusiasm, jamming his fist into the open palm of his other hand. Ox's eyes only widened at the thought. He stood up from the window, hulking massively in the room, which now seemed too small for his frame.

"Do you think we actually can?" He asked with a hint or worry in his voice. You could tell he didn't think it was possible.

"It's our job." I fired back quickly, and with authority that he wouldn't question, "Now, pack your gear, and spread out. I'll com you all later with coordinates. Get a move on!" I commanded my men, and with that, my three would-be soldiers scurried around the room grabbing their essentials and rushed out of the small run-down building. I followed behind them, holstering my shocker, and climbed into my truck. My datcom sat in the seat beside me, and as I went to pick it up, I debated on what I would tell Eddie to get what I needed from him. No doubt he wouldn't like my plan to lure Alpha into a trap. Hell, he'd probably laugh if he had seen Ox's reaction to the plan, but I had my orders. Order's given to me only hours earlier from Marcus.

I had stirred all through the night, thinking of what Eddie had told me about that *thing*. Feelings, dates, just a man like 'you or me'. Garbage. It was a monster. It had to be stopped. That next morning I had made my decision to report it all back to Marcus. I felt my convictions strengthen as I walked up the wide stairs and through the giant Paragon doorway. Remy passed me as I made my way to the familiar lift, but I did not acknowledge the runt as he beamed his eerie grin at me.

The doors slid open, I exited, and continued down the long hall to the corner office where Marcus would undoubtedly be waiting for any report that would come in. I slid my wristport on the door's receiver and they opened, as Marcus welcomed me in with a smile even more devilish than Remy's. They were certainly a creepy pair.

"Welcome, Ryne." Marcus' voice slithered out almost snake-like, "To what do I owe the pleasure of seeing you here so early in the morning? Do we already have some news?" His hands folded across his lap, and I stopped just short of his desk.

"Yes, Sir." I responded in an official manner Marcus would respect. I was still debating what to tell him in my head, but I knew I had little choice. Marcus hated having his time wasted more than anything, but he would have to know.

"Well, go on Ryne." His teeth flickered in the darkness, as his grin widened. Did he already know? How could he? Eddie wouldn't have told him. Did he just expect this much?

"Alpha never reported back in, yesterday.. It went off the grid last afternoon, and hasn't been seen since." I explained. It was very concerning to have that *thing* off its leash, running around the city, doing whatever it wanted, unchecked.

"...And, do you know what he is doing?" Marcus' voice became harsh, and I could tell the news had irritated him. The rest he probably wouldn't favor either.

"*It* is...with a woman." I was almost embarrassed to tell him. That *thing* was dating, but I barely had enough courage to talk to Reime.

"A date?" Marcus began to laugh, and it sounded just as stupid when he repeated it back to me, questioningly.

"I met up with Eddie last night, after hours, and that was what he informed me of when I asked about the upcoming mission. He said that Alpha had met a woman earlier that day, and took his car so he could go...on the date." It sounded even stupider than when Eddie had told me about it before, but Marcus only leaned back in his chair and started to laugh an evil laugh.

"Sir?" I interrupted.

"...On a date." He breathed out through his laugh, "That stupid old man, he's made it all too easy." His laughing settled and he leaned forward again in the chair, placing his elbows onto the table. His red glasses flickered and I could almost see the thoughts forming behind them.

"Ryne, I am going to need you to *kill* Alpha." He said directly, his tone evil, and his demeanor sincere. I tried to ignore the air swelling up in my throat, but the thought sent chills down my spine. I was a soldier, but *it* was the killer. There was a distinct difference.

To me, Alpha did not have remorse, hesitation, or marginal error. I had seen it in action many times. It was a precise machine; ruthless, tireless, and cold. Marcus knew how extremely dangerous his orders were, and being a soldier, I would not refuse them. I would be the first civilian to kill anyone since Alpha was created. I, however, didn't really feel it meant the same as deleting someone, *It* wasn't even human.

"Is it even possible?" I asked, disguising my concern with a questioning tone. I had never seen Alpha injured, or even bleed for that matter. No one, but Krill and Marcus, knew exactly what Alpha was. For all I knew, there was a metal skeleton under that skin, and tiny mechanisms twisting and spinning to keep him in motion. Marcus only laughed again, but not as heartily as he had before. There was doubt.

"Of course, Ryne. He is merely human like you or me. He breathes, he bleeds, and he dies. How it happens is up to you. Do whatever is necessary." He demanded, leaned back in his chair, and waved his hand for the holoscreen to come up. When it projected it still showed a collage of Estelle photographs imaged across the screen.

"I guess this will have to wait a little longer, now." He sighed, looking at the images. With Alpha gone, there wouldn't be anyone to do the Estelle assignment, except Eddie, he was still part of the deletion team, I supposed. His morals were obviously flexible.

"Estelle? Do you think Eddie will finish the assignment when Alpha is out of the picture?" I questioned, but only to get my mind on something else.

"I'm not sure Eddie will be staying in Section Seven." He replied grimly, but not like a threat, more like he questioned Eddie's loyalty to the corporation, "I'm moving this assignment to your team, as well; however; I will also be putting another unit on this assignment to assist you."

He waved his hand and the holoscreen flickered and shrank back into his desk.

"Another unit?" I asked cautiously. There wasn't another unit. What did he mean? With Alpha gone, and without Eddie, Section Seven was just my team. What was this other unit?

"Just a little addition to Section Seven. I'll introduce you to them in the morning. For now, just take care of our little problem." He explained, and there was a smirk pulling at the side of his face as he spoke the words, almost as if he was telling a joke that only he understood. I definitely didn't get it.

"So, we just need to find Alpha, delete him, and then my team does the Estelle job?" The thought of the former was still more than I could imagine, but I understood Marcus' intent. It wouldn't be safe to have Alpha roaming the city freely, especially with its new emotions, and it seemed Eddie was just as unconcerned as usual. The last part put rocks in my stomach. My team would have to delete Estelle. "So, what do we do about Eddie?" I asked again quickly to hide my hesitation. I didn't understand how Marcus would just let him out of Section Seven. It was a secret civilian sector within the company. Membership was for life.

"Nothing. I will handle Eddie's evaluation and re-assignment afterwards." he said, matter-of-factly. Then, the chair turned, and without another word, Marcus began to stare out of the windows that walled up the room behind him overlooking the city. His hand gestured me out of the room with a wave.

That was when I gathered Griff, Ramone, and Ox at one of our stakeout buildings in the Slums to try to come up with a much needed strategy. Luring Alpha to us with the girl was the best plan I could come up with. Now, I would just have to figure out who she was. I picked up the datcom that sat beside me, and punched in Eddie's number. The indicator showed him at the Ganymede. Where else would he be, I thought. I could only wonder if he had seen Alpha again. I pressed the com button, and waited for him to answer.

"Ryne, I...well, I didn't expect to hear from you, how's it going, buddy?" The voice came through the other end, abruptly. I didn't have time for small talk. I needed answers.

"Stay at the Ganymede. I'll meet you there. We need to talk." was all I said before ending the transmission. I'm sure my tone was a bit sterner than it needed to be, but Eddie wasn't a fighter, and intimidating him would probably be the best way to get what I needed out of him. I never did like him much anyway. I wasn't going to let a chance to have a little fun with him slip by.

It wasn't far to the boundary bridge and back into Central D. The rain had settled to a drizzle, which was fairly abnormal, and Central D was in full motion for the night. People were out walking the streets, and all the districts seemed to be bustling. Soon enough, I was in the Drain, and at the Ganymede. It was usually busy, but tonight it seemed more people had crawled out of their compartments, and were enjoying the lightness of the downpour.

I pulled the over-sized truck into the parking complex and got out. I lit up a vapor as I walked to the door. Inside, the music blared from a live band. The front-man, just a boy in his late-teens, held the brightest red guitar I'd ever seen and sang melodically, like nothing I'd ever heard. I had never seen a real guitar before either.

"Over here!" I barely heard him from my peripheral, and I looked to see Eddie grinning idiotically at the bar surrounded by Reime, and a few other girls I'd never seen before. He waved me over, as he leaned in talking to one of the unknown women.

"This is Ryne, a buddy of mine. He's a Paragon big shot, too. Just like yours truly." He tugged on his tie with that last statement, "Ryne, I got some people for you to meet!"

His lack of class never settled right with me, and now wasn't the time for it. He could tell I wasn't in the mood to indulge him, when I turned to him with my arms folded across my chest, nodding at him to take our business to the side exit.

"Damn." I didn't hear him, but made it out from his motioning lip, "Well, looks like we'll have to do this another time, ladies. Apparently, I'm going to have to work late tonight."

All the girls frowned, some pouted and 'awed' as he got up, but the worst was Reime still holding his sleeve as it pulled from her fingertips when he walked over to meet me at the side door.

"What is it? I'm a little busy entertaining, if you can't tell. Way to kill the mood, soldier boy. ." He puffed, but he didn't seem as put off by my appearance as I thought he would be.

"Where's Alpha?" I demanded. He must have known that Marcus wasn't happy, and he was trying to get in one last party.

"What? I don't know. The work day is over, Ryne." He said passively. He was using a coy tone to play aloof, but it wasn't going to work on me. I grabbed him by the tie, wadding a mess of his shirt along with it into the palm of my hand as I pulled him closer.

"Games Eddie? I'm not in the mood." I snarled, and he dropped the act.

"He just left; took a transport. He didn't tell me where he was going." His voice wasn't shaking out of fear. I could tell that it was just the drugs, but the pace of his speech convinced me that he was telling the truth. I pulled out my datcom, and punched in Alpha's number, then hit the locate key; still nothing on the grid. It didn't make any sense.

"I don't understand, he was just here." Eddie tried to explain, but I still had him gripped with my other hand.

"Who's the girl?" I growled again as I slid the device back into my pocket.

"Little pretty Dress? She's nobody. She's not even a citizen." He assured me, but then, I pushed Eddie into a wall that wasn't far behind him, as I released him from my clutches.

"I don't care about that, Eddie. Where is she?" I demanded again. I started to pull my shocker from its holster, to scare the answer out of him, but he wouldn't fall for it. A charge round, this close to so many people in the Drain, would send them into an uproar and cause too much of a scene. I clasped the holster pin back into place, and pulled the knife from my side. His eyes widened.

"So..." I paused for his answer.

"I don't know her. We picked her up in the slums. That's the only time I ever saw her. I swear, Ryne. If I knew I would tell you, buddy." He swore. His hands poised upwards as if to ward me off, "Now just calm down, big guy. Maybe I can help you out."

I peered at him. I was curious how he would go about doing that, but moreover, why he would. I relaxed for a minute, and he reached into his pocket, and I felt stupid for giving him the chance to catch me off-guard. I lunged, pushing him back into the wall and put the knife to his throat. His esophagus crossed the blade as he gulped.

"Whoa!" He yelled into my face, "What the hell, Ryne! datcom!" He said, as he held up his own datcom for me to see.

I pulled the knife back from his neck and relaxed again. Maybe this assignment had made me a little too edgy, and he seemed to notice, too. He straightened himself again, and punched a number into the small gadget, then placed it to his ear.

"Hey, Remy. I need you to do a trace for me." I said to the little man on the other end, and looked back to me with a sly grin, "I just need all the info on the last number Alpha com'd. We're looking for someone."

He was getting her information for me, from the database mainframe. It pissed me off that I didn't think of it first.

"Thanks Remy, I hope this helps." He ended the transmission, and then a moment later the datcom lit up again with all the information I needed, "Little weasel. See, that wasn't so hard. Let me send it to you, real quick."

As quick as he had gotten the information from Remy, he had sent it to me. My datcom buzzed, and I pulled it back from my pocket. On it was a picture of the girl, Alexxia Gyllis, and all the typical stuff; birth date, height, age, but no known address. Still, it was all I needed. I sent the information to Griff, Ramone, and Ox along with a message telling them to find her and take her into custody. When I looked back up from the datcom, Eddie was staring off into the distance, puffing a gasper. His face was hard to read, but I could tell he wasn't happy, and he didn't turn to face me.

"So, you got a new assignment, I see." His tone was low and disciplined, a far cry from the man he just was with the knife to his throat. He didn't seem to have a care in the world, but more like the world had just ended.

"You think that's real smart? Probably going to be a lot of blood, don't you think?" He said, and it was a foreboding warning that didn't hold his usual sarcasm.

"Whatever, Eddie." I shot back. I expected him to doubt us, but I didn't expect him to be so collected about it. Where was the boasting, the laughing, and the inauspicious mocking? I didn't think his concern was for me or my guys, but did he actually think that we would be able to kill that *thing*? His drifting attitude unsettled me.

"Just another job. We'll get it done." I told him assuredly. Then, there was an awkwardly long pause after.

"You sound just like him, you know." he said, still very ominous, but I didn't like the implication. I was nothing like that *thing*. My expression must have told him my thoughts; that I questioned his comparison. "Both of you have such a sense of duty, 'a jobs a job' type of mentality that closes you off from everything around you. Sad thing is, I think he finally found some freedom from that type of thinking." The way he said it was earnest, like he was trying to get me to relate to Alpha.

"You can entertain the girls with the highbrow chatter. Save it for them." I told him. I didn't have time to think about whatever philosophical nonsense Eddie wanted to throw at me. I was losing more time by the minute, "What about the girl, Eddie?" I asked. I remembered him telling me that he had taken her home. He knew where I could find her, but he was trying to make it difficult for me. His attempt to help me with Remy was all grifter con games.

"I told you, I don't know her." He was lying. He knew a little about everyone. I grabbed him by the arm, shifting his shoulder into the wall with a vice-like grip.

"Where did you take her when you gave her the ride?" I asked again as I increased the amount of pressure I was applying. He must have assumed I had forgotten that vital piece of information. His arrogance irritated me, even more, at that moment.

"It was just some old apartment building on the Main; the sign said 'Meserere'..." He groaned it out, and I let go of his arm. He exhaled hard, grabbing it himself and rubbing it to ease the soreness.

"Meserere?" I repeated. It was a very familiar sounding word, even more when I said it again.

"Geez, nice grip, sognoggin." He muttered out in insult, "You know the place?" He continued to be more concerned with the soreness of his arm, than helping me conjure the memory.

"No, but it sounds familiar." I told him as I tried, but just couldn't remember where from.

"Yeah well, Good luck with that... you apeshit." Eddied continued to curse as he shrugged, quickly passing through the doorway back into the Ganymede, but I walked around the building back to my truck. I didn't want to see the warm greeting that Remie would give him upon his return.

It was getting late and the morning would soon come. I'd have to update Marcus with some kind of results, and see this new team he had put together. It still stirred the curiosity in the back of my mind. I didn't ask Eddie about it, but then again, I doubted Marcus trusted him any more than I did.

I started up the truck. I gritted my teeth down onto the end of a vapor and steered out of the lot heading for the slums. I would check at the apartments first. I might even get a lucky break, and that's when it hit me.

"Meserere" I thought out loud. The apartments, one of the oldest and nicest in the slums. It was on the dossier for the Estelle job. It was *her* address. The girl was staying with Estelle Hart. It was even worse than I had imagined, could Alpha have grown a conscience and be protecting the target? The apartment wasn't far from the Boundary Bridge. I would be crossing it soon and would be there quickly. As I approached, I could see Alpha in the distance standing under the awning of the old apartments. I quickly turned down the closest side street, so I wouldn't be spotted. Now wasn't the time for me to make my move, but I had found them.

Alone, I was definitely not a match for that thing, even with the element of surprise. I parked the truck in a lot about a block away, and proceeded on foot to do some reconnaissance. I stopped at the corner, and leaned against the old brick building trying to see who Alpha was talking to. I couldn't make out what Alpha was saying over the drops. At a closer glance, I could see its shocker was drawn. The monster's hand seemed unsteady, and that didn't make sense to me; none of what I saw did. Alpha's shoulders slumped downward

What the hell was going on? I continued to watch, as a small hand breached the doorway and cupped Alpha's cheek, lifting his head upward. Soon after, a shimmering silky figure stepped through the threshold passing Alpha.

It was Estelle. She was practically glowing as the rain bounced off her perfect form. The posters, datacasts, and pictures in the dossier, didn't do her the justice she deserved.

A car was coming down the street in the opposite direction from me, and Estelle looked back momentarily as she mouthed something I didn't understand to Alpha. The car came to a stop in front of them to let her in. I wouldn't get a chance like this again; both of my assignments stood right in front of me. I pulled my shocker from my leg holster, and slid a charge round into the chamber. My instincts told me to go for Alpha first, but then, Estelle would make her escape. I would have to do her first, and take my chances with the monster. I only had seconds. My hand gripped the small weapon firmly, but I hesitated. She crossed the street, in what seemed like a blur from the rush of adrenaline I was feeling. Along with my immediate visual, my head filled with two different thoughts; one being the result of the other.

The first was the mathematics of how my attack would go; calculating my aim, distance from the targets, and Alpha's reaction time. Knowing the third, gave me the appropriate result; dread. Its shocker was already in its hand, and I wouldn't last a second. I wouldn't be able to get off two shots. Then, the instance was stalled, and all my thoughts had vanished, when a drop of sweat fell from my forehead onto my poised and tense arm. Gripping the small shocker, reality suddenly snapped back into place, and cured me of the illusionary time displacement.

I would have to make my move now.

My arm, still tense, straightened, and I slid to a standing position as I started my approach around the building. As my stride took me steps past the sanctuary of my corner, I could hear my ears ringing. I focused in on the singer, as she was only seconds from climbing into the car. I kept watch on Alpha from my peripheral, but he hadn't noticed me, yet. I could feel the tension welling inside of me. My ears wouldn't stop ringing. I was afraid. It was something I hadn't felt since the far bridge incident. Suddenly, the shocker in front of me was surrounded by a completely different environment. I was no longer seeing Estelle the singer, but my brother, Xack, and my hand began to shake. I was transported back to the boundary bridge, where Xack had stood in front of me before. Only this time he was smiling; he seemed happy. He slowly nodded and sent my gaze downward to his hands, and in them was a bomb with a digital timer on the front of it. It was counting down. I looked back up at his crazed smiling face. There were only seconds left on the homemade explosive that I knew wouldn't fail.

The bridge and everything below erupted into flames behind him. I looked around for Griff, Ox, and Ramone, but no one was there. Except for Alpha; standing right behind me with its own shocker drawn, but not at Xack, at me this time. Alpha was smiling eerily at me; something I'd never seen it do. I turned back to Xack still holding the bomb, and there was only five seconds left.

"Why Xack?" I pleaded and the timer ticked.

"See you soon, brother." He said it as the smile on his face started to dance wildly before bursting into full-on crazed laughter. It came from both Xack and Alpha, and then the timer hit zero and a familiar ringing started. I heard it only moments ago in my ears. I tried to shake the image from my mind, and as I did my surroundings returned, but I hadn't moved. My hand was still extended in front of me, grasping the shocker, now aimed at the car that Estelle was getting into. Alpha still hadn't noticed me, but I was almost in the middle of the street. The ringing had become faint, and I finally recognized the sound. It was my datcom, buzzing in my pocket.

It had all been a hallucination.

I shook my head once more, and retreated back to the safety of the building's corner to reach for my datcom. I kept a careful watch on Alpha. Even though he was more than fifty feet away, I had thought for sure he would have seen me. My breathing returned to normal, even though; I had barely noticed its increase. For once, the rain had come in handy. I was sure he hadn't heard the buzzing device from where he had stood, not over the drops. I was careful as I backed against the bricked side of the building and slid down to a crouch.

The transmission was from Griff. It only said, 'We have her.' I couldn't help but feel like a fool. My imagination had gotten the better of me, and I let an opportunity slip through my hands. I couldn't explain how, but now wasn't the time to go drudging around in my skull for answers.

The old relic sputtered and roared as it passed on the street, and now that opportunity was gone. Alpha was stewing on the steps to the old building's entrance, and for a half-second, I thought we met eyes from my corner, but he didn't seem phased. He continued standing on the stoop of the dilapidated building. His hands were shaking, and swinging about as he contemplated. As I watched the, whatever you would call that thing, the old man used the word "Proto Sapien", standing there; I could see nothing but torment in his eyes; a torment that gnawed at him. That is when I realized that he wasn't protecting Estelle. He hadn't even known that they lived together. Alpha's arm raised the shocker, and motioned its aim in the vacant area Estelle had been standing, and then dropped it to his side. His neck stretched as he looked up at the rain, letting it come down onto his face.

For the first time I saw him as a man; an ordinary man, probably more so than myself. Emotion clearly clouded his judgment, and if only he had deleted Estelle right then, Marcus would probably forgive his momentary desertion. Since he hadn't, it guaranteed that the plan to capture the girl would work. With a little help, he would come for her. We would only have to coax him in the right direction.

Alpha finally stopped his stirring and stepped off the building's landing, and was heading my way. The last thing I needed was for him to see me, if he hadn't already, and have him start asking questions that would lead to a shootout here in the slum streets.

It wasn't time for that, yet.

I stood, and started back to the truck as quickly as possible without alerting him to my position. He would close-in quickly at his pace, but I reached for the handle on the truck's door and climbed in. Alpha had not seen me, or he surely would have turned the corner and confronted me. Instead he continued down the street. I watched until he had vanished from my sight. Then, I drove away from the parking lot, pulling out my datcom as I continued down the rain-filled avenue. I punched in Griff's number, and he answered anxiously.

"Hey boss!" He blurted out instantly. I definitely wasn't in the mood for Griff's automated allegiance.

"Griff, what did I tell you about all the 'boss' stuff?" I demanded, but it wasn't really necessary. His continued use of the term made it clear that, ultimately, he wouldn't stop. He was the type who needed a leader, and I just got stuck in the role. "Nevermind. Where's the girl?" I was ready to complete this assignment and clear my head.

"We're back in quad B, outside of Vick's place." He said quickly, and in the background I could hear the sounds of thuds and screams being made. "She's putting up a pretty good fuss, though. What do you want us to do with her?"

I didn't really care. She was just bait. What do you do with a worm before you hook it?

"Just tie her up and keep her there, and gag her, damn it. The last thing we need is for someone to hear her. I'll be there in five minutes." I said, and a loud crashing noise came through the com. I could hear the girl scream once more.

"Ok, boss." Griff acknowledged in a tone too happy.

I let out a sigh as I ended the conversation, tossed the datcom back in the seat beside me, and pushed down the accelerator.

I was only moments away.

Her eyes widened as I walked into the mostly bare room.

She was sitting, tied to a chair, with Ramone closest to her. His eyes were trained on her, and his head was probably filled with indecent thoughts. He was the type. He could be Eddie, if he had looks and a mind that didn't pervert his attitude into a less suave, and pimative category. Ox, however, wouldn't allow anything to happen to her, especially by Ramone. He was the old- fashion type when it came to women. Griff only seemed giddy at the sight of her, and not without reason. She was very pretty with smooth skin, and a milky complexion. She was a rare and slender beauty, much like Estelle. It would fit that they were friends.

As I approached, I leaned down to meet her eyes, and pulled out my knife. I slid it along her cheek with the dull side of the blade. Her eyes widened as she stared into mine, fear permeating throughout them.

I pulled it up to the gag Griff made from a piece of his shirt, and cut it away. It fell from her mouth and landed on her shoulder, but she didn't make a sound. I pulled the knife away and tucked it back into its sheath.

"So, you're what all the fuss is about?" I asked rhetorically. I knew she was because I had seen her picture on the datcom, "Let's not make this any harder than we have to." I urged her, hoping she'd stay calm. I put my finger across my lips to motion for her silence, and stood back up. Everyone watched as me and the girl exchanged glances. Hers was probably in wonder of who I was and why she was here, and mine was trying to put all the pieces of her together. Why wasn't she with Alpha, and why did it seem he was looking for her? It wasn't long before her eyebrows arched, and she had returned to her heated state.

"Who are you and what do you want with me? Do you even have the right person? I don't appreciate your goons just snatching me up like..." She ranted, and I cautioned her once more with my finger. She seemed only appalled at my conduct with her like some debutant being treated in a way they weren't accustomed to.

"I have the right person." I stated it bluntly. Then, she seemed to understand.

"What do you people want?" She asked again, but this time in a soft whisper that held all the fear it should have for the position she was in. It was clear that she didn't know that we were from Paragon. Most people didn't.

We weren't exactly showing it off like the other suits did by putting the label on everything. As members of Section Seven, we weren't relegated to normal attire, and it was better for us to blend in with the trash. It made it easier for us to move unnoticed in the slums.

"I don't have any credits." Her small voice pleaded. She had mistaken us for common thugs.

"Don't worry. We are not after your creds." Griff shot out with unnecessary assurance, and attempted to calm the fear in her. Something I didn't want. I'd want her to stay afraid, so I shot a glance at Griff and he retracted, lowering his head into his massive shoulders. Although, He did capture her attention, and it seemed she recognized him from his former life as a shock baller.

"Griff? Griffon Brandstock? The shock ball player?" She questioned him, but he seemed to try to hide from her by pretending he didn't understand her.

"Griff! I know you. We met a couple of years ago, remember? Estelle sang at one of your games, and she introduced us. Griff, what's going on? Don't you remember me? Griff!" She was confused and hysterical. She started twisting in the chair, shaking it to turn it to face Griff directly. Before she could, I had grabbed the chair and faced her back to me, making her gaze meet mine once again.

"I'd like to know something, missy." I said in the same stern tone to regain her attention. "I want you to tell me a story. I've heard it's a good one, about a girl in the rain needing a ride."

My demand grabbed her attention as I had hoped it would. She was now more focused on me than before, and her eyes welled up, almost to the point of breaking tears.

"Vincent." The name slid out of her like she had said it a million times before. Almost too familiar to her. "How do you know him?" She asked in surprise. Her tone was still a quiet whisper, but now with a desperation hidden in her question.

"Paragon." I said ominously, but I didn't want her to have all of her answers, yet. She let out a small gasp at the name, and I could tell she knew he worked for us, but I didn't want her to know that we did, too. "He works for them, right?" I asked in ruse. She turned her face away uncompromisingly, not wanting to give any answers. It seemed she had bought my subterfuge.

"Look…" I growled as I grasped her jaw and turned her head back to center to face me, "We already know he does, but we need to know what you know, so let's just make this easy for the both of us." I released her face, and began to walk around the chair she sat in.

"Who are you?" The tiny voice had become angry and alive again.

"Me? Ryne, and that's more than you need to know, so tell me, what do you know about Alpha?" I asked again.

I couldn't be certain what he had told her about Paragon, and the assignment on Estelle Hart. If he had told her the plan to take Estelle out I couldn't let her go back and warn her. The last thing I needed was more complications.

"I don't know anything." She said smugly, but it was clearly to cover up something she did know. Could he have told her about Estelle?

"Lexxi, is it? Let's not make this harder than it has to be. Now, I know that you know Alpha. I know that you've been with him today, and yesterday. I just need to know what he's told you." I demanded once more. I kept the monotone voice as I pulled the knife back from its sheath. I slid the dull side along her knee and up to her thigh to the folds of the dress she wore. Then, I continued up to her abdomen, tracing her breasts, until I worked it around to her neck, applying moderate pressure.

"It would be a waste to have to *kill* such a beautiful woman, but don't think I'm above it." I soothed out using the term to add more deception. Her eyes widened again, but her lips poised in defiance. I could feel my brow narrow in anger. She wouldn't be as willing as I hoped, and I needed her alive. I couldn't lose any standing with her, or my men. I would have to see this game to its completion. Even if it meant having to delete her, so I turned the blade over. I started to press it into her skin, piercing it slightly. A small trail of blood started to make its way down to her collar.

"Boss, don't do it!" I heard Griff say it hastily from my peripheral. He gulped as he noticed my glance, "I thought you said we needed her." My attention darted to him and his outreached hand motioning for my pause.

"She doesn't have to be alive, and it's probably better that she's not!" I shot back at him sternly, "There is no telling what he has told her." I tried to explain, but Griff had never been a progressive thinker.

"Oh, he'd be a whole extra pound of pissed if we deleted her." Ox murmured out from under his breath. "He's already going to be pretty angry about this." he continued. I pulled the knife away reluctantly, and waited for Ramone to chime in with his two cents, but he only watched her. Almost as if he had been enjoying the show that I had put on with the knife, but she sat silently, almost in shock, studying me just as I did her.

"Ramone, Ox, outside now! Griff, you're such good friends with her, why don't you stay and keep her company." I commanded, and replaced the blade, once again, into its holster. I nodded at Ramone and Ox to go out the door, and looked back to her with a slanted and angry brow.

"You're lucky, I could leave you in here with him." I gestured to Ramone, who hadn't taken his creepy stare off of her the whole time. Then, I spun Ramone, by his shoulder, towards the door where Ox had already made his way through, and we walked out of the small dusty room.

Outside, the rain poured down off the sides of the building and flooded the streets and alleyways. We stood under the building's torn drapery awning that barely shielded us from the downpour. I pulled a gasper from inside my vest, lit it, and inhaled deep trying to calm my nerves. I hadn't realized it until I was about to delete the girl, that I was actually afraid of this assignment. It would surely mean death if anything went wrong. Death for my men, or me, or the girl. I didn't like the idea of being Paragon's new reaper either, but duty is duty. Ox and Ramone stared blankly at me, awaiting my next command. I enjoyed as much of the vape as I could, before putting it out.

"Ok, Ramone, let him know we have her." I declared in a raspy smoke-filled voice. "Ox, you're going to help me set some charges." Ox nodded, but Ramone cocked his head giving me a stern look.

"How am I supposed to do that? I don't even know where he is, Ryne." Ramone asked, and I could tell he was getting unnerved as well. His crass attitude worsened when he had to work, but this part of the plan was key, as was his involvement. He would be the only one of us who had any chance of outrunning that monster.

"I saw him before I came here, just off the Main, at the girl's apartment. He probably hasn't gone far from there, and he's on foot." I said, but I didn't like admitting that I knew where he was. It meant they would know I didn't attempt anything alone, and while I knew better, there was a lot of ego in our little group.

"What?! You saw him, and you didn't do anything? Why do we even need the girl, now?" Ox stammered out in defiance. I turned my attention to Ox with a hard look that told him not to undermine my authority.

"Leverage. He won't want her to get hurt, and as long as we have her, he will play nice like a good little monster." I reassured him through my teeth, but he only huffed in disapproval. "As I was saying, Ramone, find him and let him know we have the girl. Then, double-time it back here where we will have rigged the corner buildings to blow. We'll crush him under the rubble, and put a quick end to this assignment." I insisted. Ramone grinned at the thought of blowing up a piece of the city, but I knew the buildings were vacant. Most of this block was. Ox's lack of enthusiasm was more than apparent.

"What if it doesn't even kill him?" Ox questioned again, only not in the same defiant manner that would have him reprimanded, but instead in honest intrigue.

"I'll be on the top of that far building, there..." I gestured to the other end of the street. "...With a light rifle. If he lives through the explosion, I'll put a whole charge clip through him. I want you..." I poked a finger into the big man's chest. "...to take the light cannon, and wait on the street level for him, and we'll leave Griff in the building with the girl, as our last line of defense. You two got me?" I demanded with a question, and both of them gave an affirming nod, and I returned it.

Ramone took off down the street. He was more than twice as fast as any normal person after having the bionics installed in his legs. A gift upon entry into Section Seven, and now he would get to test them against the speed of Doc Krill's proto sapien superhuman. A task he was more than willing to attempt in the name of Section Seven, and Paragon.

Ramone was just that kind of crazy.

PAST AND PRESENT TENSION

I couldn't help but glare at the oversized ex-shockball player in disdain. I had known him in what, now, seemed like a different life. I hadn't seen who grabbed me from the street, but I would have recognized it if it were him. Estelle used to like him a little, before his injury; before he quit the game.

After that, she had told me he changed, and that he wasn't the same guy anymore. That, she couldn't waste time with someone so consumed with their own self-pity. A self-pity that seemed to have led him here to become a thug, or punk, or whatever the street gangs are calling themselves now-days. I watched him, as I twisted with the ropes that trapped my hands and arms behind my back. He looked ashamed, and stayed far away in a dimly lit corner of the room. As I tried to get my hands free, I could only think of *him*; of Vincent, and how much I needed him right now. I thought of the mistake in judgment I had made, and I wished I could take it all back. I wished that my Vincent and I would still just be sitting on our dirt hill; watching the city lights in each other's arms again.

I hoped he would come and save me. I hoped that he would still want to, but I wasn't even sure if he wanted to see me. If what the old man had told me was true, I could count on Vincent's perfect emotions to seek me out. Would he save me from this band of hooligans that were looking for him? If so, they would be sorry for who they had chosen to abduct.

The twisting was futile. The ropes had been tied too well, and there wasn't any way for me to free myself. I stared at the tall bulky man as he sat quietly, looking back at me from his solitude.

"What?" I demanded in objection to his ogling.

"Nothing, Lexxi." He muttered using a name that I only reserved for friends, and it made my blood boil at the sound of it coming from him; some common thug.

"Don't call me that, you stupid duster creep!" I shouted, and jumped the chair slightly off the ground, unintentionally, out of anger. I knew these creeps wouldn't stand a chance against Vincent, and the thoughts of him bursting in at any moment made me confident that he would come for me. No matter how big or scary they tried to be, they were nothing to him, and a smirk crossed my face.

"He will come, you know. He'll come and save me." I leaned forward, eyeing him.

"Yeah, I know." Griff stated unenthusiastically, but sincere in the fact that what I had said held some truth.

"Well, if you know so much, then you should know to be scared. He's a good guy, and he won't like what you've done." I stated, continuing my attempt to taunt the big man.

"Oh, we're ready for him." He kept the same tone, but it only made the smirk I held turn into an impish grin.

"Can you be ready for him? You should let me go now, before it's too late." I said, trying to warn him in hopes that my demeanor had caught him off guard enough to actually scare him, but it hadn't worked. He still sat in the dark corner, keeping to himself, and watching me.

"Well then, don't listen to me, but you should know that Vincent works for Paragon..." I paused for dramatic effect as he shifted his body towards mine, and his eyes became questioning, "As the phantom killer!" I shouted, hoping to evoke some reaction from Griff, but it didn't have the impact that I had thought it would, and he didn't budge.

"So he told you who he is?" He said with the same unconcerned manner, "What else did he tell you?"

Griff's unsurprised and calm behavior instantly made me more afraid. I had played my best card, but it seemed that I was still out of the loop somewhere. My stomach started to swirl in dread, as I began piecing together what I could. It would seem, from Griff's cool composure that capturing me was only to get to Vincent.

I was bait.

Would they really be able to hurt him? My stomach turned again, and thoughts of everything the so-called professor had told me swam around in my head. *Vincent was a man, the perfect man, more than human, but still human.* It was all so confusing, and I wasn't sure if I even understood it at all, or if the old man wasn't just drunk; making up fairytales to impress young women. It couldn't be. I had seen it in Alpha's eyes. There was more potential in them than I had ever seen before in anyone; even Estelle, who I had thought would be this world's savior. Now, I only wished for him to be my savior.

"It would help if you told us everything you know. I don't like it when the boss gets mad like that. He probably would delete you if he thought it was best for..." The big shadow in the corner immediately tried to suck the words back in with a gasp.

"Delete? You work for Paragon too?!" I yelled again in astonishment. This wasn't a good revelation and Vincent had used the term delete, too. It meant I was right, I was bait, but that Paragon was the one wanting to get to Vincent. I kept my stare at Griff, with my brow narrowed. I could think of nothing I'd rather do than burst out of the ropes that kept me and lunge at the oversized goon's throat.

"You used to be someone Griff. Now look at you! You are no one; just another one of Paragon's mindless puppets." I spat the words at him.

"It's not like that. We keep the city from destroying itself. We save people." He rebutted, but in a childish tone that gave off a sneer back without being damaged by the insult.

"That's what you call this?" I asked, trying to use his logic against him, as I twisted around in the chair. I glared at him, until he turned an acute brow in my direction.

"I call this doing my job. You're safe from him now. You're safe from that *killer*, don't you see?.. and once we get rid of him, you'll go back to living a normal life." He assured me, but his pitch hadn't changed once in the entire conversation. He was stone cold. This is what Paragon makes people; people who were once full of life, of dreams and emotion.

"You don't really think you can *kill* him, do you?" I let out without thinking of the secret it held. If he knew what Vincent was, he would now know that I did, too. From the look on his face, the arched eyebrow and the loosened jaw, I could tell that he knew what I had meant. He now seemed more interested in what I had to say.

"Just what do you think you know?" The large man's question had brought him to life, but I wasn't about to back down from him, now.

"I know what he is. I know you can't *kill* him. I know he's perfect." I shot out, not holding anything back, or thinking about everything Professor Krill had told me.

"Then, you know that it was made to be a *killer!* That he doesn't feel anything, and most importantly, that it's not even human! You think that thing 'loves' you? That creature doesn't love anything. It don't even know how!" He shouted, and for the first time, Griff's temper had flared. I didn't know why Vincent's origins bothered him, and I didn't care.

All I cared about was that I knew better. Inside, that's all I needed. I knew what I believed, and that was all that mattered.

"You're wrong." I said with the same apathy that he had shown me before his outburst, and I turned my head as intent to finish the discussion. Griff didn't seem to want to continue it anymore, either. The silence continued for a long period of time, each of us staring at the other; intent in my eyes, and shame in his. He had never seemed to be the type to stoop so low as to being Paragon's pet, and it didn't seem that he cared all too much about it either. My disapproving stare seemed to go on forever, until his head cocked, and he seemed to lose his focus on me, altogether. I immediately felt something was wrong.

"What is it, Griff?" I whispered out. The question barely made it from my lips before he threw his hand out to silence me, while his other hand gripped at an unfamiliar type of weapon on the table next to him.

"Ramone's back." He whispered it, but before I could think of what that meant, the sound of a massive explosion came from outside the building. A ringing went loudly through my ears. Dust fell from the ceiling; permeating the air above me in the room. The pain was like nothing I had ever felt before, and I thought I would black out from the deafening sound at any moment. The wind had been knocked from me, and the room began to spin. That was when I realized, the blast had knocked over my chair, and I was on the floor on my side. The silence from before held nothing in comparison to the absence of sound that was now.

I twisted in my ropes trying to find the ability to writhe in pain, but I could only feel their constriction. From above me, I could see a poised Griff, holding the strange weapon tight. He was crouching, and he moved from his corner to a tattered window on the other side of the room.

My hearing went in and out in waves of creaking and snapping glass echoing, as Griff moved along the wall to the window. My vision was blurry, but I could see Griff's eyes flare open in fear. The pain continued, but I tried to ignore it, so I could figure out what was happening outside. My guess was that Vincent had indeed come, and with that realization came only distress; the explosion. Did they kill him? I fought back the lump in my throat at the thought, and tried to think about what the old man had told me about Vinent; that he wasn't just a human. That, he wasn't weak or feeble, and that he could take care of himself. The sound of weapon fire broke the silence, but didn't stop the ringing sound in my ears.

He was alive, and the explosion hadn't killed him. I felt an overwhelming sensation of relief, but also a wicked sense of retribution. It had made me almost smile, knowing that this band of Paragon thugs would get what they deserved. I tried struggling against my restraints again; trying to pick myself up off of the floor to wiggle free, but it was no use. Griff stiffened, but paid no attention to me, only whatever was going on outside. He raised the weapon in his hands to take aim, but he didn't seem to have a good position, because he hadn't taken a shot.

My hearing started to fade back to normal, but I still couldn't see through the fog of smoke and dust that had filled the room. I could barely make out Griff, who was still hunched in the corner aiming through the window, wide-eyed.

"Damnit, Ox. Get out of the way," He said under his breath, but I had heard him. Visions started to dance in my head of the huge man fighting Vincent. Ox was at least twice his size, and a mountain of muscle. Any normal person would be terrified to fight him, but my Vincent was no normal person. He could win. He would win to save me, and I felt ashamed for it. It was only days ago when the thoughts of Vinecnt, Paragon, and this madness would have never entered my mind. Now, I was the focus of it all. I didn't like the thought of Vincent fighting for me because he barely knew me, but now it seemed, he could die for me. The ropes burned against my wrists and ankles as I twisted, but I went cold and still when I heard the sound of the weapon that came from the corner of the room. Griff had finally gotten his shot. He straightened himself as he looked out through the window. He seemed confident and surprised at his work.

"No!" I screamed as the tears started rushing from my eyes. I started squirming violently in the chair, and the ropes started to tear into my flesh, but I didn't care. I would get out of that damn chair. I would get free, and I would kill them all with my bare hands if I had to. Suddenly, Griff turned back to me, watching as I tried to pull myself free. A grin crossed his face, and it only doubled my efforts.

"You calm down now, Lexxi. The bad guy is gone. Your life can go back to normal, now." He stated snidely, as he strode over to pull my chair back to an upright position.

"I will *kill* you; you mutate bastard!" I slobbered it through my teeth in a fit of anger as he lifted me back up.

"Whoa, whoa, there's no need for all that, Lexxi," He said laughingly. Then, I spat in his face. The big man's expression went from jolly to rage, instantaneously, as his hand pulled back and flew, cutting the air, and turning my cheek hard. The pain seared though the side of my face as the blood rushed to my, now swollen, cheek. I could feel my heartbeat in my jaw, and my eyes started to well up with tears. I couldn't think of what to say in retaliation. I was in shock as I stared sideward at the floor. Then, bricks and boards from the tattered building exploded into the room, as Ox came flying through the wall crashing into Griff, sending them to the floor, and into my direct vision.

Blood billowed out from the mouth and ears of the bigger man, and onto the floor creating a pool of it beneath him. I turned my head, immediately, to the hole Ox had made in the wall to see Vincent standing inside of the room.

His shoulders heaved. His eyes were filled with fire. He walked over to me, gently placed his hand under my chin, and inspected my swollen cheek. I couldn't speak. I wanted to wrap my arms around him, and tell him how sorry I was for everything; all of my doubts in him, my coldness to him and for getting him into all of this, but my lips wouldn't move. He gazed into my eyes, and I could tell he was just as relieved to see me. Griff grunted, as he rolled Ox off of him.

Alpha's head snapped towards the grounded Paragon trooper, and he removed his hand from my chin as gently as he put it there. He reached down to Griff's collar, and pulled him to his feet. Griff stood almost a foot taller than him. Alpha looked deep into the eyes of the man, holding his collar tight.

"Your friends are dead." He said with a tone I'd never heard. It was as if death itself was speaking to Griff, and not the Vincent that I knew. "I didn't want to kill any of you. I only wanted to be left alone." Griff swallowed hard, but said nothing. I could only imagine the terror that he was in. Vincent gripped even harder and pushed the enormous man backwards to the wall with enough force to jog his head on the boards, "Speak!" He growled out the word, and it was a horrifying demand.

"Marcus ordered it." Griff slurred out, then took another gulp to clear his throat, "He wants you dead. You were our assignment."

Vincent's brows narrowed as he pulled Griff's face downward towards his. "And her!" Vncent shouted as he nodded towards me, "Was she part of this assignment?" Griff flinched with almost every word of the question. His fear was visible.

"Yes. She was going to be collateral, but only if necessary." Griff answered in a horrified whisper as he cowered backwards.

"Was her cheek part of the assignment? Or was that you taking initiative?" Vincent responded in a volume that even scared me.

Griff looked over to me, and then back into Vincent's eyes. He didn't answer in words, but instead only shook his head. A silence followed. Vincent lowered his head, but kept his hand clenched around Griff's vest collar, pressing him against the wall.

"If you were me, what would you do about that?" He asked low and guttural. I wanted to tell him to stop because I knew what he wanted the answer to be. I knew he was only torturing Griff with hope of a different outcome, and that he would *kill* Griff for hurting me.

"I don't know." Griff spoke softly, but Vincent's free hand pulled out the little weapon from behind his back, and brought it to Griff's face. He held it to Griff's jaw. Then, Vincent returned his stare back into the eyes of the soon-to-be dead man.

"I didn't want to *kill* anyone anymore, and because of that, I have to die? Paragon is lies... They say they are the future, but what would the future be if this continues? Tell your boss that I'm coming for Paragon, and anyone who would stand in my way." Vincent said coldly, and then with a quickness I could barely notice, drew back the weapon and brought it down against the side of Griff's face, sending him instantly to the floor. Then, Vincent turned back to me, and rushed to my side, quickly undoing the ropes. His hands moved gently, as he freed my wrist and inspected the damage done to them, and again at my ankles. He looked up at me from his knees, as the ropes were all untied.

"I'm so sorry Lexxi." He spoke to me with a voice I knew, but I still couldn't respond. The relief of seeing him, and being unbound made me throw my arms around him and start to cry.

"None of it matters now." It was all I could think to say. It was my only thought as I held him. Nothing mattered, nothing but him.

He was alive. I was alive. Everything was fine, or so I had thought. As my hand clutched at his back I felt something wet, and I pulled my hand away. I looked down over his shoulder, at my hand, and saw the fresh red blood on it.

"You've been hurt!" I shouted as I pulled away to show him my hand. I held it in front of his face, but he showed no surprise.

"It's nothing. See, there's not even a scratch." He said it without any change in his relief. Then, he scooped me up into his arms, and looked into my eyes without worry.

"I'm taking you home." He said, stepping over the bodies of Griff and Ox, carrying me out of the building.

At that moment; however, in his arms, I was home.

I watched in horror through the scope of my light rifle as the eruption destroyed the old buildings at the end of the boulevard. The top tier of the city collapsed onto its lower counterpart, and a great chasm had formed in the middle of the slums as the street melted downward into itself.

What had we done? It was the last city of humanity, and we were destroying it for the greater good, right? Was it right? Could this one man bring the downfall of the city? I had to believe it. It was my job. I wasn't in a position to question my orders, but I couldn't help but to do so as the smoke rose from the crevice to the top of the dome, making it visible for the first time in years. There was no doubt that everyone in the city would be aware. A reminder of where we were trapped, and why.

I was only a boy when I was told the stories by my father. Xack and I would sit in front of him in the living quarters, and he would entertain us with the dangers he had seen in the early years of the city during the riots, and even before, during the last wars. He had lived through all of it, and it had hardened him; a hardened father to harden his two motherless sons. He would always begin the stories the same way.

"It was Hayes, Carter, and myself..." He would grin while remembering the names, and the life he had shared with them. I always assumed that they all had a friendship that I just didn't comprehend, and I didn't until I formed the team of Ox, Griff, Ramone, and myself. Then, I knew it was about the memory of their camaraderie. "It was dusk, and we had to infiltrate the enemy's base camp, which was a lunar launch site, and lay charges. We were the best mercs the Southlander forces had. It was supposed to be an 'in and out' job. Tempest had informed us of the ten posted guard patrols, and their rounds. All we had to do was cut the fence at O' four hundred, duck the searchlights, and take out the first patrol SIBS, but Something went wrong. Hayes started snipping the fence and the light shot right on us, before we knew what had gone wrong, two patrol teams were chasing us down as we ran back into the swamps."

He would always pause there, and his face would turn grim. He would never continue the story or say what had happened to Hayes and Carter, but we knew they must not have made it out. Instead, he would just say. "So, you boys stick together and you'll make it out of the swamp."

Then he would smile and pat us on the head, as he stood up from the chair, and headed into the kitchen. It was our cue to scurry to our bedroom, and he would come in with two warm cups of boiled wheat protein. The memory was like a dream now; fading.

I felt like I had destroyed part of that memory, even though it seemed we were successful. There was no sign of Alpha. Ramone was still standing in the middle of the street, staring back at the remnants the explosion had left. I moved the scope to check Ox's position. That was when the bolts sounded. I searched quickly into the rubble, but saw nothing, then moved back to Ramone, but couldn't find him. There was only a trail of bio-oil. I followed it and found Ramone crouched behind a waste canister. He was leaking out, badly.

I pulled the scope from my eye and searched the open street for the origin of the charges. The smoke was still billowing upward, and flames surrounded the chasm of road that had spilled downward, but there was no sign of anything else. Ox had taken cover in an alley, but was vigilant. Then, a voice boomed from out of nowhere.

"Tell me where she is, or I'll delete every last one of you." It called out with a scary intent. It was *Alpha*.

Despite Ramone being downed in the attempt, our ruse had brought him right to us, almost as planned. I couldn't tell where he was, but then, Ox motioned forward to the billowing smoke, and I pulled the scope back to my eye and took aim. Amongst the rubble, a large piece of pavement had overturned, and was now visible through the clearing fog of debris.

"Ramone will die in only moments if you do not tend to him. Tell me where she is, and recover your fallen man!" Alpha called out again, but we couldn't comply. Ramone knew what he had gotten into; however, a part of me wanted to take Alpha's deal. I looked back at Ramone, who was looking up at my position. His hand clutched at his missing mechanical foot. His eyes were full of pain, but he still shook his head as if to tell me he wouldn't comply even if I ordered it. Bio-oil poured over his hand, and down into a pool beside him. A spasm shot through him, and then he steadied. That was when I noticed the second charge mark. It was in his abdomen. He had hidden it with his arm, but the spasm had made it visible. He wouldn't recover from it. A charge round produced a wound that cauterized as it passed through the victim, and a gut shot was nearly always fatal.

I couldn't watch him suffer. Alpha had guaranteed his death with the wound he had given him. I lined up on Ramone's chest. I closed my eyes and squeezed the trigger on the light rifle. When I widened my eyes again, Ramone was lifeless. I pulled back the lever, ejecting the light canister, and loaded in another round.

"You would kill your own man just to get to me? You could have saved him!" Alpha belted out through the pouring rain. The words echoed and were followed by a lingering silence. Ox's eyes were closed, and his shoulders pulled up and down as he breathed. Then, he let a howl out into the rain, and pounded his fist onto the wall in front of him.

"It's called dedication. If you had any loyalty he wouldn't have had to die!" Ox growled and pounded his fist against the wall again, and then again. Each time, it felt as if he were pounding it against my chest. I gasped for air with each blow. It was just to get to *him*. That was all; an assignment. I had killed my friend *just* for *him*, and now I would kill him, for making me do it.

"Paragon is wrong! None of this is necessary! No one has to die, Ryne!" Alpha's voice pleaded in a yell, but he remained only a voice. I waited patiently for any sign of him to appear.

"No one has to die but you, Monster!" Ox responded in the same volume, "Now come on out and fight, you coward!" Ox, threw his weapon out into the street, and went unarmed towards Alpha's anticipated location.

"Ox! No!" I yelled down to try to stop the hulking man from taking Alpha on alone. I knew better, but Ox's ego was unrivaled when he was enraged.

"Ramone is dead, and it's his fault. I will finish this!" He growled up at me, and there was nothing stopping the giant as he began his charge toward the overturned pavement, "Stop hiding and fight like a man, traitor." Ox's foot stopped just shy of the trail of fluid Ramone had left behind. Then a silhouette began to emerge from the smoke and flames.

"You don't have to do this, Ox." Alpha pleaded again, but Ox was already poised to attack.

"You're wrong. I have to do this… for Ramone." Ox bellowed out as he charged towards Alpha, and I pulled the scope back from my eye once again. Alpha hit the pavement with force as Ox tackled him, and Ox pulled him back up to his feet in an instance, then threw him into an adjacent building. The brick cracked and plaster flew from its surface. Ox was more than twice Alpha's size, and far more muscular. It started to look like it was going to be a quick fight.

"Some perfect warrior you are." Ox chuckled manically, as he walked to where Alpha had landed. Then, the massive man picked up Alpha and held him into the air by nearly the whole front of his torso. His fist smashed against Alpha's face, and then again, but the third hammer-blow was stopped by Alpha's hand. Then, a knee into Ox's chest made him release Alpha back to the ground. Ox's Face lit up with appalled anger.

"Stop it now, Ox. This is your last warning." Alpha responded in a low and eerie manner that I could barely hear, but Ox only laughed confidently.

"I *will* beat you to death, you abomination." Ox continued chuckling his insane laugh. Then, he sent his massive fist back down to Alpha, but this time I watched as Alpha caught the big man's hand in his. Shock crossed over Ox, as Alpha began to bring himself to his feet, holding the large paw of his assailant. Ox pulled his hand back, but Alpha was quick to defend his warning, ramming his fist into Ox's chest.

Normally, a man Alpha's size wouldn't be able to impact with a blow on Ox. He was just too dense, but Alpha had tremendous strength and speed, and the giant doubled over. Alpha grabbed him by the jugular, and lifted him back upright.

"It's been fun sparring Ox, now, tell me where she is." Alpha demanded of him; his voice harsh and distinct. Ox coughed up a speck of blood instead of speaking. Then, he grasped at Alpha's wrist to try to pull his hand free of his throat, but struggled, unable to remove it. I pulled the scope back to my eye. I wouldn't let Alpha *kill* Ox, too. I aimed for a kill shot; Alpha's skull as my target. My finger twitched on the trigger as the scoped bobbed. I pulled in a breath and exhaled, but just as my finger inched back on the metal, Alpha's head turned, as if he were looking down the scope back at me.

I Squeezed.

In the mili-second it took for the muzzle flash to dissipate, Alpha had turned Ox so that he was in the line of fire. All I could see was my over-sized partner's back through my sights, as Alpha released him to the ground. The light round had pierced right through Ox, who fell to his knees, with a hole burnt through him that had shocker smoke rising from the wound. Anger and horror pulsed through me as I chambered another charge. Then, Alpha looked up to the rooftop where I was prone.

"How many more of your men are you going to kill, Ryne?" He asked in a hollow tone. I could hardly breathe, because he was right to taunt me. He had bested us, and there was no point in continuing to hide the girl. If this kept going, we would all be dead. There was no stopping this monster. My greatest fear manifested; my entire team was dead in the downpour.

"Stop this, now!" He commanded once more, and a part of me wanted to defy him. A part of me wanted to take revenge for Ramone and Ox, but a greater sense of compliance and defeat rushed through me. Before I could tell him that he had won and that we would surrender, a charge bolt burst through the window of the building. Alpha went down next to Ox. Griff had caught him off-guard, and Ox shot up in a rush, wrapping his arms under Alpha's shoulders, holding him for me to take another shot. I aimed down the scope, once again, for the kill shot, and all was not lost. Ox wasn't dead, and now he had Alpha where we needed him. Alpha's face was painted with anger as I looked through the scope at him, and my finger felt for the trigger. His shirt was stained red with blood, just like any other man. Now, I couldn't see *the monster*. I couldn't see what I had hated about him as he writhed in Ox's arms. I couldn't see the destroyer of humanity that Marcus had proclaimed him to be. I could only see a man. A man that desperately wanted to save the woman he loved. I took a deep breath, and I stared at him through the scope. He could die, and he was going to.

"Shoot him Ryne! Do it now! I can't hold on to him!" Ox yelled out. The sweat and rain poured down my face. Alpha's head snapped back crushing into Ox's nose, and Ox couldn't help but to release him. Alpha's fist crashed down into Ox's cheek, and the giant caught himself on the ground with his hand. Alpha's fist came again and again in a violent, high-tempo flurry. My finger wouldn't pull back the trigger. I watched frozen in place as Alpha's fists turned Ox into a sack of broken bones. Ox's arms flailed wildly begging for an end, but Alpha wasn't stopping. There was no form; no premeditation to the blows. Alpha was an animal; a lion whipped and set free.

Suddenly, he paused and looked toward the window that Griff was hiding behind. Ox's body was lifeless as Alpha picked him up, and threw him through the window, and part of the wall that separated him from Griff. The impact was so great, that a plume of dust and debris blew into the street. Alpha had disappeared into it, and any chance I had at a shot was gone along with him. My stomach was in knots, and my mind was in shambles. I had let him kill Ox, and now he was with Griff and the girl. I had to make it back down to him, so I threw the light rifle to the side, pulled out my shocker, and ran to the fire-escape. I skipped steps, trying to get down from the four-story building as quickly as possible. As I reached the bottom, my datcom started to buzz.

It was Remy. I put it back in my pocket, and made my way down the street. It started to buzz again, and again I ignored it. I had to get to Griff. As I rounded the corner, I could see the building with the hole in it, and I ran faster. When I came to the building, Ox laid dead on the floor near the opening, and Griff was in the corner, unconscious.

"Griff! Get up." I tried, but he was out cold. I put an arm under him to bring him to his feet, but Griff was almost as big as Ox, and just as heavy. I slid him back down, seated in the corner. I could still catch them if I hurried. I could still avenge Ox and Ramone. I began to run back out of the large hole, but was interrupted by my datcom, once again.

It was Remy, and this time I answered it.

"What Remy?!" I replied furiously, and Remy cleared his throat.

"Uhm, Yes well, I'm patching you through to Marcus." The little twerp said it quickly in his snotty weasel-like voice, and then the datcom paused and beeped, until the other end of the conversation became airy again.

"Ryne." It was an unmistakable voice. It was indeed Marcus, and this wouldn't be good.

"Yes sir." I responded, but now my tone had severely declined back down to mere intolerance. I hadn't noticed until then, but I had completely stopped in my tracks.

"I take it you are to blame for the explosion in district eighteen." He slithered it out angrily.

"Sir, you said by any means necessary." I explained, and I felt like a child who was being reprimanded for playing with fire.

"And did you succeed?" He asked, but he didn't really want an answer. It was a rhetorical question that oozed sarcasm. He was wasting my time, and pissing me off.

"Ramone and Ox are dead, Griff is unconscious, and I'm in pursuit." I debriefed him, but felt ashamed that I didn't have better results, and angry at the information I did have, but I didn't need his power trip at the moment, as well.

"Don't bother, Ryne. Come back to the main office complex and regroup." He demanded, but it didn't feel like a command. It sounded more coaxing than a simple demand; like he had something waiting for me.

"But sir, Alpha and the girl will get away." I responded in surprise as I shook my head trying to comprehend how anything could be more important than my current assignment, and I couldn't give up now.

"The girl isn't important, you ignorant commando freak, and Alpha will be taken care of soon enough. Come back to the Paragon building, now. That's an order! I won't have you blowing up any more of my city." He commanded it again more sternly, and then ended transmission. I was actually a little afraid of the tone Marcus had used, and the insult he added to it. I had never heard Marcus chastise anyone so directly. When I came back to the building, Griff had started to come around.

"Boss?" The big ex ball-player stuttered as he made his way to his feet, "What happened out there?" He propped himself against the wall, and shook his head like he had water in his ears that he couldn't get out. His eyes twitched like a malfunctioning flashlight, and his nose and ears had blood dripping from them.

"Our worst nightmare, Griff. Now help me get Ox and Ramone to the bed of the truck." I commanded him, but only out of habit. I felt sorry for Griff's state as much as I did the others. Griff grumbled as he helped me to get Ox's body over our shoulders and we walked him to the truck. I wasn't satisfied with the way things had ended, and I didn't understand what Marcus was thinking; calling me off the hunt like that. Ox and Ramone deserved better. Now, they are just memories and heavy bodies.

Around the corner was my truck, and we lifted Ox's body up and over into the bed, and started back for Ramone. It wouldn't take both of us to carry him back, but I didn't have the heart to wait in the truck, or tell Griff to do the same. They were our comrades; our friends and we'd give them a proper memorial.

After Ramone was in the truck-bed, we climbed into the front and started back to Central D. Griff sat silently next to me, watching the fire from the explosion dwindling in the rearview mirror.

"She knows." He finally murmured it after we crossed the boundary bridge, but his eyes were still fixed on nothing.

"What? What does she know about Griff? She's just a stupid girl from the slums who thinks she loves that monster. She don't know nothing." I replied. The disdain for the whole ordeal lingered in my speech, and I couldn't imagine Griff telling me anything to make it worse or better.

"I don't know how she knows, but she knows what he is." He said, turning to me for the first time since we left. "She knew everything. That we were from Paragon, and that he isn't what he looks like. She knows he's a monster, and she doesn't care!" His fist pounded against the dashboard. I couldn't blame him for being as upset as he was. It didn't make any sense to me either, but it was an interesting turn of events. I already knew what Marcus would say. Griff should have deleted her, as soon as he knew what she knew. It was dangerous to let that kind of information out into the population. It would look bad on Paragon. It would be worse than the uprising he feared Estelle would bring.

"What are we going to do, Boss?" The big man asked, but I didn't know what else to tell Griff. The shock of the day's events was still too fresh in my mind; as fresh as the dead bodies of Ox and Ramone in the back of the truck. Their dead faces burned into my mind, ruining happier times with them.

"Boss? What are we going to do?" Griff repeated hysterically trying to break my silence.

"I have no idea, Griff. I got no clue how this is going turn out. This is the worst assignment I've ever taken. All I do know is that now we go back to Paragon, and see Marcus." I told him, trying to be honest, both with him and myself.

My fingers gripped the wheel tighter, twisting its leather wrapping, and it made a wet crunching noise as I did. My anger filled me, but it was a sad anger. I had made a mistake; a mistake that had cost the lives of two of my men. I didn't stay in the swamp with them, and now they are dead.

We sat in the silence of the truck the rest of the way to the main office. I watched the road in thought, and Griff kept his eyes on the buildings that passed, and the festering smoke trail in his side mirror. We pulled around to the back of the giant building and into the employee garage.

I put the truck in park, and paused a moment before I looked over to Griff, placing my hand on his shoulder to try to ease the day; to assure him that we were still here, and that it mattered that we were.

"I'm not going to tell you that it's going to be O.K. or that everything is going to turn out fine. The truth is, Griff, it probably won't. I don't know what this life has gotten us into, but we have to play it out, for now. For Ox and Ramone." I nodded to him at the end of my little pep talk, and removed my hand. He didn't turn to look at me, but nodded in acknowledgement. I pulled a gasper from the pack in the truck's tray, placed it into my mouth, and lit it.

"I've got to go up and face the music but I'll be back down soon, and we'll take Ramone and Ox to Kagan." I inhaled. It made me cough, a low lung-rattling cough. Then, I exhaled, filling the cab with smoke.

"I'm coming up with you." Griff was still distant, staring out of his window, and didn't turn to see me.

"Not Necessary. It's out of the chain of command for you to be in an executive meeting." I told him, and Marcus would surely find it inappropriate that I had a tag-a-long for what he wanted to show me. This new team, I guessed.

"I'm coming up with you." He repeated in a low growl, and then turned to look at me. His eyes held pain and anger in them, and he wasn't trying to fight it back. "It's just me and you now, boss, and if you're not inviting me into the little executives club, then, I'm inviting myself. To hell with chain of command and protocol, I'm coming up with you, sir."

The last word, 'Sir', was stronger than the rest, but I admired him for it. His loyalty to me was undeserved, and I was lucky I hadn't gotten him killed as well, and I would adhere to his newfound demanding will.

I only nodded again, before I popped open my door and stepped out of my truck. We were both covered in bio-oil and coagulated blood. We looked like we just came from a warzone when we walked into the side entrance of the Paragon lobby, and we had. Remy stood up behind his desk when he saw us enter. A grin spread across his face at our appearance. He was the type that loved blood and death, but didn't know anything about it. I wanted to punch the left half of his grin onto the right side of his face.

"Going up?" The little man slithered out of his lips.

"What do you think?" Griff growled back at him.

"Ooh, touchy touchy tough guy." Remy chortled in retort.

I just shook my head, knowing Griff would see it and not advance on Marcus' worthless peon. One day his stupid sense of humor would get him pummeled, but the war was done today, and anymore from Remy would be the last straw for Griff. I pressed the button on the lift, and it soon arrived. Fortunately for Remy, who didn't comprehend how close he had come to really pissing Griff and me off.

Luckily, we wouldn't have to walk into any of the populated areas of the office, and no one would see the mess we were. Griff had never been to the top offices before, and he didn't expect it to be as nice as it was. He ran his fingers along the walls as we walked down the long familiar hallway to Marcus' office. When we entered, the room was dim. The window shades were slid shut, bringing about an almost pitch black environment with the exception of Marcus' desk, and the gleaming red eyes that shone back at us, from the darkness.

"Ryne." Marcus' raspy devil's voice sounded out from the shadows. "What's this? You've brought company? How upset did you think I was?" His questions were sarcasm, which only his mocking laugh would show at the end of them. He knew Griff was coming up with me, Remy would have informed him. The implication that I had assumed he was upset enough to delete me was just his way of letting me know my place. I didn't give him the pleasure of my explanation of Griff's accompaniment. "So, you've blown up a part of my city, Ryne?"

This time the question wasn't sarcastic, but instead almost angered.

"Like you said, 'any means necessary', and knowing what I was up against, I thought it was necessary." I shot back.

"So you did." He said with a grin. He was acting like he didn't even care; like the city meant nothing to him. I was kicking myself inside for decimating those buildings and the street, and if I hadn't known that those buildings were uninhabited, I never would have done it. How was I supposed to know that you could drop a building on that thing, beat it senseless, and shoot it and it still wouldn't die? That pissed me off the most. All of the effort and sacrifice was for nothing, and now, Marcus just sat in front of us without a care. I had expected some sort of reprimand.

"Ox and Ramone are dead!" Griff yelled, and I looked at him in ashamed horror.

"Griff. Now's not the time." I nudged him. He didn't really understand the power that Marcus wielded. To Griff he was just a guy in a suit, who sat behind a desk, who was smaller than him, and not his commanding officer.

"No, Boss, I want to know what he's going to do about it. He sent us to die; trying to kill that thing." Griff made his point and Marcus sat patiently listening to the rant. "Well, scary shadow man? What about Ox and Ramone?" Griff huffed, posturing himself towards Marcus.

"Griff, can it." I interjected harshly with authority. He didn't understand that he was about to ruin the rest of his life, if Marcus would even let him have one, after what Marcus would claim was disrespect.

"No, Ryne, your ex-shockball flunky has a point. I did know that Alpha would be hard to eliminate, and I did understand the dangers of the assignment I gave you; however, I didn't imagine you would fail so spectacularly. Two of your men are lost. They will be replaced. You can pull from the active duty roster for your new members. Only, this time, please make sure they are field ready." He commanded apathetically in regards to my fallen men. Marcus was a cold bastard, and his reply was merely a slap in the face to Griff for his attitude, and a cut at Ramone and Ox's abilities. Unfortunately, that was what Griff deserved. The cold truth. Marcus and I both knew that Ox and Ramone were expendable corporate employees. Names on a list, lucky to have citizenship for the service they provided. This was the top floor. Things worked differently up here. That's why I didn't want Griff to come. There was no room for attachment.

"You piece of shit! I'll pull something, you son of a bitch, I pull your goddamn heart out from your throat!" Griff roared out at Marcus, who wasn't fazed.

"Griff! Stand down. Now!" I had to pull my shocker from its holster to show him that I was serious. "This isn't the place for that kind of slums-talking bullshit. Hit the truck."

I waved him out of the room. He was hesitant to leave, but the look I gave him told him he had to leave or he'd be dead, and that I'd have to do it. He drudged out of the room slowly in disgust. I holstered my weapon, and turned back towards Marcus. My shoulders dropped now that the tension was gone.

"I like him, Ryne. He's dedicated." The way he said it made it seem insincere.

"He's still a rookie. Wet behind the ears when it comes to this kind of stuff." I took a breath. Marcus leaned back in his chair, the red glass flickered reflecting the small amount of light in the room. Minutes of silence seemed to pass as we looked idly at one another. Then, out of nowhere, his devilish grin cracked the darkness.

"Ah yes, I forgot, you're an old hand. Is that why the city is on fire?" His palms smacked his desk suddenly. "Did you honestly think I would let you demolish the slums, you bumbling ogre?" His new tone burned as it emerged. "Then, you have the audacity of bringing your last remaining lummox to hide behind when I summon you, and he threatens me? He's lucky I'm not in a worse mood."

I was offended, but Marcus had become horrifying, turning back and forth in his swiveling chair as he talked. I opened my mouth to begin to speak.

"Ah, ah ah." His finger shot into the air in my direction. "Don't speak. Welcome to your last chance." Marcus said it in an elated manner, with another one of his demonic chuckles following. Before I could respond the door behind me opened letting light back into the room. For a moment, I thought Griff had returned to try to make good on his threat, but the shadow cast by the figure was significantly smaller.

"Ah, Welcome Mr. Brinnigan, come in." Marcus called the familiar name past me.

Eddie? What was he doing here?

CHAPTER FIFTEEN

SLY WITH SIDEBURNS

I had the strangest dream last night.

It's weird because I never seem to be able to dream when I'm not in my own bed, and that's not very often. Have you ever had a dream that manifests people from your everyday life, but instead of having them doing ordinary things, they are totally out of character?

That's kind of what this was like. In my dream, Alpha was pointing his shocker at me, and I had the strangest feeling he had the intention of bolting me. Estelle stood behind him. Her face was in pain. Her brows quivered in fear and she yelled out to him.

"No, please don't." She screamed in a haze of agony. My mind was telling me to wonder why Alpha's weapon was steadied on me, and I scanned the cloudy room we were in. On the walls hung pictures of my parents, and me as a child, only I didn't recognize the boy in the pictures. I just knew it was me.

Suddenly, I felt an object in my hand. An almost numb feeling, that let me know I was holding something. When I looked down I saw my Paragon issued shocker in my hand. The other hand was covered in blood. As I stared at them both, I couldn't remember how I came to be in the situation.

I looked back up at Alpha, who stood between me and Estelle. His shirt was covered in blood and his face looked saddened.

"Get out of the way, Alpha." I demanded of him. He didn't budge, but instead started to shake his head hesitantly hoping that I wasn't going to do what I appeared to be doing.

All of the sudden, I felt a pain shoot through my right leg and a grimace crossed my face. The pain was almost unbearable, and that was when I realized it wasn't only my leg. I felt something sliding off of my lips and down toward my chin. My chest felt like it was on fire.

"I'm so sorry." Alpha said it in a regretful voice, as I began my descent to the floor. The room felt like it was beginning to melt. Alpha and Estelle became blurs in front of me, and right as I started to close my eyes, they snapped open.

The room quickly came into focus as I rubbed my eyes, and sat upright in the bed. My breathing was heavy and hard. The commotion had been enough to wake up Reime, who was asleep beside me. She came to sluggishly, and her pretty eyes began to flutter open.

"Everything alright Eddie?" She whispered out, as her hand rubbed my back slowly.

"Yeah baby, I just... must have had too many of those rotten banana's last night." I assured her, and tried to blow off the vision. I'm sure it meant nothing. It was just a stupid dream, so I hoped.

"Awe, does my big tough man need some cheering up?" She teased, now wide awake and wrapping her bare leg over mine and rubbing it up and down generously, and that was all it took to push the dream to the back of my mind, and center my attention on her smooth milky skin as it flowed across mine.

I rolled over towards her and quickly grappled her up in my arms. She let out a playful scream that was followed by a giggle, before pulling the covers back up over us. She smiled up at me as I poised above her.

"Are you coming back to Ganymede tonight?" She asked, giving me a little giggle.

"Are you trying to make an honest man out of me?" I teased back down to her. She knew I would be there.

"Oh, I could never do that." She leaned up and whispered it softly into my ear. She had guessed that I wasn't the type to be tied down, but still, I didn't think she knew me that well. Not from one night.

"Oh? And why is that, Red?" I smiled playfully, as I rubbed my hand across her shoulder. She paused for a moment with a smile on her face, like she was thinking of the perfect answer. That was when I realized the game she was playing; the get close, but not too close game; a game I had perfected.

I smiled back, waiting for the answer that she would come up with.

"You're like a stray cat." She smiled, and her head bobbed around like her neck was a spring, as she began to giggle again.

"Yeah, that's right, I'm Catman." I proclaimed playfully, as I pressed my lips on her collarbone. She laughed like I didn't understand what she meant. "Alright, what do you mean I'm like a stray cat?"

I slid my fingers down her ribs, and she reared backwards, patting me on the stomach to get me to quit, and then she settled.

"Oh, you know..." She pulled her nails tenderly down my ribcage in return. "You can take 'em in and feed 'em, but you can't keep 'em from clawing up the sofa. It doesn't mean you're not cute, though." She giggled, amused with herself. I laughed a little, too. She was good. Impressed, I just pushed my lips into hers, and ended the conversation. She giggled as we tossed and turned around in the covers, occasionally knocking over what-ever little things she had sitting on her nightstands. It was a fun morning.

I straightened my tie as I walked out the front doors to her apartment. The sidewalks in Central D were partially covered to keep the rain off of them. It was a recent addition, and much nicer than the uncovered avenues of the slums. I was glad Reime was a citizen, and she was classier than I was used to.

I didn't have Penelope back from Alpha, yet. So, as I walked, I pulled my flask and a vile from my pocket, mixed them, and took a drink to get the day started in the usual way. The after-effects made me stop, midstride, as the shakes hit. They soon settled. I had gotten really proficient at mixing the right amount of *U* in after my incident a couple of years back.

After a few seconds, the world around me began to shimmer, my body felt more relaxed, and I started my walk back to the main corporate office.

The city on *U* wasn't as drab, dull, or dismal. The rain looked more like sparkles falling from the sky, and all the city's mayhem seemed like it was far away, leaving me out of the midst of it.

That wasn't the case in reality at all. I was mayhem's right-hand man, orderly, driver, babysitter, or whatever the case called for that day, and it was nice to get the chance to escape from that. The effects of *U* didn't last that long in moderation, maybe thirty minutes or so per dose. It had become a facet of the city that was never talked about in good light, but rather, anyone caught using was hauled in to detox; anyone but me at least. My corporate position had its own set of rules, and my *Uphorium* habit was of little importance to the upper-uppers which, before I knew it, was whose doorstep I was on; Paragon plaza, home of my office, where my day would start.

I opened the big entrance doors where I was soon greeted by a curious Remy. It wasn't very often that Alpha wasn't attached to me at the side. I'm sure this would alarm Remy, but that twerp doesn't know anything. I took pleasure in the fact that his bitch-job was worse than mine.

"Flying solo today, Mr. Brinnigin?" He tried to be as formal as Marcus. It didn't suit him well. He seemed better fitted as one of the punks in the slums, instead of in the fancy suit that Marcus had him dance around in.

"Yeah, Alpha's sleeping in I guess. He'll be in this afternoon." I reassured the little man, as I passed and took the lift up to the floor my office was on. I didn't really have any idea of where to start the day. Usually, Alpha would have already chosen the open-assignments and we'd be at the flavor shop, smoking gaspers, and waiting for what he considered to be the perfect moment to do the assignment.

Today, I was on my own. We didn't have a quota to meet or anything, but we had put ourselves in a position of expectation. As I stepped out of the lift and walked into mine and Alpha's office, I saw the holopacket sitting on my desk that I had left there yesterday; the Estelle job. I sat in my cushioned leather chair and swiveled it forward. I opened up the packet, and one of her pictures emerged; a profile shot of her on stage with a microphone in her hand. Her blonde hair was done up in curls, and her face was lightly dusted in various shades of make-up, in all the best places. She was definitely a sight to behold, even in pictures. She was best described as *glamorous*, a word that wasn't used for many things in this city. As I stared at the picture, the dream came rushing back to me. Now, I was wondering what it meant, if anything, and as I perused through the dossier, a cold chill ran up my spine. Most of the information on Estelle was the normal stuff; age, birth-date, occupation, and then there was residence. It was the same building that I had seen only a day earlier; "Meserere".

It was an old complex that was converted into housing, after the uprising. It was where miss pretty-dress lived; an amazing coincidence, and it made my dream all too clear. I knew Alpha had been embracing his more human aspects, as of late, and that he had been hesitating more and more on our assignments. Even yesterday, at the Vic job, he apologized to the man right before deleting him. If his new girl knew Estelle, it could be a major conflict of interest.

As I continued reading the dossier packed with pictures, I noticed more and more odd things about Estelle. Her parents for example; her mother died at birth, and her father was marked down as unknown. Paragon had a full record of every birth, and the parents of the child born. It was highly unlikely for one to slip through the system. Also, her listed known affiliates made no mention of the girl Alpha picked up yesterday, but instead had a group of not-so active anti-Paragon activists. The leader of which was a man named Benny Gloom. He was suspect in the far bridge bombing, but he was never properly associated. Now, he works as Estelle's bodyguard and entourage leader. I called downstairs to Remy to have him send up a file on Benny. Moments later, a raven-haired woman brought it up to me and plopped it down on my desk.

"Doesn't seem like too good a fella." The woman stated, as she smacked some sort of food around in her mouth looking down at me sitting behind my desk. "I read it on the way up."

She was tone, with a real affirming type of attitude, which took away from how pretty she could've been.

"Yeah, thanks." I said, but I didn't concentrate on her. I didn't want her to stick around while I was trying to figure out the mystery I stumbled onto, but she didn't seem to get the hint.

"So you're Eddie, right?" She smacked at me. "You're the guy who takes care of the scary one?"

I was assuming she meant Alpha, but I never really thought he was as scary as everyone made him out to be.

"Alpha's my partner..." I answered back, still trying to detour her interest in conversation.

"Name's Jesse. I work downstairs in the munitions office, but I'm hoping one day they'll transfer me up here to Section Seven." She continued. "Maybe I can be one of you guys? We could be a team."

I finally looked up to her with doubtful eyes. She was much prettier than my first observation, not in an elegant way, but stiffer and slightly masculine. I almost felt sorry for her. She had no idea the kind of things that went on in Section Seven, and I doubt if she did she'd still want to sign up.

"Alpha and I aren't really the team type. You'd probably want to talk to Ryne if you're looking for a promotion." I looked back down. "Besides, that guy could use some *pretty* around him." Usually a flattering comment like that makes women around me go all weak in the knees, but this 'Jesse' girl only seemed to be offended.

"It ain't all looks buddy. I'll be seeing ya." She said crassly as she turned and left my little office, and it was good to watch her go. I picked up the red data packet she had dropped on my desk. I opened the file, and Benny's rap sheet could have spilled out.

Before working with Estelle he had been picked up by Ox for assaulting a door guy in the Fader club, and again with a bartender in Kelp. He was a delinquent in one of the punk groups in his youth, and stayed in trouble with Paragon, but for the last three years he's been Estelle's go-to defense guy. He had stopped a crazed fan from getting on stage at her stadium gig, and broke another guy's nose who tried to grab her outside of the Stardust a few months back. His list of Affiliates read worse than Estelle's. If he wanted to, he could have half the city's trash up in arms with him. It wasn't any wonder that Marcus wanted this to look accidental. This man was the real threat, not Estelle. She just seemed to make bad choices in friends.

The more I read through Estelle's file, the less I thought the job was necessary. I thumbed through the pictures of her, admiring her, and thinking how unlucky the city would be to lose her. The packet also contained a digidisc.

I inserted it into my datcom and started listening to it. I had heard her live, but her recordings were just as good. Each song had a positive message, and a real mellow feel that I could get into. Her voice was as beautiful as she was, and each note sounded like it was sung by an angel. As I listened, I wondered if Alpha had made the connection from his girl to Estelle, or if he even read the file, yet.

I kept hoping his date with pretty-dress went well, and that he'd have all kinds of stories to tell me when he got back with Penelope. I knew him better than anyone, Marcus and that kooky old man in the basement combined. Ryne always thought Alpha was a monster, ever since the day Marcus brought him into the boardroom. Marcus promoted me and assigned me to Alpha, because he needed someone as an anchor for Alpha's fake memories, and I was happy to do it. Before then, I was just a use-when-you-need gopher for Killian and Marcus; Do this, do that, manipulate this or that person; it was all very unsatisfying. Then, I was taken to the basement for profiling with the professor. He asked me all kinds of personal questions and told me I had a new best friend. Hell, I never had an old one.

At first, it was all like Marcus described; monitor Alpha's actions and make sure he was going to do the job, and he did. Alpha believed that he'd known me his whole life, even though 'whole' had only been a few months at the time. He would talk to me like he trusted me and had my confidence. It was very strange, but it started to grow on me, and I opened up to him as well. He did his job and didn't question anything; not his ethics, morality, chain of command, nothing. He was perfect.

Years passed the same way, and I bonded with him more and more. He never took to my lifestyle, but accepted it all the same. Then, one day our assignment was to infiltrate a Dox-4 cooker's hideout, delete him, and burn the drugs. It should have been easy. We had done that kind of thing before, but this time something went wrong.

When we got to the apartment that the cooker was using, nobody was there. On the walls were pictures of the man, his wife, and his child; a young girl that was about six years old with brown little pig-tails and a gap in her teeth. In the back, the man had been cooking the *U*, but before we could burn what he had, he came home with his family.

They found us standing in the middle of their main room. The man took one look at Alpha and me, and immediately knew why we were there.

"Let me take my family back outside, please!" I remember the man pleading, as he positioned himself between us and them.

"None of you move." Alpha commanded the family standing in the doorway. "Close the door, and come have a seat on the couch. All of you."

The man ushered his family into the room, closing the door behind them. "Please let my wife and child go!" The man begged, but Alpha knew that he couldn't. Part of Section Seven protocol is to leave no witnesses.

"You have been found guilty of manufacturing substances in your home. You are a black mark on humanity, and you will be rubbed out." He quoted his byline given to him by Marcus.

I stood and watched in horror as Alpha worked. It was what he did, but this situation had never come up. I knew the man's wife and daughter were practically innocent, and didn't deserve what was about to happen, but Alpha only knew the Paragon code.

"They have done nothing wrong!" The man yelled in panic back at Alpha, who was standing behind their sofa.

"My only crime is trying to give people a little peace of mind, however they can get it! Let my wife and daughter go, just take me…" The man started to blather at the end of his speech, and I couldn't help but be a little touched by how pathetic he looked. The eyes of his daughter peeled tears onto her cheeks.

"Maybe we should let this one go." I tried persuading my partner, but he didn't acknowledge me. Instead, he pulled out his shocker and placed it against the back of the man's head.

"I haven't hurt anyone." The man slowly stammered out, as he reached for his wife's hand, upon feeling the metal touch the back of his skull. "It's just a harmless medicine."

But it was too late. Alpha had already made up his mind. The trigger would be pulled. The man's lifeless body fell to the floor, and a quick shot of blood splattered across his wife's face, mixing with the tears.

"Please don't…" I heard her whisper out. I turned my head as Alpha moved the shocker down the line to her. Before he could pull back the trigger, the daughter turned around and smacked Alpha's hand.

"Don't hurt my mommy!" She yelled and her little eyes burned up at him. For the first time, Alpha stopped what he was doing completely, and looked at the little girl. Their stare-off seemed to last forever. Then, Alpha pulled the shocker back and put it in his holster.

Her mother burst out into waterfalls of tears, blathering on the floor next to her dead husband. He turned to me and said nothing. He only walked past me and into the room in the back setting fire to a chemical table. When he reemerged, I was watching the mother and daughter curl over the dead man that now occupied the floor. Then, Alpha stopped and turned to me.

"Explain to them what has just happened here. Tell them they have not returned home yet. That her husband made a bad deal with a gang of street punks, and this is how they found him. Tell them that Paragon will be paying for the memorial, and they will be compensated for their loss. Make sure they understand." He insisted, "I will be waiting in the car." Then, he walked out of the room, shutting the door behind him, leaving me there to explain it all to them the way he had said to.

When I returned to the car, he was staring out of the window blankly into the rain. He wouldn't talk about it, and I never brought it back up, but ever since that day he wasn't the same. He wasn't the monster Ryne wanted him to be, and he wasn't the perfect emotionless assassin that Marcus wanted, either. That day, he did become my best friend.

I heard the lift ding over the sound of Estelle's digidisc, and I pulled it back out of my datcom. I put it back in the packet, and was trying to straighten it back up, when Alex snuck into my office, shutting the door, quietly, behind him.

FRIENDLY ADVICE

I steered the old van into the dock behind the Paragon building, but Alex seemed hesitant. After defying Marcus and helping the professor sneak out of Central D, I would be a little hesitant to walk back into that building, too.

"Are you sure you want to go back there?" I sneered sarcastically at him. Alex wasn't a fighter by any means, but ever since the rebellion in the slums, every Paragon employee was required a minimal amount of combat training. Even so, I don't think he would make it very long if Marcus knew about his secret agenda.

"I have to." He said dejectedly as his shoulders slumped down, and his head followed. "I have to do something, anything, you know?"

Do something? What can you do when the system has failed, and turned into the monster it used to fear? You're just a part of that system, you can't do anything from the inside.

"Nope." I replied. I was being honest. It wasn't his place to put himself in so much risk for just one man. I didn't know the professor that well; only met him a handful of times, but I wouldn't have done the same in his position. Defying Paragon was suicide.

"It's my fault." He continued without questioning my indifference. "The professor trusted me, and I let him down."

He sounded like a whiny child. To me, trust was one of those things we were taught, like 'an apple a day' or 'don't forget socks', that made it sound like it was better to do it, than to not. I didn't trust anyone. Well, I trusted Alpha; for the most part.

"They'll eventually find him, you know, and if you're with Krill when they do, your body will end up right next to his at Kagan's. Are you sure it's worth it?" I asked again, this time trying to be more sincere in my opinion. His resolve postured him back to a state of strength.

"Absolutely." He declared without thought to the question. I couldn't help but admire his unflinching devotion to the doc, however naïve it seemed to be.

"Well, good luck kid. You're going to need it." I replied, and he was going to need it. I could only imagine how much he would have to go through to try to cover his tracks helping Krill escape, particularly if he was ever going to make it out of Paragon, himself.

Especially, with three new Alpha-like monsters running around the city. It seemed like too much work, and I liked keeping my head low and staying out of the cross-fire.

"Thanks for helping, Eddie. I'm sure Alpha will appreciate it as well." His tone became sincere, reminding me of the treason. I didn't even know why I was doing it. Helping people without anything in return; it wasn't my style, but some things had to be done, and some things didn't need to be said.

"Whoa, kid, I just drove the van. I didn't know what was in the back. Got it?" I shot out. Besides, he wasn't going to put my head in the noose, too.

That was the least of my worries, though. I had to get over to Ganymede and tell Alpha about all this, and pick up Penelope. Just driving this big piece of junk cramped my style.

"Yeah, I got it." He shot back at me sarcastically. I guessed he didn't care much for my chosen exclusion from his little do-gooders club, but that didn't bother me, either. Life was too short, especially in this city. He hopped out of the van and scurried back inside through the Paragon basement.

I wasn't going to make an appearance at the Ganymede in this heap, but it wasn't really far from the main office. The Drain was practically below it, on the outer rim before the Boundary Bridge, and that was only a few blocks away. Just a few blocks and I'd get to see her again; my sweet *Penelope*.

Walking wasn't really my thing, but I needed the time to think. I held off on pulling out my flask and *doxing* on my trip down to the Drain. Trying to come up with what to tell Alpha, when I met up with him, was going to be the real task. I knew I had to tell him about *pretty-dress'* address and Estelle's being the same, but I didn't know what to say about Krill and his extended retirement plans. He wouldn't understand exactly why it was important for him to know. The best I knew, he only met the professor a handful of times like me, and most of them were for Krill to tinker with his parts, I assumed. Marcus tried, as much as possible, to keep the old man out of the loop on what was going on upstairs, but that didn't mean Alpha wouldn't need regular check-ups, like any other person. So, if I told him about Krill, I would probably be opening a whole can of worms, that I didn't have all the answers for. It wasn't long before the neon signs and lights drew me closer to the Ganymede, and it bustled. The rain had let up and Central D was out in force. People always got out more when the rain slowed. I guess, to them, it was a good sign. Going back there also meant that I would have to see Reime again. Not that I minded so much, she was a sweet girl, but I didn't make a habit of hooking up and hanging out. I had a reputation to maintain. Fortunately, when I walked in, the shift change hadn't happened, and Alpha was sitting where Alpha likes to sit; in the darkest corner in the place. He wasn't much for people, and he avoided being seen as much as possible. They did the same for him. It was like everyone had already known, but they didn't. His demeanor just set him apart from everyone, but he liked his solitude, or so I understood. He didn't wave me over or even give me a glance to let him know where he was. It was just an understood thing between us. I walked over and sat in the chair across from him.

"Hey buddy." I greeted him with a smile as I sat. The waitress on duty came over and smiled at me, but distanced herself from Alpha, like she was avoiding him. He wouldn't mind, he didn't drink, so it never bothered him when it happened.

"Yeah, I'll just start with a synth-ale. What are you having?" I gestured over to Alpha knowing that he didn't want anything, but I still didn't like him getting the cold shoulder while I was around.

"Nothing, ma'am." The hollow voice crept out from the shadowy corner, both eerie and polite.

"Ma'am! Well, I'll let you know that I'm only seventeen!" She gently slapped him on the forearm and smiled, but he didn't seem to acknowledge the act. "I'll be right back with that synth-ale for you, hun." She ran her hand across my shoulder as she walked away from the table.

"See, man, it's easy. All you have to do is talk to them." I played. His social obstinacy didn't annoy me, but knowing what he was, I wanted him to fit in as much as possible. He just assumed that I was trying to make him more sociable to keep up my appearance.

"What's the point? Three years from now, she'll probably just get caught up in a U-den and I'll show up, *killing* everyone. She won't be pleased to see me then." He shot out low and disheartened. He never acted pessimistic before. He really was becoming more and more human. Something had happened on the date with pretty-dress that he wasn't happy with, and he was beating himself up; I could tell.

I started to see how all of this was interesting to the professor. He really was '*growing up*'.

"O.K. man, spill it. Did things not go well with what's-her-dress?" I prodded, but was careful not to seem overly concerned. The waitress came back, and sat the glass of cold amber liquid on the table in front of me. I picked it up and took a swig from it. Alpha's eyebrows cocked up at one side. I sat the glass down, and let out a fulfilling sigh.

"What?" I wiped the leftover foam from the stubble above my lip onto my sleeve, as I noticed his odd glance.

"You're not doxing?" He asked it interrogatively, like he was divining information on an assignment. He knew me too well. I was trying to keep my wits sharp, and he had caught on.

"Nah, I'm out. I've got to go see Hilder later. You've got Penelope, remember?" It was the quickest lie I could think of. Partially true, though. I only had two vials left in my pocket, and that wouldn't last me through the night. He pulled the keys out of his front pocket, slid them across the table, and then leaned back against the seat, somewhat relaxed and somewhat frazzled.

"She's out back. I knew you wouldn't want her in the same lot with the others." He stated, and he was right. I never parked her around the citizens, out of fear of them denting her up. The reemergence of the keys made me want to go out and check on her, crank her up, and let her know I missed her, but Alpha was acting strange, and that took priority.

It was then that I realized he had used my car and my drug habit to get out of answering my question. He had learned that from me. People generally want to talk more about themselves, than someone else, and it makes for a good conversational diversion. I wasn't going to let him one-up the master.

"Alright, enough avoidance, Alpha. What happened last night?" I pursued it again. Directly, this time.

"Last night..." He paused for a long moment as he recalled. It was one of the first times I could ever remember seeing him in thought. Usually, every response came pretty quick, almost automatic, for him.

"Last night was good. It was this morning when everything went horribly wrong." He said plainly. I had never heard him describe anything as good or bad, right or wrong. Usually, when he did talk about himself, it was down to business, all gray area unemotional garbage.

"You sly dog! So, you stayed with her all night? I didn't see that one coming." I laughed out loud. I had hoped it was the case, but I didn't really expect it. I used the laugh to push him deeper into himself, still trying to take the focus from me.

"It wasn't like that." He corrected me in a very calm tone. His voice was almost peaceful-sounding as he recreated his thoughts. "It was different; real, and nice. She is different."

His face was pained, and I thought it was amusing. He had met a girl, like a real person, and now he was having a real reaction. I couldn't help but to feel like the older brother. Krill, you obviously outdid yourself.

"Yeah, yeah. They all are at first, man. You'll get over it." I assured him as I cautiously picked my glass back up to take another drink. A lull in conversation could swing it back in my direction.

"No! She was perfect, and I messed up." Alpha insisted. He was still lost in his memory, and conversation didn't sway. It was a little spooky, thinking about him being what he is, and acting like he was.

"Easy killer." I played, as I set the glass back on the table. He was having 'real people' problems. "What do you mean you messed up? You barely even know the girl."

It was true, too. He met the girl yesterday. It wasn't going to be the end of the world, it was just his first time.

"I told her, Eddie." He swallowed. I swallowed harder. What did he mean, 'he told her'?

"I wanted her to know, and I told her everything." He repeated, and I could feel my eyes widening. This wasn't good. She wasn't a citizen. She wasn't supposed to know anything about Paragon, or Alpha, or me, or my goddamn Penelope, for that matter.

"What the hell do you mean, 'you told her everything'?" I leaned forward, grasping at one of the table's edges nervously whispering to him.

"Everything, Eddie. What I do, and who I do it for. Everything." He said as calmly as he had said everything else. The silence between us passed for an eternity. The kid with the red guitar, on the corner stage, jammed that thing like he was trying to save the planet with it. It gave me an ill clarity of the future.

"Shit! Man! She can't know that kind of stuff. You know that! You're the king of protocol and this is totally against it. What were you thinking?" I asked hysterically, but I knew what he was thinking. He never was a good liar, and if he thought he had any real chance with this girl, he would be as honest with her as he possibly could be. This is why Marcus didn't want him fraternizing with the people. It was always a risk, but no one took any stock in it.

"I think...I think I might... love her." He pushed out through a stammer, and I cocked a brow. Miss pretty-dress did a real number on him. It made me interested in getting to know more about her. Anyone who could affect Alpha this much, had to be something special.

"You think you love her. Oh, well that's just great." I replied with some sarcasm, and I couldn't help but condescend him. It just came out. What did he know about love? I had a new woman every night, and I had never seen hide nor hair of love. "And just what makes you Mr. Romance all the sudden, eh? It was just one date!."

He was just being a foolish adolescent; now he would settle down, I hoped.

"I know I love her, Eddie." His voice became serious; a scary kind of serious that I was more accustomed to. "And I can't do this anymore." The last statement sent chills down my spine. This is why Marcus had partnered me with him. This was the exact sentence Marcus had been waiting for him to say, and when he did, it was my job to make sure that he didn't mean it. I was supposed to change his mind. I was to turn him around in his head, and make him see the bright and shiny Paragon future that he had been working towards.

"What do you mean?" I asked because my ass was on the line, too. This was the moment I proved my loyalty to the company, and earned my privileged citizen status.

Alpha looked down at his clothes, pulled open his coat to display his shocker in its holster, and waved his hand downward to show it off. Then gestured at me, and my clothes and around the room at the various extravagant looking people, as he released the hold on his coat; it closed to conceal his weapon, once again.

"All of this. What I am. What we do for them. I don't want to kill people anymore." He proposed, and for the first time, he sounded more human than I ever thought he could. I didn't know what to tell him. I wouldn't want his job either. No one would. I knew what he was feeling. I felt it vicariously through him all the years I've had to watch him do it. Killing people to even the status quo of the city wasn't right, no matter what future we were trying to achieve.

It just wasn't the way to do it. It was the whole reason I used *U*; to escape from what he was feeling, now. Marcus wouldn't like this report, and I didn't want to give it to him. I had decided if I could change his mind, then a report wouldn't be needed.

"I understand what you're going through. I feel the same way sometimes, but you gotta understand why we do it." I tried for the rudimentary lecture.

"You have to keep fighting for the city. It's not just about your life, buddy, or the lives you take. It's about the whole; the common good. What we do makes humanity possible. It makes the future brighter for the people who are alive." I repeated Marcus' doctrine nearly verbatim, and my conscience was kicking the crap out of me. It all burned coming out, and I didn't believe a word of it anymore. I knew the greater good for the both of us, and it wasn't telling Marcus the truth.

"That's a lie, Eddie." He said it, cold and direct. "I still see their faces, you know, and they don't agree with anything you just said. I can hear their voices; their last words and screams as I pulled back metal on them. They're future doesn't exist anymore. I'm not building the future for anyone; I'm taking it away. I'm *killing* people." He ranted.

The waitress came back by, but stopped just short of the table as she heard Alpha's remarks. I looked over to her and just nodded, so she wouldn't have to interrupt our conversation uncomfortably. Alpha and I waited, as she brought back another drink, and set it on the table.

"You boys doing alright?" She asked nervously.

"Sure thing, sweetheart, just keep bringing new ones when you see the old ones go." I said graciously so she wouldn't have to keep asking. She only nodded slowly before returning to her other tables. I picked up the new synth-ale and took a gulp.

"Sure, Alpha, what we do isn't pretty, and it might not be the way, but it's the only way we got." That was the hard truth. Paragon under Marcus had made it that way. Defiance was death. "You just need to relax and drink those voices out."

I pulled one of the remaining vials from my inner-pocket, and Alpha's brow cocked again. I poured its contents into the fresh drink in front of me. The powder danced in the liquid before settling and saturating itself throughout. "This will take the edge off. Then, tomorrow, you'll wake up and you'll go back to work, same as any day."

I pushed the glass toward him, and nodded. It was my last card to play. I knew that there was nothing I could tell him to make what we do right, but I hoped that maybe if he would just cope with it, that we would see that next work day together, but Alpha's lips pursed, and his brows narrowed. He hadn't liked my alternative.

"I won't do it anymore. I want some kind of regular life like everyone else." He demanded, and his eyes burned with an intensity that made me realize that he wasn't going to give in, and so I had to. We sat silently staring at each other, knowing that we had come to an impasse in our friendship. I thought of everything to come and everything that had passed, weighing our futures, knowing what Marcus would command; what he had already commanded me to do if this happened.

My shocker sat tucked in its holster under my arm, and if I followed orders I would be reaching for it, but I didn't always follow orders. Besides, reaching for my shocker against him would be suicide. Then, I thought of our friendship. What life with him had given me besides the car, the high life, the creds, but what it had really given me; my only friend.

I had the life they had implanted in his memories; growing up in Paragon, and being taught all the wrong things, despising it, and from that despise; the lack of real trust in people that had become so much a part of me. My conscience still kicked me as I thought of the shocker, my orders, and my friend. It was a feeling that I hadn't remembered in a long time. I looked down at the amber drink in front of us and grabbed it up, tilted it back, and swallowed it down.

"Well, buddy. It's your life. You try to be happy for as long as you can." I insisted, and the shakes kicked in as I said it, and the dimness lifted from our little corner. The drugs were quick, and the world was right again. "I'm just going to give you a little advice. Marcus isn't going to like this. It's going to be all out war. He'll probably send everyone to *delete* you, even me. So, that being said, what's your plan, Ace?"

Alpha's composure became more relaxed. He eased back into his side of the booth.

"You worry too much. I will talk with Marcus. I'll let him know how I feel, and that I won't be coming back." He explained with an innocence I didn't expect. Even with his knowledge of Marcus and Paragon, he still truly didn't understand what was going to happen.

"I don't think that's going to work." I explained and a smirk spread across my face. I was imagining the conversation Alpha would have with Marcus, and what would happen if Alpha got mad. It would be a quick regime change. That was certain.

"It has to." He sounded desperate. He wanted his life with pretty-dress more than I thought.

"Well, say it does, where will you live? I seriously doubt he will allow you to keep your citizenship." I played along with his fantasy. Dealing in all these hypotheticals was fun, but I knew what would really happen. Marcus wouldn't stop until Alpha was deleted. To Marcus, Alpha was no more than a company asset, expendable, not even a life to worry about.

"The Slums. That's where she lives." He explained as though he had already thought of everything. His innocence continued to shine through. The more he talked the more he sounded like an irrational teenager from a fairytale, planning to elope with his childhood sweetheart into the woods. I couldn't help but laugh.

"With miss pretty-dress?!" I couldn't stop the chuckle that followed.

"Lexxi. Her name is Lexxi, Eddie." He protested, giving me a stern look that compelled me to stop laughing.

"Alright, alright. So, let me ask you this. Did you ever get a chance to look at the Estelle job?" I asked in earnest. If I was going to let him run, I had to give him everything.

It was the least I could do. Tomorrow, it would be off to the gallows for me, and the fight of his life, for him.

"I don't intend on looking at it, why?" He seemed puzzled at the odd timing of the question.

"Well, I just thought you might want to know that miss-pretty...ahem...Lexxi, doesn't exactly live alone." I told him as I began to get more serious.

This would be news to him, and snap him out of his fantasy. I leaned in, over the table and into the light from above. "Are you sure you're ready for this?" I paused for dramatic emphasis. "She's Estelle's roomy!"

I pulled back into darkness, as I let the idea sink into his mind. "What?!" He shot it out quickly, after only a few seconds. He was putting it all together. How he would still be connected to the company, even after disconnecting himself.

"I only found out because I remembered the sign on the building, where we dropped her off. It's the same residence listed for the Estelle Hart job. You know that even if you do quit, there will be someone to take your place; probably Ryne or someone else from Section Seven." I informed him. I could tell he was becoming angry, and he tilted his head toward me so that I could see his eyes clearly.

"Maybe even you?" He glared at me from across the table, displeased with all the revelations. I hadn't thought of it, myself, and I highly doubted that Marcus would nominate me as a candidate for Alpha's job. The most plausible scenario, I'd be dead, but I could see how Alpha wouldn't think that.

"Nah. I've been listening to her digidisc all day. I wouldn't have the heart." I reassured him with some cynicism, but it was also true. I didn't think I could delete anyone, especially a gorgeous woman like Estelle. I celebrated what little humanity I had with another gulp of my foamy mixture.

"I have to warn her." He said in such a sudden that I almost spit out the drink.

"Or, you could finish the job, and maybe that would earn you some points with Marcus and keep pretty-dress out of danger." I just blurted it out, but it sounded good. Somehow, in my head it made a lot of sense. If he would just do the job, he could make sure that Lexxi wasn't collateral, and Marcus might actually consider letting him off the hook, but I doubted it as much as I wanted it to be true.

"I've got to go. I've got to find her." Alpha's face lit up, and he was in a hurry to leave. He stood up from the table in a rush, and started towards the front doors.

"Wait, who? Lexxi or Estelle?" I yelled out for him, wanting to know which option he had picked, but he had already made it out of the building, without looking back. I stood up from the dingy little corner table, and walked over to my usual place in the middle of the bar. The shift change had just begun, and out from the back walked Reime, wrapping her apron around her petite waist. She looked over and saw me, her face instantly burst into joy, and for some reason, I actually found it attractive instead of being repulsed, like I normally would. I didn't understand it, but Reime had somehow gotten her hooks into me, not an easy feat for any woman. She was the first, actually.

I caught myself as my hand started to come up to wave 'hello' to her, but immediately I put it back down. Instead, I smiled warmly at her. Reime had successfully turned me into a fool. I sat down at my table, and my waitress brought me another drink. She was livelier, now that Alpha had gone, and soon, one by one, the girls flocked over. Ditra, Kimber, Rache, and Icia all sat down at the table around me, waiting for me to regale them with stories of glory and triumph from the hard days of working for the man at Paragon corporate. It was the usual.

"Drinks on you, Eddie?" Kimber smiled and teased. Drinks were always on me. I had nothing else to spend my credits on, and nothing else to do with my time that I like more.

"Tell us about the duster punks again." Icia sang out. Her voice was canary gold, as she beamed a smile from under the dark curls that covered almost half of her face.

"I've told you girls that story a hundred times, now." I played back, but it was true. They never did get tired of my stories, no matter how many times I told them.

"Awe, please, Eddie." Ditra added, in a baby doll voice that just tickled all the right places. Then, all four batted their eyelashes at me as they twisted, waiting in their chairs.

"O.K., O.K." I started, but before I could begin the story, Reime walked over to the table smiling, and slid in-between Rache and Kimber, placing herself on my lap, using my leg as a seat. The other girls giggled, but didn't seem to mind the display of dominance she had made.

"I want to hear about the duster punks, too, Eddie." She smiled, and ran her hand along my inner thigh. I coughed, in surprise, as I pulled my drink away from my mouth, and wrapped my arm around her; pulling her into me with a smile of my own. Then, I began telling the story with my free hand wafting through the air as if to paint a picture.

"The Dusters pulled up behind me and Alpha on their bikes..." I spoke dramatically to give the story life, and inflected to make my characters seem real and alive, never once giving thought to the fact that my story's characters were me and Alpha. "I swerved Penelope to the left and to the right trying to get them off our tail, but one would fall and another would take his place at our bumper..." All the girls were propped, faces on palms, elbows on the table, listening longingly as I revisited my past with Alpha.

Before I could get very far into the story, the front doors opened, and in walked Ryne with a disgruntled look on his face.

"Uh oh, ladies, here comes grumpy." I observed as Ryne crossed to our table in quick strides. He looked pretty steamed about something.

I was sure this wasn't going to be fun.

ASSIGNMENT COMPLETE

Penelope hummed and vapors rose from her hood as the rain hit and evaporated off. Eddie waited for me in the driver's seat as I climbed into the back of the car. My frustration was starting to overwhelm me from the scolding I received from Krill, and moreover, I was confused about the Estelle job.

Why did the old man care so much?

I didn't understand his infatuation with hope, or why he thought that a singer was the sole cause of so much of it. There were plenty of performers in the city, and without Estelle some of them might even be acknowledged. As it was, she was the only one people even talked about. To me, it was just out of need for gossip and controversy; just something for people to keep up with, stay focused on, and spread rumors about. Still, she was hardly anything evil, nor a threat to Paragon.

I closed the car door behind me, and Eddie started down the street to the Boundary Bridge. The privacy shield soon lowered.

"So, what did pretty-dress have to say?" Eddie chuckled in delight as he asked. I couldn't tell him that I was violating Paragon protocol to see Krill, and I didn't have a decent excuse for my sudden departure. Since I hadn't commed Lexxi yet, I couldn't just tell him that I had. He would prod more for information. It was what he was good at.

Eddie could spend five minutes talking to someone and know their life story and convince them to take it in a new direction, and he was the best at it. He could tell if someone was lying to him just by watching how their eyes moved and voice sounded. He would have never let what happened to me on the Zane Blanc job happen to him, and I bet he could read me the same.

"I didn't com her." I admitted to him, but I still didn't have any explanation for my absence, and if I learned anything from him, it was that disappointing news takes precedence over furthering a friendly interrogation.

Hopefully, he would forget to ask about where I had been. I knew he had wanted me to com Lexxi because he was constantly trying to get me to socialize with him and all of his girlfriends at the Ganymede. One time, he even tried to pawn off Rache on me, just so I could have been on a date. Fortunately, she declined his offer, and stayed with him and his harem.

"What do you mean you didn't com her? You're at least going to, aren't you? It's not every day that a pretty girl like that just falls into your lap, buddy." he ranted and lectured in his own way, and it worked. My whereabouts were concealed. Not trying to do so made me think more about her. The way she had smiled and used her hand to hide it. The way she didn't shudder away from me like everyone else had always done.

"Let's talk about something else, Eddie." I wanted a detour in the conversation. I didn't need to be thinking so much about her, and I didn't like how much Eddie pressured the issue on me. I still had a job to do, and there was plenty of day left to finish it in. "What's on the agenda for the rest of the day?" I asked. I could see Eddie's disappointment through the rear-view mirror, but it didn't stop him from pulling out his datcom to find our next destination.

"The Vic's Market job is still open." He sighed as he made the statement. "That's weird; it's been open for sixteen weeks."

It wasn't good for a job to be open that long. It meant that it was originally one of Ryne's jobs that didn't get done, and had been promoted from capture to deletion. Someone must have missed it.

"It's not like Ryne to miss an assignment." I observed with careful scrutiny as I reviewed the assignment file.

"Doesn't matter now, it's in our book." Eddie assured, but he didn't seem happy about it. I wasn't really happy about it, either.

It was one thing to have to do a job, but to delete someone because one of the company's employees got lazy wasn't something that sat well with me.

"What was the assignment originally for? What did this 'Vic' do?" I asked, and hoped Eddie's concern would keep him from wondering why I hadn't given away my whereabouts. This morning at Kelp had really started messing with my head, bringing up old memories, and then she happened. Now, my head was swirling with so many different things. I just didn't feel like deleting someone else. It wasn't feeling right, anymore.

"Oh man, this is just the busts!" Eddie shot out, adding "Get this! Vic's on the books because he still owes Paragon six thousand creds for a loan he took out to open his shop, and he hasn't made a payment in five months. Damn it, Ryne."

It was absurd for this kind of detention assignment to get turned over to me and Eddie. Six thousand creds was a decent amount, but not enough to delete someone over. I could understand why Eddie was upset with Ryne. Chances were, that Eddie actually knew Vic. Eddie practically knew everyone. I didn't respond to Eddie's outburst, and we drove down the street in silence for the next few moments.

"We're not actually going to take this one, are we?" Eddie finally spoke out, but before I could answer, he continued. "I mean, I know we have to do it, but it's a shit gig. Vic's a good guy; he's probably just been having some slow business, damn it." Eddie had made his point, and he was right. I had already begun to agree before he started the tirade. It was a 'shit' assignment, and it should have been handled by a different Section Seven team.

"I'll let you talk to him when we get there. We'll see what he has to say. If it turns out he's just late on his payments, we'll call Ryne and have him clean it up." I assured, and Eddie's face lit up with excitement and relief. I hadn't ever declined a job before, or even really given a client a chance to explain themselves, until this morning. It felt good. I even felt happy that I might not have to delete Vic.

Soon Eddie's excitement turned back into inquisition. He had read me, and saw what I was feeling. The reluctance to take the Vic job had actually shown on my face, or the happiness that came with it.

"It's because of pretty-dress isn't it?" He asked with a narrow eye back at me. The squinted wrinkles gave away his grin, and I didn't know how to answer. I didn't know if it was because of her, or just from the relief, so it was better that I pretend I didn't understand the question. That's what he would do.

"What is?" I wiped the emotion from my face as fast as I could.

"You know that goofy grin you've been wearing all morning. Ever since you met her you've been acting all strange; odd disappearances, changes of heart... and that stupid grin. It's all because of her, isn't it?" He clarified, and I hadn't noticed that I had been smiling, but since he brought her up, it had begun again. I relaxed my face to try to hide it immediately. "She must be special." He deduced, and he was right. I had felt something special about her, but I didn't understand it myself. I wasn't going to justify his observation with a response. I wouldn't have to.

We could see Vic's shop in the distance down the road, and work would be back on our minds. Eddie pulled Penelope up to the curb in front of Vic's, and we both got out under the store's tattered canopy.

"He's got someone inside. We should wait until they leave." Eddie bargained, trying to put off the encounter just a few more minutes. I was more than willing to oblige him that much. "So, I'll go in first and talk to him? If everything's good I'll just come right back out. If not, I'll nod and you come in. O.k.?"

It sounded reasonable enough. I had offered him that. I only nodded my head in approval of his plan, and hoped that the former would be the case. The more I thought about having to delete Vic, a man I had never met, the more my stomach churned in disagreement with the thought, and the happier I was about giving Vic the extra time.

That happiness vanished when the door opened, and a young woman exited the market. She saw Eddie and immediately smiled at him and him to her, but she only hurried her stride as she acknowledged my presence. I was always used to that kind of thing happening. I assumed that the city had realized what I was, and that thought disgusted me further.

"I'm going in. Remember, I'll nod. O.k.?" Eddie explained again, and again I nodded. He walked through the half-glass door and into the market. Through the top of the door, I could only see Eddie approaching the counter. He was his usual charismatic self. I let out a sigh as I waited for any signal. Then, I turned and evaluated my surroundings.

I didn't recognize this part of the slums as much, and rightfully so, there wasn't a lot to it. The buildings at the end of the streets were abandoned, and from the looks of the others, they were too; except for one. I hadn't noticed until then, but we were being watched from a building across from us. It was normal. People in the Slums were very curious, especially when citizens came into their part of the city. It wasn't our place. It was a totally different society here; one where we weren't liked, and one where we didn't belong.

When I turned back to the door, Eddie's hands were in the air and he was nodding desperately. I had missed the signal. I pulled my shocker from its holster and rushed through the doorway.

Inside, Vic stood behind the counter holding a light rifle at Eddie. Upon my appearance, the light rifle then turned to me. Vic was a man in his late thirties, but time had gotten to him a little. He held the light rifle with shaky hands, clenching his teeth and narrowing his brows. It was obvious that he got the weapon from a local thug, and didn't really know how to use it.

"You! Suit-boy, get the hell out of my shop!" He yelled, and spit flew from his angry lips.

"He's with me Vic." Eddie said carefully, trying not to provoke the man any more than he already was. "We just need to ask you some questions." Eddie directed Vic's attention back towards him, and the tip of the light rifle followed.

"Questions my ass! I haven't seen you in months Brinnigin, and now you and your Paragon crony come into my store. Don't think I don't know who you are, mister, and what you two do." The man shouted, and Vic's temper was starting to flare as his grip on the weapon stayed firm. "Just leave my store now, and you can leave without the glowing orange holes in your chest."

Protocol dictated that threats were to be handled with force. Normally, I would have already acted. Normally, Vic wouldn't have been able to finish the threat.

"Put down the weapon." I commanded in a monotone voice. I already didn't like where this was going.

"Vic really, we just want some answers." Eddie tried pleading for conversation, again.

"You want answers. Fine. Yeah, I owe Paragon some creds. Creds those tyrannical bastards won't ever get to see. I'd rather make deals with the street punks any span of the week than give my hard earned money back to those evil bankers." Vic's words came out furious, and he adjusted the light rifle in his hands for grip and intimidation. "So you boys can just leave now, and go tell whatever evil shithead boss you have that I said that."

He finished by cocking the weapon and loading in a charge round. Any next second could cost someone their life. It just didn't make sense. It was all so unnecessary.

"Put the weapon down, now!" I demanded again, this time I moved toward the man to bring his focus back to me; the light rifle followed. Eddie didn't need to be in the line of fire. He was only trying to save the man's life, and this is how this man has chosen to repay him?

"Vic. Point the weapon at me... Vic." Eddie pleaded, but I didn't understand why he kept trying to keep the attention on him. Eddie didn't even have any defense. His shocker was still in its holster. "Vic, this man is going to shoot you if you keep pointing that hole-punch at him."

Vic laughed for a second, and then looked at Eddie like he was a fool. "You think your boy over there can raise his zapper, and put one in me before I can squeeze this trigger? Paragon has given you too much confidence, and they ain't gonna be around forever, kid." Vic said hollow as he ended his laugh. He then returned his attention back to me, and aimed his eye down the barrel. "Now this is the last time I'm going to tell you."

There wasn't going to be any way to convince Vic to put the light rifle down. He had already made up his mind about Paragon, and apparently when to pay his debt to them; which was going to be never. I understood now, why this job had been turned over to me and Eddie. Vic had probably tried the same thing on one of Ryne's team members, and instead of dealing with Vic, they knew they could just as easily give us the job without argument from Marcus.

Marcus hated anyone who disavowed Paragon, calling it '*treason*'. It was sad that this man's life was going to be thrown away over credits, and confusion about Paragon's direction.

I wished I didn't have to delete him, but now he had given me no choice. I couldn't just kick the job up to another department. I was the end of the line.

"I am sorry." I said to Vic, but under my breath. His eyebrows raised curiously, as I apologized for actions I had not yet taken, but I wanted him to know that I didn't want to take. I wanted to apologize to him for the fact that we couldn't just leave the store like he wanted, and for Paragon and the pain the company had brought him. I was sorry that it hadn't been the other way, where Eddie and I could have just let him go. Mostly, I wanted to apologize for taking his life; something that was precious and irreplaceable. Something that, once I had taken it; I could never return. My finger slid around to the trigger of my shocker, and in an instant my arm raised. My shocker pointed to his face. The speed at which I had done so, clearly scared the man, and his hands fumbled with his weapon. The flash enveloped the store, for what felt like minutes, and I watched as my bolt cut through the air traveling for his skull. It was the impact that made time return to normal, and blood spattered across the wall behind the counter. Vic's head snapped backwards, a hole seared through his forehead, and his body collapsed onto his knees.

"Shit!" Eddie shouted in shock. He had stopped watching me complete our assignments after a bad incident with a Dox-4 manufacturer, and I guessed he still didn't have the stomach for it. I re-holstered my shocker as I watched Eddie's expression. The shock seemed to wear-off, after a moment. "Awe, damnit Vic." He sulked, as he rounded the counter to check on the man's corpse. "Yep, he's dead." Eddie called back to me morosely from the floor as he rose back to his feet.

"Right between the eyes." He patted me on the shoulder as he walked to the freezers in the back. He opened one of the drinks and poured it into his flask, then grabbed a stick of dried meat jerky from a shelf as he made his way back to me. "Well, that's that." He said calmly. I remained looking at the dead man behind the counter. His body laid still, almost mangled looking, on the floor. His legs and arms bent, and the light rifle still in his hand. I gasped internally in horror of what I'd done. It was the first time I had felt shame.

"Let's get out of here." Eddie spouted, and we walked back outside. Eddie pulled a gasper from his pocket and put it into his mouth. He stopped under the store's awning, pulled out the keys to Penelope, and threw them into my hands.

"What's this?" I asked him, looking down at keys I had never held before.

"Com her." Was all that he answered. His tone was calm, and he was serious. He never let anyone touch Penelope, let alone, drive her.

"What?" It was enough that I needed more clarity, so I asked again.

"Pretty-dress. Com her, take her out, and use Penelope. Have fun. You know fun, right?" He lectured at me. I didn't understand why, or what had changed in Eddie just then. He seemed relaxed and didn't show me any blame for what I had just done. Instead, it was more like he pitied me. "You need it, brother."

I gripped the keys hard enough to feel their teeth gnawing at my palm. I thought of Vic, his face, and the hole that now resided there. It had already started to haunt me, but I didn't see how a girl would change that. I didn't see how I could change any of it.

"I don't understand." I told him, and he paced back and forth with the gasper hanging from his lips.

"Look Alpha, I don't pretend to know what goes through your head after something like that, but what I do know is that you need a break from it. You need some fun, or something to give you some escape from all of this. You need to com her." He explained, and he was right. I don't know how he knew that I had more on my mind than usual, but I left it at him just being good with people.

My thoughts were uneasy as it all replayed in my head. Not just the parts I had chosen to see, but the entire memory. The bolt as it was hitting Vic; his eyes rolling back into his head, and his life leaving his body. It was almost unbearable to remember, and I finally understood why Eddie was in shock for that moment afterwards. I had been blocking out these murders. I knew that now. I was *killing* people for Paragon. It was that simple. I was murdering them.

I wasn't just taking their lives and deleting them. I was stealing their existence. I wanted more than this life, and I wanted to be more than just a murderer. I wanted to know if there was more to have than just an assignment and regrets.

She was the answer, and I think Eddie knew that.

"What if she doesn't answer?" I asked.

Eddie smiled as he pressed the smoking tube between his lips. "She will." He insisted.

I trusted Eddie. He was good with people.

MORNING STAR

Through the glass, the sun became brighter as the glow began to fill the sky. She laid next to me, still sleeping, as my jacket shielded her from the dusty earth below.

The dirt hill.

The morning held hope, and I could see a need for it at last. Now, Krill's argument with me about Estelle, his anger for my assignment, and his need for hope all seemed to become clearer with the rising sun. I embodied the destroyer of what he cherished so dear, and I had been letting him down. I've never understood the connection I have with Dorian. Not so much what the connection is, but why. He is the only person in my life that has no explanation, but has always been there. My earliest memories are of him, but even he denied meeting me until almost six years ago when he was assigned to be my personal physician.

"Only the best for Paragon's elite."

He had once told me. Still, this vague need for his approval had always haunted my conscience. As far as people go, he's the most decent I had ever met, and his influence is probably playing a part in my mind's inner-war.

As I sat looking at her, watching her sleep, I felt I had found some peace. The assignments seemed so far away, like a distant memory of a former life that came to an end with little more than a smile; her smile. I couldn't imagine taking it away from her. I couldn't imagine telling her what I would, no doubt, eventually have to tell her; that I am a monster. I had come so close that previous night, but couldn't ruin the moment with little details about a life that I will no longer be partaking in. I would quit. All the thoughts I'd been having, and the confusion about my role in Paragon's order had all been weighing on me; the Vic assignment especially. It was unwarranted murder that I had committed, and I did it in the name of order.

As I gazed upon her, I wondered if she would see it that way. She was from the slums, and Paragon wasn't well liked in the slums, but tolerated out of need and poverty. With that thought, I was on my feet, and careful not to wake her. It was still early, and I had grown accustomed to sleeping less than everyone else. For a moment, I froze as I looked around and remembered my surroundings; the grass, the barrier, the old building not too far off in the distance. It was a paradise. I had never had a thought that I hadn't planned, but now I found myself wandering aimlessly through the green field of tall grass, and making headway towards the old structure. My head was clearing, as I left her, and thoughts of leaving Paragon had manifested Eddie's voice inside my head.

"You're crazy. It's suicide. You want to die, buddy?"

He would be right. I knew Marcus. I knew our assignments and what I did for Paragon. They wouldn't just let me live a happy life outside of all of those things. For me, there's no such thing as a happy life.

The wooden doorway to the old building was rotted and falling off the hinges. The architecture was old and it gave off a pre-migration era feel. The city didn't have many wooden structures left, and this one seemed to have been forgotten along with the place that surrounded it. An absent-minded curiosity sent me through the threshold of the old building. It was only two stories, but wide with wooden floors that spanned several hundred square feet. It was empty; except for a few tattered rugs, and the dust that had collected on the floor; probably blown in from the dirt hill. The light danced in through the dust-darkened windows, and it gave the big room a strange majesty. The boards creaked as I walked across them, and in the corner I noticed light pouring in from a patch of broken wood along the wall, and in the center of the light was one small red flower; A single life living in the darkness. It was beautiful like something I had never seen, or hadn't seen, until yesterday. The only comparison I could make was to the girl who was still sleeping on my jacket atop the dusty hill.

I leaned down to inspect the flower closer, and decided that it would have to be hers. I carefully pulled the little wildflower out from the crack, and made my way back outside to the tall grass, wondering if she had ever seen this. She would be the only one that would know of its existence other than me, and that too reminded me of her. She was my wildflower.

The closer I came to the dirt hill and to her, the more my head became clouded with thoughts of her; her silky hair, her smooth alabaster skin, and her indelible smile. The memory of the previous night played in my head; watching the lights of the city, the sunset, and how perfect everything had been.

The perfection is what snapped me back into reality, and the fact I am a murderer for Paragon; a fact I couldn't ignore. No doubt, the promises I had made were in vain. I couldn't leave Paragon, Marcus would never allow it. Dorian had told me of how things had been before my recruitment, and the rebellion. Even if Marcus did let me leave, I couldn't let the city become that again. I was torn. I sat down on the small dirt hill next to her side, and watched as she slept peacefully without the knowledge of my worriment. Suddenly, her eyes began to flutter open to the new day, and it brought a smile to my face. I was in love with her, and I knew it. If there was anything I could be certain of, it was that.

"Good morning." Her soft voice crept out gently as she stretched. Her eyes met mine, and I could see a change in her. She was less guarded, and it put me at ease as well. I held the flower in my hand hiding it from her, but instead put out my other hand for her to take. She took my free hand with a smile, and I turned it over and placed the little red wildflower into her palm. Her smile beamed, and a sense of happiness surged through me.

"Good morning to you, too." The response came much easier than conversations from the day before. Now, everything seemed much more natural; more destined and easy, almost like the actions were programmed into me.

"It's beautiful." She soothed out, but my gaze was not detoured from her, as she was the same to me as she saw the flower, and in an instant the words came out.

"Almost the most beautiful thing I have ever seen." I told her, meaning every word, and had planned none of them. Her smile stayed, and her cheeks filled with the subtle rose color that I adored. She tried to hide them from me, but I adored that too.

She held the flower in her hand, the roots hung through the bottom of her grip, and that was when I realized it would die. I had pulled it from the earth, and took it from where it flourished. It wasn't like the rest of the flowers in the city. It wasn't in a grower's datalogue to be ordered up for arrangement; it had been special. Its beauty was natural, and grew in a place where only it could.

The thought meant more than the flower to me. It was a metaphor for what I was doing with her. I found her in the slums, flourishing, with an unequaled beauty and uniqueness. Now, my selfishness was pulling her towards me and out of her natural state. Out of her life, and into mine. It was a scary thought; a terrifying thought.

I picked my glasses up from the dirt next to her, wiped them free of the dust, and placed them back on my face.

I couldn't do this to her. I couldn't allow her to wind up in danger because of the life I had led, and no doubt she eventually would. The blood on my hands was too much, and there was a trail of it that led back to Paragon; back to Marcus. In an instant, I had made up my mind.

I would not involve her in my departure from the company. It would put her in more danger than I could prevent, and I only hoped that I hadn't already. I would have to leave her.

I would have to continue working for them until she wasn't a thought anymore, not to Eddie or Marcus, or anyone. Then I could leave, and not worry about her being part of Paragon's reprisal. Then, she would never have to know what I had done for them, and I could plant my roots in the slums.

Then, I could keep growing there; with her.

MINOR PENALTY

How was I going to explain this without taking a bolt to the head? Not only did I let Alpha off his leash, I had made no attempts to clean any of it up. That is exactly what Marcus would say, but if he knew that I was actually half-way encouraging Alpha, I'd be dead for sure. I'd have to think of something quick.

The transmission came in, over my datcom, only a few minutes earlier. Remy's snide little voice told me to head into the office with or without Alpha, and it would be without. I was still uncertain of what Alpha's epiphany had been back at the bar; whether he would complete the Estelle assignment or if he were out for good, and on the run with pretty-dress. I knew what the latter would mean. It would be a Manhunt. If that's what you could, technically, call it.It won't come to that, I'm sure. After seeing Alpha in action as much as I have, who knew if it would be a manhunt or just a bloodbath? Could Paragon even bring him back in if they wanted? How many lives would they waste trying?

That's not what this meeting was about, was it? It probably has something to do with the bomb that went off in the slums minutes ago; another riot patrol, another investigation, and another open assignment. Just another day at the office.

I pulled Penelope into the Garage, and saw Griff huffing and pounding his fists on the bed on Ryne's truck. I pulled in and parked, and watched the stout guy hammer his hands down on the truck, again and again. When my engine had stopped, I could hear him cursing. I got out and closed the door, and walked over to him, but before I got close the smell almost floored me. I knew the smell very well, but I would never get used to it; death.

"What the hell, Griff? Are there bodies in that truck?" I shouted, with one hand over my mouth and nose. The large man turned to me; his eyes were as hard as stone. His shoulders rolled back and he stiffened. His meaty hand shot out and grasped me at the shirt, wrenching it tight as his fingers closed, knotting the front into a bunch in his palm.

"What's it to you, hack?" He growled, violent and angry. His eyes squinted, and I could see something trigger in his mind, suddenly he recognized who I was. "This is all your fault, grifter!" His grip tightened as he chewed out the words. "You were supposed to keep an eye on him, keep him out of trouble..." I could feel him shaking as his forearm twisted like a nest of snakes, clinching his hand tighter, as he pulled me closer. "...I should put you in the back of this truck with them."

In an instant, I felt my back slam hard against the truck and my head snapped to the side. Out of the corner of my eye, I could make out one of the metal pneumatic boots Ramone wore, but the tarp was wrapped over something much bigger than Ramone. I only guessed that since Griff was alive, that it had to be Ox under the tarp with him.

"Ramone...Ox? What the hell happened?" I muttered, in shock, as my mind raced to piece together what I had missed. Not many people in this city could take out a Section Seven member, let alone two. The explosion? Alpha. Was he implying that Alpha had done this? Shit.

"Like you give a cred. Maybe if you were doing your job, your buddy Alpha wouldn't be running around streets deleting his own people." He cried out, and the spit flew from his teeth as he spoke, and now his other hand grasped symmetrically at my collar, and I was being lifted off of the pavement.

"Wait...wait Griff...wait. This isn't my fault." I stammered out the lie. Of course it was my fault. I encouraged him to see the girl. I gave him the keys. I knew it could lead to this, whatever this was. "Griff..." My voice tried to free itself from the tightened clutches of the monstrous man in front of me, but he only squeezed harder, burning his eyes furiously into mine.

The world around started to become a blur, his face was just shades and hues all becoming out of focus. I started to feel faint, then suddenly, I was slammed against the truck again, and released. I slid back down the side of the truck, and found a seat on the concrete to catch my breath.

"You're right." He muttered out in a low growl. The pulsing in my ears started to fade, and I looked to Griff, who had turned away, thankful that he hadn't killed me. I guessed, he just needed a little sense talked into him. I was amused and relieved. He didn't say anything for the next few seconds while I recovered. When I did, I stood up and looked in the back of the pick-up once again, only this time to inspect the bodies. I lifted the tarp. "We pissed him off, and this is what happened. He said he didn't want to fight...He said he was going to *Kill* all of us."

Griff's voice was much calmer and much more monotone, like he was replaying the events in his mind and reading them back to me, in horror.

"Why?" I didn't understand. I knew Alpha, and I knew he wouldn't delete a citizen without good reason, and this was worse. These were Paragon troops. "It doesn't make sense."

It didn't make sense. The wounds weren't made with a shocker. Ox had been beaten brutally by the looks of it, but both he and Ramone had light rifle wounds.

"We asked for it." I could hear the guilt he felt in his words, "Boss said it would give us the best tactical advantage against a foe with unknown potential, but he didn't think this would happen. Marcus was pressuring him to get results; told us to take whatever measures necessary." He continued in the low dull voice that droned on, but he suddenly paused and looked at me blankly; the stupidest blank look.

"What did you do?" I asked in an angry tone, that let him know that I knew something was off with their little plan. This was unbelievable, but now the story was unfolding in my head. Ryne would've had to have gone back to Marcus with the information I had given him, and knowing Marcus, he would've given Ryne orders to try to delete Alpha.

It was a sick thought that I knew had to be the truth, but I still didn't get the whole *tactical advantage* part. The big man took a gulp of air, and exhaled with a sigh.

"We took the girl as bait." He admitted solemnly. The air went silent and I was torn. I felt the thumping of my heart in my ears, as I hypothesized different scenarios.

"We lured him into a trap hoping he would try to rescue her, and we were right. We set charges in some of the old buildings down the street." He continued to explain. They were responsible for the explosion in the slums; not a band of activists or the thugs or punks, but Paragon. My division even. His voice became dull background noise as my imagination pieced together the events that had occurred, and I searched my feelings.

My hand slid inside my jacket, and unhooked the clasp that held in my shocker. Thoughts of them kidnapping that innocent girl, and what they might have put her through, raced through my mind. Then, my friendship with Alpha and the dedication that comes with it. As my arm extended, I thought of the city, humanity, and what it all was supposed to be for.

A quick flash of light, and a spatter of blood smacked the wall of the garage. The sound echoed, like a brilliant electric crackle. Griff's body stood for split-seconds, until slowly toppling over onto the pavement. I steadied myself and holstered my weapon, feeling my flask in my inside pocket with a shaky hand. This was a time to stay sharp, but the stiffness was starting to set-in. If I didn't dox, I couldn't do what I needed to; put that moron in the back of Penelope. I had to be in that meeting in a couple minutes.

I couldn't think straight. I pulled out the flask and my last *packer*. I swallowed and in seconds, the dull surroundings had become alive and bright; the red blood was vibrant on the pavement. *Alex!* I thought to myself. He owed me one, and it was time to collect. I couldn't use my datcom to contact him. It would be traceable. I'm sure Ryne would wonder where his last moron went. He might try to track Griff's adjacent signatures. My only hope was that Alex was still in the building. I hooked my hands under the giant shoulders of Griff's new corpse, and slid him to Penelope. My stomach started to churn at the thought of Griff's raunchy corpse on sweet Penelope's leather seats, but I couldn't spare her. He was too large to fit in the trunk.

I folded Griff's legs into the back of the car, and stuffed him in closing the door. I was thankful for the dark tint on the windows; no one would notice a large ex-shock ball player's body in there. Now, I just had to get to Alex. I made my way into the garage lift, and took it down to the lab. It would look strange that I had entered the lab first, but by the time the security sweep had noticed, I would probably already be dead anyway.

The doors slid open, and to my surprise the lab was almost empty. A few techs stood around checking gauges and blinking lights, or whatever it is those smart-type guys usually did.

"Looking for me?" Alex's voice came from a bench against the wall, and I turned, relieved to hear it.

"You don't know how glad I am that you're still here!" I exclaimed, probably seeming overly enthusiastic. My adrenaline kicked back in, and the immediate need to salvage my situation.

"You haven't been upstairs, yet?" His eyebrow lifted, and he stood up. "So, you haven't seen them?" The new Proto Sapiens... That's what this meeting was about.

"He woke them up?" I asked as an eerie hollow turned my stomach. My surroundings began to make sense. This was merely the clean-up shift. I had missed the big ceremony. I tried not to smirk, as I thought of a giant switch with Marcus tugging at the lever, which dropped a curtain. Now he would want to put them on display. The pieces started fitting together better now. The arrival of these Proto Sapiens, the distrust of Alpha, and the Doc's escape all now seemed so perfectly synchronized. The Doc had known for far longer than he had let on, about what Marcus had in mind.

"Only a few minutes ago, actually." Alex's attitude was less than desirable. He talked in almost mutters that were barely discernible as sentences. "I just pushed a few buttons, and woosh, the doors slid open and then their eyes..." His face tried to mimic that of the creepy Proto Sapien awakening. I didn't have time to listen to him ramble.

I had gotten lucky with my timing, and if my luck continued, I could be upstairs in that meeting in minutes, while Alex cleaned the rest of Griff off the parking garage. I grabbed Alex by the shoulders and shook him to bring back his focus.

"Listen, I need you to go out to the parking garage." I said as I tossed my keys to him, something I would never normally do. His quizzical look told me he knew that, too. "Griff is in the back. I had to delete him." I explained plainly, and Alex partially snapped out of his catatonic state with a moderate amount of alarm.

"What! Why?" He asked in shock. Alex never liked the idea of deletion. He was more like the professor in that area.

"I can't explain that right now, but I need you to get rid of him and the mess outside before anyone notices him missing. I have to be in Marcus' office soon, or it will look suspicious." I told him, leaning myself into his side of his little revolution. Alex pushed up his glasses in moderate defiance.

"And just what do I do with him?" He asked sternly. He wasn't pleased, but at least he was willing.

"Take Penelope and head to Kagan. Tell him you have a normal drop-off from Eddie. He will know what to do from there." I explained, and it seemed a bit morbid to have a guy for this type of thing. Alex only nodded in disdain, and we both stepped into the lift. The door dinged open, just as quick as it had closed, and Alex was in the parking garage. It didn't take him long to see the mess that I had made.

"At least, it's just a small radial spatter." Alex assured me with some sarcasm. He looked back with doubt on his face as the lift doors began to close, again.

"You got this!" I smirked, high and happy that everything was working out just as I had hoped. As long as no one interrupted Alex, Griff would just disappear. It wasn't uncommon in this city, a lot of people disappeared, or seemed to. I knew where they went and it was the same place Griff was going; down the Drain. At the bottom of the Drain was a facility for garbage dumping, a furnace of sorts that vented out of the dome. That's where bodies were taken for disposal.

The lift dinged once more, and ended my thought process. The doors slid open and my focus was back on the meeting. I didn't have time to ask Alex about the Proto Sapiens, but he didn't seem too happy, so they must be operational. That's a scary thought.

The long corridor to the office passed too quickly. Before I knew it, I was walking into the big office and being greeted by Marcus' hollow voice as it boomed through the dimly lit space.

"Ah, welcome Mr. Brinnigan, come in." He commanded from behind his desk. Then, I noticed Ryne's surprise. He postured himself upright, and quickly wiped any emotion from his face. He obviously wasn't happy to see me, not that he'd ever been.

I quickly filed in next to him in front of Marcus' desk. Alpha's absence didn't go unnoticed, but it didn't seem unexpected.

"Well, it seems we're all here, so let's begin." Marcus' words were snide and unnerving as he spoke, "Eddie, where are we on the Estelle assignment?" A smile ran across his face, and a chill ran up my spine. I didn't have an answer, at least not one that he would like to hear.

"The job is still open." I replied hesitantly. The air in the room became stale, and I began to feel less and less comfortable in the ensuing silence.

"I see." Marcus wasn't pleased. "And what of Alpha? Anything new to report?" Marcus seemed like he was toying with me, and asking me questions to which he knew the obvious answers. His ego was never a hard read. "Still absent, I suppose?" He asked coyly. I knew I couldn't let him know I was responsible, but there wasn't a way around it. I would have to confess to needing a break from Alpha. It would be a risky excuse, and I didn't know how Marcus would respond. Without Alpha, my necessity to Paragon was very minimal. Before being indentured to him, I was little more than an errand boy for Paragon elites.

"I know that he is, Eddie. You are not the only one with more information than people assume." He exposed and I gulped. How much did he know? "Have you heard from him? He has removed his datcom, and disappeared into the slums due to Ryne's miscalculation." Marcus continued.

This was my chance. I could use Ryne's mistake to try to turn the attention back to him. They didn't know that I ran into Griff downstairs. That he had told me every stupid detail of Ryne's failed attempt to capture Alpha. They didn't know that my right hand held Griff's shaking retribution.

"Miscalculation? Ryne miscalculated something? I'm sure that's not what happened, is it, big guy?" I mocked a grin out of the side of my face at the merc. It was almost too simple. "Something to do with the explosion I heard in the slums earlier?"

I shot a condescending glance to the disgruntled soldier who only sneered off my visual attack, but it did not go unnoticed to Marcus either, who was buying the whole cow.

"It isn't important." Marcus shot out in obvious contempt. As evil as he was, Marcus still wouldn't condone the actions taken by Ryne; whatever the reasons. I knew that, and I used it to turn any resentment he felt for me losing Alpha back to Ryne, hoping to push Marcus to continue on, without reprisal at me. For now, it had worked. Marcus cleared his throat, and pushed the button on his desk that opened the oversized blinds that covered his window to the city.

As the light poured through, three silhouettes were left standing behind him, and then he stood very ominously. The three figures moved forward, and the light from his desk illuminated their pale faces. Each of them held only a slight variation from the others. They all wore sleek tinted glasses, and uniform paragon long-jackets with suits under them.

"Let me introduce you to the newest members of Section Seven; XO-One, XO-Two and XO-Three. Their names are their designations and level of authority. A new form of executive rank." Marcus sneered with some delight. The men had a creepy presence about them; cold and detached.

It reminded me of the first time I had met Alpha. Only, the way these men stood held an obvious obedience. An obedience only to Marcus. Ryne stood straight and still, but his eyes studied them. He was not impressed, but I was terrified.

If these three things were anything like Alpha, and Marcus could control them, the city would enter a new era of fear; starting with the death of Estelle. I could see that future clearly, for the first time.

Marcus' future.

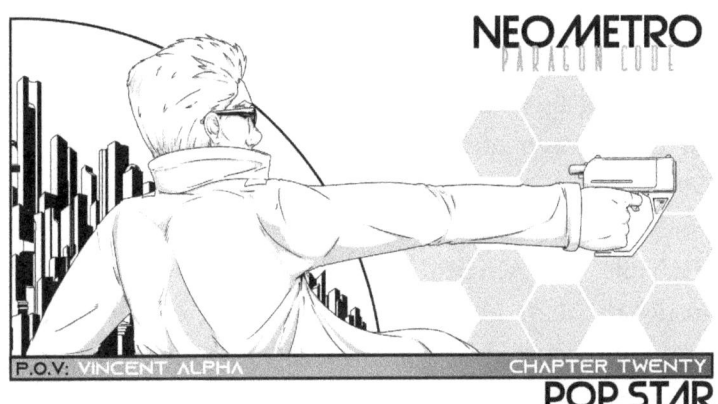

POP STAR

Eddie's words of warning rang through my head, and I had choices to make. Marcus wasn't going to like my sudden change in career plans, and finishing the Estelle job was out of the question. I couldn't imagine hurting her. If she and Estelle were close, I really would be the monster she saw this morning.

I couldn't be that. Marcus would have to wait. The slums were calling me back; back to her. I had to find her and make sure she'd be safe. Marcus was serious about the Estelle job, and Ryne's admittance into yesterday's briefing was proof of that. He was sending more than just me to make sure this job was done, and that puts her in the crossfire. I'd have to protect her. As I exited through the doors of the Ganymede, I noticed a Paragon labeled transport sitting in the lot across the street. All of Paragon's vehicles were wired to start with the wristport system, and Eddie would be all too happy to see Penelope again.

I couldn't take that from him. So, I climbed into the old transport, tapped my wrist to the dash, and it came to life.

I was on my way to the slums. My only thoughts were to find Lexxi or Estelle. To warn them about Paragon's vigilance, and to keep Lexxi safe. Then, I thought of Estelle's safety as hers would come easier. All I would have to do was keep her from playing the concert and keep her out of Paragon's sight for a while. The rain pelted the maintenance truck as I barreled through the alleys and streets of the slums. It wouldn't take long to get back to their apartment building. That's when I remembered that I was in the maintenance transport, and that the Paragon logo was on the side. It would stick out in the slums, just like I did.

I cut the wheel, and I traveled down the Main. I would have to lose the truck if I were going to approach Estelle or the old apartment complex. The people would have it ripped apart, and dismantled within minutes of me parking it. Not for its value, but just on principle. They disliked Paragon, and damaging company property was their only real retribution. I parked in a lot down the street from the old apartment. I went over in my mind what I would say as I stopped the odd van in place. The engine whirred an electric hum as it idled. I sat, looking down the road to the old building. I thought for a moment that if I did finish the Estelle assignment, like Eddie had said, Lexxi would be safe. I could disappear with her, and Marcus would have gotten his kill. Maybe he would even leave us alone satisfied that I had saved his city, one last time.

I thought of her face at the end of that scenario, and the tears that would no doubt come from the loss of her friend. I had made her cry before, and it had felt painful, intolerably painful, but not in a physical way. It had put me at a loss for words that I hadn't felt before, a helpless sense that filled me with fear and dread. Krill had described the pain before. He had called it *empathy*.

I tapped the dash again, and the truck's mechanics began to cease, slow and quiet. I stepped out, and I could feel the eyes on me. This part of the slums was well populated, probably by people trying to be close to Estelle. It made sense that the population would localize around their symbol of hope. The rain pattered around me as I walked. I took the few steps that led under the building's awning and put my hand forward to buzz the com. Before my finger could make it to the pad, the door swung open, revealing Estelle. She wore a dress like I had never seen, and her beauty almost rivaled that of Lexxi's; only artificially. It was the decorations and the make-up products that did most of the work for her.

"Excuse me, can I help you?" She said it in a tone that let me know I wasn't welcome, and I had guessed that she knew who I was. "If you're here to hurt her more, then you just wait right there. Benny will be here any moment. You can take it up with him."

My head fell towards my chest. She did know who I was. She knew that it was my fault that Lexxi hurt, and that she felt the pain that I had caused by not telling her the truth when I should have.

"No, I didn't come to hurt anyone." I could barely muster a voice to speak with. The way she looked at me, was something I'd never felt. Her eyes peered down at me, wide and deliberate.

"Then, what the hell do you want?" the tall blonde demanded. I could barely give an answer. I didn't know why I felt this way, and it was starting to make me angry. I thought of the woman in front of me, staring disapprovingly at me with wild eyes.

"I just need to talk to Lexxi." I explained as calmly as I could, and her foot tapped on the stoop below.

"You can say whatever you want to me, and I'll give her the massage." She offered, and my mind stuttered. There were so many things to say to both of them; Lexxi and Estelle. "Well, I'm waiting..." Her foot seemed to pound into the stoop as my eyes kept fixed on the ground in front of me. I wasn't able to look at her through the shame I felt, and what I would have to tell her. The rain beat down around the awning, keeping us from silence.

"I love her." It explained everything, and I didn't know what else to say.

"Sure you do...They all do. You got a little taste, and you just want the next bite, is all. Get one thing straight, Paragon boy...Lexxi ain't the type of girl you can just get your fix on. Just because she's not a civi doesn't mean she's gonna get used, and I'll see to that!" Her voice scolded hard, and the words seemed like knives in my chest.

Had I been insincere? How do you put love into words? My mind raced to come up with the answer, as I lifted my eyes back up towards Estelle.

"Then, just tell her I'm sorry." I soothed out in defeat. Estelle sighed, and unfolded her arms.

"You'll have to tell her yourself. She left a few minutes ago. She didn't even say a word because she was so broken up about whatever you two go into." Her foot stopped pounding, and she began to take a step forward to come down towards me, but I stopped her by pulling out my shocker. I held it in my hand, but kept it pointed at the ground. She quickly stepped back into place, confused most likely "What!? I'm telling you, she's not here!"

I shook my head to let her know that Lexxi wasn't the reason I had pulled my weapon. Thoughts of finishing the assignment played in my mind, as well as, the thoughts of Lexxi's sadness.

"I'm supposed to *kill* you." I told her in a small whisper. She gasped, but calmed pretty quickly. The silence continued for a moment, as I thought of Lexxi, Paragon, and our happy life afterwards. Estelle's eyebrows raised.

"Well then, go ahead and do it. What are you waiting for?" Her voice asked low and plain, holding a hint of fear and something else. It was as if she knew this moment would come, whether by me or someone else, and she was ready to die.

"I can't." I told her, and her eyes widened, as did mine.

"What?" She asked as plainly as she had before. I steadied my hand, gripping the weapon tighter. It was a lie, I could. The instrument in my hand would make it all too easy, but the truth was, I didn't want to. I just didn't want to take another life, ever again.

"I mean, I won't do it; not for them. You're too important to her. I can't see her cry, not again." I explained to her.

At that moment, I felt a trickle travel down my cheek as I remembered Lexxi's pained face. It wasn't the rain, but instead it was something I had never felt before. My hand shook the little shocker, as my eyes squeezed shut, stopping any other tears that wanted to emerge. My body shook as I fought them.

The emotion had almost made me forget my surroundings, and that Estelle stood in front of me. I felt her hand as her palm touched my face, and in that instance, time froze and I could see it all. The past, the present, and the infinite future. I could see further back than my memories would take me, and I could see everyone in the city at that moment; who they were, what they did, and the lives they wanted. The future appeared the same.

It was as if I had somehow entered another dimension. I could see the world outside, both dead and barren, and full of green life. It was as if time had layers, and I could peel them all away.

"Do it now, Omar!" I heard a woman's voice call out from beyond the folds. Suddenly, a young man appeared in front of me. He had a familiarity about him that I couldn't understand.

"You sure, he can't see me?" he asked, but not to me, instead to someone I couldn't make out behind him. I could see him; however, his hair fell down to his cheeks, holding a strange bluish-black tint, and his eyes held a strange focus..

"We won't be able to hold it open much longer, you have to do it, now!" The woman's voice yelled out again, from a place unknown to me.

Though I could see everything throughout time, and this young man, I still could not see the origin of the second voice.

"O.k. Hold on!" He said, and the young man placed his hand on my cheek in exactly the same location Estelle's had landed in the split seconds before. As he did, time and its folds began to unravel back onto themselves, until it had become linear again, and my perception of it, normal. Estelle's hand withdrew from my face. She began to giggle a little as she watched my expressions.

"You have a good heart. It would seem that I owe Lexxi an apology." She said with a smile. Had she seen everything that had just happened? Was she the cause? An old automobile sputtered through the rain towards us. "Well, if I'm free to go..." She asked with a beaming grin, but it wasn't a question. I could only nod in acknowledgement. Then, she made her way past me down the steps. "She's probably at the Zigg. She really likes that place." She continued into the rain as she popped open her umbrella, and made her way to the old car. A rough-looking man was driving, and I assumed it was her bodyguard, Benny, whom she had just mentioned.

I still couldn't speak as I watched the car roll away down the rainy street. I could only think of the moment she touched my face, and the weird vision I had seen. It was vague, and I had no idea what it meant. I thought of how familiar the young man looked, even though I hadn't ever seen him before, and his clothes were different than anything I had ever seen. It was as if he was from another time and place, altogether. My mind dwelled on it for minutes, before I began to think of my surroundings again, and the time I had wasted.

Time had instantly become an odd concept to me. I hadn't really given it much thought, but I had noticed that time seemed to move differently for everyone else. It wasn't until I reflected back, that I began to understand. My age, Eddie's age, they were the same, but I hadn't changed. He had started to get a few gray hairs and a couple wrinkles on his face, but I had not, and I became somewhat suspicious of that fact, and time itself. I made my way to the lower levels on foot. She would have been walking, and I would do the same. I had made it to the down ramp in moments, and the rain let up. This part of the slums was even more dilapidated than its above counterpart, but not nearly as bad as below. The Zigg was on this level, but I had never been there before. I started to become nervous in anticipation of seeing her again. How would I apologize for what I am? I had tried. I would have to tell her that I only wanted to keep her safe. That Paragon would come after her because of my actions, and that I was her only hope, if that was any hope at all. People peered from their windows, watching me walk down the main of the second tier. I stuck out even more, here. Above, the buildings were vacant. A lot of the slum population had retreated to the lower levels to avoid Paragon.

Kids were playing in an alley as I passed, but they quickly froze upon seeing me. Their eyes followed as I disappeared around the corner. Then, a strange noise came from behind me, a rapid metal on metal sound that seemed almost mechanical.

"Hey, monster..." A hand tapped my shoulder. I turned, but saw no one.

"Are you looking for your little girlfriend?" I turned again, and Ramone stood in front of me. He was one of Ryne's crew. His face was scarred worse than Ryne's, and his curled hair hung down into his eyes. He was smiling at me. He had meant Lexxi by his question. It wasn't a good thing for Ryne, or Section Seven, to know about her. I had to assume Eddie had been talking. Ramone's pneumatic feet bounced as he shifted his weight back and forth from one to the other. He was keeping a pace, one that was ready to run. It was what he did.

"Where is she?" I growled angrily. I knew that his appearance only meant one thing. She wasn't at the Zigg.

"Oh that's funny. You think you care about her." His feet continued to bounce as he laughed. "Well, just how fast are you?"

In a blink, Ramone had dashed down the street about fifty feet. He was far faster than any normal person. I knew that, and he was trying to make me clearly aware of the fact.

"You think you can keep up? For her?" He yelled down the alleyway. I pulled my shocker to slow him down, but before I could aim, he was gone.

I began to chase after him. As I rounded the corner, I could see him standing on the main, waiting for me. His shocker had been pulled from its holster. I raised my arm to take aim once again, and again, he disappeared down another alleyway. I pursued him again, but as I got to the alley where he had vanished, the kids who were playing all ran out screaming as they passed me. All except for one. Ramone held him by the shirt.

"Oh, monster wants to play?" he said as he dug his shocker into the boy's face.

"Let him go!" I yelled through the alley, and my voice echoed. It had scared both the kid, and Ramone. I didn't raise my weapon out of fear of the boy getting harmed. I walked cautiously towards both of them. "I said let him go!"

The boy squirmed in Ramone's grip, but Ramone only tightened it, grinning wildly. Then, he pulled up his shocker and fired into me. A pain seared through me as the charge round sliced across my shoulder. I grimaced, and raised my shocker and fired into the brick wall beside Ramone's face. The dust and debris blasted into him, making him release the kid.

"Run kid!" I howled, and the boy made his way to me, and then kept going. Ramone regained himself, and laughed. He was having fun with me.

"You want the girl, murderer, you're going to have to catch me." He said, and then Ramone sped out of the other end of the alley. I could hear his metal legs clanging against the street as he turned back onto the main, towards the ramp.

I thought about time, and the sound his feet made on the pavement. It was rhythmic, and changed in volume, the closer and further from me he had gotten. I could use that to my advantage, since keeping up with him had become visually difficult. When I came out of the alley, he was at the bottom of the ramp; bouncing from one leg to the other. I aimed the shocker, and fired, but the distance had given him time to dodge. I started to run towards him.

"Come on, monster..." he taunted me. The clanging of his metal feet made their way up the ramp, and out to the upper tier as I followed. I gritted my teeth and pushed my legs harder than I ever had before. The distant noise of his metal became closer. I was making up space between us. The buildings around me became a blur as I ran. It must have been how Ramone had always seen the city.

Ramone's face spread wide in shock, when he looked back to see me on his heels. I pulled up my shocker to take aim. It would be difficult to calculate at this speed, and before I could, he had varied his trajectory. The city went by at a tremendous pace, but it started to become familiar. I was there just yesterday. The last place I had deleted anyone, '*Vic's*' was coming up ahead of us. It reminded me of what it felt like to murder someone. It reminded me of the difference in that, and what I was doing now. I was going to find Lexxi, and change everything.

I took aim down the sights of the shocker. In only seconds I would put a bolt into the back of Ramone and get answers from him. What was this game he was playing? Why did they have Lexxi? What in the world was going on?

Then, a loud boom filled the air. The ground started to give way from under me, and I began to fall. Above me, I could see the buildings of the slums toppling towards the ground; ground that I was falling through. My arm stretched, and my hand grasped a piece of rebar that jutted out from under the nearly destroyed street. Debris and rubble pelted me as it made its way to the tier below. Then, I watched as it destroyed that level, its buildings and people, and continued downward. They would have never seen it coming. They were all crushed by the buildings from above. I was fortunate that my speed had taken me to the edge of the blast, and that I wasn't at the epicenter of the explosion.

The dust made a cloud that would shield my ascent back up topside. I pulled hard on the rebar, and shot myself up and out of the hole, landing behind some adjacent rubble. I could see Ramone through the dirt. His legs had stopped bouncing. He was looking for me, to make sure that I hadn't remerged.

They had tried, extravagantly, to *kill* me.

I felt light in his arms. The lightest I had ever felt. I could only smile at how stern his face looked, as he carried me down the street through the pouring rain. The smoke billowed from the crevice in front of us, and the slums were separated now. We would have to make a big loop around to get back to the other side.

"I still have my legs, you know." I smiled. I couldn't let him carry me the whole way, although I was sure he would try. His hard demeanor hadn't let up. "Come on, I think you scared them all pretty bad. They're not following us, and I'm fine now. Let me down." He paused in his steps, and let me down gently. I dusted the debris from my dress.

"I'm sorry." He said it as stern as he looked, but I could tell he meant it. I just didn't know what he was sorry for. I had to take the blame. It was my fault I hadn't listened when he tried to warn me.

"I am too, you know." I assured him. His shoulders pulled back, and his chin came up.

"It is all my fault." He said blankly. He continued to walk down the Main, and I followed. His exterior was cold, and deadly. It only upset me more that he didn't seem more happy to see me. The rain poured down like a million tiny knives.

"Oh, my day? Thanks for asking. It was pretty interesting, actually." I found that the sarcasm crept out easily after everything I had just gone through, and he stopped abruptly.

"We have to get you somewhere safe." He insisted. His stare held a strange and ominous warning, and ended my need for banter. I could only nod with eyes like perfect eggs, I'm sure. Then, he returned to his brisk pace.

"I'm just glad I'm not deleted...psh." I stated, as I attempted to blow a hair out from in front of my face, but the rain had stuck it to my forehead.

"That word means nothing." He said, as he marched onward. "A fancy phrase that Paragon used to use to commit murder." The way he said it made it sound as if the past tense was a recent development. His way of telling me that he was leaving them.

"Used to?" I asked, and he turned back to me again, back-pedaling effortlessly in the rain.

"Don't you understand? They just tried to *delete* me!" He said angrily with intent. I continued to follow him, until he stopped suddenly at a corner, turning his head to look down an alleyway. He held up his hand to have me stop, and then motioned his hand for me to be quiet. I leaned against the brick next to him so I could see down the alley. A car was sitting idle with a group of gang members sitting around it.

"Stay here." He motioned for me to stay, and nodded slightly. It was gentle and cautionary. His eyes connected with mine, but this time they weren't fierce. I nodded and pursed my lips tight to motion my silence. He began to walk down the alleyway. A gangly kid covered in an odd-looking type of moldy and worn leathers began to approach Vincent.

"What are you looking for, suit? Couple scars to take back to the civilized world. You'd look really cool, then, huh?" The kid asked, and I found it ironic. One of the punks crawled out from behind a dumpster, behind Vincent, and the car's brake lights came alive.

"I just need the car." Alpha's voice was almost too low for me to hear in the distance. One of the hooligans began to laugh and howl.

"Looks like he's a funny man. Funny, he didn't look like a funny man!" The scrawny gang member bellowed out. Vincent postured slightly, raising his right arm as a sign of peace. His left went into his jacket pocket, and the gang members all twitched and froze.

"Now, I'm sure we can come to some kind of arrangement. A heap like that's worth what, ten thousand?" Vincent's left hand returned, full of credit coins.

"We don't want your money, company man!" one of the other gang members shouted. Suddenly, all the doors on the sedan opened, and out crawled three more members of the troupe. With the appearance of the new members, I could tell that they all wore matching leather uniforms, and painted their faces in similar green and black skulls.

"You think you can just buy off the green death? You think we'll just bow to the man whenever he comes around demanding our shit?" The punk shook out spit as he spoke. "Mister corporate, suit and dumb-ass tie, thinking 'I'm sly', bout to get his ass cut like rehomiginized wheat loaf!" He laughed and cackled as he called out.

The man behind Alpha pulled out a blade as long as my forearm. He began to lunge at Alpha from behind, but as he stepped forward, Alpha's right hand raised and flew backwards, smashing into the man's face. From where I stood, I could only see a spray of blood in every direction, and chunks of no telling what from the man's head. I could only imagine what the rest of his crew saw, as their mouths gaped open, horrified and disgusted; one man even vomited. The man's body fell to the ground like a bullet ricocheting into the dirt. It was almost comical. The rest of the men soon began pushing each other into the alley walls, trying to leave faster than the rest. It was as if they had run upon a snake, and thought it was a worm, and now they couldn't get away fast enough from their folly; leaving us their humming automobile.

I didn't look down at the fallen man as I walked to the car, and climbed into the passenger seat. Vincent was there waiting, his face still holding the same stern look, as he put the car into gear.

"Well, that was easy, huh?" My sarcastic statement sliced through the thin air of our newly acquired car, as we made our way towards the Main. "Did you just know he was going to jump out all 'stabby' like that?" I reenacted the motion the punk had made with the knife. I added in a few sound effects, as I mimicked Vincent's winning blow. He actually smiled.

"When he came out from behind the dumpster, his foot hit a box. I knew he was there. Then, I just listened to his footsteps in the puddles to calculate his distance away. From there, it was easy to predict his angle of attack." He explained, and I couldn't help but stare into him. Even as I studied him, I couldn't tell if he was taunting me back, or if he was serious about his confidently timed strategy. He compensated for things that no ordinary person imagined, and it reminded me of everything Krill had told me. Vincent wasn't ordinary by any stretch. As we drove, he held the wheel with the same precision he had the day before; correcting for every minor divot in the street. I realized now, that they were timed calculations; tactical decisions that guided us along the path he chose.

"Before I found you, I saw Estelle. She was leaving your apartment, but I still don't think it would be safe there." He explained, trying to think of places to hide me. I could barely make out an expression on his face, but what little he did show, said panic.

"There's an abandoned top floor. It has a lookout, with glass windows, almost invisible from the street below. Only Estelle and I know where the key is." I nodded with a smile, as I tried to help. Estelle used that room for something she called 'inspiration'. She would sit up there, and look out over the city as she wrote her songs. Sometimes, she would let me sit up there and listen, and watch the rain with her.

"They know you live there. Eddie said it was in her file. We'll have to find somewhere else for you to stay, while I go work everything out." he said, and I gasped. He was planning on leaving me again.

"But...where will you be?" My voice didn't want to make the journey across to him. I couldn't think of him leaving me after everything that had happened.

"I have to go make sure they don't follow us anymore. I have to show Marcus the truth." His tone was dark, but full of hope. It reminded me of the last place I had felt that kind of hope. The hope that the future holds when you're not alone, and I felt that hope at our dirt hill. I would be safe there in the old building.

"You know, you don't have to go back. We could stay in The Outskirts; at our hill beyond the grass." I offered, and I could see his eyes widened at the thought. His hands steered the old clunker towards one of the ramps to take us down a tier.

"It's perfect." he said almost as if he were thinking aloud, and the undercarriage scraped along the dusty pavement, sparks flew from the bottom of the car, and it felt like the thing would fall apart at any moment.

"Good! So, you're going to stay, too? We'll make rose tea, and watch the dust fly by." I soothed out sarcastically. His hand felt for the dash, and keyed the sound bar. Ironically, Estelle's latest song started to play. He was trying to avoid my question.

I let it play as we passed through the old district, not wanting to hear him reject my perfectly delightful plans.

As we entered the outskirts, we passed through the wall of rain, and headed for the tall grass. The car sputtered and died as he parked it at the barricade, and we got out.

He made his way through the tall grass, and to the top of the hill. I followed slowly behind, watching him, as he made the journey. The light poured in around him as he gazed through the glass, and the grass danced around my waste. As I became closer, he dashed to the glass wall, and pounded on it with his fist. It almost seemed as though I could see it vibrate as he hit it, but it must have been my imagination. It wasn't until I stood where he had, atop the hill, that I realized what he saw in the reflection of the glass.

A dark and evil city, gnawing up like giant teeth, distorted by the curvature of the dome. His shoulders heaved as he took deep breaths, and he paced around the little hill.

"We'll be safe here." I promised. While he saw the city's reflection, I could only see the beauty of our hill; our paradise.

"You don't know Marcus. He won't stop hunting me down." He said leaning against the glass, "Defying Paragon is punishable by deletion. It is protocol."

I always hated rules, and as far as rules go, that was a pretty stupid one. The thought of him leaving was torture, but the thought of him never returning was death.

"You can't go back, you're special." I shot out before I could understand what I was saying, and his eyes widened.

"Special!" He laughed, but not in a way that had made me happy, but an angry laugh that stopped short of rage. "Tell that to the guy whose face is still on the back of my hand."

He started to walk back through the grass, towards the old dead sedan. "You won't be safe. They will, eventually, find us." He called back over his shoulder, "Marcus has to be stopped; he has to pay for what he's done to this city. If not for you or me, but for Ox, and Ramone, Vic, Zane, and the rest of the people whose lives he's destroyed. Don't you see? He's tearing it all down. He's lost his compassion for the people; for humanity. He only sees Paragon."

His speech sent ominous chills down my spine. He had made it through the old barricade, and back to the car, opening its door.

"Your father, Dorian Krill; he said he made you to save the city." I shouted out, but the sedan growled angrily as it started up again. I watched as he reversed into the wall of rain, letting it cut the car down the middle, before turning back into the rainy city. I picked up a rock and threw it into the wet street beyond the small field, where the clunker had been.

I turned back, heading for the old tattered building. It wasn't far away; just a few hundred yards that I used to clear my head. The old door creaked as I entered, and dust flew into the air, but hung like it was suspended in time, until it slowly settled back onto the floor. The red daylight outside bled in through the windows. It felt like walking into a two-tone painting of red-orange and blacks.

In a far corner I could see a small crack in the wooden floor. There, a small bud crept out from below. I knelt down, and twisted the water from my hair onto what would soon be a new flower.

The building wasn't all that bad. It could have used some work in places, and maybe some curtains. I began to imagine what the future would look like there, with him.

Then, the old door creaked open wide, blowing in dust from the hill outside.

I reversed the old sputtering car, and watched as she stood in the tall grass on the other side of the barricade. At least there, she would be safe. I didn't understand what she had yelled. Krill? My father? It didn't make any sense. How did she even know that name?

After I crossed the Boundary Bridge, this car would stand out horribly. It was rusted and could barely keep its engine going. In Central D, vehicles were refurbished by Paragon's engineering team, and issued as rewards to citizens. The slums residents would then purchase them from those citizens, after they started to break down again. There, they never lasted much longer. I remembered the Paragon transport I had abandoned. It wouldn't have been far from the bridge, and I could transfer vehicles, making my entrance back into Central D and Paragon much more covert. I hoped the residents hadn't pulled it apart, yet.

I had parked it just off the Main, down the street from Estelle's apartments, and when I pulled up to the lot, it was still there. It had been vandalized with paint, where someone had turned the circular Paragon logo into a smiling creature with horns. It wasn't an uncommon occurrence in the slums. I was lucky it was still in one piece. I ditched the old clunker, and headed back to Central D.

There, the lights burned into the dark sky above as the rain poured down. What I once saw as vibrant life, now looked like an array of warning indicators. The rear view mirror gave a better likeness than the glass in the Outskirts had. I could see the monster even better in it. I could see myself, and everything I had done with my life. The bridge lights flickered by. How could I have let myself become this thing which had ravaged humanity? I didn't deserve whatever happiness she thought would come.

My hands gripped the wheel tighter trying to form the fists that had battered the glass. My victims all coursed through my mind. I could see their faces at the moment I took their lives. Vic's was angry, ready to kill me for what I had done. Zane's wore a sneer, as if he knew something I didn't. The rest were all the same; a familiar expression, distorted in this new reflection.

I parked in the rear garage, and the lift took me to the twenty-ninth floor. The ride up felt like minutes, although it would only be a couple dozen seconds. I tried to think of what I would tell Marcus, but nothing entered my mind but anger when I thought of him. I could only think of how he had used me.

The lift sounded and the doors slid open. The long hallway wasn't as familiar as it had always seemed. Now, it held a foreboding distance that felt unnecessary. Every step now angered me, as I made my way towards Marcus' office door. It slid open to show him behind his desk. The windows behind him let in a darkly tinted red illumination that matched his chosen style.

"I've been expecting you, Alpha." His voice was calm and relaxed as I entered. "Go ahead, you can have a seat." He gestured to the chair I had only recently used to regularly report to him. The scene was all too familiar.

"That's O.k. This won't take long." I told him in anticipation. Marcus shot out of his chair, angrily.

"Sit down!" He demanded as much with his hand as he did with his voice. It was insulting; like he had commanded a dog. I only cocked a brow at him in further defiance. After a short pause, he eased backwards with a single laugh huffing out of him. His grin grew wide.

"Let me ask you something, Alpha." He said as he began walking towards the large windows behind his desk, folding his arms behind his back along the way. "How many people do you think live in this city?"

As he turned back towards me, I could only stare out of the large pane of glass behind him. The city sat covered by a thin fog cloud that misted down on them.

"The people living in this city are my responsibility." Marcus' voice began to fade into background noise. The office became distant in my peripheral, and the city outside slid even further into focus. It was a horrible place. I could see that now. The lights were dim through the thick rain, but I could almost feel them trying to fight to fill the space around their bulbs.

Their glow was constant, never dying in this dark city. It reminded me of humanity's will, and how it was the same; a glowing beacon in a dark void, trying to fill the space around it. It made me think of how I was the extinguisher of that light. It didn't matter how many people there were left in the city. I only care about the ones that weren't here anymore, because of me.

"Do you know what kind of chaos would ensue if they all just did what they wanted? We would have nothing! There would be no order, and no Paragon to give them what they needed." He walked slowly past the city skyline, bringing him back into my focus. I felt my eyebrows digging into my sockets, and my fist clenched tight.

"This company is Order, and I have been charged with its preservation. Now tell me, Alpha, where are we on the Estelle assignment?" He grinned widely, and for the first time I saw through him; through the stupid and eerie facade he projected. I could see he was just a man, who had been given more power than he could handle, and now was afraid to lose it. It had made his judgment irrational.

"I have reservations about that assignment. It is unnecessary to delete Estelle Hart." I made the observation knowing it would enrage him. Marcus stepped forward examining me from behind the red glasses he wore.

"You don't think it seems *necessary*? It was a direct order!" He shouted into space between us. His hand waved over his desk, and holoscreens ejected into the air above it. Details about the Estella Hart assignment flickered by; the same information that would have been in the holopacket.

"Her known associates, the rise in anti-paragon activism, and the music. A child could see the correlation. She is the lynchpin; The downfall of our society!" He condescended me with his tone. I watched as his hands motioned his words when he spoke, like he was conducting some great masterpiece with every sentence.

"Sorry, Marcus. I just don't see it." I interjected, hoping to end his composure. His hand wafted through the datascreens, dissolving them.

"It's not your place to see it!" His voice roared. "You weren't made to think! You were supposed to do as you were told, and cleanse this city of human waste!"

As his voice rose, the room seemed to begin to shake. From behind him, I could see an explosion erupt in the entertainment district through the windows. Marcus turned abruptly, waiving his arm to display the inferno outside.

"Everyone has a role to play. If you don't play your role, then somebody else will, and then who knows what could happen?" He said calmly, despite the fire raging across the city outside the window.

"What did you do, Marcus?" I interrogated as I watched the fire dance along the skyline. "Ryne is destroying the city! This is what you call order?" Marcus turned back to me, still displaying his grin.

"You just don't get it. Krill was wrong. You do have a flaw." He let a small laugh bubble out, but nothing he said made any sense. Why bring up the old man, now? What did he have to do with anything? Marcus liked to talk in circles to confuse people. He felt it made him appear more intelligent, but I had assumed the attack was on the Stardust Amphitheater, and Estelle.

Had this meant that he had succeeded in killing her? He had obviously sent another team; I had assumed Ryne because of the use of demolitions being used.

"Sometimes, to save the whole you must sacrifice a little. An offering to the people. A show of faith. You don't understand humanity at all." He cackled, but I understood all too well. I knew how Marcus thought. He was sinister, and he would do anything for his vision of order. He would see Paragon as the leader of humanity until the end of time; no matter what was best. Anything less would starve his ego.

"You would *murder* her just show the people your power?" I asked in a demand, and he snapped forward over his desk.

"I would murder whoever it takes to ensure humanity's future." The words snarled from his lips. His attempts to intimidate me started to wear on my patience. "Today, it just happens to be her." He walked back to the giant windows. Smoke billowed from the amphitheater. It had dissipated much quicker than a regular electric-charge explosion would have. It was smaller. It must have been tactical. I could only imagine Lexxi's face as I told her of Estelle's death at the hands of Paragon.

"I don't want any part of this, or Paragon, not anymore." I decreed, and the clouds had become darker as they filled with smoke. Marcus's office began to dim, and his shadow sprawled on the open floor. He began to laugh a hollow laugh.

"And what else could you do?" His laughing continued, but only became more eerie as it proceeded.

"You think you're just going to run off to the slums with some stray you've found? Live a normal life? Maybe become the quad janitor, and have little dumpster kittens?" He laughed harder, but then he stopped instantly. He approached so that his face would be inches from mine. "Do you think you know morality better than I do, monster?"

His breath carried the words to me, emphasizing the last one. Instantly, my palm thrust into his shoulder, and he spun away only to catch himself on the corner of his sleek desk.

"I know that I didn't kill Estelle Hart, and that you may as well have. That makes you the monster, Marcus." I drew my shocker from behind my back and took aim at him. I thought of what a future would look like without Marcus, how bright it would be. To most, taking his life at that moment, would have been justice. He regained his stance, but his ominous red glasses had fallen to the floor.

"Look who's the hypocrite, now." He said, backing away slowly behind his desk. I followed him with my weapon. Without the glasses he looked ordinary and weak; not the evil leader of a powerful governing corporation.

"No, I'm not going to *delete* you." I smirked. It seemed almost puerile to call it that now. I took a step back, keeping my posture. "I probably should, but I'm trying real hard not to."

He sighed a small laugh. It only made it more sinister.

"People are going to know what you've done. You can't hide behind Paragon forever, and you'll be lucky if it isn't me here when judgment does find you." I told him as I took another step backwards. Marcus bent down and picked up his glasses, replacing them on his face.

"Oh, I don't intend to hide, so don't think you're just free to leave. You are Paragon property, after all." he sneered out, but the thought was sickening. Section Seven Protocol Seven. Section Seven membership is a life-long assignment. Defiance of Paragon was punishable by deletion.

It made him think of me as some kind of servant. I began to find his ego repulsive, and I fired a bolt into his desk, electricity traced jagged lines across the surface. It had made Marcus stagger, and that made my point.

"I'm no one's property, Marcus. Don't come looking for me, or I will make you regret it." I warned as the door slid open, and I quickly made my exit. Marcus took his seat as the doors slid shut. I turned my aim down the hallway, but it was empty. I hurried to the lift, but as I slid my wristport a new noise sounded, and the doors wouldn't operate.

I slid my ID again, but again, the strange negative alarm sounded out. I crossed the hall to the corner emergency stairwell. They had been made to be used if the building ever lost power, but to my knowledge it never had, and now they were a forgotten means of descent. From the twenty-ninth floor, the view down was a hole of white light from the fluorescence dancing off the white walls. The stairs were a pale ugly green.

"There he is!" I heard a man shout, and a charge bolt embedded itself into the wall next to my shoulder, and I ducked behind the railing.

"He's on the twenty-eighth floor. Move in all teams!" The man yelled again. Another volley of shock rounds kept me in my position. They would use one team to fire, while another moved up the stairs, interchanging as they climbed.

"Section Six, on you!" Another shouted, and I could hear their boot steps echoing in the metal stairwell.

I fired over the rail, only to receive another barrage that forced me back into cover. I could feel my datcom buzzing in my pocket, but it would have to wait. Any second spared and the Section Six guard team would gain ground in their quest to apprehend me. The boot steps were louder as they made headway up the stairs. The lower team laid cover fire.

The datcom continued to buzz obnoxiously. Suddenly, the lights in the stairwell switched to a faded red and orange color. It was to show a state of emergency. I used the environmental change as cover, and moved quickly down to the twenty seventh floor. I had glimpsed the Section Six team's positions along the way. They hadn't seen my advancement. I took cover in the corner, and my datcom vibrated harder, I pulled it out and flipped it open. A message was being broadcast over the Paragon Emergency Datastream; an old form of mass communication that Paragon initially tried to employ to help after the riots. It didn't get used much anymore, but all com devices would receive it. It was a live streaming feed of Marcus.

The broadcast began to play. Marcus was in the middle of speaking, and I had missed a portion of the video.

"...I assure you that Paragon will not stop, until we find these radicals, and..." Marcos spoke over the stream, but a charge bolt took the datcom from my hand, sending it down the center of the stairwell. Above, I heard the door where I entered, slam shut. More Paragon citizens charged into the stairwell, and I was surrounded.

It didn't matter who you were. If you were a citizen, you were given some tactical training and weapons proficiency courses during your educational years; a leftover precaution from the era when Paragon had saved humanity. Now, target practice and mathematics were given similar marks of accomplishment. Marcus wouldn't run out of trained citizens to send for me. Another blast sent sparks along the rail in front of me.

"He's on floor twenty-seven! We've got him cornered." Another random voice declared anxiously. I could assume the position of the team below. They hadn't made much progress, and were still several floors down. The team above was closing in.

No doubt they would have deletion orders. Even though citizens were trained, most weren't activated. I could feel their fear as I moved along the wall. They mumbled amongst themselves and hesitated, moving only when absolutely positive it was safe. I moved to the steps leading down to the twenty-sixth floor.

As I did, the team above me came into view. I pulled up my shocker, and fired. The charge hit the team leader's auto-rifle. The electric current from the round incapacitated him, and sent him flailing down the steps. The second man turned his aim over the rail, but would only see my charge bolt for a millisecond before it then exited his skull. His body hung across the railing as blood spattered in strokes across the ceiling above him. I moved down a floor, and the boots from below stopped echoing.

"Holy shit!" I heard a man scream. A volley of charges came from below. I was still two floors above the next team. The door above me opened. Another team of Paragon pretenders piled through into the stairwell, quickly ducking behind the rail.

"Just come out and die!" One of them demanded, and then they all moved up a floor, as the team above covered them. I was stuck in the corner of the twenty-sixth floor. Then, I heard something clanking against the steps as a light mine bounced towards me. I dove quickly, and threw it down the fluorescent white pit. When it ignited, it had barely made it to the floor below.

Light erupted, pouring into the stairwell. The blast wave traveled vertically throwing me against the wall. Heat rose through the open levels. I stood, and when I descended to the floor below, the rails had melted and bent inward. A chalky white residue covered the walls. I had never seen a light mine at work before and it was a sight to behold.

"Team two?" The men yelled down from above. I fired a round back up at them.

"You just killed your own men!" I yelled up, and another round of charge bolts fired up from the leftover teams below, pelting the wall behind me. The light mine had removed all cover from this section, so I dove into the middle of the stairwell. As I fell, I fired my shocker into the remaining three lower section sixers. Twelve floors went by fast before I caught the railing with my free hand.

The remaining thirteen floors down didn't seem that much further, and I could hear the door pop open on the floor above me. I let go of the rail, and caught the one on the floor below. I worked silently, as more citizens joined in the hunt. I moved down another floor.

"There he is! In the middle!" A yelled sound to alert the others to my location. I looked up to see two more teams only a few floors above, aiming back down. Then, a hand shot out over the railing.

"Come on! Come on! What are you waiting for?" The hand shook intensely, but the voice was familiar.

Iit was Eddie.

NO WAY OUT

It followed me down the long corridor just as Alpha always had, but this thing was nothing like him. Its presence was cold and lifeless, and it moved precisely in an almost mechanical fashion. Its eyes were blank under the brim of the fedora that Marcus had decided was a good accoutrement.

The lift doors opened and we both entered, me and that thing. It was unreadable. It made no facial expression, and moved to look at nothing; studied nothing. It had no point of focus to give it away. As we exited the lift, Remy waited at the front desk grinning his snide little grin.

"Mr. Brinnigin, and Mr..." He looked quizzically at the Proto Sapien trooper, trying to decipher which one it was. I sarcastically motioned two fingers to the little twerp.

"Ahem, XO Number two. Should I have *Penelope* brought around front?" The way he said her name made my stomach turn. She was too beautiful for his voice to say correctly.

"Don't bother, runt. I'm just giving Frosty here the grand tour. Besides, our orders are downstairs in retirement. I just thought the new guy here would like to know where he worked, so I'm just showing him around." I waved out a hand as if to show off the lobby's decor. "This is the Lobby, and this miniature human being is Remy. He's a glorified doorstop, he just doesn't know it."

Remy fumed. He didn't like my little show, but I didn't care. I was buying time. The assignment given to me by Marcus for this thing's trial run was going to come up bust, and I already knew it. He had given me my replacement partner, and our first gig; delete Dorian Krill, anti-paragon extremist. I could almost laugh.

He was being charged with treason, based on evidence accusing him of tampering with Paragon research and development. It was all a bunch of trumped up bologna so Marcus could finally kill the professor for choosing Alpha over Paragon.

"The Paragon main office complex has one main entrance, two internal lifts, one external, and two emergency staircase access points." The lifeless being beside me spoke regularly, too regularly, like it was putting on a show and over-acting, but doing it convincingly. It then looked down at Remy.

"Remy Taird. A class three civilian. Minimal combat training." I read off his file, and I couldn't tell if the thing was making a joke, or if it only operated tactically. Remy began laughing obnoxiously as he returned to the front desk.

"They gave that one a personality." He laughed again, only more amused with himself this time.

"I know the layout of the entire Paragon facility, Mr. Brinnigin. Our assignment is on the floor below." It stated abruptly. I could only nod, as it led me back towards the lift. My only hope was to waste as much time as possible to delay the inevitable. I knew what this assignment meant. It wasn't just a deletion order for Krill, but I was sure Marcus would have told that thing to kill me, too.

The doors slid open again, and we made our way through that level of closed doors and hallways that all looked the same. It seemed more like a prison than any retirement I'd ever heard of.

"His quarters are..." I started to speak, but his creepy voice interrupted my step, and I halted in place..

"Dorian Krill resides in sector thirteen. Eight doors up on our right, Mr. Brinnigin." Its hand motioned me forward. Its presence behind me was uncomfortable and foreboding. Marcus knew I wouldn't like this, and that's why he gave me this assignment. He just wanted to scare the hell out of me.

I didn't think there was any possibility of him knowing about the professor's absence, but I couldn't be sure. I could only imagine what the spook behind me would do when the door slid open and there was no Doc to be found. It would only expedite my demise.

"So, Two...I can call you, Two, right? I don't have to say the full exo thing every time, do I?" I asked, and the pale man only turned his head slightly to acknowledge that I was speaking. "Right, O.k. So, Two, since we're going to be working together, I thought maybe we should get to know each other."

The professor's empty quarters approached quicker than I would have liked. The Proto Sapien held its wristport to the panel to open the door, and then looked back at me.

"You're Eddie Brinnigin, Class two civilian, reprobate, caretaker of the Proto Sapien model Version A, current employee of the Paragon Corporation, smoker, abuser of the chemical Dox-4, also known as Uphorium. Don't worry, I know who you are, Mr. Brinnigin." It stated plain, and it was almost cruel how simplified it had described me. I fumed. Marcus had uploaded my entire file to the thing, and no telling what else.

"Yeah well, I bet you didn't know my favorite color is..." I started to say, but it cut me short again.

"Purple. Mr. Brinnigin." It answered, and I couldn't imagine how it had known. I pulled out my shocker, and cocked it, pulling in a charge round. I huffed. It didn't flinch. I stared into the dark glasses that shielded its eyes.

"Very funny. After you, comedian." I motioned forward into the room, and the stoic man merely began to walk, completely disregarding the exchange of banter. It hadn't drawn its weapon, which was against protocol. At the point of any incursion, a citizen's weapon must be ready.

It stood in the middle of the small living space, looking for signs of life. It gave up and turned back to me, all too quickly.

"Where is Professor Dorian Krill, Mr. Brinnigin?" It asked, and its voice stayed at the same level tone, as it began walking back towards me.

"How the hell am I supposed to know? It's Thursday, maybe he's at bingo, or getting a massage. Do I look like his caretaker?" I shout out in sarcastic ruse. The pale creepy figure scanned the room again, but continued to speak to me, although I held none of its attention.

"The probability of Dorian Krill escaping the Paragon retirement floor without help is nearly non-existent. He wasn't allowed access to the Database Mainframe, he would have to have been let out of his room...Mr. Brinnigin." It suggested, and its eyes shifted under the fedora at the floor, and the mess that had been left behind. "Mostly likely candidates to aid him in this endeavor would be Version Alpha, if he has complete awareness, Alex Rexon, who would comply out of probable guilt, and you, Mr. Brinnigin."

My brow twitched. I could feel the sweat about to drop from it. This thing was good. This thing was real damn good. It knelt at the floor checking for who-knew-what.

"What? Me? Why the hell would I go and do something like that?" I asked, trying to understand how it formed its suspicions. The Proto Sapien rose back into stance. Its neck cocked its head to the side, but only slightly to make it seem more intimidating.

"A favor for a friend, perhaps? There are no other candidates who have motivation or access." It assured me, and I felt the grips on my shocker in my palm. It was suicidal, but it was my last recourse. I had to be fast and accurate, so I raised my shocker to my waist and fired. A hole steamed into the chest of the false man's trench coat as he fell to the floor.

"...And, the favors just keep on piling on up." I mocked, as I turned to make my way back to the lift. I would have to get out of the building before anyone noticed the missing Proto Sapien trooper. It was time for me to make my exit from Paragon, as well.

Or, so I thought. Then, the ground rumbled and I caught myself against the lift panel. It felt like an explosion somewhere close by. The shock only lasted a second, and the lift doors sounded as they opened. I stepped in pressing the garage button, which would take me several floors up.

Just as the doors began to slide shut, I could see a figure emerge from down the hallway. It was XO Two. It had lived through the bolt to the chest, and undoubtedly wanted revenge, but it wouldn't be able to make it to me before the lift doors closed. I felt like the lift couldn't go up fast enough. Then, I felt the lift jostled like something had thrown off its balance. The XO had jumped onto the bottom of the lift car. The lift had to have easily traveled up three floors before that monster could even get the lower doors open. I fired a round through the floor. The lift car shook, again.

Suddenly, the emergency lights flashed on, and the lift was filled with orange and red hues.

"Shit, what now?" I asked aloud. My datcom began to hum in my pocket. When I flipped it open, the emergency datastream had been activated. The lift car shook again, and I almost dropped the device as Marcus began to speak over the airwaves.

"People of the city, citizens and residents alike, I come to you today with great tragedy..." he said, standing in front of his window view as he addressed the entire city. "...It is regrettably my responsibility to inform the people, that only moments ago, a terrible crime was committed that resulted in the lifeloss of one of our city's most beloved entertainers..."

They had succeeded so fast. It hadn't been fifteen minutes since Ryne and XO Three were sent to the Stardust by Marcus. I remembered the explosive shock from before, and had to assume that they were the cause. I fired another bolt through the floor of the lift car, and suddenly the doors slid open behind me.

I could hear my datcom still emitting Marcus' speech in a low volume as I ran into the garage floor lobby. A team of Section Six Paragon Guard entered the stairwell access in my peripheral.

"Set light rifles to max charge!" One of them commanded, and they breached the door and were gone in seconds. I ran to where I had parked Penelope, but she was also gone.

"Damnit, Alex." I cursed, and walked back to the little enclosed lobby, regretting the fact that I had loaned out my carm, yet again.

As I opened the door, I could hear a twisting and crunching metal sound. Then, the doors to the lift spread apart. XO Two crawled out from the hole below and onto the lobby floor. When it stood it was almost mechanical. It pulled a shocker from inside its coat.

"You are only confirming my suspicions, Mr. Brinnigin." It said in the same monotone voice as it started moving fast, almost as fast as I shut the door, closing it in the little lobby. I had to get to the floor above, so I started to run up the ramp. I heard the door slam open behind me as I ascended to the next level above.

I hid behind a nearby Paragon courier truck as I watched XO Two run up the ramp. It moved like Alpha, nothing but precise coordinated effort of its body and mind. It stopped as it noticed it had lost me.

Its pace became a slow walk. Three cars sat dormant next to the truck I hid behind, and I thought of backtracking down the ramp in the shadows. In the new silence, I heard my datcom still playing the emergency broadcast. I quickly muted it, thankful that my hunter hadn't been alerted; although, it had given me an idea.

I placed it on the back of one of the cars, and moved along the wall behind them. I had set the alert for ten long seconds, and hid as I watched and waited for the proto sapien to find it.

"Come out, Mr. Brinnigin. There is no need to make this difficult for yourself. Struggling will only prolong the inevitable." It warned. I still couldn't believe the thing had taken a charge round to the chest and was still walking.

I knew I would have to have a better shot. I positioned myself, poised to take aim, behind the truck. Then, suddenly, the alarm sounded on the datcom, but I hesitated. I had thought the XO would have walked around the car where the datcom sat, but it grabbed the vehicle by the hood and slid it out of the line-up by hand. I was on the wrong end of the truck, my shot wouldn't be as good, but moving would give away my position. I was frozen in place by the feat of strength the thing had displayed. XO Two picked up the datcom from the trunk of the car. I thought about making a run down the ramp, but I was too late to make any kind of move. I could be made at any second. It was almost as if it looked right towards my hiding spot, and at me.

"Very clever, Mr. Brinnigin." It said, still not knowing where I was, and I used the truck's rear-view mirror to watch as it threw the datcom onto the garage floor. In the reflection, I noticed the charge port on the car. If I ignited the fuel cell, that thing would be so close to the explosion it wouldn't have a chance. This was my better shot, but I had to keep him in position.

"OK…" I shouted out, as I moved out from around the truck, holding my shocker tight. "You got me. That was my best move, and you saw right through it." I pulled the shocker up as I took aim. It didn't flinch.

"Put down the weapon, Mr. Brinnigin." It ordered, and you could tell Marcus had made these things by their arrogance. They didn't feel fear, worry, or hesitation. I couldn't either, or I would lose. I squeezed the trigger, and the charge bolt pegged the fuel port.

The resulting explosion happened so fast that the next thing I knew, I was sitting against the wall of the garage. One of XO Two's arms twitched beside me as I regained consciousness.

I stood, kicking it away from me as I made my way back down the ramp and into the lobby. I could hear charge rounds being fired on the other side of the stairwell door. Through the little glass window I saw a falling blur, and I entered the stairwell. When I looked up, I noticed several bodies hanging in the white vertical tunnel, and more Section Six guards making their way down. Then, when I looked below, I saw a familiar face and a hand gripping the railing. I instinctively threw my arm over the rail, offering my hand. It hung there for moments longer than it should as the Section Six team descended.

"What are you waiting for? Come on!" I shouted out the command to Alpha, and his grip was unbelievably tight as I helped him over the rail. We slid up against the corner of the stairwell. The next team was more than nine floors up, and they wouldn't be able to see where we were.

"I can't believe you actually came back here!" I told him, as I took in his more comfortable atmosphere. I was glad to see him, but Alpha only looked back at me blankly.

"What else was I supposed to do?" He asked, in an innocence that only he had. He held his shocker up as he leaned out over the rail, firing upward at the Paragon troops pursuing him. Then, ducked back down behind the railing.

"I don't know. Hide?" I told him. I made sure to emphasize my sarcasm. "I warned you of how Marcus would react."

Alpha moved along the wall to the door from where I had entered. He looked out the little window, and scanned the garage.

"I had to do something. Marcus is deranged. How many more people is he going to send to die for him?" He questioned as he looked back at me, and I could only sigh. He just didn't get it, but I understood why Marcus couldn't let him go. It was more than just duty; more than Section Seven protocol. It was both business and personal.

"For you, he would send the entire force of the company, buddy." I joked, but it was the truth. To Marcus, Alpha symbolized his inadequacy. The professor had made Alpha to be perfect, but to Marcus perfection stopped at him. He had never liked how pleased Krill was over Alpha's completion.

He claimed that the professor had undermined Paragon since Alpha's inception, and that the old man planned to use Alpha to bring down the corporation, somehow. He had made that opinion known to Stoddard, but he never validated it with any proof. The sound of boots grew louder from above, until they were drowned out by a familiar humming roar coming from beyond the door. I pushed Alpha aside, and peered through the glass-covered hole.

"Oh, my sweet girl." I let out as I pulled the handle and swung open the door to see Alex parking Penelope. I walked towards my missing love. Alex opened the driver's door and stepped out. "It is so good to see you, baby."

Alex tossed me the key, and I caught it without paying attention to him as I inspected Penelope for any alteration that may have occurred in her absence from me.

"Good to see you, too." He sounded a little disgusted at my admiration, but he trailed off into silence. I hadn't noticed that Alpha had followed me, and Alex was now standing next to Alpha, inspecting him.

"Alex Rexon...I've heard so much." he shot out, and stuck out his hand for Alpha to take. It shook like he was meeting his childhood idol, and his voice wasn't much sturdier. Alpha cocked a brow at the funny man, and cautiously took his hand. Then, returned his attention to me.

"What do you mean, he'd send everyone just for me? Why?" Alpha asked, but then I noticed Griff's body was still in the back of the car, and turned to Alex, deflecting Alpha's question.

"Hey, why's Griff still in here?" I asked, and Alex's finger came up to signal a coming explanation as he stutter-stepped to me, causing the three of us to form a huddle.

"Did you know that the Drain access doors shut during the Emergency Signal? I couldn't get out." He informed me in an oddly humorous way that wasn't very funny. I smacked my hand on her rear quarter-panel.

"Damnit. I'll never get that smell out." I declared, but before I could protest any further, the stair access swung open. Alpha turned, firing three more bolts into the wall around it. Alex and I ducked down, and slid in close to Penelope. Alpha walked back toward the lobby, ejecting the clip from his shocker.

"He seems...normal." Alex noted as we watched Alpha pull a Section Sixer out from the access door, and into the glass enclosed lobby. Then, he fired a few more bolts up, and a few more down. Marcus really was sending everyone.

"He is normal, dweeb. It's the world we live in that's messed up." I assured Alex with some philosophical insight that I guess was lost on men of science.

Alpha took the utility ax and braced the door with it, before crossing over the top of a stunned man on the ground as he walked back to us. We all stood around each other, again.

"Why is he doing this?" Alpha demanded, and his anger was apparent. He glared at me and Alex as if he knew we had some answer he longed for.

"Krill." Alex's voice was a low gulp as he said the name. Alpha's head snapped in his direction.

"What?" Alpha asked in genuine curiosity. I wasn't going to add anything to Alex's vague explanation, but he had Alpha's attention. Alex postured himself, and It was as though he had prepared for this moment. I could imagine him deciding it was a good idea for Alpha to know everything.

I could imagine him thinking it was his job to tell him. He probably figured he owed it to Krill, somehow.

"It's all because of the professor; because he chose you. More than that, he chose humanity over...this..." Alex motioned his hands to air in an all-encompassing manner, and as he did, a hole burned through his chest as a charge bolt exited his back. Blood smacked against Penelope's metal, as he began to fall to the ground.

Alpha and I both ducked and dragged him as we moved behind the car. I could see our assailant over the hood; a one armed, shocker holding, proto sapien assassin.

"Shit. Of course, it's not dead." I accidentally said out loud. Alpha looked at me with an odd raised brow.

"I see Version A is with you, now, Mr. Brinnigin." The thing's voice echoed through the garage. It fired another bolt, only this time into Penelope's side. Alpha stood, and fired a bolt back into the overglorified henchman. It continued to walk, as it fired back. Alpha dove behind a column to escape the thing's aim.

I looked over to see the blank eyes of Alex looking up at me from the concrete. He had felt obligated to the Doc, to the professor's crusade against Paragon's corruption, and to Alpha. Enough so, that it got him killed. Another round hit Penelope's metal.

"Eddie, what the hell is this thing?" Alpha shouted the question over to me and it drove a spike into my brain, more so, because of who had asked.

Normally, I would reply with 'a monster', or 'a thing' that Marcus had created to destroy us, but as I looked into the blank eyes of the dead honor-bound man, I could hardly breathe. Another ping sounded against Penelope, but Alpha returned fire putting a new hole through the proto sapien, and It drew the thing's aim back to him.

"Eddie?" Alpha asked again, louder this time; only calling my name. A chunk of concrete flew from the column as another round hit. It didn't let up. It fired round after round, without hesitation, and then another pop went into the side of my beautiful girl. Alex's eyes were so vacant, and lifeless. All that dedication. Now, just lying there. Alpha fired again, only this time, the monster's shocker flew from its hand, and slid along the garage floor.

The creature howled in defiance.

I couldn't take it. Every bolt that had pierced Penelope only reminded me of the man who made her, who now laid dead on the concrete next to me. Alpha stepped out from behind the column pointing his shocker at the monster. I stood, filled with rage, commanding a war cry of my own, filling the armless proto sapien with electro-bolts as I cursed.

"You stupid, no count, worthless, one-armed, piece of shit!" I screamed, as I unloaded the entire charge container. Alpha's head swung towards me, as he took a step back. The light that had danced in the dim parking structure had stopped as my clip went empty, and pieces of Marcus's creature laid all over place, in chunks. My shoulders heaved up and down, violently at first, as the sound from the last bolt still resonated in the garage.

The adrenaline began to rush out of my system, and my surroundings came back into focus. I was still pointing the shocker towards the space the thing once occupied. I hadn't noticed Alpha moving closer to me, until his hand lowered my weapon. I turned, suddenly, as I became aware of him. He was now looking down at Alex, whose body sat crumpled at Penelope's rear.

"Was he a friend?" He asked as he placed his hand on my shoulder. I pulled out a gasper from my inside pocket, and pursed it between my dry lips. It shook as I spoke.

"I wouldn't call him that. He was better than any *'friend'* I deserve." It was true. I had never gotten the chance to be Alex's friend, and I took note of that in my mind. I had broken out in a sweat from the intensity, and it dropped down onto my gasper before I could light it. I pulled the soggy thing from my lips and flung it across the garage.

"This is all so much bullshit." I declared, as I beat my hand down on Penelope's trunk. Alpha knew something was wrong, instantly. He knew I would never strike my lady. It had been too long since I last had a dox.

"You want to start telling me what's going on, Eddie? Like, who this guy is, and who that guy was? You want to tell me why Griff is in your back seat? I let him live." Alpha remarked, making me think about all of it. The city, Marcus, Krill; the stupid little game they played for the fate of humanity. I thought of Alpha, and the day he was assigned to me. I gave my memories to Krill, so that Alpha would become who he is.

I thought of Alex, and how he had been blinded by Marcus' truth, and how he had used the professor's teachings to create the XOs; only to have one of his creations be what killed him. I thought of how Marcus hunted Alpha now, all because he fell in love with a girl. It was all so stupid. What a way to end the world.

"Yeah, well I couldn't let that moron take another breath." I shot back, taking a deep breath of my own to convince myself I had done the right thing. "You want some answers? Well, me too, man. I live in this garbage heap, shoveling the shit just like everybody else. Is there going to be a brighter future? Are we making it? Bullshit...those aren't questions. How long do I got left? Now, that's a good damn question, I want that answer."

Alpha holstered his shocker. It had become quiet again, almost too quiet.

"What was that thing?" He pointed to the bits of proto sapien still twitching on the floor. I could only look at the oversized man in the back of my car with Alex's matching shocker wound.

"You know, Griff was the first person I ever deleted. Don't even know why I did it, really. I just got angry and felt my weapon under my arm. I thought it would change things, but it hasn't. Paragon will always find someone else to do whatever evil it needs." I explained calmly, trying to give him the best answer I could. Alpha studied me over, and I could feel it. I just wasn't paying him much attention. I couldn't. My mind filled with reality; infinitely perplexing reality. I needed a dox like never before.

"But you're with Section Seven." Alpha stated in an odd disbelief of my insubordination. I understood why Alpha questioned what I was saying. He was in the dark about everything; Section Seven, Paragon, the riots. Hell, the whole reason he existed was a mystery to him. I never thought about it, but he probably thought he was just human like the rest of us. No human had killed anyone since the riots. That's when we realized how precious human life really was. In the beginning, Killian had saved close to a quarter-million people in the dome, but after the riots, there was only a fraction of that. Killing became outlawed and Section Seven was created as an enforcement team to apprehend those who did or would kill.

Eventually, the population started to rebuild itself, and as it did the violence started again. We had all been told the stories.

"Yeah, well, so was he. He was supposed to know better, am I right?" I asked my always prepared superhuman partner. Supposedly, the doc created Alpha so we could find a way outside of the city, but that's when I got called in. I was working my way around the slums. I was Paragon's guy on the other side. I knew the city, and Paragon had lost touch with the people on the other end of the bridges. A couple of personality tests later, I had a new best friend, and humanity was put on auto-pilot.

I walked around Penelope inspecting the damage. Deep holes had scorched and bent back the metal on the driver's side. I became infuriated.

"Son of a mutate! Do you see this shit?" I yelled as I touched the still-glowing orange hole.

Alpha grabbed me by the shoulder, to turn me. I don't know how wild I had become, but I had lost myself for a moment as I fumed over the top of Penelope.

"Eddie, cut the act." He said as his eyes burned into me. He had been around me long enough to know when I was dodging his, or my own, feelings. As much as I didn't want to admit, the car was just another attachment I used as a crutch to maintain the character I perform.

"Marcus made that thing. He wants you dead." I rang out in quick explanation, and his hand dropped from my shoulder.

"I understand as much, but what does it have to do with Dorian Krill? Why did Lexxi say that he's my father?" Alpha asked bluntly in a way I didn't expect. His father? He backed away disappointed in the answers I had given him. I pulled another gasper from my inside pocket, and lit it quickly.

"The truth is, you think you've known me your whole life, right?" I stammered out, and the tip of the stick began to burn an orange glowing ember, and he nodded slowly as his brow began to furrow, I guess at the thought of what I was to unfold. "Well you have, but your whole life has been a lie." I didn't know how else to tell him. "Paragon, Section Seven, Krill, Me, even you. It all got twisted some way or another before they put it all in your skull. I was just supposed to make sure nothing unraveled." I explained. Alpha postured his shoulders backwards and retreated a step.

"What the hell are you talking about?" He asked angrily in shock of what I was saying. I took another deep inhale.

"It was my job to act like everything you do is normal; to convince you that all the insane things you do are everyday human shit, but come on, man. You never thought there was something different about you?" I asked because I had thought about it for years. Ever since the Far bridge incident. I had thought that, one day, he would just realize that he wasn't like everyone else; that not everyone can jump thirty feet or run forty miles an hour. He would do something amazing, and I would act like it was just a normal day at work. "You weren't made to kill people, Vincent." I tried to make him understand.

I realized my role in the whole game. I was only Marcus' stall tactic. He knew he had lost all those years ago. The moment Alpha woke up, he knew what Krill planned for humanity couldn't be stopped, only delayed until he could control it.

"What is that supposed to mean? Made? You said Marcus made that thing." Alpha stammered out, and it was one of the only times I had seen him flustered, but not without reason. Alex believed that Alpha should know. He was about to tell him everything. I tried to imagine what that would change, but couldn't think of anything worse than the way things were now.

"Six years ago, they took me to Marcus. He offered me a job, a car, and a new life. Then, he showed me you, only at the time, you were in a vacuum sealed tube and barely had any hair, anywhere." I tried to imagine what Alex would have said, but instead, I could only give him my experience. His arms crossed in disbelief like I was attempting some twisted joke on him. I leaned back against Penelope as I recalled the story.

"Then, he took me into a white room. There, Krill studied my personality, and I studied his. He had decided that I wasn't the best option for compatibility or whatever, but Marcus overruled his decision and gave me the job anyway. For the next few months, they asked me questions about my childhood, modified my identity, and trained me as a Section Seven member. All to better adapt to your life." Alpha's head lowered. He couldn't look at me. I could understand the betrayal he must have felt. "They put me in your head, and we were best friends. Always had been. No one suspected otherwise the way I played along, not even you, and not even me, sometimes." I flicked out the gasper, and exhaled. "Six years. We've been going for almost six years. I've watched you kill people for that long, but that's not what the old man made you for." I continued. It was my attempt at telling him how guilty I felt. He moved quickly, grabbing me by the jacket, and holding me against Penelope.

"Stop saying that." He growled an inhuman sound, as he pressed me back, but it was then I noticed the bolt hole in his jacket. He had been shot. Any normal person would have been greatly affected by a hole made by a charge round, and not nearly have his range of motion.

"You're shoulder, you've been shot!" I tried to detour his attention back to himself. He paused momentarily, looking at the hole in his jacket, and back to me.

"Getting sentimental now, Eddie?" He tightened his grip on my jacket to the point that it made it hard to breathe.

"The wound...you don't have a wound..." I pointed out as I flailed my arms against his vice-like hands, and he suddenly let go. I could breathe again, and I let out a big sigh of relief that none of my ribs had been crushed. "Any normal person would have a big gaping hole in their shoulder. I'm telling you, you're different. You're special."

He pulled his jacket off, and his shirt collar aside. There was a small blast scar, a tiny circle with a jagged star around it. It was a kill shot to any human being, and as he peered down at it, I could see the wheels turning behind his eyes.

"I have to find Krill." he blurted out of nowhere. He closed his jacket, looking at me in a new kind of disbelief. Then, he turned back to the lobby entrance.

"Wait, he's not there." I halted him, and his face lit up in anger as he turned back to me.

"What do you mean? Where is Dorian?" He asked as he returned his grip to my jacket with one hand. It was something instinctive he did to seem more threatening. It worked on everyone, including me. Something about someone choking you to death with ease did that pretty convincingly.

"We've hidden him in the slums; lowest tier. He'll be safe, but that's not the worst of it; that wasn't the only one of those things Marcus has made." I gestured to the bits of XO still on the garage floor, when suddenly, I heard banging coming from the little glass lobby door. The utility ax bounced against the wall, and the door handle opened. Muddled voices mumbled behind the dancing door frame. Alpha pulled his shocker from its holster as he watched the door trying to give way.

"How many more of them are there?" He asked in a gulp. I grabbed his arm, trying to ease it back, but he only exerted more force to keep me in place. He had changed in those past few seconds. I could tell his priorities were different, and that I no longer made it on the list of them.

"Two more. One with Ryne at the Stardust. The other was sent to the slums to find her." I admitted. His eyes grew livid at the idea. His shocker pressed into my thigh, and he squeezed the trigger without thought. I felt the bolt rip through the muscle above my knee, blood spattered against Penelope for a second time, and the bolt bounced against the ground. I howled in pain. The cauterized hole was big enough I could stick the tip of my pinky finger through. It burned a deep and internal searing pain. I grasped at the new wound, and slid down beside Penelope.

"Tell Marcus that you tried, but you couldn't stop me." He said sternly, and then ran off through the garage. The door burst open in the little glass enclosed room, and Section Six guards poured through the door, coming towards me, with their light rifles charged and ready. A vintage *lightster speedcycle* roared to life, as Alpha made his way out of the garage. The guards wouldn't be fast enough to take a decent shot at him, not that some didn't try.

"Hey! Over here!" I waved down one of the Section Six commandos, and he ran over as I tried to pull myself up the side of Penelope. "He shot me in the damn leg! Can you believe that? Give me a hand, will ya?" The young innocent guard extended his arm, and finished helping me to my feet. His eyes were wide as he looked through my leg.

"You're really lucky, sir. We've had several casualties." He said encouragingly, so I slapped him on the shoulder, and looked him dead in the eye.

"It's a shame he got away. Nothing you could do, though. Don't worry, I'll tell Marcus the good you've done here." I smiled to lay it on. This idiot wouldn't suspect shit.

Section Six members didn't even see the twenty-seventh floor, or meet Marcus. To them, he was just a name synonymous with power. My little pampering would be enough for him not to ask any questions.

"Here, lend me a hand to the lift, will you?" I steered the innocent doofus to the entrance, and that's one less active Paragon drone after Alpha.

I really hated these idiots.

I quickly made my way out of the dust-filled room, and further into the old building. The wood cracked and split as I walked. They had said the early structures were wood because that's all the world had to build with at the time. It wasn't until years later, that the needed resources were harvested to build the slums. It gave it an ethereal feel.

I don't know why, but the further into the building I went, the more uneasy I became. It was like walking back in time. Less and less had been touched, walls still held maps of the New Axis and images of Southlander mercenaries. Tables sat covered in dust and unmoved. In the main hall, there were photo prints stapled along a section of the wall. Suddenly, I came upon a woman in her mid-thirties, standing next to a strange military vehicle in armor, and looking at the distant sky through some odd glowing glasses. The name Tempest Gyllis was printed below it.

"She could be my grandmother." I thought out loud. I didn't realize how quiet it had been until I broke the silence, and my voice bounced along the old wooden walls. I wondered what it would have been like to live in a world outside this glass dome, on a planet that wasn't dying. I wonder what granny Tempest would have been like. She seemed strong, and had a stern look, but also kind.

Only one other picture stood out. A very handsome man in some kind of old-fashioned combat uniform. It was just a portrait, but it stood out because it was painted. A printed tag hung below it that read 'Noma Faust – Hero of Mankind', and I thought it was odd that I had never heard of such a person. I made my way back to the entrance of the building. I hadn't seen it when I came in, but above the door was a mural of a woman floating in a sea of electric light. I recognized her as the Countess of Meridia. People in the slums passed out fliers with her face on it, still. They say at one point she was a great ruler of the people, leading a vast and unstoppable army of enhanced warriors, but they say they never even fought. Instead, she mitigated warfare as an arbitrator. Some believed she even spoke with the Universe, but even she couldn't stop humanity from destroying the planet. The pictures on the flier make her seem less sophisticated than the mural as it gave off an almost angelic presence.

I began to worry as I left the building and started to wander through the tall grass. Time felt different here. Minutes felt like hours as I waited. I sat down on the dirt hill where I had last spent any real time with him, but I didn't look out at the dead earth beyond, I stared back at the ominous city.

"This really is the only beautiful place left in the world." I reassured myself as I picked up a rock, and threw it at the barricade. As it collided with the stone wall, smoke erupted into the skyline and the ground shook. I remembered the sound from only hours earlier. It was an explosion, but it was far away. Maybe even in Central D.

From the outskirts, I couldn't see anything but a plume of black smoke trailing to the top of the dome. The trail from earlier still faintly lingered as well. I had to get closer; at least to the next tier.

I headed for the ramp that would take me up to the Main. I burst through the wall of rain, and continued down the street as it poured around me. As I ascended to the top tier, I could now make out the Stardust across the Boundary Bridge. It was on fire.

I stood under the awning of a *datajack* as the rain pelted the pavement, when my datcom began to buzz. I opened it and the screen displayed the Paragon Emergency Datastream. The message began with the Paragon logo, a simplified outline of the city, spinning until a man faded into the background. I knew the man on the screen as Marcus Creed, the new chairman of the Paragon Corporation. He had replaced Killian Stoddard, six years ago, and was seen on almost every piece of propaganda that Paragon released. He was a face, and that was about all I knew.

"People of the city, citizens and residents alike, I come to you today with great tragedy. It is regrettably my responsibility to inform the people that only moments ago, a terrible crime was committed that resulted in the life loss of one of our city's most beloved entertainers, Estelle Hart."

My heart jumped as he said her name. I couldn't believe it. My mind had to be playing a trick on me, and I must have only thought that I heard him say her name.

"It saddens me to no end to see acts of violence such as these committed by rebels and activists with agendas against civilization, and I personally want the people of the city to know that Paragon will not stop until we find these radicals, and end this new terrorist threat. We have reason to believe that the explosion in sector eighteen earlier was also caused by these same activists, and again today in the Paragon main office. We are currently doing all we can to track these criminals, and any assistance will be rewarded with citizenship. There is no cause for alarm. Paragon is the future." The face of Paragon stated, and the transmission ended. I could feel my bottom lip battering against my top teeth as I blathered. I covered my hideous face with my hand. It couldn't be true. Estelle couldn't be dead.

My legs carried me, defiantly, to the apartment I shared with her as I wept. I had to see her absence for myself. I had to feel the empty space where she would have been. It wasn't far. I had to go back to the Meserere. I ran hard and fast until I got there, and I pushed open the old creaking door as my legs pulled me up the stairs to the apartment door.

I threw it open and ran inside. I could feel the tears landing in my ears as I ran. The air inside was silent and still.

"Essy!" I shouted. It was the kind of quiet that made it hard to breathe. "I'm...home." My knees buckled, and I sank to the floor. My chin buried itself into my clavicle, and my hands curled back into my arms. I felt my whole body heave as I poured out tears into the silent room. My wet clothes pooled around me as I sat in the middle of the floor. It reminded me of all the times I had come in soaking, and Estelle would lecture me about getting the floor wet; how it would rot the floorboards. I immediately stood up, and began pulling off my wet clothes as I marched to the bathroom for a towel.

As I entered, I noticed the gown Estelle was going to wear for the concert, and at first, my heart began to beat fast. She always wore her concert dress to rehearsal. She said it brought her luck, and if her dress was at the apartment, then maybe she wasn't at the Stardust, and maybe it was all a Paragon lie. Then, the tears reemerged as I noticed the tear on the seam of the dress, and I remembered her ripping in on the sofa the day before. She wouldn't wear something that wasn't perfect. My stomach turned. I thought of all the dresses that I had borrowed. How she would always smile and pretend that she didn't mind.

I guess I thought that if I put it on, she would come home and find me in it. She would tease me about stealing her clothes, tell me how she was working on a new sound, or sarcastically ask how my employment crisis went. I guess I thought I would never get to do it again; borrow her dress. This was the last one.

I could not stop the tears as I slid my arms through the lace straps. It floated down around me. I took the small staircase up to the top floor of the Meserere; a small room with one glass wall that was almost like a bubble. Estelle had put carpet on the floor, and spread pillows around throughout making the room a giant cushion. She had installed a digidisk player into the wall, and would sing along with her new album in preparation for the concert.

I pushed the start button, and 'Hope for the Future' began. The guitar bled a feverish tune that lasted a breathtaking moment, before allowing the drums to really start the song. Then came her smoldering voice.

'look deep into the shadow
To find the light of tomorrow
It's been way too long now
That we've seen this sorrow
And with you, it can end forever
Just believe, hope for the future,
Is all I see.'

I always had loved that song, but now as it played through the small room, I could only sob. I tried to think about how she must have felt writing it, and who it was about as I stared out through the glass wall. The rain looked like it melted along the sheet of glass that separated me from the world outside. I was four floors up, and in the slums that was something. The rain made it impossible to really make out much from below, but from here, you could see almost everything in the city skyline.

In the distance, the Stardust smoked, and I agonized in heartache. People had started coming out into the streets to see the pillars of smoke filling the top of the dome. The sky grew darker, and then I heard the door creak open and close below.

I jumped to my feet, not realizing that I still wore the fancy performance gown, and fell over onto another series of cushions. I stood up again, this time balancing myself, and slowly made my way to the staircase. As I came to the bottom, I looked forward to see a man standing down the hallway.

He wore a trench coat and a fedora, and had very pale weird-looking skin. He was looking back at me, too. I instantly recognized the signature Paragon style.

"Can I help you?" I asked nervously. He stared blankly back at me. There was something familiar about him; familiar and cold. I remembered the last time I had felt that way was when I saw Alpha for what he was.

"Alexxia Gyllis. Age, twenty-four, resident of sector nine. You have been chosen for deletion." It remarked casually.

The thing's hand reached inside of its coat and pulled out a long blade. It seemed to glow hot, and electricity danced as he flicked it out to his side. I quickly retreated up the stairs, pushing down as many cushions as I could along the way, but it carved them in two, igniting them into flames, as it followed.

I didn't have anywhere to run, and nowhere I could hide. The shadowy figure emerged from the staircase. Lightning crackled across the sky bouncing off the dome. It had never happened before.

"Why? What have I done?" I could barely ask. I knew what this thing was. It was death and it had come for me. Its blade hummed as it closed in. I stared into its darkly covered eyes, but there wasn't even a hint of expression.

I dashed to the far side of the room hoping to slip by and get back down the stairs, but it adjusted perfectly to cut off my path. It didn't feel hot, like I thought it would from how it looked. Instead, it was cold. It had happened so fast, I didn't comprehend enough to look down. I only felt a massive force stop me as I dashed forward. Then, I didn't move.

I watched as the black tinted glasses that I stared into move away from me to show the full view of the henchman holding the blade. I thought there would be blood, but there wasn't. My hands instinctively palmed my sternum, as I felt the back of my head and shoulder collide with the glass wall; shattering it.

The shards of glass sparkled in the dark sky above and around me they began to combine with the rain. I coughed, and I felt the blood land on the crease of my lip, and then I closed my eyes. The world around me began to disappear. There wasn't any rain, and no glass. There was no black suited henchman to escape. There was only peace. I felt like I was floating, and I was.

I begged my eyes to open again, and fought against the desire to stop breathing. I could feel his hands touching me, and his arms wrapping around me. I knew it was him by the way I felt his touch. He was the only one who had ever been so gentle. My heart felt like a slow ticking clock about to stop.

I wasn't ready.

I had just met him. It wasn't time. It wasn't supposed to be like this. I begged my eyes once more, '*please open to see him*'. I knew it would be the last time, but I had to.

He was everything; perfection. Not just for me, but for everyone. He had so much potential, it beamed from him, making him glow like the red sun of the outside world enveloping this small city.

Now, his touch was just as warm, and I was able to open my eyes one last time to see him.

TOGETHER IN UNISON

The dark glasses hid their eyes, and the trench coat and fedora ensemble was a little cliché. Marcus paraded back and forth in front of the new monsters. The dark clouds kept much of the light from coming in through the massive windows behind them.

"The future, gentlemen, is now in my hands." Marcus said, and his voice was almost a hiss. Marcus had become, on some level, mad with his own concept of power. He took a step towards me and Eddie.

"Because of Ryne's stupidity, I'm moving up the timeline. XO One will accompany Ryne. I'm sure you'll find that he's very capable. Use him to ensure the completion of the Estelle assignment. XO Two will join you Mr. Brinnigin." Marcus explained as he laid out his plan. Marcus wasn't ever really fond of Eddie. At first, he had thought Eddie would be able to con Alpha into being a company man, but after Eddie started bonding with Alpha, Marcus began to distrust his motives.

"Join me for what? If it's dinner, he's paying. I'm still waiting on my paycheck." Eddie's defiant sarcasm was apparent. Marcus just grinned.

"You are being given a new assignment." He said to Eddie, and then, Marcus turned his gaze back to me. "Did you forget something, Mr. Lutz?"

I gulped. The weird XO hadn't made a move, and so neither had I. I had just been listening to Marcus and Eddie continue talking.

"What about the other girl? Alexxia Gyllis?" I postured myself straight with the question, "She knows about what Alpha is." It was a good cover for my hesitation, but truthfully I wasn't sure why I didn't move. It was as though my body forgot where it was going, or had refused to take me there. I felt the same fear I had earlier, before my team was dead in the back of my truck, before Alpha had killed them. I didn't like this assignment.

"That's just splendid. I imagine that's somehow also your doing?" Marcus asked infuriated. I could tell he wasn't thrilled with how I handled my earlier assignment, and now I had this thing babysitting me. "Why don't you let me worry about the other girl. You have your assignment. Now move." I snapped my boots together and turned; an old habit I had gotten from taking squad training too seriously. "...and Ryne, try not to blow up anything else." Marcus mocked as I walked out of the office followed by the pale skinned, darkly shrouded pseudo-human. We silently made our way down the long corridor; me and this new thing.

I didn't like the idea of having Eddie's job, either. Carting this zombie around and making sure it did as it's told didn't sound like my idea of a good time.

We took the lift down to the parking floor, where I had left Griff to watch over the others. When we arrived, Griff was nowhere to be found. I looked inside the cab of the truck, but there wasn't anything different than the way I'd left it. I slapped my hand against the fender.

"Is something wrong, Ryne Lutz?" The XO asked ominously. I knew he was having a hard time with everything; losing Ramone and Ox, it made sense that Griff would take off now. After his heated exchange with Marcus, he was probably scared for his life, and decided to hide it out in the slums. I even tried to tell myself that disappearing was his best option.

"It's nothing. Come on, we have to see Kagan." I said as I pulled myself into the truck, and gripped the wheel. Part of a gasper still laid in the tray. The creepy dark man eased into the passenger seat in a robotic fashion, closing the door behind him in an oddly perfect timing. Its head turned to me as I ignited the engine.

"Kagan Shank, Citizen, Undertaker, Central D drain access caretaker and recluse. It is an unnecessary delay. I must insist that we continue onward to our current assignment." It redirected, and I looked through the back window and put the truck in reverse to pull out of the parking space. A utility tarp covered Ramone and Ox's bodies in the bed of the truck.

"You insist?" I turned back to the scary new recruit in my passenger seat. "You, first day in the world, and you think you can insist shit? You might insist I not cram my fist down your throat and pull out some manners." I said, cocking a brow and a wide eye in the thing's direction. Its head merely turned forward in the same weird rhythm. I put the truck in gear and drove out of the lot and onto the central turnpike.

"The corpses in the back of the vehicle will not become toxic in the time allotted for assignment completion, and can remain in their current location a little longer. I must insist we continue on our way to our current assignment." It added with a second insistence. My hands gripped the wheel tighter as I turned to enter the crossway between the drain and the entertainment district. The leather stretched and cried in my palms. I continued to stare at the rain that melted into the windshield in front of us. The thought of Griff abandoning the team filled my mind, and I didn't think he was the quitting type, but something told me there was something weird going on. I grabbed the gasper from the tray and bit down on the stubby thing, chewing it into place. Then, I lit it. In the new light, I got a much better glimpse of the strange man riding with me. His skin was so pale that it was nearly see-through, showing blue and red veins just under the surface.

"Are you in some kind of hurry to do the job? Do you even know what it is? Do you know what you're going up against? She's practically got an army of slum punks and dimwits worshiping her, trying to keep her safe." I explained to the zombie in the passenger seat, but no expression came. No fear or reluctance, it just stayed the same cold hard nothing.

"Probability of assignment success is one hundred percent. Assignment completion is the desired outcome." Its eerie voice was monotone, and it gave me chills. How the hell could this thing think it would be so easy to just walk in and kill Estelle and walk out again?

"What do you mean, one hundred percent? They have weapons too, you know. They'll shoot back...did you even get the packet? We need a plan, dammit." I demanded as I slapped my palm against the steering wheel. I didn't like this. That thing would just walk right through the front door, blasting up the place. It wasn't my style not to have a plan. It kept its intense forward gaze on the road ahead.

"I will enter through the civilian terminal. You may provide cover with the light rifle, if you wish. Success rate factors are based on calculated data and predictions based on causality." It continued to explain.I merged onto the turnoff.

The entertainment district wasn't very big; an over-sized amusement area filled with different cuisines and games. The Stardust Amphitheater was the largest part of the district. It sat at the back after a gauntlet of tiny placations, sunken into the ground floor with room for several tens of thousands of people to fit inside. I had been once before, when I was a kid. My father took Xack and I to see some circus act where the acrobats swung from ropes and long strands of cloth. I remembered it being one of our better days, even though our seats were in the very back section. We all just seemed happier watching the show.

"Whatever you say, partner." I indulged. The thing had a creepy aura. It sat in the passenger seat, stoic and calm. Too calm to be walking into what was sure to be a fight. Marcus had been vague on just what this thing was capable of, just that it was that; capable.

The entrance to the district was a large semi-oval archway lit in neon and fluorescent lighting meant to attract the city's population. Beyond that was all electric nonsense; giant signs lit with bulbs the size of a man's head. The Stardust was the most ostentatious part of the district, light shot into the skyline through its half-roof, flickering and changing colors to wild beats and sounds. I pulled the truck into park down from the entrance, in front of the Mental Park Arcade. I hoped the distance would give me a chance to scout out our targets. XO One opened its door and stepped out in mechanically precise motions, shutting it quickly behind him. I grabbed the light rifle from the back and followed behind it, as we made our way to the entrance of the Stardust. One man sat on a carved column of the ground's lit entrance. He looked down as we approached.

"The concert's sold out, but I can get you guys' tickets...if you got the creds." He shouted down. The cold XO ignored the man and continued through the small plaza entrance.

"Hey, you can't go in there!" The little man yelled out from behind us as XO One passed through the gateway. It pulled a shocker from under its coat, and fired a bolt into the man sending him down from the column.

All his yammering would surely blow our cover, and sure I wanted the element of some sort of surprise, but if this thing didn't even care about Estelle's bodyguards, my ass was in a jam.

As we entered, the arena opened up to a half-circle lobby with multiple entry points that led down several flights of stairs to a circular stage, benches lining them in-between. The half-roof hung over the stage to keep the entertainers dry, but the audience, with the exception of a few, would stand in the rain with umbrellas. XO One stopped, replacing his shocker in its holders and looked around; taking in the layout. I had heard that the spectral light emitters were quite a spectacle. They danced along the drops reflecting like starbursts as they fell. As I saw them for the first time, I felt slightly paralyzed by the effect it had. That's when the familiar song began to play. It started with the strum of a guitar that sang out alone.

"Hey! You in the hat. The doors are closed til Saturday! Beat it!" A man called out. I snapped out of the mesmerized state to notice that we were being approached by two rough-looking punks; all beards and bandanas, tattoos and horseshit.

XO One kept the same pace as it continued towards them.

"Didn't you hear me, boy?" The cocky guy paused, and took a step back as he got a better look at the transparent skin of the XO trooper. The second man, a particularly muscular guy who carried a collapsible rod, stopped as well.

"What the...There's something wrong with this guy." He pointed at the thing like it was a grotesque abomination. You could barely see XO One's uncovered flesh, but I agreed that it was notably unappealing. The second man flicked out the telescoping baton.

"Yeah, he's ugly and stupid." He remarked as he approached. His muscles tightened as he swung at the proto sapien, but as the baton came down, XO One's hand caught the rod and ripped it from the man's hands. In the same instant, it had retaliated with a swing of its own, across the man's jaw. Blood shot across the wall, and the man hit the ground with force. Without hesitation, XO One delivered another blow into the knee of the smaller aggressor. As the man fell, grasping at his shattered knee, XO One caught him by the jaw; twisting his head around until I could hear his spine pop. Then, it dropped him and the baton. It had done it all in a single motion, and continued to walk forward as if its path were unhindered. It had been quiet, and the music had hid its actions. I stayed in the back row, setting up the light rifle, as I watched the horror descend down the aisle of stairs.

I looked down at the two dead men. It had happened so fast it was almost unbelievable, but looking at them, I couldn't deny the gruesome thing Marcus had created. It made its predecessor seem like a mere child with its apathetic indiscretion. Then, the drums kicked in.

"Hey, you there! Stop!" Another man shouted out to the proto sapien. As I pulled up the scope, I noticed the voice coming from Benny Gloom.

He pointed up at the XO. Several other men scattered into place behind Benny, who had now come to a sprint. Benny was a bulky man, tall and massive. His size, even at a sprint, would build up some power. I scoped around as the song screeched to a halt, just as the light popped on, revealing Estelle. She looked the same as she had earlier with Alpha. I pulled the scope away, and the distance made her small.

I heard the smack, rows back, as Benny collided with XO One. His fingers clasped together as he attempted a second hammer blow, but the XO didn't budge, instead returning with a strike of its own, into Benny. The force and position of the hit launched Benny down the rows. Estelle fumed as she watched.

"What in the red world, you guys?!" She screamed out.

I pulled the scope back up, and followed XO One as he made his way down the steps. The rest of Benny's crew caught up quickly, but XO One dispatched them in the same deadly and exact manner he had the men before. Killing one just as quickly as the next.

Benny regained consciousness, and jumped on the back of the XO sending them tumbling down the steps over the top of one another. Benny landed on top as they lost momentum, and began battering his fists into the face of the pale monster, who had now lost its hat and glasses disguise. Benny paused, as he looked at his punching bag in horror, and the hesitation cost him.

The XO pulled its legs upward, kicking him through the old brick wall of the amphitheater, and into the backstage area. Then, it continued to make short work of the rest of the rebels, until one pulled out an old light pistol. He fired it into the XO at close range, and a beam of light pierced the creature, but it still did not phase it. Instead, XO One pulled an *Electroblade* from inside its coat. It crackled as it lit up. I had only ever seen them in telecasts. They were weapons of a previous era; crude instruments that were difficult to wield. The XO moved extremely fast, quicker than any human could, lunging into the pistol wielder. Electricity popped and arced as it withdrew the blade. I could do nothing but watch, stunned and mortified, as the little entourage dwindled through the distorted eye of the scope.

Estelle screamed a terrified and loud scream as the proto sapien made its way to the stage. I put in my earpiece so that I could hear whatever was said down below. I had gotten lost in the intensity of the carnage. I took a deep breath. It had already killed seven men. There was only one left, and the band.

"Man, just...you know, chill out..." A little coward of a man quivered as the XO approached the stage.

"You have violated Paragon law and aided in an activist movement, you will be deleted from humanity." The creature spoke out, and it pulled the electroblade through the smaller man, brutally carving him across the waist, with nothing but a flick of its wrist. Estelle had retreated to the back of the stage, and her bandmates formed a trembling shield in front of her. It slaughtered them, instantly, like it was cutting down a forest.

A trail of bodies made a path to this moment. Estelle tried to run to the side of the stage, but the XO blocked her path at every turn. Its blade crackled and sparked currents across the floor below its grip.

"What the hell do you want!?" The blonde singer screamed. Estelle picked up an instrument and threw it at the approaching figure. The terrible noise it made came through the speakers above. I could see her tears sparkle in the stage lights as they flew through the air.

"Estelle Hart. You have perpetrated crimes against Paragon, including beginning a terrorist movement and spreading anti-Paragon propaganda. You have been selected for deletion." It spoke out devoid of emotion as it came closer to her and the stage, climbing up a small section of steps.

"Terrorist!? It's just music!" Estelle cried out as she tried again to make her escape, but again it cut her off. It was as if it was toying with her. "Well, what are you waiting for?"

The XO's blade popped again, and it cocked its head to the side. It was now less than ten feet from Estelle, but it had paused and stood staring at her, poised to strike.

"Factoring in unknown variables. Unidentified anomaly detected." It said, but wasn't making any sense. I didn't understand what it meant. It had just froze, and so had Estelle. They had come to a stalemate, only to be interrupted when Benny reappeared through the side stage door, bruised and covered in blood, pointing a Light Shoulder Cannon at the paralyzed Proto Sapien.

"Hey asshole, you missed me!" Benny yelled out as he took aim. I was almost relieved. I couldn't believe that I had done nothing, but sat, hidden, watching the grisly show. For a second, I actually wanted Benny to fire. The LSC hummed as it began to charge, and at that moment, XO One turned to see him. It lunged, what had to be twenty-five feet, and lashed the blade across the ground sending sparks into Benny.

Benny recoiled and the blast collided with the ceiling above, resulting in an explosion that enveloped the amphitheater. The light burned into the sky above us, and I quickly shielded my eyes. I heard the giant metal ceiling squeal and roar in my ears, as it twisted and ripped downward towards the stage. It felt like the whole city shook at that moment.

When I uncovered my eyes, I tried to see through the clearing dust, but it and the rain made it to where I couldn't make out anything. I pulled the scope up to my eye again to see if it helped. Now, I could make out silhouettes amidst the chaos, and a flicker of electricity danced vertically from one of them to another.

Benny was big, but the XO wielded an unmatched power. As the dust settled, I could make out Benny still dodging and pounding on XO One like he was fighting for his life.

"Estelle!" He yelled out as he looked to the performance area. His distraction allowed the proto sapien a chance to make its deathblow, and I watched Benny twitch as he grasped at the blade plunged through his stomach. Blood popped out of his mouth as the XO pulled the oversized knife out from him.

I focused on XO One, and I could make out the debris-filled stage. Beams from the rafters lay one over another, and concrete and stone littered the ground. XO One stood over some of the rumble. As I panned the scope down, I could see Estelle, wedged under a steel shaft. XO One stared down at her, holding the buzzing flickering blade in his hand. She had been crushed, and a pool of blood began to form around her torso. I watched as her eyes searched for anything and nothing. Then, she seemed to look up at the monster.

"Please, it hurts." Her voice shook the words loose as her arm reached out. I could imagine the pain she was in. Giant pools of tears began to form around her eyes. As she tried to move, she cringed painfully and small. The XO just continued to stare down at her.

"I cannot." It stated cold and stern. Blood began to flow over her lips, and she bellowed out in pain. Then, I noticed a piece of rebar protruding from her thigh, and another through her other calf. She had been pierced several times by the part of the ceiling that fell on her.

"But...why?" It was almost a scream, and I flinched down the sights..

"I...Don't know." It said affirmatively, but also like it was confused. It stared at her for a moment longer, until it seemed to confirm whatever thought it had. Then, it turned around, and began to walk off the stage. It wouldn't even finish her off, and instead she laid there viciously maimed, and dying. It didn't make any sense. Deleting her was the assignment.

She was the assignment. I watched her writhe under the debris, spitting up blood onto the floor, as the XO carelessly made its journey back to me. I couldn't stand it. It knew she would die slowly, and it did nothing. I could see her pooling tears marry the pooling blood on the floor below her face, and she cried out again. I closed my eyes, wishing I could do more, and I pulled the trigger on my light rifle. I couldn't watch the bolt enter and exit through her beautiful face. I kept them closed while I pulled the scope away. I didn't look back down at the stage until XO One rejoined me. I spun the clamps that unlocked the light rifle from the rail. We walked back out into the half-circle lobby and through the main entrance doors; neither of us saying a word until we had reached the truck.

"You really are an ugly piece of shit, you know that?" It oozed out of me in hatred for the hideous thing, which now sat replacing its hat and glasses, as he entered thes seat.

"The assignment has been completed." The door clicked shut behind it, and I got in, too. I pressed the igniter and it hummed up. I pulled back out from the parking slot, steaming. I could hear the sound of the bolt firing, over and over, in my mind. I thought about how much of a waste this XO thing was. It didn't do its job. I did it. It wasn't going to keep me from having to feel the shame of it, either.

"Why didn't you finish her off?" I asked as It sat staring out of the windshield at the rain.

"I could not." It said plain and exact, as if it were any kind of real answer. I slapped the steering wheel, grinding my teeth, trying not to spit.

"What the hell do you mean, you 'could not'?" I demanded, and the XO turned slightly at the neck to face me.

"An unknown singularity. Now irrelevant." it explained, making less sense than before. I could have shaken the wheel off of the column as I gripped it in my hands. What a bunch of crap. It didn't have an answer. It was just a monster. It could murder a whole gang of people in minutes, and then, when the practical human thing to do would be to end suffering, it ignores that instinct. There was some kind of flaw in Marcus' new design. These new Alpha's were the real monsters.

"I will com in the report." It said abruptly.

It pulled out a datcom, and I knew who would be on the other end. Marcus had to know every little detail, and he'd probably blame me for the new explosion at the Stardust. It didn't take long for it to make a connection.

"XO One reporting on assignment six eight seven four four nine one. Estelle Hart, resident, song writer, performer. Deleted." It said like it was filling out paperwork. Then, it ended transmission just as quickly. It made no display of emotion, nor even seemed aware of the scene we left. It couldn't care less.

A few moments passed, and the datcom buzzed. The emergency datastream began to display it reopened its com. Marcus came across the screen, and the thing watched the telecast without blinking, but I just heard the same Marcus sales pitch babbling in my peripheral. I drove through the rain ignoring it, as I still had the sound of the shot I took ringing in my ears.

"...Paragon is the Future." He said at the end, and the way he said it made my stomach turn. The telecast ended and the XO closed the datcom and replaced it in its pocket. Then, it continued facing forward as though the event had never happened.

"So, that's the plan, aye? Have everyone believe it was a bunch of terrorists that blew up everything?" I asked rhetorically as I turned the wheel to go down the Main round-about. It was a pretty good lie, I had to admit. Especially the part where it exonerated me.

"Estelle Hart and Benny Gloom both carried agendas that undermined the authority of Paragon. From the corporation's point of view, they were terrorists." It lectured me. The turn-off for the drain was coming up, and I thought again of Ramone and Ox. It wouldn't take long to get to Kagan, and have their bodies commemorated.

"Yeah well, what about the point of view of the guy who's got to clean up that mess." I asked the pale creature. Paragon was good about promptly sending clean-up crews after every assignment. Most of the time, you couldn't tell anything had ever happened, and some person just vanished from the city. "We're going to see Kagan, now. Ox and Ramone deserve better than this." I demanded as I pulled off at the diversion, and took the ramp down to the drain. This time the thing didn't argue, and instead kept its gaze through the windshield. As we descended, the rain let up a little.

I thought of how the proto sapien had never seen the city, or anything really, and yet it didn't care to ask questions; it had no curiosity. How much did this thing know about anything?

Was it like Alpha, could it feel? I didn't think so. This thing seemed more mechanical, and less alive.

We reached the Drain, and passed by the Ganymede. Kagan was the last stop before the exit bay door, down in the junk. He got rid of everything really, people included, and he stood by the tall bay door as we pulled up. I got out of the truck, and walked around to the tailgate, but the XO didn't move.

"Ryne! Hey, don't see you much no more. You still looking to unload those light rounds? I got two guys wanting to trade me some synth for my old light rifle, but not without the rounds. I was thinking to myself the other day, who might have some light rounds? Then, it hit me like a shock bolt, you were trying to unload some light rounds when you picked up that new charge beamer." Kagan was a talkative guy, and loved to ramble on about nothing. He didn't get a lot of company down in this part of the Drain, and people were his favorite form of entertainment.

"Nah, the beamer fried. Got two for you, today. They'll need to be commemorated." I told him. I pulled the tarp back to show Ramone and Ox, and Kagan's eyes went straight to Ramone.

"Them those new-style Paragon issue pneumatics?" He let out an odd whistle. "Never seen nothing like them before. What's a fellow have to do to merit a couple of dancing shoes like them? Bet you, you gotta do something pretty fancy to earn the creds to make them joggers happen." I put my arms under Ramone and pulled him out from the back of the truck.

"They were my crew. My team. Paragon elite." I told him, hoping he'd show more decorum. Kagan's hand flew around and around in a circle towards himself suggesting the direction in which to bring Ramone's body. He then jumped into the back of the truck, and pulled down a harness and rope. He tied it around the big man in the bed.

"This is one big boy, right here. Don't think his momma didn't keep him on that wheat protein. Pumped him up like a balloon animal, just bulging out of all his creases." he mused, and then shook his head as he pressed a button that hung from the ceiling. The rope began to pull Ox's body up and out of the bed of the truck. Ox hung lifeless from the rope harness.

"You're all set. I'll take care of all the commemoration ceremonies and dispose of your friends here." Kagan's apathy for the dead wasn't as unnerving as it probably should have been. He seemed just slow enough to forgive for things like that.

"I'll be back in an hour to pick up their personals." I told him, but Kagan just scratched the back of his head as he looked up at the big man tied up above us.

"Yeah, I can do an hour, maybe a little more, this one's one big mother, you know. Might take some extra time. Maybe a few extra Paragon creds. If you catch what I'm saying." He tilted an eye up to me while he twisted the tips of his fingers around. I grimaced, but nodded to the greedy little man before heading back to the cab of the truck. Kagan slammed the tailgate shut, and the truck roared back to life.

"We are needed at the Boundary Bridge. Sector four B, top tier." The monster commanded, but I didn't listen at first. I was still shaken and its stupid monotone voice aggravated me more than whatever accent Kagan had. It was almost like it hadn't said anything at all, until my memory replayed its words.

"XO Three pursues Version A as we speak. We must aid in XO Three's assignment. Turn onto the Boundary Bridge, here." It pointed as it prompted my every next move.

Alpha was fighting the other one of those things, and that was a scary thought that I had to see. I accelerated onto the ramp and back up to Central D, heading for the Boundary Bridge.

It was show time.

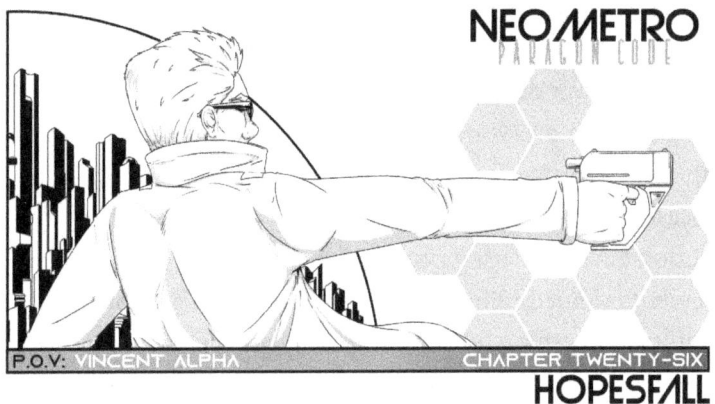

"Damnit, Eddie." I growled, but I should have known better knowing him, of all people, I may have trusted him most. It made sense why they would use him against me.

The rain pierced the air as I roared through it on the light cycle that shook and clambered, and had parts jostling free from untightened fasteners. It made sense that the speedster wasn't very well kept in a city full of rain. I only had to make it back to the tall grass, and to my green beautiful world where it didn't rain at all. Where she waited for me. It would have to hold together until I could make sure she was still safe, and then, I would let her tell me what to do about Estelle and Paragon.It wasn't right, and I realized that now. The way that Paragon steered the people's future, and claimed it was for the betterment of humanity. They murdered people, but used their position to avoid judgment, and hoist themselves above everyone else. She had to know that it was Paragon who killed Estelle.

The Boundary Bridge felt longer than ever before. I thought of how many assignments I had completed. Every time I had ever deleted someone, I believed that it was to make life better for everyone inside this city. The idea was to cut evil out of the population, like a disease, but it only made the disease spread worse. In the five years that I had worked in Section Seven, deleting people, the crime and other bad elements seemed to have only worsened. The assignments didn't stop coming, in fact, they only grew in number. So, how could what I was doing be a solution?

I kicked myself at how stupid I had been before that epiphany. There was no way to fix the problem Paragon had created; not by killing anyone. Paragon feared any pretender. It was as clear as glass. Instead of dealing with the problems they created, Paragon deleted them.

"Creds! Kill a man over some stupid creds!" I shouted as I pierced through the rain remembering the assignments. Paragon was a corporation, and acted as such. One of its main implementations after the rebellion was the re-introduction of a monetary system that it monitored and controlled. Credits weren't actually backed by anything of value, just the value of Paragon's word. Most of my assignments had been for some kind of debt, and most people were deleted for the credit they owed.

I thought that maybe that's why this assignment was different. It wasn't like Zane Blanc; it wasn't about some stupid loan. It was about life, and its value. Something Paragon shouldn't get to decide.

Humanity had to choose for itself which direction it went. If it wanted to follow some pop singer into the glowing red dawn of the outside world, then it should. To change that would be profane, but that's exactly what Paragon used me for.

Krill made me. I had no idea how to begin to comprehend that. How do you make someone? I had trusted Krill, too. Perhaps, more than Eddie. I would have to find him as well, and get him to give me some answers. No doubt he would have them, he was well on his way to being the oldest citizen, and probably had more secrets than Paragon itself. Some of what Eddie had said did make sense. I had always noticed little differences over the years. I tried not to pay any attention to them, but I was stronger than men twice my size, and I never understood why. I could always run faster. No matter how fast I was going, I always felt like I could go faster. I'm not sure if that's how normal people feel. People seemed slower. Not that people were dumb or stupid, but that they calculated information at a rate that I had surpassed long ago. The way they moved was lazily thought out, often leading to clumsy mishaps. They let irrational priorities divert their lives into disarray. They wasted time filling their lives with things that only made them feel complete, but never to become happy.

It was all becoming clearer now. I was different, or at least, I wanted to be. I was consumed with self-perfection. Not in a vain way, but to the degree that I wanted to make sure my existence had meaning; that the world was better for having had me in it. I only wanted to make my impact, and I had thought Paragon was the way to do it. At least, that's what I had been told, but now I am to believe that Paragon, and Krill, made me in some laboratory like a science experiment.

The perfect little machine designed to kill whoever they wanted. I wasn't even human, no wonder I didn't have a problem feeling superior for so long. I couldn't stop the thoughts as I sped down the Main. The rain beat down into my face making it hard to see further ahead, but I knew I would pass the *Meserere* apartment building in seconds. It made me think of the first time I saw her. She was soaking under an awning, trying to hide from the drops. She didn't look displeased and struggling, but rather, flourishing and happy with a faint smile that lifted the drops of water over and around her cheeks.

I had seen something in her. I felt something I didn't understand. I couldn't deny it, and my body wouldn't let me. I remembered how my mind betrayed me by filling itself with thoughts of her, and still did. In the car she had shown such strength and confidence. It didn't surprise me that she could survive an encounter with Ryne and his Section Seven misfits. Ryne would be lucky if I never saw him again. I was almost relieved when I saw Griff's body in Penelope. It gave me an odd fulfillment, and peace of mind to know that I didn't pull the trigger but that the job was still done.

As the familiar stoop approached in the distance I felt an odd sensation.

'Deleted. Assignment Complete.'

I looked up as the rain turned into hard sparkles as the glass fell. Through the gray hues of water, I could see the shadow of her body falling from the sky above. My hands released the rickety handlebars of the Lightster, and I let it slide out from under me as I planted my boots into the pavement.

Her weight was nothing as I had accounted for her rate of descent upon catching her. The bike collided into the wall of an adjacent building, catching fire. She had changed into an elegant dress. I had to guess it was Estelle's. Her eyes trembled as she stared into mine. Her face tried to push out a smile at the sight of me, but her expression became wry, forcing a tear instead, and her hand grazed over my face. In a moment, her hand fell back down, lifeless, and I noticed the wound in her chest. There was nothing that could have been done for her. There was no blood, other than the little bit that crept from the corner of her mouth. There was only a cauterized hole in the middle of her chest. Her head fell slowly down onto my shoulder. As I felt her body become lifeless, my knees seemed to lose all strength, sending them to the glass-covered concrete below. Still holding her in my arms, I bellowed out an angry roar. It felt primal and necessary.

"Lexxi!" I shouted at her, and I shook her, but I already knew she was gone. "Lexxi! No! Wake up!" I didn't want it to be real. It couldn't be. What was she even doing there? It was some twisted nightmare reality. The Lightster hummed like it was building a charge, and then it suddenly exploded.

I shook as I held her body crumpled in my arms; twisted like some half-assembled shop mannequin, and me trying to hold her together. My shoulders heaved. I couldn't understand. I replayed the instant over and over again. It had happened so fast, now, all frame by frame, as my mind searched for some answer in the madness, but there was none to be found.

The love I had just discovered, so new, was now lifeless in my arms. Then, I heard boots hit the pavement in front of me. I looked up from her delicate face, to see another one of an oddly fashioned man. Eddie had said there were more, but I didn't understand what he had meant until I noted the similarities between this one, and the one from the parking garage.

"Version A. Prototype genetic research avatar. Section Seven, dispatch operative. You are accused of treason against Paragon, and as such, are to be deleted." It said to me with a cold indifference that I understood deep within myself. Even after it finished talking, it was like I could hear inside of its mind. I could tell what it was thinking. It had one simple mission, and that was to kill me. It wasn't discrete in the way it thought, and it acted like it didn't know that I could hear it thinking. The thing's thought pattern only repeated itself like a replicating command as it approached. It carried an electroblade that crackled in its hand. I slid Lexxi down from my arms to the concrete, and pulled my shocker from its holster inside my jacket. As I went to aim, it moved fast. I quickly came to a stance holding my weapon, and scanned for the odd looking man who had dodged to my left. I adjusted quickly, and fired.

Its arm ripped apart from the elbow down, shredding its sleeve, and taking the blade with it across the pavement. It didn't flinch, merely recoiled, almost surprised. It retreated just as quickly to the spot where its severed arm had fallen.

I fired again to distance it from the weapon, and it stuttered backward, looking back at me. I fired again, but this time it had gotten ahead of my timing, and dodged backwards into an alleyway.

XO Three. In need of assistance. Version A sighted.

I heard it, but it wasn't as if it had said the words. It felt more like a distress signal sent across some sort of sixth sense. I began to chase after it, but stopped, thinking of Lexxi laying on the ground in the rain. I turned back, and scooped her up from the ground into my arms. I walked up the stoop, and placed her inside the door and out of the rain. I took off my jacket, and pulled it across her body. She didn't deserve any of this.

My chest began to ache, a dull throbbing heavy thumping. It took several deep breaths to make it stop. I thought there would be tears but none came. I still didn't believe it was true. I thought of the wildflower I had plucked. I thought of how right I had been. It was all my fault, and I couldn't make it right, not anymore. There wasn't any way to fix it, but I could still kill every last one of them.

Suddenly, life in this city had become meaningless. Life at all was meaningless without her. I had seen a better future, and I couldn't go back. Now, that future didn't exist, and I was stuck somewhere in a void between. I gripped the shocker firm in my hand.

I was just some *'thing'*. I wasn't one of them, one of her. I wasn't human, and that's what got her killed. I was some monster created in a Paragon tube who barely had any hair, or whatever that comment meant. I started putting things together.

I thought of Krill, and what I knew of him; what he had done for Paragon, and our little visits over the years. I had felt bonded to him, and now I knew why. He would have all the answers. I would find him and make him tell me everything, but first I would make them all suffer for her. I would make them pay for the memory of her, because now that's all she was.

I ran my fist into the wall above her as I stood. I thought of Eddie, and how he should have said something sooner. How the betrayal of that information was what had cost Lexxi her life, and if he had told me earlier how I might have been different, maybe not even met her, and she would still be alive.

Then, I thought of Paragon, and how their rules had created a world that allowed such horrible things to happen, and of Marcus. He had given Eddie the orders to stay quiet, and it was really his doing that had caused all of this. He had created the monster that killed her. He had created me, and lied to me my entire life, making me believe whatever he wanted. He created a theater of the world, and used me as a puppet.

Proto-Sapien was a funny term that I didn't understand, but that thing seemed pretty sure of what it was talking about, calling me *'Version A'*.

The odd sensation of hearing its thoughts was something I hadn't experienced before with anyone else in the city, but the sensation had stopped since the thing had fled. The clarity was striking as the new information calculated in my mind. I was different. I was sure of it, now. I looked down at the coat that covered her. It had become tattered and worn. Her hair was the only thing sprawled out from below it. It shimmered even still.

"I'll come back for you. I promise." I told her. I felt the tears try to pull at my eyes, but still nothing came as I opened the door and walked back outside. I remembered the alley that the ugly man had escaped down, and took to it slowly. The fire from the burning cycle was dying down against a nearby wall.

The streets of the slums were oddly quiet. Everyone had retreated inside to keep from the chaos. When I came out of the alley, I could hear it thinking, and it directed my attention down the street to where it stood, watching me.

'Section B.'

It stood near the merge to the boundary bridge. I pulled my arm up to aim, and fired several rounds. The bolts danced through the rain as they traveled. The shadowy figure charged to the side in anticipation of my attack. Then, it lunged at me. It must have been a block away, but it covered the distance like it was nothing. Its speed was like nothing I had ever seen from a person before. As it closed in, I was barely able to move from its path and predict where it would stop. I fired a round into its chest, high right, and it spun to the ground.

It quickly popped back up to its feet, and gargled a howl at me as it hunched into a fighting stance. I watched as the hole that the bolt made in its shoulder slowly started to close.

"What the hell?" I pondered aloud.

It was a whisper I had made to myself. The scar that was left was the same as the one on my shoulder, only pale and translucent. A small circle with a jagged star around it. It watched me, anticipating my shocker's movements and waiting to dodge my next volley. Its thoughts were a mess of calculations, which I followed. They were my movements, and alternate scenario predictions based on causality. Then, it dove, and I pulled the trigger. It pushed off of the ground and started to run along the side of the nearby building wall. It was almost beast-like. It had dodged my shot, and I took aim again, but its speed was unreal.

I fired.

The henchman's fist collided with my face, and my whole body turned. I cut through the air in a spiral, hitting the ground hard on my back. My shocker slid out of my hand, and before I could grab it, I was being lifted back off of the pavement. The monster's thoughts clustered with my own, and I tried to drown them out, but its mind was full of survival and finishing the assignment. The thoughts were familiar on a basic level, and resonated within my own mind. I grabbed its arm and twisted myself free, grappling him into position in front of me. I had its arm bent behind its back snapping at the bone. It didn't act as though it felt any pain.

It spun, twisting and breaking its own arm at the elbow, freeing itself, but not without sending its stump into my chin with enough force to push me backwards. It growled again, and bent its arm back into place, moving it back and forth, as it stared at me. The rain started picking up to a hard drizzle.

It launched itself at me, its fist cutting through the drops. I dodged, and retaliated with a strike to the ribs that crushed and crunched. A downward blow came at me from its opposite arm, and I parried instantly, striking again, this time at its knee with my boot. It gnarled downward, and I sent my fist into its face. It thundered as the knock sent the pale bald ugly to the ground.

'Deletion imminent.'

The henchman's thought startled me. It was right, I was a split-second away from ripping its head from its neck, but I had never heard the thoughts of someone or something as it died before. The next seconds were painful. I had barely heard Ryne's truck in the background of scattered rain. I saw sparks erupt from the collision that the beam had made when it hit the wall in front of me. There was a new voice in my head as I spun and landed on the pavement with a new hole in my chest. I gasped for air, momentarily.

'Targeted strike successful.'

I writhed in a familiar pain. I had felt it earlier when Griff had shot me from the window. It burned for a moment, and then the searing pain began to subside. I looked down to see the wound healing, just as the henchman's had moments before. If I had any doubts left, they were gone.

The truck spun sideways as it rounded the bridge access ramp, and came to a stop several blocks away. Now, with both of the shrouded figures' thoughts in my head, and my own, it had become hard to concentrate.

The injured one took off toward the truck and his cavalry. I stuttered back upright. My shocker laid across the pavement, in the alleyway near a trash canister. I backed slowly towards it, keeping my eye on my new assailants. This new henchman stepped out of the truck still holding the light rifle. In the same motion, it reached in its jacket, and pulled out another electroblade, tossing it to the disarmed one.

I shot an angry glance at Ryne, who sat in the driver's seat watching the two black coats rally their next attack. I increased my speed towards my weapon. Their thoughts echoed in my head. They now thought in unison. Dividing the math that allowed them to conceptualize their next attack. It was almost too much for my mind to handle. The rain beat down around us, and I reached down and quickly yanked up my shocker from the garbage. They had begun their advance. The one with the light pistol approached slowly taking aim, while the one with the blade made a mad dash towards me. I raised my weapon, but only to have a bolt jazzed over my left shoulder. I had to retreat partially into the alleyway, and the blade-wielder followed, electricity trailing him the entire way.

The light jumped along the alley walls as he advanced. My thought was to use their varying speeds to separate them. By the time I had made it to the end of the alleyway, the electroblade wielder had started to make up some space between us, and I turned to fire a bolt into him.

As I pulled the weapon up, mid-turn, another light round pierced me through the side from an upward angle. I tumbled through to the converging street with the electricity following my roll. Fortunately, the one had missed with the blade as it swung, but the static trail had burned through to my chest leaving a black line across me. I managed to catch myself quickly, and push myself back up to my feet. I dashed down the street, looking behind me to keep an eye on my followers. I could see the rifle-toting coat moving along the rooftops. The bladed henchman was close behind me on the ground. They made no display of emotion. No facial movement except when talking, even now, as they pushed themselves to chase me.

An awning gave me the height I needed to make a jump from the front of one of the buildings to the roof. In doing so, I moved ahead of the rifleman. I turned back to him, as he pulled up to aim, but this time I was quicker, and the shot I made was square to his chest, and sent him down the backside of the building into the alley. I could hear the pain it felt, in my mind, as it hit the floor of the alleyway. It kept me from noticing the second henchman ascend to the rooftops behind me, until his step crushed a small rooftop turbine. I turned to see him speeding at me with the electric blade. I aimed, but too slow, and I felt the blade cut into my side. My bolt flew just over the henchman's shoulder, narrowly missing him.

I pulled away fast as I felt the blade's cold touch, but I could already feel the damage it had done. He brought it down again, as I crumpled to the ground from the first blow. I managed to roll out of the way, but the static burned me again, this time across the back.

I ran to the edge of the building and jumped to the next, turning in the air firing my shocker back at him. This time, the round pierced it at the shoulder, tearing a chunk from the limb, leaving it barely attached. It howled. The blade flailed around searing and sparking along the rooftop. My eyebrows narrowed. I fired the rest of my clip into the grotesque thing, blowing it to pieces, like Eddie had ended the one before.

I jumped down from the building to search for the other one. A silence had entered my mind, and I felt a relief. That was when the truck collided into my back, sending me sliding across the street. I turned over to see Ryne, stepping out of the truck with a Light Cannon over his shoulder.

"Ryne! We're fighting for the same thing..." I said, but it did not deter him from taking aim, and I was out of bolts.

"This is for Ramone and Ox!" He growled out, and it was almost as if I could feel him squeeze the trigger with the tightening of my throat. The kickback pulled him against the truck, and I tried to jump out of the line of fire. The explosion propelled me even further through the air. I felt heat radiating throughout my body as I smacked against the brick of an old store. The warmth made me feel weak and sluggish. When I tried to move, it felt like my arms were too heavy and my legs wouldn't respond. I lifted my head, and my vision was a wash of whites and oranges.

"Get him now! While he's just lying there!" I couldn't make out Ryne, only hear him. Then, I felt another burning light round enter my chest. I mustered the strength to barely stand, but my vision hadn't returned to normal.

The last henchman was a white blur that quickly came into view. I dove, trying to dodge the rounds it fired, but my escape had become a crawl as the light rounds continued piercing my body. The pavement felt cold and unforgivingly wet. Every time I tried to pull myself up, another round would pierce my arm or leg, sending me back down, and I pulled myself across the street.

'Maintain incapacitation to ensure deletion.'

I wished I couldn't hear its thoughts. I was the most afraid I had ever been. I had never feared for my life before, and it gave me a weird sense of relief. If I was going to die, then that meant I had been alive. Everything was real, and I was going to be with her. Even if we had to die to do it. We were going to escape this city together. I was suddenly bathed in light, and a familiar hum gargled to a stop.

"What the hell is this, now? What is he doing here?" Ryne shot out in protest, and the light flicked away as a car door shut. Then, my eyes began to flutter shut as well, when I felt another light round pierce my body.

"Just how much of the city did you plan on destroying, asshole?" I knew that voice. It was probably the most familiar voice I had ever known. "Hey, you! XO-whichever? You think he's *deleted* yet? He's chunks, a torso. You fire another damn round and I'm having you overhauled. You boys have made a real mess, you know." It was Eddie, but I couldn't coax my eyes back open. I couldn't feel my lungs move, even if they had. I couldn't do anything. I was just aware, pulsating with heat.

"Can the shit, Eddie. Who died and made you, Mr. fancy-pants." Ryne argued, and the rounds stopped being shot into me.

"I'll shit-can you, Ryne, you stupid ape. Meet your new boss, Fancy-pants Eddie, and if you don't want to be waxing my car until retirement, you'll take nimrod and the light cannon back to corporate for debriefing." Eddie responded with authority, "That's right lug wrench, you got some explaining to do to Marcus about how you're going to pay for the Stardust, and now this shit. Another half a city block on fire." The light cannon made a metal clang when it hit the bed of Ryne's truck.

"What? You? Head of Section Seven? That's a laugh riot." Ryne responded, and I could still hear the thing's thoughts.

Incoming transmission – change of office – Section Seven – Eddie Brinnigin – Command Operative

"The change has been logged in the Paragon Corporate system. Eddie Brinnigin, Class one civilian, Section Seven Commanding Operative." The proto sapien confirmed what I had heard in its mind, and the truck door closed behind the henchman as he entered.

"Don't worry, I'll take *it* to Kagan, he'll know what to do with what's left." Eddie assured as he ushered Ryne back into his truck and back to the corporate office. Then, Ryne's door shut a moment later. The truck's engine roared to life, and took off down the road, leaving me with Eddie.

"Well, old buddy. Looks like you owe me a few more." I heard him say as my consciousness dimmed. I felt myself become weightless, and the world became black. The darkest black I had ever seen, and the rain suddenly stopped.

I could feel nothing, anymore.

JUST FOLLOWING ORDERS

I tried to ignore the burning pain that seared through the bolt wound in my leg. It had barely been more than a graze, but it was enough to sting like hell, and I'd probably be walking funny for a while.

I had stopped and grabbed one of the first aid supply kits from the sixth floor training hall, and cringed as I sprayed the antibiotic foam into the wound. I dressed it with a little bit of dermal mesh cloth, and I continued to the lift. I swiped my wrist lazily and the doors slid open. I was hesitant to enter, as I thought of the previous events, and being chased up a lift by the monster from before. I pressed the button for the second-to-top floor. Marcus and I were going to have a little chat. I was going to tell him about some of the changes I thought we should implement, and see what kind of health insurance policy upgrades I could make. I pulled my shocker and loaded in another cartridge in anticipation of our conversation.

When the doors dinged open to the long familiar hallway, it seemed quiet. It wasn't much different than normal, but the day's activities had made it seem almost peaceful. I limped my way down the hall, and opened the doors to the oversized office. Marcus wasn't anywhere to be found.

I approached the large windows and looked out over a city that now burned. Smoke trails entered the sky, hitting the top of the glass and mixed with the clouds. From here, you could see it all swirling together. The image and my solitude was more than enough to pontificate. Thoughts of Alpha flooded my mind. I had lost my friend, and it was probably my fault. I tried to give him what he wanted, but I wasn't watching out for him, not like friends do. I probably should have told him what he was, sooner. Maybe even on day one, but the man had a gift; a forte. He was good at doing his job. It made me good at mine. Sure, he was my friend, but I was selfish. I rode his coat tails like a Dox-4 high that I thought would never wear off. Now, I was having a bad trip.

Krill and Marcus' little game had become postmodern warfare, tearing apart humanity once again, and I understood at last. I understood war, and what it meant. I thought of the last wars, and how I had always perceived everyone fighting each other; a whole world in arms ripping itself apart, but as I looked out the window at the smoldering buildings, I could only see my role in it all. Everyone wasn't destroying humanity. Just a few of us. Some people, like the professor, actually cared about us. All of us; humanity as a whole entity. Marcus only cared about humanity if it suited his ideas, and otherwise tried to conform it into them.

I had been a victim of that, but Paragon had started long before him. The company's grip on this city was so tight you could hardly anything but the hand anymore; Paragon's hand. I sat in the chair behind Marcus' desk and spread my hands across the smooth surface in front of me.

"What the hell do you think you're doing, Mr. Brinnigin?" The doors slid shut behind Marcus as he entered the room. I popped up with a jaunt, and walked around the desk to the other side. Marcus' eyebrow pulled up over one of the lenses that covered his face, and he seemed a bit surprised to see me as he walked around the other side of his desk to his chair, standing by it. I made sure to acknowledge my newfound difficulty getting around.

"Oh, the leg? Thanks for asking, Marcus. You wouldn't believe the day I've had." I sneered out, letting him know I wasn't pleased. I eased into one of the chairs in front of him.

"What do you want, Mr. Brinnigin?" He asked, seemingly surprised to see me. I thought of how he always called me that, and how he used it as some kind of insult instead of it carrying the appropriate respect. I pulled out my shocker, and pointed it at him.

"Me? I just want you to sit your ass in the chair for a minute. Go on, have a seat, Mr. Creed." I pointed the shocker in the direction I wanted him to go, and he just grinned at the sight of the weapon, and slowly began to sit in the chair I had only recently vacated. I wiped my forehead with the hand that held the shocker, taking its aim off of him to show that I didn't need it to be intimidating at the moment.

"Whew, thanks, all that hovering was starting to make me nervous." I told him sarcastically, but it was also true. I didn't like it when people stood over me. Maybe, it was a new development. I returned his maniacal grin, but in a mocking manner that I tried to imbue some scorn into the gesture. Then, I let my hand lazily lay back down on the armrest. He looked at me in bitter contempt.

"Is that really necessary, Eddie?" Ha asked as he nodded to the shocker I gripped loosely.

"You tell me." I said as I widened my eyes to look at him, "I've given my life to this company, sure maybe not in the way you or anyone else wanted me to do it, but I did it my way, just the same."

He eased back into his chair, leaning it backward.

"What's your point?" He asked in condescension. His fingers wrapped the edge of his desk, and I pulled my hand back up quick; shocker at his face. He gulped. I could hear it as loud as the far bridge explosion.

"My point is... I followed orders for years, and yet you were going to have that thing kill me, like I was just anyone else to delete." I urged, as I pushed the shocker forward. His hands shot out as if to stop me from blasting a clips-worth into him. I wanted to, and of all people, he deserved it.

"You were compromised...it was protocol!" The words slithered out of his mouth. He seemed pathetic. All of his tyrannical yammering and commands, and pointing a shocker at him turned him into a sniveling coward. I stood to get an even closer aim.

"Compromised? No one even asked. You let Ryne run around, blowing shit up? You do realize the slum stunt from earlier killed countless people on the tiers below? And the Stardust? Should we even talk about how bad that went...an explosion in Central D? That's home turf...but, no...I let someone borrow a car, and I'm compromised?" I explained in a fury as I strode over to him.

I pushed the end of the barrel into his chest. I could hear his breaths as he took them, and sweat beaded up on his cheeks and forehead around his glasses.

"Now, ask me about my damn leg before I put bolts through you." I insisted. The pain of neglect was feeling worse than the hole in my thigh. It really seemed like no one cared these days. He stood quickly, pushing his chair backwards and his chest into the barrel. His tinted eyes burned into mine.

"I don't give a shit about your leg. What I want to know is, if you think I was having you deleted, then why the hell are you even standing here? I would have put an order out, and have had your buddy Alpha do it whenever I wanted." He gloated, puffing his ego, even now. I turned, pulling the shocker from his chest, laughing. I cringed as I put pressure on my leg to walk.

"That's what you think." I laughed out, and his eyebrow rose so hard you could almost hear them.

"What's that supposed to mean?" His anger came through in his tone, and I turned back to him with a sarcastic smile on my face.

"You really should have just asked me about my leg, because you see, he didn't kill me. He told me to just tell you, that I couldn't stop him." I paused for a breath. I would give a full report. "He knows everything. I told him, as kind of a reward for saving me from your creep after it went all haywire and tried to kill me. I told him how we weren't really friends and his whole life was a lie, and do you know what he did?"

I tapped my thigh with the hand that held the shocker, and laughed an acknowledging laugh as I nodded to him. "But, he didn't kill me." I explained again, shaking my head, changing my motions abruptly, "he just took off on a *lightster* towards the slums." Marcus grinned, and took his seat again.

"Ryne and the XOs are already in position." He assured me, and I hadn't told him anything that he didn't already know. His hands folded across his sternum as he sat, looking at me still holding the shocker. I looked down at the weapon, and then back to him.

"Oh, if you don't mind, I'm still going to hold it." I smiled, but he chuckled slightly, and it was disgusting. "Don't you think you've left things in the hands of that monkey, long enough?" I tempted him by insulting Ryne in a way that I knew he would appreciate, and I had caught his attention as he leaned forward.

"What would you have me do, Mr. Brinnigin? Put you in charge?" He laughed, but I had had enough. He had really started getting under my skin with the backhanded surname insult. He'd even had his underlings doing it, but it was still creepier coming from him.

"You don't think you might need someone with a lighter touch? Especially now that the city's blowing up people are going to look for someone to blame. Look outside, you can almost smell the rebellion firing back up." I insisted. He grinned, almost splitting his face a part. I knew I could play his ego like an old horn.

"Oh, and what? You'd have done so much better? You couldn't even control one person, let alone an entire city." He mocked, and I adjusted in the uncomfortable chair to posture myself.

"I did for five years, and I did it without blowing anything up or setting the city on fire. I was a loyal company man for five long years." I said as I gripped the shocker tight, still trying to make up my mind on a few things. I tried to turn the blame back to Ryne. He was an incompetent dullard anyway. He knew what was good for the city like he knew how to please a woman. Pointing out his flawed strategies was easy.

"Fine, Eddie, I'll make you a deal." Marcus soothed out using my first name, but that small effort wasn't going to make me start trusting him, now; his word and a couple of Paragon credits could get you a ticket to the moon.

"What's that?" I asked. He stood up and walked towards the window holding the city's burning skyline in view.

"If there's even one more explosion, even just one tiny one, I'll make you head of Section Seven, and you can take over the whole operation." He slithered it out with remarkable confidence, but it was what I wanted to hear him say.

If Ryne blew it again, I would have real power. I could make a real difference. I stood from the chair ignoring the pain in the burning thigh, but as I did, a circle of light enveloped an overpass, through the window, crumpling it to the lower tier, and a new dust trail rose to the top of the dome. Marcus only began to laugh an almost crazed full bellied laugh, before letting his dramatic display settle.

"Well, I guess it's your mess now, Eddie. Now, go out and make the chairman of the board happy. Oh wait, that's me!" he exalted as he continued his maniacal laughing. I turned, holstering my shocker, and walked out of the office as he continued staring out of the window at the pandemonium beginning below.

Now, I was going to create some real changes in the city. Now, it was my turn to run the show, and I knew just where I wanted to start.

GIVING UP THE GHOST

The city rumbled, and the old dusty building felt like it could betray me at any moment, and collapse crushing me beneath it. It was really quite exciting. I had rarely seen the slums from within them, and to me, this was the beginning of a great adventure. One that I had set in motion so long ago that I could barely remember when, in my old age.

The place that Eddie had selected seemed livable enough, and even had room in the back for some of the things I couldn't leave behind. Most importantly, the Beta system. My newest and most important project.

I now realized that you can't solve every problem with brute strength, and while Alpha was the best physical representation of humanity, he lacked emotional development. This newer unit would be what the city needed, more now than ever.

Hope couldn't be hammered into the human psyche. It was a song that had to be sung. People needed a softer touch, and I should have anticipated that. None of this would have happened if Marcus hadn't stolen Alpha from me, and perverted my science.

I picked myself up out of the old chair. All of the commotion had woken me to unpleasant first thoughts. I made my way into the makeshift kitchen. Really, it was just a sink and a small countertop stove to fix myself a cup of hot water. I could still feel the effects of the synthohol in my system, but unfortunately it was wearing off.

The kettle began to boil after a moment, and seconds later it gave a little whistle to let me know it was ready. I poured my cup, and added in one of the last packets of *flavoring* I had found into it. I had never liked the stuff, but I grew up on it and had acquired a taste for it because of my father. I stirred it with an old plastic spoon. One of the only pieces of tableware I had seen here.

The steam rose from the cup, and I began to think of Alpha, and what he must be doing now, and when Alex would return. I dreaded sending him back, but it had to be done. The sooner I knew he was safe, the better I would feel.

Then, I thought of the young woman I had met, and how nice she had been. I hoped that she and Alpha would return, as well. The thought of hiding out in the forgotten city until I died, was almost the most appealing plan I had ever had. It was too bad that I felt more obligation to humanity than that.

I pulled the cup up to my mustache, and took in the scent before taking a sip. It burned my sinuses a bit, and my throat a bit more. Just the way mother always used to make it. I had set up an old holocom against the wall when we first arrived. One of the lights was blinking on the front, as though I had missed a recent broadcast. I ignored it, and went to the back to fire up 'Xoe'. I could check the broadcast later.

Right now, she was just a few million lines of code that needed a host. I didn't have access to a specimen, like I had with Alpha, and a human host would have to suffice. I only hoped that whatever body we created could withstand the amount of data it would have to contain.

I took another sip from my cup as I stared at the data I had been working on, when I heard the squeal of the old front door opening. It slapped shut quickly behind Eddie, who now stood in the front room.

"Professor, we've got a big problem!" He said, excitedly throwing his hands into the air as he entered. He was soaked. I quickly made my way into the front room to greet him.

"What's happened? Where's Alex?" I asked a bit too impatiently. He heaved as he breathed, and his hands flew around him wildly as he talked.

"He's dead!" He yelled, and I gasped audibly. My hand automatically covered my mouth, and I dropped my cup of flavoring. Its collision with the floor, and subsequent destruction, seemed trivial.

"What?! Oh, my Countess." I cursed. He began to pace around the room, nodding at my reaction.

"All the shit is breaking loose, Doc. Didn't you see the Paragon Emergency Datasteam? They killed her!" Just as he said it, the holocom started displaying a new broadcast. It began just as any other Paragon datastream, with the corporate logo, and then, Marcus faded into focus like Killian used to do during the riots. He stood in the executive office on the twenty-ninth floor, in front of the open windows to the city. The skyline was polluted with dark smoke rising into the sky.

"Citizens and Residents. I am pleased to inform you, that I have just received confirmation that the terrorists behind today's attacks have been dealt with, and no further attacks will be coming. You may all return to your normal everyday lives without fear. Paragon is the future." Marcus commanded the usual salutation at the end, but the way the spires of smoke behind him began to disappear was almost theatrical.

"It is with a heavy heart, that we look to the future after suffering such a tragic loss, but as the last bastion of humanity, we will prevail into a brighter tomorrow. Estelle Hart was a perfect example of a great human being, and as such, Paragon and I would like to commemorate her as a citizen of the city. The ceremony will be streamed live in place of the concert she was planning to perform, and will be provided credit-free by Paragon." The transmission ended abruptly. I could only stare wide-eyed at the bushy sideburn-wearing youngster. He stared at the holocom, until he slowly raised his finger to point at it.

"Where'd you get that pre-revelation piece of garbage?" He said it with an almost snide sarcasm. I hated the term *'pre-revelation'*, but it was what people called my father's generation, now. They don't really even know why they do, but it was another one of Paragon's deceptions, stemming from an early attempt to end the rebellion by discrediting the United Northern Alliance and the Countess. They convinced the population that the lunar rewards program was a lie, but my father swore, if you could still see it, there would be a colony up there on the moon.

"Estelle, too. Oh my." I had slept through so much. My heart pounded. I leaned up to walk, attempting to stumble to my chair in shock. Eddie gripped my arm, aiding me, but instead of going to the chair, we continued to the front door. He opened it, quickly leading me outside to Penelope.

"I don't have very long, professor. A lot has happened today." He explained quickly having to yell through the pouring waterfalls that drizzled down rapidly from the tier above as he opened the driver door. I noticed he had a tarp over whatever was in the back seat.

"One of the new proto sapiens Marcus created, blew a hole through Alex, and chased me up a lift shaft like some kind of horror show." He continued, almost inexplicably as he reached for the handle to unlatch the trunk of the sedan, but paused as he looked back at me. "Don't worry, I killed it."

Eddie continued around to the back of the car, where he pulled open the trunk. He still looked at me as he held the lid open, and there was a sadness in his eyes behind his glasses.

"You have Ryne and another one of those ugly henchmen to blame for Estelle." He told me, in an effort to bring me some sort of comfort that it wasn't him, or to alleviate his own guilt in some way.

I walked around to the back of the car where he stood, directing me to look inside. Along the way, I noticed the side of the sedan had been punctured with a ridiculous amount of holes.

"I think he got one of them, too." He said as he nodded down into the trunk. It was almost too much to see when I looked down. Eddie gave me a wry unnerved look. It was Alpha, missing a whole arm and another hand, and little bit of everything else laid in a plastic sheet. His wounds were all cauterized shock types, and the excess amount of them was keeping him from healing.

"Quickly, get him inside." I commanded, probably seemingly less concerned than Eddie would have imagined I would be. I helped Eddie pick him up, and we carried his mangled body into the back room of the old building, laying him on the old surgical table.

"What can you even do, Doc?" Eddie said as he paced around the table while I ripped off the charred bits of his clothes and some of the dead flesh. I could see Alpha's body slowly repairing itself. The cells sluggishly replicated themselves to reform the destroyed tissue and bone. The massive amount of burn injuries and dismemberment had put his body in a stunted regrowth state. I pulled open one of the drawers to find nothing of use, and then another, until I came across an old rusted kitchen knife.

"He'll be fine." I said with a smile, looking at the rusted thing. Eddie's mouth hung open for a second as he peered at me.

"What do you mean, fine? He's barely alive!" Eddie shot out. I took the knife, and carved off a piece of Alpha's cauterized wound around his wrist. The new wound bled, but only momentarily.

"What are you, sick? What the hell are you doing professor?" Eddie cried out again, and I cut again, and then another time, completely removing the obstructing dead cells. Eddie watched horrified. Then, as I cut, the blood began to stop, and the new wound started to close as it reformed Alpha's missing hand. Eddie's mouth was so gaped it could hold a shockball.

"Like I said, he'll be fine." I assured him again, and Just then, Alpha's eyes sprang open.

"Lexxi!" he called out. Alpha slowly searched his new surroundings before reaching out and grasping violently at Eddie's arm. Eddie squirmed in Alpha's grip. "You! You're the reason she's dead." Alpha said sternly looking up at Eddie.

Eddie tried to pull himself free, but Alpha had him tight around the wrist. I had to act fast. I heard Eddie's bones crunching, as he let out a high pitched scream. The *nuerocomm* from my old lab was in one of the boxes I had brought. It was the device I had used to program Alpha for the first time, and I could use it to put him in a stasis mode.

"Krill...do something." Eddie begged as he grunted and moaned. Alpha turned his head to see me pulling the nuerocomm from a box. It was a green-lensed eyewear apparatus that connected to the user's temporal lobe through electronic pulses that it emitted and received. It was originally designed by a Southlander as a combat augmentation, but I had used it to regulate Alpha's brain wave patterns during his creation. I quickly slid it over Alpha's eyes.

As the nuerocomm clicked into place, and it begant to initiate as binary data flowed across the illuminated lens, and Alpha released Eddie's hand. Eddie fell to the floor, rubbing his wrist aggressively.

"Yeah, it's broken." He moaned, holding his wrist. He stood back up making pained faces. Alpha was catatonic. I didn't know what to think. Alpha would slowly start to heal himself completely back to normal. When I had used the nuerocomm to program him before, he was a blank slate, but now, he had his own experiences.

Experiences that had made him dark and tormented. I thought of how much good he could still do if he hadn't been corrupted.

"He could have been so much more, you know. He was meant for more." I murmured to myself as I looked down upon my creation. Eddie twisted his hand around in circles, popping the bones in his wrist.

"Is he just going to stare at the ceiling now?" Eddied asked cynically. Alpha laid on the table with the code scrolling across his eyes. I thought of how much pain he must be in. Then, what he had said hit me.

'She's dead'

Did he mean the young girl? I felt the pounding in my chest again.

"The nuerocomm is acting like a sedative while it integrates with his mind. Then, I'll see what I can do about the rest of him. My poor boy." I explained to Eddie, needlessly. I placed my hand along Alpha's cheek, patting it. Dead skin continued to flake from his blackened wounds as the nuerocomm initialized. Eddie seemed a little weak in the stomach at the site of his regrowing body.

"Well, I have to get to Kagan. I have to make sure both of your bodies make it to the drain before Marcus wants to see any proof that you're dead." Eddie replied with an explanation of his own. I arched my brow curiously at him as I remembered the tarp-covered back seat of the sedan outside. He started to continue to explain, but I began nodding as I started to guide him to the door.

"You have done well today, Eddie. All of humanity owes you a great debt." I told him as positive reinforcement, coaxing him outside to his car.

"So, he is going to be alright right? I mean, he's alive? That's crazy, right?" Eddie asked in mumbles as he got into the sedan. Then, the rain raised my volume once again.

"He's fine, it's everyone else I'm worried about. You go do what you need to do!" I insisted. I closed the door behind me as I made my way back inside; back to Alpha. I grabbed the rusty blade again and began to carve off the charred flesh from his severed arm. Within a minute, twenty-percent of it had regrown. I watched in delight.

"Amazing. Alpha, can you hear me?" The nuerocomm had made Alpha's mind blank. I had it set to default parameters, and was awaiting its next use on a new avatar. I didn't want to admit to Eddie that it was luck that had saved him. When the nuerocomm went operational, Alpha would have still been in control, and Eddie might have been missing that hand. Even in default, the avatar can still respond.

"Yes, Professor Krill. I can hear you." Alpha replied. I looked down and his arm had almost completely finished reforming.

"Alpha, who is Lexxi?" I asked, and I could see his eyes wrench to a squint behind the lens.

"I... love Lexxi." He stammered out, and his words seemed haunted as I continued to work on his wounds. The ones to his back and ribs were extensive and took time to cut out. His legs had received a lot of damage as well.

"Alpha, what is love?" I asked again, and Alpha's face went blank, as if the nuerocomm had returned to default. "Alpha?"

I stopped cutting, and leaned down to inspect the nuerocomm's interface.

"Hope..for the future." He said as tears began to stream down the sides of his face, and under the nuerocomm. The liquid from them short-circuited the input connectors, frying them. I tried to pull it from his face, but the tines wouldn't retract, and the device was stuck. He sat up suddenly from the table trying to pull it off himself. Binary continued to scroll across the lens.

He twitched violently as the nuerocomm electrocuted him. I tried again to pull them from his face, but this time his arm sent me into the building's brick wall in self-defense. The room began to become blurry, and Alpha rolled off of the steel table.

The last thing I saw was the rain, before the world dimmed out of sight. It dripped into pools in front of the old creaking door as it swung closed behind Alpha, who had run out into the dark wet streets, naked and alone.

But also, alive.

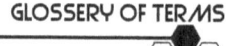

Shocker - A handheld electrical based ranged weapon that uses an electrically charged bolt as a projectile. The wound made by this weapon cauterizes itself upon penetration.

Light Rifle - A long range light beam weapon that deploys the enegery from a shock round, but does not project the bolt from the chamber.

Electroblade - A brutal short range melee weapon that emits electricity from its blade.

Shock Charge/Light Grenade - An explosive device that uses a shock round as its detonator.

DatCom - A device used for communication, data storage, and location services within New Axis. Each citizen is issued a DatCom, and each DatCom is linked to the Database Mainframe.

Lightpen - An attachment device for the DatCom that allows the end-user to write on the liquiglass screen.

Digidisc - A storage drive for the DatCom unit that allows the user to store additional mainframe data and create new data.

Holopacket - A virtual file system that manifest itself onto a liquiglass surface for easy viewing.

Holoscreen - A liquiglass display that emits from and data projector, such as a datacom or datajack.

Datajack - A stand alone portal created for use in the slums to connect to the Database Mainframe. A datajack can interface with a users DatCom, use Digidiscs, and display holopackets

Wristport - An attachment given to Paragon employees to access a variety of compnay-only areas of both Central D and the Database Mainframe.

Gasper - A synthetic tobacco product consumed by the people of New Axis. The effects cause mild stress relief.

Uphorium - The street name for the chemical mixture DOX-4. A mild sedative abused by most of the city; the hallucinogenic effects of which are called "stargazing" by residents due to how the lights of the city appear to sparkle to the user.